THE MEMORY CONCIERGE

A NOVEL

LAUREN W. ROACH

*Sunflower*ROSE PUBLISHING

Copyright © 2023 by Lauren W. Roach

All rights reserved.

No part of this publication may be reproduced, distributed, or transmitted in any form or by any means, including photocopying, recording, or other electronic or mechanical methods, without the prior written permission of the publisher, except as permitted by U.S. copyright law. For permission requests, contact Lauren W. Roach at Sunflower Rose Publishing.

The story, all names, characters, and incidents portrayed in this production are fictitious. No identification with actual persons (living or deceased), places, buildings, and products is intended or should be inferred.

Cover Design by Jared Roach at DRMR Creative

Editing by: Literary Pearl Editing Services and Naya Powell

Cover Art by rawpixel

ISBN: 979-8-9894618-0-6

To the younger version of me with notebooks full of stories she was too scared to share, this one is for you.

Author's Note

Alzheimer's disease is a complex and devastating neurodegenerative condition that predominantly affects the elderly population. It is named after Dr. Alois Alzheimer, who first identified and described the disease in the early 20th century. Since then, research into the causes, symptoms, and potential treatments for Alzheimer's has made significant strides, yet many questions remain unanswered.

The purpose of this work is not to diminish or dismiss anyone's struggle with the condition; it is meant to acknowledge that your pain is real. We see you, we hear you, and we support you however we can. We must realize Alzheimer's is not solely a medical issue; it is a human issue. It permanently and profoundly impacts the lives of those diagnosed and those who love them.

While in research was done in the formation of this story, I did take creative liberties wherever possible to push the plot forward. With that being said, to be on the safe side, you will need to suspend your disbelief just a little. In fact, go ahead and grab it with both hands, open the nearest window, and yeet it into the wind. You won't need it.

Prologue

They say that the smell of death is one you will always recognize, even if you have never smelled it before. They say it is a mixture of putrid meat with rotten fruity undertones. When Henry stepped into the dimly lit room sheathed in cobwebs from years of non-use, that very smell permeated the air. Something in there was dead. The entire room was blanketed in dust and rot. It was so thick that it made his eyes sting and he could taste it with every deep breath.

Henry raised a hand to cover his nose and realized it was trembling. He should not have come; he knew that now. He inched further inside, checking over his shoulder every few seconds to be sure nothing was creeping behind him. In this room, which looked like it had once been an office, there were floor-to-ceiling windows with tattered and discolored curtains. The wallpaper peeled off the walls, revealing a stained grayish paint underneath. A shiver crept up Henry's spine. He could not tell if it was from the chilly air or fear. He felt as if someone or something could be watching him.

"You should not be in here." The sudden voice made Henry trip over a discarded wooden plank near his foot. Even with the windows allowing in the sprinkles of moonlight, it was so dark that Henry had not realized someone else was in there with him. He whirled around, searching for the source of the voice. In the farthest corner, under one of the windows, a black mound sat hidden just out of view. At first glance, it looked like a pile of fabric, but a pair of glowing white, pupil-less eyes stared back at him, clocking his every move.

"H-Hello? Who's there?" he demanded, taking an unsteady step forward. "Show yourself! I have a weapon!" He did not have a weapon. In his anxious preparation for the trip there, he had forgotten to bring something for protection. All habits of self-preservation had flown out the window. The creature shuffled and stood to its full height, sending white-hot panic pulsing through Henry's body. He let out a small squeak in shock. This thing was huge. From what he could see in the shadows, the head of the creature almost skimmed the ceiling. It hunched forward to give itself more room to stand. Its unnaturally large wingspan could undoubtedly touch both corners of the room without moving.

If it could sense the panic that surged through Henry and made him quiver like a chihuahua, it gave no indication. When it tilted its head, its white eyes remained fixed on Henry. Something niggled at the base of Henry's brain… his flight-or-fight response kicked in urging him to turn around and run back in the direction he came. His subconscious begged him to abort the mission and take off running; there was still time to escape. The creature had not moved towards him yet, so there was a slim chance he could run before it reached him.

He could tell the others that he had not been able to find anything. No one would know the difference. Maybe he could try again during the day. He wanted to kick himself for coming to an abandoned building at night. He made this situation so much more dangerous for himself. He had not even thought to bring a flashlight. He was terrified, but instead of running, he stood where he was, his feet firmly planted on the dusty floor.

Doubt flooded his mind, followed by the common sense he had been missing when he decided to come out here in the first place.

He was in search of something called The Memory Concierge. Henry wasn't convinced that it had truly existed, but he felt better knowing that he had tried everything before giving up. A few years prior, he and his wife were blindsided when she was diagnosed with Alzheimer's disease. He had every intention of weathering the storm with her, but as time passed, the distance between them increased until he could no longer recognize his marriage. He had heard whispers about a mythical creature that could restore and replace lost memories. He didn't believe the stories and chalked them up to a silly fairy tale, however, as time progressed, he became frustrated.

No matter what advice he received from others, articles he read, or discussion forums entered, he could not shake the feeling of bitterness. That frustration morphed into desperation until he found himself entertaining the idea of a memory concierge even more. If it were real, it could solve all his problems. The possibility gave him hope. As he stood in the abandoned hotel, staring at this abnormally large creature (and praying it didn't have a diet that consisted of humans), the hope that had driven him forward seemed so far away.

"Why did you come?" the creature asked, ignoring Henry's attempt to look intimidating. It shifted forward, allowing some of its face to be visible from the shadows. Pale greenish-gray skin stretched taut over the beast's body. It looked like just enough to cover the bones if it had any. It seemed to be a weird combination of a snake and a human - like a horrible science experiment gone wrong or something from the depths of Henry's nightmares.

"Are you...are you him?" Henry's voice shook. He was irritated at himself for sounding as terrified as he felt.

"Am I who?" the creature asked, stepping further out of the shadows. Henry bit his tongue to keep from letting out a petrified yelp. Its voice was so uncomfortably loud that Henry felt like he was standing next to a speaker at a concert. Each word made his eardrums jump.

"Are you The Memory Concierge?" He felt stupid saying it out loud. He suddenly felt insecure, worried that he had come all this way just for the entire thing to be a lie. The creature remained silent, watching him. A slow smile spread across its face revealing sharp and jagged teeth.

"Hello, Henry..."

PART ONE

1

Henry stared at the bulky orange and black costume his girlfriend, Lynette, had laid out for him. Despite the protesting and bargaining he had done in the weeks leading up to this party, Lynette wouldn't let him get out of going. Henry hated Halloween. He hated dressing up but, most of all, he absolutely despised couple costumes. He had repeatedly told Lynette this, but it never seemed to stick in their years together. Henry picked up the costume between his thumb and his forefinger, holding it close to his face so he could examine it. It had a funny smell and looked like it had been put together by someone who didn't have the best control over their own hands.

They were going dressed as the Flintstones, her as Wilma and him as Fred. He was already counting down the hours and the minutes until he could return home and relax. He had contemplated staying at work late, so Lynette would have no choice but to go to the party without him, but he chickened out at the last minute. Henry wanted nothing more than to kick back and relax after the day he'd just had at work, but he had promised Lynette he would go to this Halloween party because a friend of hers was throwing it. It felt weird celebrating this holiday after being raised in a devout Christian home his entire life, but he was a man of his word.

If he was being candid with himself, Henry would admit that he had checked out of this relationship months ago, and the guilt that came with it was the reason he even agreed to go to the party in the first place. Henry stuck around because he couldn't determine the best time to end things. When he first planned to tell her, Lynette had lost her job, and since he wasn't a total monster, he stuck around to ease her through the transition.

When Lynette found another job, her car broke down. So, Henry hung around to make sure she could get to and from work long enough for her to get her money together to get a new car. After her car was replaced, her grandmother passed, and as much as Henry wanted to cut ties and run, he stayed by her side to be sure she was okay. Even though everything seemed to have settled down, he didn't want to be a jerk and dip out right before the holidays. So here he was, begrudgingly putting on a Fred Flintstone costume and wishing he could figure out a way to make himself disappear in the next few seconds.

"You ready, cubby bear?" Lynette asked, giving him a kiss on the cheek. He bit his tongue to keep from recoiling. Her breath smelled like a revolting mixture of bologna and chocolate. He couldn't, for the life of him, imagine a food combination that would inspire such a horrid smell. Had she always smelled this badly? Or was this a recent addition to the list of reasons why he would much sooner lick the side of a public toilet than continue in this relationship? His stomach churned dangerously, but he managed to smile and nod. "Almost ready."

The ride to the party was quiet aside from the radio playing softly in the background. Neither one of them had anything to talk about. They had stopped bothering to ask each other about their day weeks ago. The conversation stayed superficial. He couldn't pinpoint when they both decided to stop trying and let the romance die out, but he was grateful to not have to make the continued effort. It was exhausting.

When they pulled up at the party, Lynette perked up almost immediately. "I see my friend Eric from work! I'll catch up with you later, babe!" She barely gave him a chance to respond before she went bouncing out of the car and over to a man dressed as a pumpkin. Henry watched for a second, noting the lack of jealousy he felt watching his girlfriend interacting more enthusiastically with another man than she had with him in months. Instead, he was grateful for the downtime. He didn't have to pretend that he was interested when he was by himself.

Cars lined up on each side of the sidewalk, making it almost impossible to find a parking space. Henry was tempted to turn around and go back home. He could always swing by and pick her up later. Would she even notice his absence? She seemed more concerned with Eric than she was with him. A block and a half later, he found a vacant spot behind a monstrosity of a vehicle with a broken door handle and tape over the windows. It looked like a death trap on wheels. Henry sighed to himself and began the trek back toward the house.

Halloween decorations littered the front yard and doorway of the home as Henry made his way inside. Fake, fuzzy spiders on cotton spiderwebs covered most of the walls of the front entrance. Henry stared in awe at the variety of costumes in front of him. Someone had truly gone all out for Halloween. A woman dressed as a black Wonder Woman with an impressive afro passed in front of him and glanced down at his costume, her disgust written all over her face. He couldn't find it in himself to be offended. He was disgusted at his costume too. He shrugged and smiled at her.

"Where is the kitchen?" he asked. He could at least fill his stomach with good food if he had to be judged for his costume. She rolled her eyes and pointed behind her. A trail of robbers spilled out of what he assumed was the kitchen, carrying hotdogs in both fists. His stomach growled angrily as he made his way toward the food. He hadn't had the chance to stop for his lunch break that day, and Lynette was too excited to get to the party to let him stop for something to eat on the way to the party. Speaking of his girlfriend, he had lost sight of her. The last time Henry spotted her, she was grinning up in the face of Eric the Pumpkin. He glanced around the room, trying to pick her out amongst the sea of adults dressed as Disney and other television characters, but eventually, his growling stomach won his attention. Lynette would turn up eventually; if she didn't, he could just sniff the air for her rancid breath and follow the trail of her scent.

There was an impressive spread of food laid out on the kitchen counter. Wings, hotdogs, hamburgers, fruits, small sandwiches, and any other finger food combination possible were somewhere in this kitchen. He turned sharply, looking for a plate and something to grab the food with, and bumped into soft flesh. "Oof!" he exclaimed as he smacked into the person holding a mustard-loaded hotdog. The mustard smeared all over the front of his costume. He looked at it absentmindedly, wondering if Lynette could still return it with a condiment stain on the front.

"I'm so sorry, here - let me help you clean that." the person said. Henry finally looked up to see who was talking, and when he did, he almost melted into a puddle. The most beautiful woman stood in front of him.

She had soft brown eyes that crinkled at the corners as she smiled politely at him. Her hair was pulled in a low ponytail, which drew attention to her sharp cheekbones and unique facial features. She was dressed in all white, with red splatters all over the front of her outfit. He vaguely wondered if their collision had caused that but then shook his head. When they collided, he had nothing in his hands; it must be a part of her costume. Henry was dazed, completely thrown off by her beauty.

"You okay, Fred?" She asked. When he didn't answer right away, her smile faltered a little. Most likely because he was standing in front of her like an idiot, open-mouthed and dangerously close to drooling. He closed his mouth and accepted the napkins she had been standing there holding out to him, thankful he had something to do with his hands. He wanted to reach out and touch her, to see if her skin felt as soft as it looked, but that would be weird.

"What are you dressed as?" he asked as he swiped at the mustard on his costume, watching the yellow condiment settle deeper into the fabric. He would do anything to distract himself from staring at her. He didn't want to seem creepy. She chuckled a little and tossed her plate in the nearby trash cash. "I'm a used sanitary napkin."

"You're...a what?" He stopped scrubbing at the mustard and stared at her. Part of him wanted to laugh because he assumed she was joking, but looking down at her costume, it made sense. He was both impressed and confused. Most women used Halloween as an excuse to wear something provocative to garner attention. Yet, she was easily the most beautiful woman in the room and dressed as a used feminine product.

"I'm a used sanitary napkin. A pad." She burst into laughter. "You look disgusted."

"I am disgusted. That's a gross costume."

"It is, but it's a conversation starter." Her smile widened, flashing her blindingly white teeth at Henry. He caught himself staring and shook his head imperceptibly, hoping she hadn't noticed his ogling.

"So, you dressed as a dirty pad to start a conversation? A simple 'hi, how are you?' wouldn't have done the trick?" She tilted her head at his question, allowing him to see the tissues hanging from her earrings covered in some of the same red substance.

"Look around; everyone here is wearing the typical costume." She waved her hand around the room. As if on cue, another Wonder Woman costume floated by them. "Why not be different? Stand out? It's more creative than being a knock-off of Fred Flintstone." She retorted, pointing at his ill-fitting and now mustard-stained outfit.

"So, what you're telling me is that you hate my costume so much you bumped into me on purpose so you could spill mustard on it?" Henry smiled. He leaned over to toss the soiled napkins in the trash can. A few people moved around them, trying to get to the food. Henry barely noticed. The woman laughed; the sound made him swell with pride as if he had accomplished a lifelong goal.

"That's exactly what I'm telling you." She stuck her perfectly manicured hand out towards him and winked. "My name is Clara. Tell me yours, or I'll keep calling you Fred."

"My name is Henry. But you can call me whatever you want to." He took her hand in his, noting that her skin did actually feel as soft as it looked. This woman was gorgeous, and he was immediately jealous of whoever she had come to this party with. Her eyes sparkled as she smiled at him. All thoughts of food completely vanished from his memory.

"You are stunning. I... I love your outfit." He blurted. He hadn't meant to be so obvious, but he couldn't help himself. Clara smirked.

"Henry, I'm dressed as a dirty pad, and you just said it was gross." He immediately felt his cheeks grow hot with embarrassment. He had forgotten, just that quickly, that she was dressed as a period product.

"Yes, but you're still the most beautiful woman at this party. By a long shot." His voice sounded more confident than he felt. Clara bit her lip, trying to conceal her laughter, but Henry saw it anyway. He wanted to take a picture of that smile. He wanted to capture it and hold on to it forever. In all his years of living, nothing had made him as happy as seeing this smile directed at him. It was like winning the lottery.

Henry had been at this party for hours longer than he had planned. He had stuffed himself full of hotdogs, burgers, and various chips while he and Clara talked as if they had known each other forever. He had never had a conversation that flowed so effortlessly before. She was a wealth of knowledge and intelligence. All of his attention focused on her as she spoke. He studied her eyes and her lips; memorized the dimple on her left cheek that jumped out when she smiled, and took in every word she said as if his life depended on it. - like he was stranded in the middle of the sea, and her conversation was his life raft. What made it even better was that she seemed just as invested in the conversation as he was. Her gaze was fixed on him whenever he spoke as if he was the most important man in the room. It made him feel important, like he was better and more interesting than anyone else at the party.

Henry had always made fun of those movies where the love interests claimed that they felt like the only ones in the room, but here and now, with Clara standing in front of him, he couldn't see anyone else. He couldn't hear anyone else. The music quieted, the crowd faded, and the lights around them dimmed just enough so the one light above her head shone bright like a spotlight. He vaguely registered that he was incredibly cheesy at this moment, staring at her like they were in a romantic comedy, but he honestly didn't care.

"When I finish med school, I will become an anesthesiologist. I can put the people to sleep and ensure they stay asleep during their surgery, but I don't have to do the cutting," she said, popping a strawberry in her mouth. Henry leaned against the counter and sipped the drink he had managed to pour himself. His eyes never left her face. He was sure he had memorized every inch of it by now. If someone were to test him on her features, he would pass with flying colors. He would see it in his dreams until the end of time.

"How long have you known that was what you wanted to be?" He asked. Clara chewed on her lip; a thoughtful smile spread across her face.

"Ever since I learned about Jesse Owens," she said.

"The track and field athlete?" Henry asked, slightly confused. When she nodded, he furrowed his brow, silently asking for more information.

"When he was five years old," she tossed her thick curls over her shoulder, "he had a tumor in his chest. His parents couldn't afford a doctor, so his own mother had to cut it out. His and his mother's bravery in that moment is what started my interest in medicine. We need more people like us in the medical field."

The way her face brightened while she explained the story to him made his heart flutter in his chest. He watched her, captivated by every word that came out of her mouth. Before he could respond, a loud chorus of clapping erupted from the living room. From where the two of them stood, they could see directly into the room, where a man dressed as a pumpkin was dapping up a few of his friends as he led a woman dressed as Wilma Flintstone up the stairs. Henry froze as he and Wilma made eye contact.

It was Lynette.

He had forgotten that Lynette existed, let alone that he came to the party with her. As soon as he spotted Clara, all thoughts of bologna breath escaped him like waking from a bad dream. Henry watched her over the rim of his cup as he took another sip. Lynette glanced between him and Eric the Pumpkin, unsure what to do. Henry stood still as he watched them head up the stairs, feeling completely unbothered. Those who knew they came together turned to stare at Henry, waiting to see how he'd react. Would he run after them, punch Eric the Pumpkin in the face, and triumphantly reclaim his woman?

Henry did neither. He didn't want to. Instead, Henry raised his cup and nodded at Lynette. He was thankful to be rid of her and would happily pass the buck to Eric the Pumpkin. Henry had been contemplating how to dump Lynette as soon as he and Clara started talking. Now, he wouldn't even have to. Henry almost wanted to thank her.

He was so excited he could have hugged her right there as she walked up the steps with another man. A wave of relief washed over her face, and she smiled back at him with a silent "thank you." Both knew their relationship was over. It had been over for a long time. It was a shame it had to end this way, but from the looks of it, neither of them would be hurting over it. Clara placed a hand on his arm and leaned close to his ear. He tried to ignore the chill of her breath on his neck and in his ear. It was way too early for that.

"Do you know her?" she asked. He turned to look at Clara; she looked concerned as she searched his eyes. He smiled at her, feeling a new sense of freedom.

"I used to." He placed his cup on the counter behind him and again faced her. "Can we continue this conversation? Possibly over some dessert elsewhere?"

"How do you know I didn't come with someone?" She crossed her arms and stared at him. The corners of her mouth twitched like she was trying not to laugh.

"Did you?" He asked simply. Clara narrowed her eyes at him before breaking out into a grin. She remained silent. He held her gaze with a confidence he wasn't quite feeling but was determined to find.

"No, but I don't usually go out with men dressed as Fred Flintstone."

"I don't usually go out with women dressed as bloody pads, but I'll make a special exception for you."

"And why is that?"

"Because I plan to make you my wife someday, Clara." He hadn't meant to say that out loud. As soon as the words left his lips, he wished he could grab and swallow them. He had no idea where that sudden burst of confidence came from, and the look on her face almost made him want to apologize for overstepping.

Clara stood impossibly still, staring at Henry but saying nothing. So many different emotions danced across her face. Henry wanted to disappear, almost sure that Lynette would be creeped out by such a forward comment. It felt like she could see inside his mind and recognize how nervous he was. Something in her expression relaxed. She laughed and playfully smacked him on the arm.

"Yeah, okay, sure, Henry." she grinned, rolling her eyes. He smiled back at her and grabbed her hand. Her skin was still just as soft as it was before.

"You don't have to believe me now. I'll show you."

2

"Are you excited?" Clara asked as Henry walked her to his car. He had just arrived at her house for their first official date. They had gone out as friends and spent most of their nights talking on the phone since the Halloween party, but tonight was the first time they would go on an actual date. Henry planned the perfect night for them: A taping of Soul Train in Hollywood was about a twenty-minute drive from where they were in Los Angeles. Henry heard that the special guest was Shalamar, and he was incredibly excited to see them perform live. When he extended the invite to Clara, she excitedly accepted and told him that Shalamar was one of her favorite groups.

"I am," Henry said quietly as he opened the passenger door for her. He was excited, but he was also nervous. He wanted to make a good impression but wasn't sure if his dancing skills were up to snuff. At the Halloween party, Clara told him she loved to dance and go running, which required a person to be in pretty good shape. Henry was no slouch, but he wasn't the most athletic either. People would see his large, six-foot-two frame and assume he played football or basketball. In reality, Henry preferred sitting at his desk, taking apart electronics. He was a gadgets guy.

Looking at Clara, examining her lean, athletic body, Henry knew he couldn't just go in and improvise. He had been practicing since the night he called her and asked her to accompany him. Nights he would usually spend tinkering with his gadgets and gizmos were spent practicing the same few steps to impress Clara. He wanted tonight to be perfect.

"Are you always this quiet?" Clara grinned at him as he pulled out of her driveway onto the road. Henry felt his face flush. Was he not talking enough?

"I- sorry. I'm excited, but I'm also a bit nervous. I just want tonight to be...smooth."

Clara's expression softened. A shockwave pulsed through his body when she reached out to touch his leg. He shivered slightly under her touch. He had never been this affected by anyone before. Lynette was never able to make him melt this way, even when things were new between them. He glanced at Clara, taking in her outfit and admiring her beauty. She wore a sleeveless black crop top with matching black capris that hugged her legs and hips. Black heels made her calf muscles pop. Her curls bounced around her shoulders, sending small whiffs of vanilla his way with every movement.

"Just relax. We're going to have a great time, especially if they play 'A Night To Remember.' That's one of my favorites."

Henry smiled at the familiar Shalamar tune. It was also one of his favorites. He briefly wondered if Clara, in all her glory, was too good to be true. Can someone be too perfect? The way her skin glowed and her eyes sparkled made him want to pull over to the side of the road and kiss her repeatedly. He turned to her, ready to ask about her other favorite songs, but her expression made him freeze. She had gone rigid, staring out the window at a group of men standing on the street.

"Do you know them?" he asked, glancing back at the road. Clara seemed to snap out of her trance at the sound of his voice. She cleared her throat, her smile forced and uncomfortable.

"Only one of them," she replied stiffly. Henry raised an eyebrow.

"My brother. He was one of the guys in that group."

Henry slowed, "do you want me to pull over so you can talk to-"

"No. Just keep...keep going." Tears filled her eyes. Henry swallowed down the anger that bubbled up in his chest. He wanted to harm whoever it was that made her cry. Henry blinked, surprised at his own reaction to Clara's emotions. He barely knew her but was willing to burn the world down to ease her pain. That can't be normal.

"My brother got mixed up with that group he was standing with. They sell drugs. I can't...I can't look him in the eye anymore, knowing what he's doing to our people." She shook her head. Her hands balled into fists in her lap. Henry took a deep breath, unsure of what to say. He understood her anger. Drugs were ruining their community. He had a cousin who was hooked on something heavy. They were close as children, but Henry watched the cousin he once knew fade into a husk of himself. It was too much. He quickly swiped under Clara's eyes, catching the tears before they fell.

"We are supposed to be having a good time. No crying allowed." He smiled at her. "Tell me something."

"What do you want to know?" Clara asked, giving him a watery smile in return.

"What made you say yes to a date with me?"

"Obviously, I wanted to see Shalamar."

The look he shot her made her bark out a laugh. He shook his head, pretending to be annoyed, but could feel a smile tugging at his lips. Her laughter made him soar.

"I see you," she said simply after her laughter died down. He tilted his head, unsure of what to make of her answer. "I could tell from our conversation at the party that you were something special, Henry Tubeck."

He felt his insides buzz at her words. The desire to pull over and kiss her grew more powerful. He tried, without success, to reel himself in. Instead, he focused his attention on the road, not wanting to let her see how much she had affected him.

"When you asked me out, saying yes felt as easy and as second nature as breathing. Of course, I would go out with you. I would be foolish not to." She reached up and touched his cheek. He resisted the urge to close his eyes and lean into her touch. He had to remind himself that he was driving and must keep his eyes on the road. So many emotions were swirling through him; he had trouble pinpointing just one. He wanted to respond with something as beautiful and heartfelt as she had said, but the words wouldn't come.

"Wow," he whispered. Clara giggled and shrugged.

"Too much?"

"No. Not at all."

"Dance with me!" Clara shrieked, grabbing Henry's hand. He resisted the urge to pull back and hide. Logically, he knew no one was paying any attention to him, but he couldn't help feeling like all eyes would be on him and his lack of dancing skills. Every move he had practiced for weeks completely evaporated from his memory.

"I'm no good at it!" He had to practically scream in her ear over the volume of the music. She shook her head and tugged his hand again. He allowed himself to be pulled over to the soul train line, praying that he wouldn't do something stupid in the heat of the moment. The neon Soul Train sign glowed a bright orangey red against the purplish hue of the walls. People were everywhere, bouncing to the music in a dance that looked choreographed. Everyone but Henry seemed to already know the steps. The room was hot and smelled of sweaty bodies. Henry felt utterly out of place.

"Come on! Don't think so hard about it! Just relax!" Clara threw her hands up and swayed to the music. He admired how easily her body moved to the beat of the song.

Give it to me, baby! The Rick James song thumped through the room. Henry took a deep breath and closed his eyes, imagining he was home listening to his records. He could feel his hips begin to sway and his legs begin to move timidly at first, but as the song thumped through the room, he leaned into it, not letting himself worry about how he looked or whether he was doing it correctly.

Skilled dancer or not, Henry was having a good time. He could feel his muscles loosening. His heart jumped and bumped in rhythm with his steps. He took a chance and opened his eyes, half expecting to see others laughing at him.

Instead, he saw a crowd of people enjoying themselves. His eyes found Clara's, and she grinned at him. The pure joy on her face made this all worthwhile. Sweat trickled down his forehead and back, dampening his white suit, but he didn't care. Henry couldn't remember the last time he let himself go like this, all thanks to the gorgeous woman twirling around him. He felt dizzy with happiness. He grabbed her around the waist and dipped her forward. Clara let out a squeal of delight at the movement.

The room glowed, the people moved, but all Henry could see was Clara. He couldn't remember what life was like before her, and he couldn't fathom what it would be like without her. In one moment, his life had become forever changed - completely altered by the impact of Clara. Her smell, her sound, and the feel of her body in his arms was seared into his memory. He would forever chase the high of this moment. His arms snaked around her waist and pulled her closer to him. A light sheen of sweat coated her arms.

"God, woman. You are absolutely perfect," he murmured against her neck.

"I bet you say that to all the girls." Her lips gently grazed his ear as she spoke. Henry shivered and pulled her even tighter. He could spend the rest of his life in this moment easily without question. All his insecurities about dancing in front of her melted away. All worries about whether they would have a good time faded into the distance. Henry pulled back just enough to look at her face, memorizing every detail. He committed to memory every line, blemish, and bead of sweat at that moment.

"There is no one else like you." He meant every word. Clara rolled her eyes playfully and pushed his chest. Henry smiled.

"You're laying it on a little thick, Casanova." She tried to look serious, but her face immediately broke into a smile. Henry threw his hands up in mock surrender.

"Calling it like I see it, is all." He laughed. The music around them lowered, and Don Cornelius moved back to the middle of the floor, his skinny microphone held tight in his hand. Henry barely registered what he said as he watched Clara take everything in. The light hit her face in a way that made his heart beat wildly in his chest. When he talked about Clara to his friends, they joked that Henry was already so far gone over this girl, and they hadn't even been on a date yet. At the time, he had laughed it off, but now, as he watched her, he knew they were right. He was so far gone over this woman.

"When can I see you again?" Henry asked as they pulled into Clara's driveway after a night of dancing. They grabbed food at one of the diners nearby before he brought her home. Clara leaned back in the seat in mock seriousness.

"How do you know I want to go out with you again, sir? Quite presumptuous of you."

"Call it a hunch." He grinned. His confidence had grown as the night progressed. He looked down at his outfit, he was slightly sweaty, and the clothes stuck to his skin in certain spots. Still, he had never felt surer of himself or anything else than he had in that moment.

"A hunch, hmm? Well, who says the night has to end here?" she asked, raising an eyebrow.

"What do you mean?" He watched as she leaned back in the seat and put her legs on the dashboard, crossing them at the ankles.

"I'm not tired yet...but I can go if you're ready to end the night." She made a movement as if she was going to exit the car.

"No! Don't leave." He reached out and grabbed her arm. The smile on her face made him mentally kick himself for sounding so desperate. "What I meant was...I'm cool to hang out for a little longer if you want."

She settled back into the seat. The edges of her hair around her scalp were slick from sweat. Some of her makeup had begun to smudge and drip off, but Henry didn't mind. In his opinion, she still looked perfect.

"So, where do you want to be in five years?" he asked after a moment of comfortable silence..

"Hopefully done with school and finishing up my residency."

"Do you want to still be in Los Angeles?" Henry rested his head against the headrest and closed his eyes. He was still fully engaged in the conversation, allowing his body to settle after the exciting night.

"I don't. Drugs are taking over this community, and I think it will only get worse from here. This will be a dangerous place to raise kids." Clara said.

"How many kids do you want?" He asked.

"Three." She replied. Henry tried to imagine himself as a father. The thought seemed so foreign to him. He wanted a family, but after being raised poor and watching his parents barely scrape by, he wanted to at least ensure he was in a good financial position for them first.

He thought about Clara being a mother. The thought excited him in a way he had never felt before. The idea of starting a family with this woman, someone he had just recently met, made him want to smile.

"How many kids do you want?" She asked.

"As many as we can comfortably afford." He responded. Her eyebrow arched.

"We?" Her voice was playful. Henry glanced over at her, taking in her appearance, studying the curves of her hips and the lines of her face. Henry was a quick learner; Clara had just become his favorite subject.

"We."

They sat outside her house, talking in Henry's car until sunrise. Neither one wanted to be the first to end the conversation. They talked about everything, laying it all on the table for the other to see. Henry had never felt so open and at ease with anyone else. He didn't even care that they hadn't known each other long.

Later that morning, after getting ready for work, bleary-eyed and running on no sleep, he made a quick detour to the store to pick up a gift for Clara. He left roses on her doorstep with a note to meet him for dinner after she finished her day. He headed to work, counting the minutes until he could see her again.

"Tubeck, why are you smiling like that?" Henry had been so engrossed in his thoughts he hadn't noticed Tim, a coworker sidling up to his desk, watching him with a curious expression.

"What?" Henry asked, with a quick shake of his head. Tim folded his arms across his birdlike chest and narrowed his eyes.

"I haven't seen you smile this hard in... well, ever. What's up?"

"Just in a good mood, I guess," Henry replied. He took a sip of his coffee and shrugged. He wasn't about to divulge the events of his night with this man. It would have been the talk of the office by the end of the day, and he had no interest in being the latest gossip. After realizing Henry wouldn't share anything else, Tim stalked away from the desk in a huff.

Henry had only been with this company for about a year, but that didn't stop his coworkers from trying to glean as much information about him as they could. Henry remained tight-lipped, focusing on keeping his work life and private life separate. He never understood workplace gossip. They were being paid to do a specific job, not make friends.

By the time his lunch break rolled around, the high from the night before had worn off and been replaced with heavy tiredness. He was no longer a teenager that could run on two hours of sleep and be fine. He settled into his car to take a quick nap before going back in. He had just managed to drift off when a knock on his window pulled him out of his sleepy state. He squinted as he sat up.

"Lynette?"

She waved at him and swiped under her nose awkwardly. As he opened the door to get out, she stepped back and wobbled unsteadily.

"Hey, Cubby Bear." She hiccupped and shot him a lopsided smile.

"Are you alright?" Henry asked, tilting his head. She didn't look well. Her skin seemed sallow and dull, a light sheen of sweat coated her face, and her hair was tangled on her head. Lynette ignored his question and stepped towards him, placing her dirty hands on his chest. Henry turned his head slightly, repulsed by the smell seeping from her pores. It seemed to drip off her skin and coat the air around them.

"Do you have thirty dollars I could borrow?" she asked, leaning in too close to his face. He stepped back, increasing their distance, and patted his pockets.

"No. I don't. How did you even get here?" He glanced around the parking lot, "where is your car?"

"Eric has it," said Lynette, swiping under her nose again. Henry stared at her for a moment; something seemed off about her. Concern coursed through him. He and Lynette may no longer be together, but he still cared about her as a person.

"When is Eric coming back?" He asked.

"Do you have the money or not?"

His brow furrowed at her tone. They hadn't seen each other since that Halloween party, but that was less than a month ago. Lynette looked like she had aged a few years in just a few weeks. He peered at her, trying to understand the change in her appearance and demeanor. Then it clicked.

"Lynette, are you high?" Henry asked, his stomach twisted in knots. Lynette's head jerked up at the question. She stared at him in glassy-eyed defiance. Her cracked lips curled into an ugly smile.

"You always were so uptight. Never could get you to relax or open up," she said. Henry remained silent. "Eric is much more fun than you."

"Answer my question, Lynette."

"So what if I am? I feel better than I ever have with you" she hissed. Her words were meant to hurt him, but the only thing Henry felt was pity. The woman in front of him was a stranger. Maybe she always had been. Part of him wondered if this was somehow his fault. Had he driven her to this?

"Oh, Lynette..."Henry shook his head. The words lodged in his throat. Even if he didn't want to be with her, he didn't want this for her either. She stared at him, and a flicker of embarrassment crossed her face for a moment before she blinked and the wall went up. Her face became blank and unreadable. Henry vaguely registered some of his coworkers in the window, watching, foaming at the mouth for a chance to get a glimpse into his personal life. He'd be annoyed about it later, but he wanted to confirm his ex-girlfriend was safe. He still felt responsible for her.

"I don't need your pity, Henry. You always thought you were better than me."

"That's not true."

"It is! Don't you think I noticed when you stopped wanting to be with me? You only stayed with me out of pity, or obligation. Or maybe it was to make yourself feel like less of an asshole because you wanted to break up with me when my life was falling apart!" She took a shaky step toward him and pointed a finger at his chest. Henry averted his gaze. He opened his mouth to protest but then closed it. There was nothing he could say at the moment. She was right.

"I'm sorry." He mumbled. Guilt swallowed him.

"Screw you." Lynette spat. He said nothing as she turned and stalked off in the distance.

3

January, 1981

Woman, why do you stop in every clothing store we pass?" Henry grumbled half-heartedly as Clara dragged him toward a small boutique. His feet throbbed in his shoes, and he was dying for something to eat. It was rare for Clara to have a free Saturday between work and studying for her classes, and Henry jumped at the chance to spend time with her, even if it meant shopping in stores he had no interest in. He didn't care what they were doing as long as he was with her. Clara stuck out her tongue and stepped inside the shop. Henry shook his head and followed her inside. The two had spent almost every night together since that trip to the Soul Train taping.

He would spend nights tinkering with his gadgets while Clara poured over her textbooks and drilled herself on medical procedures and terms. It was a level of comfort and ease that came naturally between them. They had fallen into a rhythm. Henry found it hard to remember what life was like before Clara. Even now, as she mercilessly dragged him into store after store, he still couldn't imagine his life without her. Everything about her set his soul at ease, brought him peace, and quieted his mind.

"Hush, Hen! I just want to look at one thing. They have an excellent shoe selection in here."

"You said that about the last three stores!" He whined. Truthfully, he didn't mind shopping with her. He like to watch her try on outfits and parade around before him, but he loved giving her a hard time about it just as much. She ignored his protest and gently pushed him down in the chair nearest the dressing rooms.

"I promise I'll be done soon" she said. He shook his head, knowing that was a lie. He had fallen for that same line four different stores ago. Instead, he made himself comfortable while he waited. Clara disappeared into one of the racks of clothing.

"Excuse me, there is no loitering in this store," a thin voice said from behind him. Henry looked over his shoulder to see a small white woman glaring at him with her hands on her hips.

"I'm a customer, ma'am," Henry said quietly. He didn't want to cause trouble, but he knew what he must look like sitting in this store alone. He glanced around. He was the only black person within viewing distance. Clara had disappeared entirely somewhere in the back of the store.

"If you aren't purchasing anything, you'll need to leave, and I'll need to check your pockets before you walk out that door!" The tiny woman continued to glare at him over her wide glasses. Her lips flattened into a thin line on her face. Her bird's nest hairdo made her look old and haggard. Henry wanted to protest, but he knew this woman's word would trump anything he could say to the police. He took a deep breath and stood. When he unfolded himself from the tiny chair and stretched to his full height, he could see the fear flash across the woman's face. She stepped back defensively.

"I'll call the police!" She shrieked. Henry sighed.

"Ma'am, I haven't done anything wrong, I was just-"

"Don't come any closer!" Her voice grew shriller with each word. Henry glanced around nervously. Patrons in the store were looking in their direction. At this point, Clara was nowhere to be found. Where was she?

"I don't want any trouble," Henry spoke slowly, keeping his voice as calm as possible with the growing anxiety in his gut. He hated how guilty he felt, even though he had done nothing wrong. He resisted the urge to put his hands up in surrender.

"Get out of here! You...you ni-"

"Is everything okay over here?" Clara's voice sent a wave of calm through him but had the opposite effect on the woman. She noticeably flinched at the interruption. He turned to see Clara holding a pile of clothes and shoes. The white woman turned as well and eyed Clara.

"I was telling this man that he needed to leave," she spat. Clara stepped closer, keeping her eyes trained on the woman. Henry said nothing.

"Why does he need to leave?" Clara's voice was calm, but the coolness in her tone sent a wave of ice through the room.

"He...he looks suspicious!" The woman stammered and began wringing her hands together. "You both do."

"He was sitting there, patiently waiting for me to finish shopping. He wasn't touching anything, nor was he being loud or disruptive. What made him suspicious to you?" The tension in the room was thick enough to cut with a knife. Henry stood frozen in his spot, feeling stuck in an intense battle's crosshairs. Store patrons inched closer, anxious to see what was happening.

"Look, I don't have to explain myself to you." The woman snapped. Clara took a deep breath and stepped even closer.

"What made him suspicious?" she repeated, deliberately pausing after every word. Henry shivered at the venom dripping from Clara's tone. This was the first time he had seen her like this. The shop woman swallowed, clearly understanding that she had been caught in a lie. She glanced around nervously at the rest of the shoppers in the store.

"It must have just been a misunderstanding. There's no need to get aggressive. Can I ring your items up for you?"

"You can give me your name. I'm sure Marcel would love to hear how his employees treat customers who are minding their business." At the mention of her boss's name, the woman grew pale. Her eyes darted around helplessly. Clara wasn't tall, but her presence could still make others sweat. When the woman didn't offer a name, Clara laid each item on the floor at her feet.

"No matter. I have an excellent memory. I'll just have to describe you. Let's go, Henry."

Henry followed Clara as she marched out of the store. When they hit the fresh air, Clara huffed and relaxed her shoulders.

"That was impressive," Henry said, admiring her. She turned to look at him, eyes still ablaze with anger.

"Racist witch." she muttered, shaking her head. Henry stepped toward her and grabbed her face with his hands. She softened under his touch, her face breaking into a mischievous grin.

"You didn't have to do that." Henry gently kissed her cheeks and then her chin. "I could have just waited outside for you to get finished."

"You shouldn't have to wait outside. You were doing nothing wrong." Clara glanced behind him at the store. Henry was almost sure the woman was at the window watching them. He felt slightly embarrassed and guilty, even though Clara was right; he had done nothing wrong. This is why Henry avoided the small, snooty stores like this. He always felt like he was committing a crime just by existing.

"Are you really going to call the store owner on her?" Henry asked, grabbing her hand. Her skin felt soft against his fingers. He swirled his thumb in small circles against her knuckles.

"I don't actually know him." Clara grinned. "I was bluffing." Henry stared at her in disbelief.

"You don't? You called him Marcel."

"I overheard her on the phone mentioning Marcel as her boss. Took a chance." Clara shrugged.

Henry threw his head back and let out a deep laugh. The sheer confidence and audacity emanating from Clara were something to be studied. It was risky, but judging from the panic that had spread across that woman's face, it paid off. He shook his head in complete amazement.

"Woman, you are absolutely unbelievable." Henry wrapped his arms around her waist and pulled her close to him. When their lips touched, that shockwave he had become familiar with shuddered through his body. He would happily spend every day kissing her if he could.

Clara eventually pulled away, laughing. Henry found himself laughing along with her; her joy was contagious. He felt a deep sense of contentment just being around her. Is this what love felt like? Is this what all of the songs and poems were about? He could see his future in the sparkles of her eyes.

"Let's get you something to eat." Her gentle voice broke through Henry's thoughts. His answering stomach rumble made her giggle. "Clearly, you're hungry." As much as he wanted to profess his unwavering and undying love, Henry couldn't deny that he was starving. It had been hours since they had breakfast, and with all of the walking, it had long since been digested.

"I'm dying for some fried chicken, collards, mashed potatoes, biscuits, and-" Henry stopped short, "What?"

"You want all of that for lunch? What about dinner?"

"Well, for dinner, I was thinking we could probably do some steak, macaroni and cheese, green beans, and-"

"Henry!" Clara shouted with a laugh; she placed a hand over his mouth. He smiled around her fingers and raised his hands in defeat. Clara squinted at him; she raised her hand to shield her eyes from the sun. There was a slight chill in the air, even though the sun continued to shine bright. They turned and headed towards his car; Henry slowed his walk to give Clara a second to catch up. It took her three steps to match his since his legs were much longer than hers. He resisted the urge to grab her and put her on his back.

"Let's stop by the grocery store. Sounds like I have some cooking I need to get started on."

"Have you made fried chicken before?" Henry asked, peering in her direction. She narrowed her eyes at him, mock offense contorting her expression.

"How dare you question my cooking!" Henry smiled. The last time she had cooked resulted in a grease fire in his home. He had taken a nap only to wake up to smoke filtering into the living room from the kitchen. Henry was terrified that something happened to Clara, only to find her sheepishly fanning the flames over the stove.

"You remember the last chicken you tried to make?" Henry said gently. When she rolled her eyes, he tugged at a curl and tapped her chin with his finger. "I'll give you another shot just because you're so pretty."

"Flattery gets you nowhere, Henry." Clara deadpanned. He looked over at her just in time to catch her smile. He chuckled but stopped short when they reached his car. The laughter died in his throat.

Lynette.

She looked even worse than he had seen her two months ago, leaning against his car. How did she keep finding him? She seemed to pop up at the worst times. Her skin looked sallow and dull, her hair was matted and seemed missing in some spots, and her clothes were tattered and dirty. His heart cracked a little. Henry couldn't help but feel responsible every time he saw her. He glanced over at Clara, hoping he could redirect her before they got too close, but it was too late. Lynette locked eyes with her.

"You his new hoe?" she asked lazily. Clara observed her cooly, saying nothing.

"Watch your mouth," Henry replied, his irritation immediately overshadowed his pity. He could see that Lynette was struggling, but he wouldn't tolerate anyone bad-mouthing Clara in his presence. Lynette dragged her eyes over his face, her reaction time severely delayed.

"You look like you have money. You got forty dollars I can borrow? I can pay you back." Lynette turned back to Clara and swiped a hand over her forehead. A layer of sweat coated her skin even though it was chilly out. Specks of blood dotted her shirt. Henry's heart jumped in his throat.

"What's your name?" Clara asked. Lynette glared at her for a minute and then looked around warily.

"Why you want to know?" Her voice was hoarse and scratchy like she hadn't done much talking in the past few days. Henry wasn't sure what drugs she had been doing, but it was intense. She had changed so much in such a short period. Or had she always been this bad off, and he hadn't cared enough to notice?

"I'd like to know the name of people asking me for money," Clara responded. Henry watched the two of them interact, his stomach in knots. Would Clara view him differently for having associated with her? Lynette scratched at her arms and shrugged.

"My name is Lynette."

"I don't have any cash for you, Lynette, but I can feed you. Are you hungry?"

Lynette gave a slight nod. Tears welled in her eyes. Henry watched, unable to speak. Clara wrapped her arms around Lynette and rubbed her back.

"Come. Let's get you something to eat."

Later that night, Henry stared in disbelief as Clara bustled around his living room. Lynette laid on the couch covered in blankets with a half-eaten sandwich on the coffee table in front of her. It was mind-blowing to see the difference in Lynette's appearance. Not even six months earlier, she was walking around the house as if she owned it. Now it was Clara, running around searching closets and grabbing blankets to ensure Lynette was comfortable. She offered Lynette some of her newly purchased clothes from their shopping trip and let her take a hot shower.

Clara unmatted Lynette's hair, washed it, and braided it down. Without judgment and hesitation, Clara stepped in to care for a woman in need, even though that woman was Henry's ex-girlfriend. Even though that same woman had called her names just hours before.

Tears pushed at the corners of Henry's eyes at Clara's selflessness. He wasn't sure before, but he knew now, without a shadow of a doubt, that he loved her. Her name was etched onto the fibers of his soul. She was in his bones and in his blood. Everything in him was forever changed by this woman. He felt unworthy and so incredibly lucky all at once.

"How can someone be so perfect?" Henry asked quietly. Clara, paused to look at him as she folded the extra blankets.

"What?" she asked, tilting her head. Henry stared at her, taking in her casual beauty. She had changed into his sweatpants and a black tank top that hugged her curves in the right places and threw her hair into a messy top bun, and wispy curls sprang free on her head. It was wild and unkempt. It was confidence and beauty. It was everything.

"Marry me," he said. The words surprised both of them. Clara stared at him as the blanket she was folding fluttered to the floor.

"Did you just say what I think you said?" she whispered. Henry nodded and gathered her in his arms. Lynette tossed on the couch in fitful sleep. He gently guided Clara into his kitchen to give them some privacy.

"Clara, we haven't been together long, but this feels different." He grabbed her hands in his. "You are the sun, the moon, and the stars. You are everything beautiful about this world in human form. And I want you—no, I need you to be my wife."

"I'm still in school" she said weakly, staring up at him. He placed a kiss on her forehead.

"We can wait until after you finish if you'd like, or we can wait a few years. It doesn't matter. As long as you promise me that you will be my wife one day."

Clara pulled away from him, tugging absentmindedly at some loose curls in her bun. She paced before him, nerves bubbling off her in waves.

"Your ex-girlfriend is addicted to something and is currently on your couch," she said.

"She is."

"We have only been dating for three months. How can you be sure?"

"I've found the one whom my soul loves," Henry whispered. She whirled to face him, eyes narrowed.

"Did you just quote Song of Solomon at me?" she demanded. He smiled and nodded.

"I did."

"Henry!" Clara ran a hand over her face, "This is insane." Henry cupped her face, forcing her to stop pacing and look up at him.

"Do you love me?" He asked simply.

"Of course. So much."

"Then say yes. We will figure the rest out." Lynette snored from her position on the couch, but both ignored it. They stared into each other's eyes, saying everything they didn't have the words to say out loud. Henry knew it was a big jump when they hadn't known each other long enough to gauge each other, but he had seen everything he needed. He witnessed everything he needed to witness, and he knew without a doubt in his mind or soul that Clara was the one for him. She was his wife. Something flickered in Clara's eyes as she looked at him; her mouth opened and closed wordlessly. Henry held his breath as he waited, ready to go out and purchase a ring at that exact moment if she agreed. He prayed to every deity imaginable that she would.

"Ask...ask me again," Clara whispered, a sob caught in her throat. Tears rushed down her cheeks. Henry swiped them away and kissed her gently on the lips. His heart and stomach flipped, meeting in the middle of his body with a thump.

"Clara Linwood, I love you more than I ever imagined loving anyone. I may not have much to offer you right now, but if you give me a chance, I promise to spend the rest of my life making you as happy as you have made me." He kissed each cheek, tasting the salt in her tears.

"Ask me again," she demanded.

"You are all together beautiful, my love; there is no flaw in you. Marry me, woman. Make me the happiest man on this earth. Please." Both were crying now. Henry could count on one hand how many times he had cried in his adult life, but as he stood here now, cradling perfection in his hands, he couldn't help but be overcome with emotion. Clara nodded; tears fell freely from her eyes and dripped down her neck.

"Yes."

PART TWO

4

So many people believe that love is only about finding the right person to spend life with, when in reality, it's about finding the right relationship. People are not perfect, even when they have the best intentions. Love, even with the right person, is never easy. There will be storms and there will be hard times. That is inevitable in this life, but the real key to love is developing a relationship with a person that can sustain you during hard times. Otherwise, it can ruin your entire life.

Henry had seen so many people trapped in loveless marriages or toxic relationships that he was skeptical about love until he experienced it himself. His brother married a woman he hadn't known long and got scammed out of his entire life savings. Luckily, Henry married a fantastic woman. Clara Tubeck, formally known as Clara Linwood, and every moment with her felt like a fairytale. They were married for almost thirty-five years. He married her when he was thirty years old, and even though he was a completely different person back then, the part of him that never changed. was his love for Clara. It kept him going. He fell more hopelessly and madly in love with her by the day.

It's funny because he never believed in love before he met her. He had been in a relationship headed nowhere fast when he met Clara at a party. He was trying to figure out a way to gracefully ease his way out of that relationship when he literally stumbled into his answer: Clara. From the moment he met her, he was unable to focus on anyone else. His friends and brother relentlessly teased him about how wide-open she had him. He knew from their first conversation that he was going to marry her. He was even bold enough to tell her. She laughed at him then, but a year later, he proved himself. That was thirty-five years, three kids, and one whole lifetime ago.

Their anniversary was coming soon, and Henry was working on a surprise trip to Paris. Clara always wanted to go to Paris. That was the one thing she asked of him when they first got married. At the time, he was still new in his career field and couldn't afford it, and then they started having kids. The dream kept getting pushed back until they eventually forgot about it. Now, as he set the table for their dinner, he smiled to himself at how excited she would be in a few weeks when he surprised her with the trip.

It felt like a massive accomplishment in more ways than one. He was able to afford it on his own, and he was finally able to gift her with the vacation of her wildest dreams. He had everything planned out perfectly. Even down to the way he was going to surprise her. He would take her to her favorite little French bakery and get her some macarons in all the different colors and flavors she loved. Then he would ask if they tasted the same in Paris. When she shrugged, he would pull out the tickets in a grand sweeping, "Ta-Da!" type of moment.

He heard her car pull into the driveway just as he put the finishing touches on their dinner. He watched her from the kitchen window with a dopey grin as she walked up the driveway to the front door. The sight of her still made his heart flutter. Even decked out in her scrubs and messy hair, she still looked radiant in Henry's eyes. She had just come home from an unusually long day at the hospital where she worked as an anesthesiologist. She was usually home before he was, but he liked to have dinner ready for her on her long days by the time she got home. He set the table for the two of them and waited for her to enter the kitchen. After waiting a moment, he walked a few paces toward the front door and opened it. She stood, front door key in hand and arm outstretched in the process of unlocking the door. He smiled at her.

"What took you so long?" He laughed. She stuck her tongue out at him and entered the house; the front door squeaked a little as she closed it behind her. She glanced around the foyer at the scattered pictures of their family throughout the different stages of life and let out a small sigh. She barely made it to the living room before kicking off her shoes. Henry followed her, amused at how much she resembled their eldest daughter at that moment.

"I forgot which key it was for a second," she said sheepishly. "It's been a long day." She tossed her work bag on the couch and sniffed the air. Henry smiled. He knew she would be excited to see that he made her favorite, Chicken Marsala. It was the only thing Henry learned how to make. He forced himself to learn when they married so that he had a go-to meal whenever he wanted to help out.

Her brown eyes sparkled as she stood on her tiptoes to kiss his cheek. He wanted to grab her around the waist and take her directly to the bedroom, but he resisted. He'd at least let her get a couple of bites of food first. "This smells amazing," she sighed. Her eyes closed as she savored the smell.

"Only the best for you, baby." He grinned with a seductive wink. She rolled her eyes at him, but he could see a hint of a smile on her plump lips. The remnants of the lipstick she had put on that morning stained the edges of her mouth. The two of them sat down together at the kitchen table and began to eat. Clara closed her eyes, savoring each bite. "If I didn't know any better, I'd think you were an amazing cook based on this dish alone." He chuckled and gave a quick shrug.

"It's about quality, not quantity."

She playfully smacked his arm, which made him laugh again. Clara began to hum as she ate. It was the one thing that seemed to annoy him. Humming would have easily been at the top if someone asked him to list her negative qualities. Very little time passed without her humming or singing the lyrics to a song at the top of her lungs. It annoyed him most in moments when he preferred silence, but he learned to live with it. Everyone had annoying habits, and if she could deal with him leaving his clothes all over the house, he could certainly deal with her humming.

"I heard from Rose today" she said after a moment, breaking him out of his thoughts. Rose was the eldest of their three children. She and her husband moved to the next town over recently. She claimed she wanted to get a fresh start and separate herself from the house and city where she grew up, but every day since they moved, she called her mom to complain about what it was missing.

"Is she settling in okay?" he asked, already knowing the answer.

Clara raised an eyebrow at him and smirked. "You already know she was complaining." They both laughed. Their daughter was nothing if not stubborn.

"I talked to Junior earlier," Henry said, putting another bite of chicken in his mouth. He cursed himself for not making enough for leftovers. Even if it was the only dish he knew how to make, he made it well. He had years to perfect it. He resisted the urge to lean down and lick his plate. Clara tilted her head and looked at him, expecting an update. He purposely took his time chewing, knowing she would get frustrated with him. Like clockwork, she smacked his arm. "Don't leave me in suspense!

How is he doing?" He laughed and set down his fork.

"He's good. He is still working on the concept for his restaurant. He just signed a contract with a wine vendor. According to him, it's an incredibly classy vendor that not many people score," Henry replied with a small shrug. He knew nothing about wine or vendors, but the excitement in his son's voice as he explained was enough to let him know how big a of a deal it was. Clara smiled; her face glittered with pride. Henry was incredibly proud of Junior as well. It was hard not to be, after everything he had accomplished and pushed through on his own. Things were a bit touch and go for a while as he struggled to find his place in the culinary industry, but he was blossoming in the field and making quite a name for himself.

Junior had shown interest in being a chef since he was a young boy, favoring trying out new recipes in the kitchen with his mom over sports and roughhousing with the neighborhood kids. After graduating from culinary school, he talked about opening his own restaurant. He had briefly partnered with a friend planning to open his own place, but the funding fell through. Henry was worried Junior would let it get to him, but he bounced back much quicker than expected. He almost immediately started drafting the plans for his new spot.

Henry encouraged him to take a few business classes before he really got started to ensure he had enough resources to succeed. Most restaurants don't make it past the first two years, and ones owned by black men make it even less often. Henry was impressed with how things seemed to fall into place for his son. He expected to have to step in at some point or offer some funding, but so far, Junior was handling everything on his own. All he needed Henry to do was be there for support. Henry felt a mixture of pride and sadness at the fact that his only son no longer needed him, but that happens as kids grow and come into their own. They no longer need their parents as much.

"Rue is good. She is taking some interior design classes," Clara continued. Henry tried not to wince. Rue was their youngest and in Henry's opinion, the most difficult. Like her mother, she was a strong-willed firecracker, but where Clara remained focused and determined, Rue seemed a bit aimless. She could never decide what career path she wanted, could never stick to a hobby for more than a few months, and never seemed to know what she wanted to do next. It was exhausting and expensive. She was still in college, but only because she changed her major more times than Henry bothered to count.

If he was being honest with himself, he really couldn't relate much to Rue. Her brother and sister were both older and much easier to get along with. By the time Clara had the baby of the family at forty years old, Henry was well established in his career and was trying to push for a higher position. He felt like he spent more time working than at home and missed most of her childhood. When he realized that he made a mistake in neglecting her, she was no longer interested in hanging out with him. Clara admitted to Henry during their late-night conversations that sometimes Rue escaped her too. She was hard to pin down. Her interests changed so often. He remembered getting her a Bratz doll for her tenth birthday because she had been obsessed with those big-headed, bug-eyed monstrosities for months. He was confident she would love the gift and spent the day almost too excited to give her the present, finally certain he had managed to pick something she would actually like. He couldn't wait to see the look on her face. His nerves buzzed with excitement as her tiny fingers unwrapped the box, but when she looked up at him, the disappointment in her eyes shattered his soul.

"Daddy, I don't even like these anymore!" she said with a stomp of her foot. He felt incredibly embarrassed at that moment like he somehow failed her. That is how their relationship had always been. He struggled like an idiot to keep up with her ever-evolving interests and style. Eventually, he stopped attempting to figure her out and just let her be. He tried not to act like the distance between them didn't bother him.

"Did I tell you I heard from Rose today?" Clara asked. He blinked, not realizing he had allowed his mind to wander during their conversation. Henry frowned and glanced over at his wife. She really must have had a long day.

"Yes, honey, you told me that already."

"No, I didn't. I asked if you had heard from her." His frown deepened. She had been doing that much more lately, repeating herself or switching small details. He assumed they were working her pretty hard at her job. She covered a few extra surgeries recently because her colleague was out on maternity leave. Henry made a mental note to try and schedule a spa day for her next weekend off. He knew she would never ask for it herself, but she needed the downtime.

After finishing dinner, Clara headed to the gym for some cardio. While she was gone, Henry caught up on some of his favorite shows, but only the ones that Clara had no interest in watching with him. She would have his head on a platter if he dared to watch any of the shows they had started together without her. His phone buzzed with an incoming notification.

At the store, do you want anything?

Henry glanced down at the text message from Clara. He wondered what was taking her so long at the gym. She usually only stayed for about an hour at night. She claimed the cardio helped her sleep better. Henry didn't object as long as she didn't expect him to accompany her.

No thanks, I'll see you when you get home. Drive safe.

He tossed his phone on the couch beside him and settled in to finish his show. By the time Clara arrived, he had fallen asleep on the couch. She leaned over and shook him gently to wake him.

"I brought you the ice cream you wanted." She grinned, holding up a gray Walmart bag. He rubbed his eyes and sat up.

"I didn't ask you for ice cream, babe." He said gently. She turned back from the groceries she was unpacking and stared at him.

"What? Yes, you did." Her brow furrowed in confusion. He shook his head, which only made the frown on her face deepen. She crossed the room and touched a hand to his forehead, staring at him as if he had grown another head while she was gone.

"Are you okay, honey? That's the second time today you've mixed up the conversation," Clara said, moving her hand from his forehead to his cheek. Henry stared at her in disbelief. He wanted to protest, but instead of pushing the issue, he shrugged and took the bag with the Ben and Jerry's carton of ice cream. At least he gota treat out of the confusion.

"How was the gym?" h asked. He stuck a spoon in the cold treat and then licked it. The ice cream melted as he moved it around in his mouth. Chocolate Fudge Brownie - his favorite. It looked a little like dirt, but it tasted so good. She grabbed a bottle of water and sat beside him on the couch. She smelled like perfume mixed with sweat. Call him weird, but he didn't mind the smell at all. To him, she always smelled amazing, even in her smelliest moments. He chuckled to himself. Maybe he was as wide open as his people had teased him about.

"It was good. I ran a mile in less than the time before."

"Are you going to tackle that 5k again this year?"

She nodded and grinned at him. He admired her commitment to fitness. At sixty-five years old, she still hit the gym several times weekly.

Henry was a lot less committed. He tried but could never stick with it. He used to be more into building muscle when he was a bit younger, but he was never interested in it for the right reasons. He had only done it to garner the attention of as many women as he could. He didn't care much about the physical benefits. He stuck with it for about two years and then eventually stopped going as often until one day he looked up and realized it had been months since he even stepped foot inside a gym. Luckily for him, he had a slender build. so people assumed he stayed in shape, even though he didn't.

"Have you talked to the kids recently?" she asked absentmindedly. He watched as she untied her shoes. Her shirt slipped up a bit to reveal her back's smooth and blemish-free skin. He resisted the urge to touch it and instead focused on what she asked. He stared at her, wondering if he should be concerned. When a moment passed, and he still didn't answer, she glanced up at him.

"What?" she asked, giving him a weird look. "Why are you staring at me like that?"

"We talked about the kids over dinner." He said, watching to gauge her reaction. She tilted her head to one side as if trying to remember the conversation. He watched her, mildly concerned. After a moment, Clara snapped her fingers.

"Oh! Right. Yes, I remember now. Whew. I must be tired. I'm going to take a shower and get ready for bed." Henry shook his head. He kept telling her not to work so much, but she insisted on picking up extra shifts to help out and now she was too tired to remember simple conversations. She was always willing to extend herself to others, even when that meant she spread herself too thin. It was a blessing and a curse.

He turned back to the episode of the Netflix show he was watching, getting ready to press play on the next episode. Clara took a few steps toward the bedroom and then turned toward him with a mischievous grin. He raised an eyebrow.

"Are you coming?" she asked. He hopped up from his seat on the couch as quickly as his body would allow and hurried towards her. She let out a playful shriek and took off running towards the bathroom. He caught her around the waist a moment later and tackled her to the ground in an awkward heap. They laughed, entirely out of breath from the effort. She gazed up at him, the laughter faded from her eyes and replaced with a look full of longing and desire. His body began to heat up just from the intensity of her gaze. He kissed her lips and sighed against her mouth when she slid her tongue against his and wrapped her arms around his neck.

"I love you," she said breathlessly, her eyelids low. He bit his lip and grinned at his wife.

"Keep talking to me like that, and you'll be too tired to go to work tomorrow." He laughed. She kissed him again and pressed her body against his. He melted under her touch. Any concern he had felt moments earlier was long gone.

They say hindsight is 20/20, and looking back on those small moments, the signs were right there in his face taunting him. Instead, he chose to ignore it and look the other way, unable to accept that there could be an issue. Henry had always been the king of denial. He felt most comfortable in it, and when life had moments that were too hard to process, he would deny that there was anything wrong. Deny, deny, and deny. He would pretend it wasn't happening. They say that once you admit it out loud, that's when it becomes real but that's only true sometimes. In those moments , your mind is telling you that something is wrong and you need to pay attention to what's happening. That is when it becomes real.

5

A few days passed without incident; Clara went to work like usual, and they had been without issue for almost a week. No memory lapses. No confusion. Conversations passed by without a hitch. There were no miscommunications between them, but when Henry started to believe that maybe it was just a fluke, it circled back around and planted itself right in front of his face, daring him to acknowledge it.

He sat at his work desk, gazing at the passing cars out the window. The sun started to set, leaving the sky streaked in beautiful shades of purples and pinks. Henry glanced at the clock and nodded to himself. He had about half an hour left until it was time to leave. The day had been long and laborious, leaving him exhausted and looking forward to going home to relax.

Clara promised him they could catch up on *The Blacklist*, one of their favorite Netflix shows. He had been begging her for the last few days to watch it, so they could avoid spoilers on the internet. He was ducking specific social media timelines because he didn't want to run the risk of someone spoiling the show before he could get to it. It was exhausting work trying to make sure he remained spoiler-free. If she didn't watch it tonight, he would just do it without her and pretend he hadn't seen it yet. Clara called him while he was sitting at his desk, wrapping up his work for the night. The smile that lit up his face when he saw her picture on his phone vanished as soon as he heard her voice.

"Henry?" she asked. He knew immediately that something was wrong.

"What's wrong, beautiful?"

"Oh, Hen! Today has been the worst day. The absolute worst. I can't even believe I still have my job."

"It couldn't have been that bad! Talk to me. What's wrong?" He frowned at the phone and closed out his emails. He had a few clients trying to touch base with him at the last minute, but he would have to get to that later. He had already given most of his clients his office hours, so there was no point in worrying about it now. They'd have to learn when to reach out and when they could expect an answer. The frustration in Clara's voice brought him back to the conversation.

"I made so many pointless mistakes. I have been doing this job for years. I know this place like I know my own name, and today it felt like it did almost fifteen years ago when I first started." There were tears in her voice; Henry could tell she was beating herself up. His heart squeezed. He packed up the work he had decided to finish at home, grateful that the day was finally over for him.

"Oh honey, I'm sorry. You've been stressed out lately with all those extra shifts. That's all," he said, balancing the phone between his ear and his shoulder so he could grab the rest of his things. "I told you that you needed to relax. You don't owe that job anything. You don't owe them you." Clara sniffed into the phone. Her voice sounded small and unsure.

"Yeah, I guess you're right," she said quietly. He heard a rustling in the background, like she had moved or dropped the phone. He nodded at his boss on the way out and headed for his car. On his way home, he'd stop and get Clara some roses to cheer her up after having such a hard day at work. He would book that spa appointment he had meant to set up for her this weekend. After a relaxing weekend, she would be good as new by the time she returned to work on Monday.

"We can talk more about it when you get home. Are you almost done for the day?"

"Yes. I've got one more quick procedure, and then I should be on the way in about an hour." After they hung up, he took a deep breath, trying to shove his concern out of the way. She was just stressed, that was all. She had been working a lot, which had taken a toll on her memory. She would be fine once she had some rest and could recharge. Their anniversary was coming soon, and his plan to take her to Paris was still underway. That trip would be perfect for her to finally take a moment to breathe.

He talked to their travel agent, a pleasant heavy-set woman with an odd obsession with floral prints, who had sent him an itinerary of all the art and culture available where they would be staying. He knew that Clara would be over the moon to finally experience some of her favorite places in person. He had the day he would surprise her marked off in his phone. Each day it pinged with a countdown to the big reveal. He hadn't been this excited about anything in a while. He felt like a little kid in a candy store, eager to touch all the colorful candies on the shelves.

By the time he got home, it was already dark. He hated the winter months when it would get darker earlier. It felt like he wasted his entire day at work on those days. When he arrived, it was dark, and it was dark again when he left. The prettiest parts of the day occurred when he was stuck in the office. He absolutely understood why people became depressed during these months. The cold weather was definitely no help, either.

Clara still hadn't made it home yet, so he placed the flowers he purchased in a vase on the kitchen counter. It would be the first thing she'd see when she came home. He knew it wouldn't erase her trouble at work, but it could at least make her smile for a bit. He pulled out the stack of takeout menus they kept in the kitchen. His stomach grumbled as he looked through the items, trying to decide what he wanted to eat. He hadn't eaten since breakfast earlier that morning because he was so busy at work. Days like this left him so hungry he would probably eat plastic if enough salt was sprinkled on top. Clara always fussed at him for not taking the time to eat. She'd tell him that his body was convinced that it was being starved. He listened, but it mostly went in one ear and out the other.

What are you and Mom doing for your anniversary? A text from his oldest daughter momentarily distracted him as he headed to the office to set his work stuff down. He planned to tackle some of it later, but for the moment, he wanted to just relax and not think about it. The clients could wait.

Paris trip. Don't tell her, it's a surprise.. A few seconds later, another text made his phone vibrate.

Fancy! I'm jealous. Bring me back a croissant!

Henry smiled to himself and placed his phone in his back pocket. Clara should be home soon. When she arrived, he would order some takeout from the Chinese restaurant around the corner; their menu looked the most appetizing and let her vent about her day. That was the usual routine when she had a rougher day than average. He learned long ago that pumping her full of her favorite foods and letting her vent her frustrations would almost always do the trick when she was upset. If that didn't work, she would snuggle with their dog Chauncy for a bit. Almost as if he could sense being thought about, Chauncy lifted his head and stared at Henry with a quick thump of his tail. His left ear had flopped inside out. Henry reached down to give him a quick scratch and fix his ear. He sat down on the couch and turned on the television. The news station droned quietly in the background. Without realizing it, Henry drifted off to sleep.

He popped awake to someone knocking on the front door and Chauncy barking hysterically. It took him a second to register where he was and why it was so dark in the house. Apparently, he had fallen asleep. He grabbed his phone in the dark living room to check the time. 10pm. Clara still wasn't home. When he talked to her earlier, she said the last procedure would only take an hour. That was six hours ago.

The knock sounded again. Just as blue lights began to flash from the driveway, Henry looked up. They bounced off the walls of the house. Henry's stomach dropped to his knees as he hauled himself off the couch and raced to the front door. Something happened. Why were the police here? Was Clara alright?

He threw open the front door to see an officer standing with his hands on his hips. Looking wholly disheveled and distraught, Clara peeked from behind the officer's shoulder. Henry stared at the both of them, his mouth open in shock.

"Are you Mr. Tubeck?" The officer asked; his voice was gruff with an air of irritation. Henry nodded dumbly.

"Is this your wife?" he asked, motioning to Clara. Henry nodded again. "Someone called the police after she was seen driving back and forth down the street about three blocks over." Clara burst into tears behind him. Henry vaguely registered the neighbors staring from a few doors down.

"Thank you, officer." He turned his attention to his wife. "Baby? What happened?"

"I...I...I couldn't find you." She collapsed in his arms and sobbed. His heart sank. The stress was getting to be too much for her to handle. If she kept going at this rate, she would make herself sick. He made a mental note to discuss with her about cutting back at work; he was starting to worry about her. The officer watched the two of them, an unreadable expression on his face. Henry felt uncomfortable, suddenly aware that they were being observed.

He gently guided Clara to the couch and sat her down. Her hands were wrapped around his shirt, hanging on to him for dear life. He gently pried her fingers off of his clothing so he could address the officer, who, at the moment, was still standing in front of the wide-open door, just watching them. She began to sob even louder, wrapping her arms around herself for protection. Henry blinked away his own tears and turned his attention back to the officer.

"Thank you for bringing her home, sir," he said. The officer nodded; his face relaxed into a knowing expression that Henry didn't like. How dare he assume he knew what was happening in this home?

"It's no problem. My mother had the same struggle. I...I know what you must be feeling." The officer reached forward to place a hand on Henry's shoulder, but he stepped out of reach, annoyed by the officer's assumptions. It didn't make him feel any better.

"What do you mean? She's just stressed. She's fine." He snapped, glaring at the officer. His voice came out much more tense than he had meant it to. The officer looked at him briefly, shocked at his reaction, but then his face softened, and he nodded. "Yes, well...you guys have a good night." He offered an awkward smile that Henry didn't return and retreated to his vehicle.

That man had no idea what he was talking about. Clara was fine. There was nothing wrong other than that she needed to relax. Clara continued crying while Henry held her, stroking her hair and kissing her forehead, unsure what to do or say. After what felt like an eternity, she leaned back and looked up at him.

"Henry, something is wrong," she whispered. He recoiled and shook his head.

"Don't be silly, baby. Nothing is wrong. You just need to rest." He patted her hair, hoping they could change the subject. He didn't want to think about this, not now. She shook her head, and when he tried to guide her back down to his shoulder, she pulled back and looked at him; her eyes were desperate and pleading.

"We need to see a doctor."

"We have the results from the tests, Mr. Tubeck and Dr. Tubeck." Henry and Clara sat in the small office, huddled together, holding hands and hoping for good news. Clara had been whispering silent prayers since they woke up that morning. Part of Henry thought she was overreacting, but a small piece of him, in the back of his mind, was worried that maybe he wasn't reacting enough. He tried to be positive for Clara, but she was so worried that what he said didn't matter. In the days leading up to the appointment, she had been so jittery and off balance that he had to ban her from the kitchen.

He came home to find her cell phone in the refrigerator beside the milk. He laughed it off, but Clara was panicky and inconsolable. He hated seeing her so upset, but he wasn't sure what to do to improve things. So, he came with her to this appointment, even though he didn't think they needed it, and sat with her in the waiting room. They had been waiting for twenty minutes for the doctor to be ready to see them, and in those twenty minutes, Clara managed to come up with every worst possible scenario her brain could conjure up. Henry watched helplessly while she bubbled with anxiety and paced the room, trying to run down the list of possible explanations.

Maybe she had a tumor that would need to be removed through surgery. Perhaps she was too stressed at work and would need to take a break for a while. If that were the case, they would need to revisit their finances and create a new monthly budget. They would survive, but the hit to their monthly income would require some adjustments. Henry did his best to keep her calm while they waited, but once she had an idea, her mind was not changing. He breathed a sigh of relief when Dr. Mizzelle finally entered his office and sat at the desk before them. Finally, they could get this over with and go home. He would ease Clara's mind and tell her that her forgetfulness was due to being stressed or overworked at the hospital. He'd ask her to take it easy and make a point to relax a little more. Everything would be fine.

"Please tell her that nothing is wrong and it's not a big deal. It's just stress," Henry said, folding his arms across his chest. Clara shot him a sharp look. He knew she was becoming irritated with his flippant attitude about the situation, but it was the only way he could handle it without freaking out himself. He had been struggling to accept the possibility that this wasn't just a misunderstanding. What if something was actually wrong? What was he supposed to do then?

"It's just stress, right?" He said again, with much less confidence. He sat back in his chair, trying to force his suddenly buzzing nerves to relax. Dr. Mizzelle looked at the two of them, pausing as if he needed to choose his words carefully. His mouth twisted in a slight frown.

"Don't keep us in suspense, Doc. What is it?"

Dr. Mizzelle smiled gently as he settled in behind his office desk. It was a large mahogany desk with a computer screen on the left and a haphazard stack of papers to his right. Henry finally sensed that whatever he was about to say wasn't good. He would have eased their worry by now, but instead, Dr. Mizzelle was fidgeting with the buttons on his lab coat, looking everywhere but at the two of them.

"Out with it," Henry snapped, his frustration growing. The sooner they got this appointment over with, the sooner they could pretend it never happened and get something to eat. Or they could laugh about it and use it as a fun dinner conversation. "Do you remember that time your mom thought she was losing her mind? That was funny, right?" He imagined their kids laughing at them over the next holiday dinner. This entire ordeal would be a distant memory. Dr. Mizzelle looked up at him and sighed heavily before leaning forward.

"Now, I need you to understand that, while this may be difficult to accept initially, you have options. New medications are being created daily, and while there is no cure, there are ways to manage it successfully." He took a deep breath. Henry's brow furrowed, and Clara reached for his hand; her own was trembling uncontrollably. Henry's heart began to pound.

No cure? New medications? This didn't mean what he thought it meant, did it? He swallowed, realizing that his own hands had started to tremble slightly. Dread stiffened his muscles.

"Wh-What are you talking about?" he asked. "What did the results say?"

"We have resources. We have support groups. We have-"

"Dr. Mizzelle, please."

"Mr. Tubeck, I'm afraid it is rapid early onset Alzheimer's." He paused, letting them take in what he had just said. Clara let out a small squeak and covered her mouth with her hand. Henry's appetite vanished immediately, replaced by nausea. He blinked, stunned. He hadn't prepared himself for this. He fought the urge to get up and leave the room.

Alzheimer's?

6

W hat?"

Maybe he misheard. He had to have misheard. Henry shook his head quickly, refusing to accept that as the answer. Alzheimer's? While they waited for the results, Clara had run down the list of worst-case scenarios, but Alzheimer's wasn't on the list anywhere. He hadn't even considered the possibility that the sudden changes in memory were this serious. He thought it was just stress from an extra workload or normal aging. It couldn't be this serious. It had to be some type of mistake.

Henry glanced around the office, searching for something out of place to let him know that this was just an ugly nightmare, and he would wake up in his bed with his wife sleeping next to him, completely fine and free of any disease. He blinked, waiting for his surroundings to morph into their bedroom. He listened for the familiar sounds of their home at night -cars passing, their dog snoring at the foot of the bed, the sound of the television playing in the background. Something. Anything. But nothing changed.

"I understand that this may be hard to hear," the doctor said. His voice had a syrupy sweet tone; it sounded almost condescending. Henry wanted to reach forward, wrap his fingers around the man's thick neck, and squeeze just to wipe that look off his face.

"We have a list of resources we can provide so you'll have an idea of what to expect in the upcoming months," the doctor continued to talk to them, trying to ease the blow of the diagnosis they just received. Clara listened intently, occasionally dabbing her eyes with a tissue she grabbed from somewhere, but Henry felt far away- like he was watching this happen on a screen. The doctor's voice sounded muffled, like he was talking underwater. The walls in the room suddenly felt way too small. He stared at the ugly pale blue wallpaper with faint hints of flower designs. The harder Henry stared, trying to block out the conversation, the more the flowers seemed to dance and swirl around the wall. He felt the vague beginnings of a headache easing up the back of his neck.

Alzheimer's. How was this even possible? Both were still young. Their 70th birthdays had yet to come around. She was only 65 years old. They both were. How was this happening now? The memory loss and forgetfulness hadn't been that bad. Sure, she had forgotten obvious information and had started doing absentminded things like leaving the house without turning off the stove or forgetting to turn off the shower and flooding the bathroom. They were minor inconveniences in the grand scheme of things. He didn't expected this diagnosis when she sat beside him and told him she thought a doctor's appointment needed to be made just in case. He figured she was overreacting, and things would eventually smooth out again. There must be some type of mistake. Maybe they should have looked at the results of her tests more closely. Or perhaps they mixed up her results with someone with a similar name.

That made more sense.

"Do the test again," he blurted. Dr. Mizzelle and Clara turned to look at him, surprised at his sudden outburst. Henry vaguely registered that Dr. Mizzelle had been in the middle of explaining specific symptoms to expect when Henry had interrupted him. He smiled sympathetically, folded his hands over the stack of papers on his desk, and stared at Henry, looking like he was trying to cherry-pick his response. It made Henry even angrier. None of this made any sense. After a moment, he removed his glasses and placed them on the top of his head with a sigh.

"Mr. Tubeck, I understand that this may be very hard for you to hear, but I can assure you that we've-"

"I said do the test again!" Henry bellowed, standing abruptly. The dull purple chair flipped over from his sudden movement. Clara grabbed his arm to calm him down. Tears spilled out of her eyes and down her cheeks. Henry briefly felt remorse flood through him, but he was committed now. Dr. Mizzelle remained seated, unbothered by his outburst.

"We have completed the tests multiple times to ensure we had the correct diagnosis. If you wish to put yourselves through the stress of this ordeal again, we can, but I wouldn't recommend it." His voice was calm and steady. The exact opposite of what Henry was feeling at this moment. He felt like he had somehow failed to protect his wife. He stood, staring at Dr. Mizzelle as anger pumped through his veins. His blood pressure spiked, sending a sharp pain through his head. He winced a bit, knowing his anger was misdirected somewhere in his subconscious, but he couldn't seem to swallow it nor control who he directed it towards.

"Henry, honey, please." Clara's voice snapped him out of rage; the anger fizzled out of him like a deflated balloon. Her pain mirrored his own. He leaned over to fix his chair and sank in it, defeated. Dr. Mizzelle watched Henry silently with that same sympathetic expression that irritated him. He glanced away.

"Sorry," Henry muttered. He sounded eerily like a petulant child. He was only partly embarrassed for his behavior. Dr. Mizzelle nodded and reached for the stack of papers on his desk. He motioned towards the form on the top of the pile he had given Clara and Henry. Henry glanced down reluctantly, feeling almost as if he could block out this entire visit if he refused to take in any of the offered information. Denial, denial, denial. That was the key to surviving this whole thing. If he didn't accept it, then it couldn't be real.

"Here is a list of resources. You are both going to need a lot of support. We have a stunning team of home health aides that-"

"There is no need. I'll handle this on my own." Henry snapped. He was still trying hard to grasp his anger, but it was spilling out of him faster than he could stop it. Similar to that whack-a-mole game, it popped up again as soon as he smashed it down in one spot. It taunted him. He didn't want anyone in the house other than his family. He didn't need anyone to tell him how to care for himself or his wife. He had been doing so for the past three and a half decades. He would be able to handle anything that was needed on his own. Dr. Mizzelle stared at him briefly, visibly struggling with what to say next. Henry held his gaze in a steely one of his own.

"Well, you'll have the information available to you anyway." He smiled softly, nodding at the packet he had given to Clara. "Just in case you change your mind." Henry stayed silent while Clara leafed through the information. She gave a teary-eyed smile of appreciation. Henry glanced around at the office, desperately searching for something to focus on while his temper simmered inside of him.

A rack of pamphlets that sat behind Dr. Mizzelle on the wall caught his attention. The packets offered information about Alzheimer's and other dementia diagnoses, and each brochure was inundated with smiling couples and families. They were filled with sweet nothings about how they would find a way to get through the struggle together, and how they were not alone in any of it. Henry struggled to resist the urge to rip them to shreds one by one. None of this was anything to smile about.

He refused to speak for the rest of the appointment and most of the ride home. Not because he was angry at the diagnosis, but because he wasn't sure what he could say without collapsing into tears. Clara didn't need this from him. He didn't deserve to break around her when she was the one who would be suffering. She needed to know that she could count on him. So, he did his best to swallow down the rage, the devastation, and the confusion, no matter how badly he wanted to pull the car over, shake his fist at the sky and curse God for making this how their story ends. On the outside, he looked calm and in control, but on the inside, he struggled to reel his emotions in. He wanted to tuck them inside a neat little box and put that box somewhere deep in his subconscious that couldn't be reached.

He didn't want to and couldn't afford to feel it, not when Clara needed him for support. He wanted so badly to erase these last few hours from existence. When they pulled up to their beautiful, Victorian-style home that Henry had built for Clara a few years after they married, he put the car in park in the long winding driveway and stared, remembering the day he had brought her here for the first time.

The Victorian era was one of Clara's favorites. Henry struggled to understand the appeal of the sharp edges and castle-like features. Still, she constantly gushed about how much she loved the gothic influences and the intricately designed woodwork of homes during that era. When they started dating, she told him it was her dream to one day live in a house inspired by that period. As soon as his finances allowed, he built the house of her dreams. In his opinion, their home resembled a dollhouse with elaborate trim and bright colors, but all that mattered to him was that Clara loved it. He would have lived in a shoe if it had made her happy. Nothing could compare to the smile on her face and the joy in her voice when she saw the final product. It was one of his proudest moments, even many years later.

"You remember when I built you this home?" he asked, reaching for her hand.

"No."

He turned and looked at Clara, his thoughts swallowed by panic. She looked back at him with a severe expression that only lasted for a moment before her face softened into that beautiful smile that still made him weak in the knees. He relaxed, but only slightly.

"Is it too soon for jokes?" She smiled, tucking a cinnamon-colored curl behind her ear. He didn't understand how she could find a way to joke about the seriousness of this situation. But it was just like Clara to try and lighten the mood by trying to be funny. He wanted to stop wondering how long she could joke like this. How long would it take for her to forget her own personality? Their children? His face? He wanted to cry, scream, and kick himself for being unable to stop this.

"How can you joke at a time like this, Clara?" his voice cracked with pain. Her expression softened slightly as she lifted a hand to rest it on his cheek. Tears slipped down his face.

"It's hard for me too, Hen," she whispered. The sound of her unique nickname for him made his heart clench with grief. How long would it take for it to be completely forgotten? She wiped a tear from his face, her expression turning somber.

"I'll understand if you want to leave." She held up a hand to stop him from protesting. "This is going to require a lot of support. It will be exhausting. It's going to be ugly. It's going to be unfair… painful, even. I understand if it's more than what you signed up for. I wouldn't fault you for backing out."

"Clara, I have been in love with you from the moment I first saw you. You'd be foolish to think that I would choose to be anywhere other than right here with you."

"I'm letting you know you aren't obligated to-"

"I'm not leaving you. I can't handle the thought of us not being together. There is no life without you. Whatever we must do, whatever we must go through, we will do it as a team."

The two of them sat together in the car, looking out at their house, at the memories they built over the years. They would start to slip away soon, leaving one of them to carry the weight of everything on their own, but he would be strong for his wife. He would carry them both as long as he needed to. Silence washed over the car, both thinking about different things. Henry wondered how his children would take the news.

Their eldest daughter had just gotten married. The ink had yet to even dry on their marriage certificate. Henry didn't want to call and burden her with this news, but he knew she would expect an update. Their children had noticed the moments of confusion and little memory lapses as much as he tried to shield it from them. They tried to sit down with him several times and discuss their concerns about what was happening, but Henry refused to listen. He didn't want to think about it then, either.

He didn't see the point in making a big deal out of a few forgotten dates and misplaced household items. Everyone forgets things. Even when Clara started to get concerned, Henry tried to brush her off, terrified of the possibility that something could actually be wrong. However, at her insistence, he conceded to a doctor's appointment. He had hoped it would be nothing serious, so he could rub in their children's faces that they were worried for nothing, but here they were with the weight of this diagnosis in their laps.

"We need to call the kids," Clara whispered, breaking the silence. She pulled at a loose string on the seat cover. She had read his mind. Henry turned to the window, glancing out at the weather. The sun beat down on the car, making it almost unbearably hot.

"Not yet," he said, turning back to his wife. "I want a few moments with you to let this settle first."

They stepped out of Henry's black SUV and headed towards the house. He had no idea what would come next. How long would it take before his entire life was completely different? How much longer did he have with his wife? Henry looked at Clara, admiring how her cinnamon curls flowed around her shoulders. She was in her sixties but could easily pass for someone in their late thirties or early forties. Black don't crack, as they say. This may be why it was so hard to accept. It didn't feel like it should be happening to either of them.

It had been a few weeks since that doctor's visit. Henry watched how his wife handled each moment with the grace and poise she was known for. The same grace he had never been able to muster. She navigated through the conversations with each of their children while Henry sat dumbly by her side, nodding occasionally, and squeezing Clara's knee in support at the appropriate times. Each time he heard the words it felt like a punch in the chest. She handled the tears of their children with compassion and love, breaking only when it was the two of them alone in their room at night. Henry felt useless. He knew he could be and should be doing more, but he never felt like he knew what to say.

Those moments when Clara would forget a word and would struggle helplessly trying to force her brain to recall what she was trying to say, he would just watch her with a stupid smile on his face. He wanted desperately to find a way to help her. His usual mode of denial wouldn't work anymore. They had moved past the point where he could close his eyes and forget. When she was asleep, he would slip out of bed and head to the computer in his office. There he would spend hours researching Alzheimer's disease. If there was a theory or a possible solution out there, he had read about it.

The condition continued to worsen. It felt like everything started falling rapidly as soon as they had gotten the diagnosis. Memories declined almost overnight. Henry would have to repeat things constantly, sometimes multiple times in the same conversation. Things would be misplaced, and he would find them later in odd spots. The smell of burning plastic often had him rushing into the kitchen only to find her trying to heat up leftovers in the oven but forgetting to take the food out of the plastic container first.

Even now, as he watched her style her curls in a bun on the top of her head, he could feel the distance between them growing. The woman he loved was slipping further and further away. Eventually, the distance between them would swallow them both whole. It felt like the earth had cracked between them, leaving them both on opposite sides. The thought choked him up sometimes, leaving him gasping for air like he was suffocating. Naturally growing apart from someone you love is one thing, but no one ever truly prepares you for the possibility of watching your soulmate fade in front of your eyes. No one prepared him for the grief of losing the life he had imagined for the two of them. All the moments with his family that he had ignored to advance in his career were fading in front of him. He wasn't ready to let go.

7

"Henry, honey, are you ready?" Clara stood before the bathroom mirror, pinning her hair atop her head. She wore an elegant black dress that accentuated her curves. They were headed to a work banquet where they would honor Henry with an achievement award as one of the first in the company to secure the Kittrell Account. This was a huge accomplishment as a black man, one of the few in the pharmaceutical sales market. Henry worked tirelessly long nights and sat through countless tedious negotiations to ensure he could land this account.

He missed out on family moments to be sure he could get the funding. When he finally did, the stress melted off his shoulders almost instantly. As a thank you for earning the company so much money, they threw a small awards banquet dinner for his immediate team.

Henry hadn't told any of his coworkers or clients about the recent diagnosis, and he was so nervous about how tonight would go that he was sweating through his shirt. He loved his wife too much to be embarrassed by her, that could never be the case, but he was sensitive about her. Things were better than they had been those first few days. A few months passed, and they fell into a routine that worked for them.

After Clara's initial appointment, Dr. Mizzelle placed her on a medication regimen meant to stave off the effects of the disease. Finding a dose that worked best for her took a while, but the newest dosage was doing well so far. She still forgot things, and Henry did his best to fill in the blanks whenever he could, but sometimes it was difficult. He could only hope that tonight would be a good night.

"Always ready. You look beautiful. Are you sure you want to go? We could have our own little party here." He sauntered over to her, wiggling his eyebrows playfully. She turned to him just as he wrapped his arms around her waist.

"You're such a cornball. Of course, I'm going. Who else is going to make sure you behave yourself?" She giggled. Her smile made his heart thump a little harder. Henry smiled back with a shrug. He was trying his hardest to seem like he wasn't freaking out about her giving a speech, but the way she was staring at him now, he knew she could tell exactly what he was worried about.

"The medicine has been helping. We've been doing good lately. We can do this," she said, gathering his face in her hands. She stared at him; her expression was full of determination. She was right. With the new medicine, she had been doing well. He nodded.

"You can do this." He watched in awe as she returned to the mirror to continue getting ready. Watching her prepare for outings was an event in itself. She confirmed that every piece of hair and every stitch of clothing was in the proper place before she would even step foot out of the house. When she finished with her hair, she turned to him, holding her arms out slightly to give him a better view of her outfit.

"How do I look?"

"Absolutely incredible." His voice came out soft and thick with emotion. She tilted her head in confusion at the sudden change in his voice but didn't question it. He couldn't help but be emotional. Since her diagnosis, he was keenly aware of every moment between them, taking mental notes obsessively to recall the small things when the days became rough. He would tell her she was beautiful numerous times a day. He meant every word. Clara was gorgeous, just as beautiful as the day they met.

Her curvy frame was covered in chestnut skin that seemed to sparkle and shimmer under fluorescent lights. Her thick hair fell around her shoulders. Her natural hair color was dark brown, almost black, but she kept it dyed cinnamon during the fall and winter months. The color faded to a sandy brown during the summer. She had eyes you could get lost in, and he often found himself swirling in the depths of them, thanking God for allowing Henry to love her. Wherever she went, she turned the heads of men and women. When he was younger and a bit more immature, it made him feel self-conscious that so many people were staring at his wife, but now he would shake his head and puff his chest with pride.

Henry had the prize that everyone else wanted. Clara planted a kiss on his cheek, her eyes scanning his face. She had been doing that a lot herself lately. Observing things, observing him, paying extra attention to things she usually wouldn't have cared about. The two of them headed down the stairs and towards his car. The closer they got to their destination, the more his breath caught in his throat. He could only hope that the night would continue to go as well as it had been. Now was not the time to explain to his colleagues that his wife was suffering and losing her grip on her memories by the day.

The banquet was at a five-star restaurant in downtown Brimdale called *Le Fugue*. It was one of Henry's favorite places to eat, but he and Clara tended to save it only for special occasions. It was the only restaurant in town that served crab cakes with authentic jumbo lump crab meat instead of the odd-tasting imitation crab. They spared no detail when making delicious foods; their prices reflected such. Thankfully, the company was paying. The restaurant was in the heart of downtown and was often chosen to host the town's high society events.

Next door to the restaurant, on the busy streets, was a boutique clothing store that Clara liked to frequent on her days off. Henry often joked that they should buy stock in the store since she spent so much time walking the aisles, but the beautiful clothing she consistently found made it all worth it. Henry glanced over at Clara, admiring how the silky fabric of her dress clung to her skin. Yes, it was all definitely worth it.

The town sparkled with nightlife as the clubs on the adjoining streets opened their doors to college-aged patrons. Brimdale was a quiet place for the most part, except for downtown. College kids migrated towards the bars and restaurants as soon as it got dark outside. Henry smiled nostalgically at the sight of the carefree young adults chattering while they waited their turn in line.

He was never much of a partygoer at their age, but he had friends who frequented all the hot spots. He'd listen intently as they recounted their wild and carefree adventures. Seeing the groups of kids now made him miss the friends he used to spend a great deal of his time with.

Once college was over, they settled down in different areas, ready to start their lives as adults. Every now and then, they would catch up with a Facebook post or a quick email, but it had been months they'd spoken. All his focus was split between caring for Clara and holding it together at work.

Another wave of nervousness settled on his shoulders. They prepared weeks in advance for this night, but he still felt like he was going into the situation completely blind. His secret would be out if it didn't go perfectly, and everyone would look at him differently. The thought of being pitied made him angry. He had worked too hard to keep it all together to deal with the sympathetic smiles and the looks of sadness. The idea of it made his stomach flip. They had to get through tonight, and he could buy more time. Henry wasn't quite ready to let everyone know about his personal life. Not just yet.

He shook his head and turned his attention back to Clara; she looped her arm through his and smiled at him. His heart thumped in his chest, and the growing nervousness subsided just a little.

"Have I told you how proud I am of you?" she whispered as they made their way to their table. The place settings had their names written in loopy cursive writing, sitting atop beautifully embroidered cloth napkins. The room had been transformed; twinkling lights hung from the ceiling, making the entire room look like a starry paradise. Whoever decorated truly outdid themselves. Henry glanced over at Clara, who was looking around in awe at the decorations.

Henry smiled at her as heavy sweat soaked his suit. When his supervisor asked Clara to present the award to him at the banquet, Henry was apprehensive. He worried this would be too much for her to take on at once, but she hastily accepted. Every attempt to persuade her otherwise was met with argument and stubborn indignation. He let it go; after all, her medicine had been working well. Her memory lapses were fewer and farther between, but they still flared in moments when he least expected it. Right around the time he allowed himself to relax enough around her, something would trigger a moment, and he would have to struggle to bring her back.

As he watched her fiddle with the embroidery on the tablecloth, he wondered if he should have informed his supervisors of her condition. He stupidly thought he could handle it all on his own. He couldn't stomach the idea of anyone looking at his wife as anything other than the beautiful and intelligent woman she was.

Is. The woman she is.

Speaking about the situation felt like condemning her to a life of disability and weakness. She didn't deserve that, but at this moment, he couldn't help but worry that in his desperation to make everything seem completely fine, he had backed Clara into a corner she couldn't get out of unscathed. He leaned over, bringing his lips to her ear so no one nearby could hear them.

"Do you still want to give the speech? I can talk to Sullivan before it starts and see-"

She placed a hand on his arm to stop him. He leaned back so he could look at her. Her expression of stubborn determination lit a fire behind her eyes. The same fire that made his stomach clench whenever he saw it. The fire that Alzheimer's hadn't yet wrapped its suffocating tentacles around and snuffed out. "I know you're worried about how this will work out, but we can do this. We will do this." She whispered back. The confidence in her voice made Henry relax a little.

He nodded. If Clara believed she could do it, so did he. He kissed her lightly on the lips, careful not to smudge her perfectly applied makeup. He needed to stop worrying about her so much. They watched waiters spill out from the back rooms carrying trays high above their heads. He always admired the skill of holding a tray of plates above the head. He was confident he would have made a mess and spilled everything on the floor had he tried.

A waiter set their plates in front of each guest with a polite smile. They picked their preferences off a postcard sent in the mail months ago for tonight's meal. Henry's mouth began to water as the aroma of his favorite crab cakes swirled around his nose. In his opinion, the crab cakes were the best dish in the restaurant, even though their other menu items tasted delicious. He glanced over at Clara's plate. Her salmon and vegetables had been plated beautifully.

Henry took a deep breath. The tension that had been building up in his shoulders and neck slowly started to dissipate. Things would be fine. They would have a lovely evening at the banquet and then go home and enjoy the rest of their night together. Movement out of the corner of his eye caught his attention. His boss, Zander Sullivan, was approaching the table, his rotund belly draped over the top of his pants in an uncomfortable way. Beads of sweat dotted his brow, even though the room was exceptionally cool. His fiery red hair clung to his forehead in stringy clumps.

He looked like he had come directly from the gym without bothering to shower or freshen up first. Henry could see the beginnings of sweat stains soaking the underarms of the shirt under his suit jacket. Henry smiled stiffly. He didn't particularly care for Sullivan. The man was loud and abrasive in his best moments and downright unlikeable in his worst.

"Tubeck! You handsome bastard! How are you?" Sullivan yelled. His voice carried over the music and the hum of the guests chattering among themselves and ping-ponged off the walls like a pinball. He clapped Henry on the back with such force that it knocked the bite of crab cake off his fork. Henry glanced down at his plate, trying to stifle the sudden flare of irritation.

"Hey, Sullivan. You clean up nicely!" It was a lie. Sullivan looked like a disheveled mess. The soft chuckle from Clara let him know that she could tell he was lying through his teeth. Sullivan grinned at the two of them before returning to his table, where a beautiful and slightly confused young woman sat. Clara and Henry watched as Sullivan flopped heavily in his seat and planted an unnecessarily sloppy kiss on the woman's lips. As he turned to wave at some other guests a few tables over, the woman gagged and wiped his kiss off her lips. Henry shook his head.

"New flavor of the week?" Clara whispered in his ear. They laughed. It was no secret that Henry's boss cycled through women like ill-fitting pairs of pants. He never quite understood how Sullivan managed to snag such attractive women when he was so grotesque and disgusting. Henry shook his head and turned back around just as the speaker for the night took the small stage set up in the front of the banquet room.

"Good evening, everyone! Thank you for coming!" Clara squeezed Henry's hand, excitement bouncing off her in waves. They had been preparing for this night for months, and in those months, Henry wouldn't allow himself to let go long enough to feel anything other than nervousness. He just wanted to make sure everything went well, but now, with Clara by his side and the string lights above them twinkling romantically, he felt excited. He had always been a hard worker and resigned himself to the fact that his dedication would often go unnoticed. It felt awkward to finally be recognized for a part of himself that was ingrained in the fibers of his being by his own father.

As a black man, if you ever want to get anywhere in life, you have to work. Nothing will be handed to you. When they are resting, you need to be working. You need to be working when they are goofing off with their friends. Life is full of time you can't get back. Don't spend it letting opportunities slip past you.

His father was a complicated man of few words, but Henry took that lesson from him and tucked it away deep in the back corners of his mind. It was always lurking in whatever he was doing. He would feel guilty if he rested or took a second to enjoy his surroundings. Meeting Clara kept him from spiraling into a miserable life of strokes and heart attacks. She took him by the hand and forced him to look up from his work and take in the world around him. She pushed him to learn how to relax.

"And now, we'll have a few words from Henry's beautiful wife, Clara

Tubeck!" The mention of his name snapped him back into the present moment. Clara smiled, holding her notecards tightly in her hand, and headed towards the microphone. Heads turned in her direction, admiring her appearance. Clara never disappointed when it came to dressing up for events. Her beauty was a spectacle to those who were not used to it. He watched as she made her way to the front of the room. The fabric of her dress glittered under the lights.

"Hello, everyone." Clara's voice filled the room as she spoke into the microphone. Henry detected a slight shake in her tone, almost imperceptible to anyone other than him. She was nervous. They had prepared for her to give her speech, they rehearsed it constantly, but they did not prepare for the blinding lights and the numerous stares from everyone in the room. He swallowed back the sudden panic that filled his throat. She could do this. "As you know, my name is..." She paused for a moment. It was fleeting, but it was all Henry needed to realize they had made a mistake.

"My name is Clara Tubeck, for those who don't know. My husband is the wonderful Henry Tubeck. We have been married for a long time, and he has been an exceptionally hard worker for as long as I've known him." She smiled at the crowd, searching for Henry. When she spotted him, her smile grew wider. "I am so glad you all came out tonight to help me celebrate his birthday!"

The crowd grew quiet, confusion and uncertainty thick in the air. Henry wanted to shrink in his seat and disappear under the table, but he couldn't. He looked around at the people in the room. Some looked at him, and others looked at Clara with furrowed brows.

"I didn't realize today was your birthday!" a coworker leaned towards him from a nearby table. He swallowed. "It's not." He said simply. The coworker tilted his head and stared at Henry, expecting more explanation, but Henry offered nothing else. He couldn't look away from Clara.

"I- no. No, that's not right. I'm so sorry. I meant to say I am so glad you all came to...um...to-" Clara glanced down at her notecards, fingers trembling. Henry stood and made his way over to her, not caring for a second about the whispers and the reactions of the other attendees. Clara's eyes welled with tears as she stood there, struggling to regain control of the situation. Just before he reached her, Clara took a deep breath, closed her eyes briefly, and then smiled at everyone. Henry froze where he stood.

"Please excuse me. We pre-gamed a bit before we got here." She glanced over at Henry and gave a slight shake of her head. He stayed glued to where he was, holding his breath. The audience seemed to buy her joke and tittered with laughter. She gave another award-winning smile and looked down at the cards. Henry's throat was dry. He swallowed silently and sent up a quick prayer.

"As I said, my dear husband has always worked incredibly hard. If anyone deserves this achievement award, it is him..."

Henry slunk back to his seat, unable to focus on the rest of the speech. He wanted to kick himself for letting his guard down. Things had been going so well; he allowed himself to enjoy the night, even if just for a moment. As soon as his muscles unclenched and his body relaxed, this disease reared its ugly head to taunt him.

8

So, your wife has Alzheimer's, huh?" Henry sat in Sullivan's office the following Monday, counting the moments until he could leave and finish working. Henry eyed his supervisor warily, unsure of how deep into his personal life he was willing to go. He had been hoping he could hold off on having this conversation for a while, but that past Friday night's events made that impossible. Sullivan had been blowing his phone up all weekend, demanding to know what was up with Clara's blundering during her speech. He tried to disguise it as a concern, but Henry knew he was looking for information because he was nosey. Sullivan loved a good story. He would happily jump at the chance to gossip, no matter who it was about. Henry took a deep breath and nodded.

"Yes. My wife was diagnosed with rapid early onset almost half a year ago." He watched as Sullivan ran a hand through his hair and winced when Sullivan wiped his hand on his suit jacket. The hair products he had generously gooped all over his head that morning left streak marks on his suit, but there was still so much product left in his hair that it stayed in the position it fell in when he stuck his hand in it. It looked ridiculous. Henry braced himself for the insensitive comment he knew was coming.

He clenched and unclenched his fists, trying to get a head start to calm his nerves.

"Wow. Tubeck, that sucks. I'm so sorry."

Henry froze, unprepared for this response.

"What?"

"Yeah, my second wife's father went through something similar when we were still married. It was a rough couple of months." Sullivan sniffed a bit and shrugged.

"What ended up happening to him?"

"No idea. We got divorced, and I never bothered to check after that. I had to keep it moving. She was irritating. She couldn't cook to save her life. But anyway, her father was suffering. He couldn't remember how to wipe his ass." Henry stared blankly at his boss, unsure of what to say. It wasn't quite the disrespectful comment he expected, but it was still crude and insensitive.

"I mean, it's certainly tough, but we're managing," Henry said, suddenly wanting this conversation to end. It was uncomfortable sharing his personal life with people at his place of work, especially Sullivan. This was as close to a heartfelt discussion as he was willing to have with this beast of a man whose belly pressed against his shirt dangerously, begging for release. One sneeze would turn one of the buttons into a weapon, and Henry didn't want to be around to see the damage they would cause.

"What have you tried so far?" Sullivan asked, turning towards the computer on his desk. He pushed a stack of papers to the side to type comfortably. Henry sat in stunned silence, still reeling from the comment about his ex-wife's father and unsure how much to divulge here in his boss's office.

"So far, um, we've just tried medication. He shifted uncomfortably in his seat, "And just making sure we set little reminders so she doesn't forget things." Sullivan stopped typing and leaned toward Henry, the smell of his hair products making him cringe. It smelled like a synthetic version of mango. That, mixed with the salty smell of Sullivan's sweat, made Henry want to cover his nose. Instead, he remained still, watching Sullivan with wary eyes.

"No, I mean...have you tried...anything else?"

"Like what?"

"You know! There are unconventional methods available. There's a medical trial that is supposed to restore whatever memory you've lost. Have you heard of it?" Sullivan tilted his head, surprised Henry didn't know what he was talking about. "It's a doctor. He calls himself, The Memory Concierge."

"Sullivan, you can't be serious." Henry stared at him, annoyed at this conversation's sudden, unrealistic direction. Quack doctors and their ridiculous trials were popping up all the time. It never panned out. Frankly, even entertaining the idea of being able to restore memories seemed cruel. Of course, Henry would jump at the chance to save his wife from her struggle, but it was impossible. Doctors and specialists reminded them time and time again that there was no cure. No backing out, just pushing through. Holding on to that kind of ridiculous hope would do nothing but make him miserable down the line.

"You wouldn't consider trying it? It could help you out..."

"No, because there is no such thing. Life is not a fairytale. If you'll excuse me."

Henry stood up and left the office before Sullivan could respond. Part of why he didn't want to divulge his personal information to anyone at work was for that exact conversation. A mythical man that could miraculously restore someone's memories seemed like a joke. That had to be the plot of a poorly done Lifetime movie. Henry shook his head as he made his way back to his office. He had a few clients to follow up with.

Anya, his assistant, was perched in the chair across from his desk, looking at the framed photos of him and Clara. He didn't expect to see her so soon; she usually didn't come in on Monday mornings. He was counting on her absence so there would be one less person to explain his personal life to. Henry sighed quietly, trying to reign in his annoyance. She hadn't done anything to him and didn't deserve to be the target of his anger or embarrassment. He never realized that his wife having Alzheimer's would mean he'd have to clean up the mess her memory lapses made.

The pamphlets and the articles he was obsessively studying since that day at the doctor's office did nothing to prepare him for the amount of damage control he had to do. The only thing they managed to do was to confirm what he already knew. Denying that anything was wrong could no longer be his course of action. He couldn't hide his head in the sand, not if he wanted to keep the home safe for the both of them, and not if he wanted to make it through this with his last thin grip on his sanity. Henry cleared his throat, hoping to catch Anya's attention. She turned, her brown skin tinting a shade of pink almost identical to the dress she was wearing. She put down the picture and blinked as her eyes refocused on her surroundings.

"Hi, Mr. Tubeck!" She smiled cheerfully. He smiled stiffly in return as he took his seat at the desk. His emails were pinging loudly on his computer with work he had been pushing off since last week. Clients were demanding answers and follow-ups.

"How can I help you, Anya?" he asked. Anya paused for a long moment, then looked up at him, her expression unreadable.

"Are you doing okay today?" Her voice was soft, unassuming. He froze, unsure of what to say, and suddenly felt open and exposed in front of the world, even though he and Anya were the only two in the room.

"I'm sorry?"

"You seem troubled. Just checking in to make sure you're okay." Anya's voice was gentle, almost as if she were talking to a child. He said nothing. Anger rose in his throat. Had Sullivan started gossiping about his personal life that quickly? It had only been a few minutes since their conversation. Had word spread around the office that fast? "I overheard your conversation with Mr. Sullivan about Alzheimer's disease. My father was diagnosed with it. We're at the end stages now." She continued, offering a small sympathetic smile. The tension in his shoulders dissipated a little. He felt guilty for assuming the worst of her. Anya was new but hadn't done anything to prove herself untrustworthy. Not yet.

"It's been six months for Clara."

"How are you coping?"

Henry paused momentarily, surprised at the emotions that question stirred up in him. His primary focus had been ensuring everything was as Clara needed; he hadn't taken the time to examine his feelings about the situation. Henry turned towards the window to hide the tears that began to slip down his face. They were still in the early stages, and he was already struggling to hang on.

An overwhelming sense of dread plagued him daily. Would he be strong enough to handle this when it inevitably got worse? The articles he had been reading terrified him. He read stories of loved ones whose personalities were altered entirely by the disease, coupled with the frustration and loneliness that the caretakers usually felt spiked Henry's anxiety. It was coming, but he wasn't ready for any of it. He wasn't sure he ever would be.

"There is a support group that I go to. They meet on Thursdays. It has been unbelievably helpful with sorting through my emotions."

"I'm fine. I don't need help. I have it under control." Henry snapped. It was a lie, he knew it was, and judging from the look on her face, Anya knew it was too. Henry began to fidget under her gaze. He felt like she could see through him, down to the deeper parts that he was terrified to say out loud. Maybe she could see it.

"One of the first things we learn is that needing help is okay. It's common to feel like you must handle it alone, but we all need people. There is nothing wrong with that." She smiled gently, waiting for him to respond. When he didn't, she paused momentarily before nodding and turning towards the door. She slipped out of the office quietly, closing the door behind her. Henry's fragile resolve broke utterly as soon as he heard the click. The tears were coming fast and heavy as he struggled to reel his emotions.

He glanced at his cell phone as it lit up with Clara's picture. She was calling him again. They had already spoken three times that morning. He was never going to be able to get anything done today if he had to keep stopping to carry on conversations and trying to keep himself from collapsing into a ball of tears.

"Hi, honey. Everything okay?" He wiped his eyes and plastered on a smile, even though she couldn't see him.

"Where are you?" she demanded; she sounded worried.

"I'm at work, honey. Remember we talked about this?"

"You're...at work? Why?" The confusion in her voice made his stomach clench. They talked the night before and that morning about how he desperately needed to show his face at work and check in with his clients. He was running out of PTO, and the upcoming deadlines were approaching faster than he was ready for. At the time, she nodded and said she understood.

"I have to work, Honey. I will be back home this evening. Will you be okay?"

"I think so." She sounded uncertain. He imagined her sitting on the couch in the living room, detangling a section of her curls. She always reached for her hair whenever she felt anxious or unsure about something. Lately, he had to make sure she didn't accidentally pull her hair out by the roots. Henry glanced at his computer; the emails were coming in by the second. "I'll call you a little later to check on you." After they hung up, he sat in his silent office for a moment, letting his memories take over. He tried not to let himself reminisce for too long because it became painful so quickly. Mourning the loss of the woman he married while she was still physically alive made his heart throb in pain.

"Dance with me, woman!" Henry demanded, cranking up the music. John Legend's familiar raspy voice filled the room. Clara looked up from where she was sitting and shot him a crazy look.

"What song is this?" She asked, tilting her head. Henry shrugged and twirled clumsily, attempting to appear smooth. John Legend crooned in the background.

"I don't know. It was a playlist your son made. I kept telling him that music these days doesn't have that same all-consuming love as ours."

He danced over to her and offered his hand. Clara studied him for a moment before smiling and grabbing his hand. She squealed as he yanked her up and into his arms in one fluid motion.

"You knew he was going to take that as a challenge to prove you wrong." She laughed, nestling deeper into his embrace. Henry knew Dee would jump at the chance

to send them his favorite music. The truth is, some of it he didn't mind even though he would never let them know that. Clara rested her head on his shoulder as they swayed to the music in the middle of the living room. Even after being married for so long, they still knew how to sink into each other. He could feel her presence in the room before he saw her. Their eyes always found each other in a crowded room. It was like traveling through life with his heart on the outside of his body.

"You're still pretty light on your feet for an old man." A smile tugged at the corner of her lips.

"Watch it- before I show you how light on my feet I can be." He dipped her forward and planted a sloppy kiss on her neck. Chauncy barked and danced around their ankles as they swayed to the music. It had been a stressful day at work for Henry; he'd spent the majority of the day counting down the moments until he could come home and be with the one person that gave him peace. Clara had taken time off- helping Rose shop for a wedding dress- and at home waiting for him when he arrived.

"Did I tell you we found a dress today?" She said after a moment.

"No, you didn't. How much is it going to cost?" He cringed, bracing himself to hear the price. Clara rolled her eyes at him.

"That's not the point. Our daughter was beautiful in it. It reminds me of the dress I wore on our wedding day."

"I don't remember it," he said. When she glared at him, he smiled and grabbed her hands.

"I don't remember it because I was so distracted by your beauty. I didn't see the dress,. I saw you." Clara glared at him briefly, but her face relaxed into a beautiful smile.

"Nice save." She laughed and stepped back into his arms as the next song began to play.

"I'm serious. No matter what is in front of me, I will only see you."

His phone vibrating on his desk broke him out of his thoughts. Clara was calling. Again. The call ended before he could reach for it, and the screen remained lit for a few seconds. There were twelve missed calls from his wife. He paused for a split second, wondering what would happen if he ignored it and continued about his day as if nothing was wrong, just for a second. Eventually, she would be fine. She would busy herself with something until he came home and reminded her that he had been at work all day. The thought was tempting, but in the end, as the screen lit up once again with an incoming call, the guilt won out.

"Hello?"

"Where are you?"

"Clara, honey, I'm at work. We talked about this before I left this morning."

"I-I don't remember. That's not what you told me. You said you were going to the store." He sank into his chair, suddenly feeling weighed down by this same conversation.

"No, baby, I'm at work. I told you I was coming in for a few hours to catch up on some of my deadlines." He bit the inside of his cheek, fighting to keep his voice calm and friendly despite the bubbling anger in his belly. Is this what his life would amount to? Repeating conversations and reminding his wife of things they had already talked about so many times before? Clara paused for a beat, so long that he had almost thought he had uttered his thoughts out loud, but then she sighed quietly.

"Right. I remember now. I'm sorry I keep bothering you. I'm so sorry."

"It's no problem, beautiful. I will be home soon, I promise. I love you."

"Will you still love me when this gets worse, Hen?"

"Always." The distress in her tone made Henry's heart sink. A wave of emotion swept through him; he desperately wanted to grab her in his arms and shield her from this struggle. His gaze fell on his computer screen once again. The email Sullivan sent was still at the top of his inbox. He opened it, reading over the information in the email's body. The bottom contained a list of instructions on how to contact the Memory Concierge. Henry found himself scrolling through the directions, mentally noting what he needed to do. It was a preposterous concept, but he would save it for when things got too hard to handle alone.

"Hey, Mr. Tubeck. A few of us are grabbing a drink after work. Are you interested?" Anya poked her head into the office and interrupted his reading. A drink would be excellent. It had been a while since he went out with work friends or personal friends. He wanted to be able to hold a conversation with someone who could remember it later, but he promised Clara he would be home after work.

He contemplated what it would mean to sneak out and grab a drink with coworkers. He could tell Clara that work ran late or he wanted to catch up with his coworkers. He thought about what it would do to Clara's fragile mental state to change the plan at the last minute. Guilt coursed through his veins.

"I appreciate it, but no, thank you." He smiled at Anya, who shrugged and closed the door behind her. He thought about going anyway and leaving Clara to figure it out alone for a bit but decided to stick with the original plan.

The guilt always won.

9

"Tubeck! Tell me you've heard about this!" Sullivan burst into Henry's office, breaking his concentration. His eyes narrowed as he glanced up from his computer, but Sullivan didn't notice. It never failed with this man; whenever Henry wanted to be alone to stew in his thoughts or to catch up on work with his clients, Sullivan suddenly had something he wanted to talk about that couldn't seem to wait. He waved the paper back and forth, rambling animatedly. He was too excited to notice that Henry wasn't in the mood for conversation.

He huffed and puffed as he crossed the room to stand before the desk, making Henry wonder when Sullivan last had a checkup with his doctor. Being out of breath after so little movement couldn't be healthy. Before he could ask what was happening, Sullivan slapped a piece of paper on his desk with enough force to make him flinch slightly, then folded his arms and waited expectantly. When Henry didn't move immediately, he pointed at the paper and impatiently tapped his foot.

Henry could tell he wasn't leaving until he was satisfied. With a small sigh, Henry picked up the paper. It had food smudges over some of the words and was slightly crumpled; it looked as if Sullivan had been clutching it tightly as he read it during a meal. Henry resisted the urge to turn up his nose and instead squinted at it trying to make out the words under what looked to be chocolate stains. It was half of a printed article from a website he had never heard of. So, this is what Sullivan is in his office doing while everyone else was doing all the work. He shook his head.

New Experimental Drug Said to Restore Memories Stolen by Alzheimer's Disease. Drug Trial Participants Claim it is the New Miracle Drug!

Henry ignored the little thump of hope in his chest and glanced at his boss. Sullivan stared back at him. He was so excited he was almost vibrating.

"Why are you showing me this?" Henry asked, feigning confusion. He returned the paper to Sullivan and tried his best to look disinterested. He didn't want to read too much into it, fearing it would give him false hope. He didn't need that right now. In frustration, Sullivan threw his hands up and let them slap against his thighs. The force of the slap made his belly shake a bit, making him look like a red-haired version of Santa Claus. Sweat stains peeked out from under his armpits. Henry tried not to wince at the sweaty smell that seemed to pour out of his skin from the movements. Did he ever take a shower? Why did he always smell like he had just come from the gym and didn't clean himself off?

"Don't be coy. You know exactly why! The whole Alzheimer's thing. If you don't take my word for it when I tell you about The Memory Concierge, you obviously need proof that this is real. So here. Bada-boom bada-bing! Problem solved."

"I'm not giving my wife any experimental drugs," Henry said. Sullivan stared at him for a moment, his mouth open in shocked confusion. Henry folded his hands together and placed them on his desk. He wanted this man to leave his office, but he couldn't say it without being disrespectful. Especially not using the words he wanted to use. It would get him sent home for the day almost immediately, if not wholly fired, depending on how generous Sullivan was feeling. Losing his job was the last thing Henry needed with everything going on.

"No, Henry, I'm talking about-" Sullivan started and stopped. His expression changed suddenly, and his face reddened. Henry watched as he opened and closed his mouth a few times, struggling to find something to say. After a moment, he gave up. "You know what? Never mind. I'm not about to try and convince you to want better for yourself. It's your choice. Just know that you could make things so much easier for everyone around you if you just tried it."

"I'll keep it in mind."

"Yeah, you do that." He sniffed, rolling his eyes like a bratty teenager. Henry resisted the urge to give him the middle finger. Instead, he plastered on his best professional smile and waited for him to leave. He hesitated momentarily, waiting to see if Henry would change his mind. He didn't. With a frustrated huff, Sullivan turned on his heels and headed for the door. When Sullivan left the room, Henry tried to put the entire conversation out of his mind and get back to work. It was more complicated than he thought it would be. His mind kept drifting, fixating on the possibility of a drug being able to cure his wife's memory. They could go on that trip to Paris like he planned. After her diagnosis, they had to cancel the trip. He was even more heartbroken about it than she was. It had been her dream since she was a young girl, and it was taken away from her permanently.

A knock on his door made him glance up. His assistant, Anya, stood in the doorway with muffins from the bakery down the road in her hands. She smiled when he looked up, and he involuntarily smiled back. Clara was usually the only person who could make him smile without trying.

Maybe that was why he enjoyed talking to Anya so much. She reminded him of a younger version of his wife in so many ways. They had the same spitfire energy never afraid to say what needed to be said, no matter who got their feelings hurt.

"I come bearing gifts," she said, peeking in the doorway. Henry chuckled and waved her in, grateful for the temporary distraction. She placed a napkin on the corner of his desk and then gently sat the muffin on top of it. It was blueberry, his absolute favorite flavor. When she settled into the chair in front of her desk and took out her muffin, he slid his closer and sniffed it.

"This smells amazing."

"I should hope so, as much as it costs." He glanced up at her, fully prepared to reimburse her for the muffin, but noticed the sparkle in her eye. Instead, he grinned as he took his first bite. The muffin was still warm, with the slightest hint of steam pumping from the center.

"How's your dad doing?" he asked, wiping the crumbs off the side of his mouth. Her smile faded almost instantly.

"He...it's difficult," she replied quietly, looking down at her hands. He nodded. He knew exactly what that felt like. It was difficult for him, too, even more difficult trying to verbalize what he was feeling. He never knew what to say whenever he was asked about it.

"I bet it is. Clara has been getting worse recently." He took another bite of the muffin. Anya said nothing, just listened intently, allowing him the space to vent. She never pushed the conversation; he could talk as little or as much as he needed. "Some days, I don't even recognize my wife anymore. Feels like I'm watching someone who looks familiar, but I have absolutely no connection with. That's what I've been having the most trouble with the most. Trying to reconcile this version of her with the version I fell in love with so many years ago."

"How have you been coping?" Anya asked. The deep brown of her eyes sparkled with intensity. Henry squirmed a bit in his chair. He always felt uncomfortable whenever anyone asked how he was coping or how he was dealing. The truth is, Henry could have dealt with it better. He wouldn't need to work if he had a nickel for every time he wanted to give up. Maybe he had been able to hide it well enough on the outside, but he felt like he was drowning in quicksand. Every day was a struggle. With every passing moment, he felt as if he was drifting closer and closer to being swallowed up by the weight of it all. Every minute was like a fight to the death, and he was losing.

"I'm...fine," he said after a moment of picking at his muffin. He refused to meet Anya's gaze out of fear that she could tell that he wasn't being honest. If she could tell, she gave no indication. Instead, she finished her muffin and stood. A few crumbs fell from her lap as she lifted herself from the chair. Henry swallowed, mentally kicking himself for always trying to hide his feelings. He had ruined his first genuine conversation in a long time.

"I should go. Make sure you're taking care of yourself, eating and staying hydrated like you're supposed to. It's easy to neglect yourself when focusing on something else."

"Sullivan mentioned a new drug," he blurted suddenly, feeling desperate to continue the conversation somehow. Anya lifted an eyebrow, waiting for him to continue. "He says it's supposed to completely restore memories."

"That almost sounds like magic." She smiled.

"If it works for Clara, maybe you can try it for your dad?" Henry observed her face, trying to make sense of her reaction. Her lips spread into a thin line like she was trying to suppress her first thought. After a beat of silence, she sighed and shook her head.

"It would be nice if someone could wave a magic wand and give my daddy back to me." She smiled wistfully. "But unfortunately, I think it's too late for that." With that, Anya turned and left his office, shutting the door behind her. He sat still momentarily, letting his mind conjure up the possibilities.

By the time the end of the day rolled around, Henry had two thoughts swirling in his mind: experimental drugs and memory restoration. As hard as he tried, he couldn't focus on anything else. He hadn't been able to get any work done for the day. He didn't want to admit that what Sullivan said got under his skin. If there was a cure, then didn't he at least owe it to himself and to his wife to try? If they had a shot at normalcy, why wouldn't Henry take it? As if his Spidey senses were tingling and he could sense Henry was debating at that moment, Sullivan poked his head in the door.

"You changed your mind yet, Tubeck?" he asked, wiggling his eyebrows. Henry gave him a sidelong glance, not wanting to admit that what he said, mixed with the conversation with Anya, had him wondering if he should at least give it a shot. If it didn't work out, then no harm, no foul. But if it did, his entire life could change in the best way possible.

"Tell me more about it," Henry said with a defeated sigh. Sullivan's grin stretched across his face before Henry fully got the sentence out. He glanced back and forth down the hallway like they were a part of some kind of conspiracy and slipped into the office. Henry rolled his eyes at the theatrics. Sullivan closed the door behind him and sat down in the chair; he pressed his fingertips together and leaned forward like he was divulging a deep, dark secret.

"Okay. So, it's this new drug that is supposed to change the outcome of dementia and whatnot. This one doctor created it. He's been experimenting with trying to give people certain memories back or taking certain memories away."

"That sounds dangerous." Henry made a face. "It's a doctor doing experiments on brains. Where did you find this information?" Sullivan waved a hand, dismissing Henry's concern.

"Do you want to talk semantics, or do you want the information?" Sullivan crossed his arms and stared at Henry, daring him to question what he was being told.

"I'm just asking how you got this information and how you seem to be the only one with it."

"I know people," Sullivan sniffed. Henry made a face but remained silent. The two men stared at each other in a stubborn standoff. After a moment, Sullivan shrugged and heaved himself up. "If you don't want to hear what I have to say, then I can just go." Henry watched as Sullivan hefted himself towards the door.

"Christ. Alright, alright! Fine go ahead." Sullivan whipped back around with a wicked grin on his face. Henry folded his arms in frustration. Sullivan enjoyed this way too much, and Henry didn't like it. The chair groaned in protest as Sullivan flung his oversized frame back into it.

"He's the keeper of all memories, almost. He's like the point of contact between the patients and their memories. People call him the memory holder, like a butler or something."

"You mean a concierge?" Henry asked. Sullivan snapped his fingers and pointed excitedly.

"Exactly. So, apparently, this drug hasn't been approved by the FDA yet, but the ones that have tried it say it works." Henry stared at him, trying to figure out whether he was serious. A small smile tugged at the corners of his mouth. There was a mischievous gleam in his eye. Henry narrowed his gaze and leaned toward Sullivan, keeping his voice low, almost whispering. His father used to do this when he was younger to convey his seriousness in the moment. It used to make Henry terrified of what would happen if he were to get in trouble. When he became an adult himself and then a parent, he learned to master his own version of the voice. He had used it many times over when his kids were growing up.

"Are you messing with me?" he asked. His voice was quiet, but his tone was menacing. He rarely spoke this way, but it seemed appropriate at the moment. Sullivan's eyes widened slightly then he shook his head with his hands up, feigning innocence.

"Hey, you don't have to believe me. I'm just telling you what I know."

"What you've heard. Not what you know."

"Same thing, Tubeck. Have a little faith for once!"

"Fine. How do I find the doctor?" Henry asked. He couldn't ignore the skepticism that crept into his thoughts. Sullivan was a sleazy man that only looked out for himself. It seemed stupid to trust anything he said. The man had a face like a supervillain. Even his regular smile looked like he had just gotten done torturing innocent victims.

"It's a top-secret location." He whispered, wiggling his bushy eyebrows and looking around the room even though he knew he and Henry were the only ones around. Henry wanted to laugh at him but decided against it. He needed help figuring out if this was worth paying attention to. He was never able to trust Sullivan as far as he could throw him; it would be foolish to start now when there was so much at stake.

"Sullivan, get out of my office. I really don't want to hear this." He had the sneaking feeling that Sullivan was lying, and even if he couldn't prove it, he didn't feel like wasting his time. Sullivan shrugged and stood up.

"I was just trying to help."

"It's unnecessary; I've got everything under control." Henry snapped. Sullivan paused by the door and looked at him. For a minute, neither of them said anything; they just stared at each other. A look of pity settled onto Sullivan's puffy face.

"I really do hope that's true. For your sake."

"What's that supposed to mean?" Henry asked, slightly offended. Was he trying to imply that he didn't have everything under control? He narrowed his eyes at Sullivan, daring him to say something else. He knew he wasn't angry with Sullivan, but since he was here, he was the target. His boss gave him a sad smile before leaving the room.

"I think...deep down, you know exactly what I mean." The office door clicked gently behind him.

When Henry arrived home, Clara was in the living room, asleep on the couch. He wanted to wake her up to say hi but didn't want to disturb her. He watched her for a moment, savoring the peaceful look on her face. She had been sleeping a lot more lately. The doctor said that this is normal behavior. Sometimes the dreamworld is easier to cope with and understand. Things don't have to make sense in there. You don't have to remember names or faces in there. He couldn't imagine how she felt. He wanted to help her but had no idea how. Should he try to get the experimental drug? Clara was already taking so much medication it seemed almost cruel to add another. What if it didn't work or if it counteracted with one of her other medications? There were so many risks involved.

He couldn't shake the idea of there being something out there that could bring his wife back. Everything around them changed so suddenly. Who knew that one doctor's appointment would absolutely upend their entire lives?

He lay awake that night, staring up at the ceiling. He hadn't been able to get much sleep lately, stressing about Clara. Anya's warning to ensure he cared for himself popped back in his head as he lay there, denying his body the much-needed sleep. He was perpetually exhausted, but he could never seem to rest. No matter how hard he tried to let go of things long enough to wind down, his mind wouldn't let him. It wandered constantly, his thoughts full of anxiety and stress. Had he told Clara he loved her enough? Had he told his kids that he loved them enough? Did they know their mother loved them, even if she couldn't remember them? Was he doing enough for them and his wife? Was he enough?

What if it got worse? What if he was no longer able to be a good husband? He could already feel his patience growing thinner with her, even though he tried to reel it in. He promised for better or for worse and in sickness and health, but he had never imagined a life like this. What if he had to get some help to take care of her? What if…What if he ended up alone? What if she forgot who he was?

All the pamphlets and welcome packets in the world couldn't have prepared him for that. Those same eyes that used to hold so much love and affection for him were now so empty. She was fading right before him. Soon she would be gone entirely. In some moments she was already gone. As if he was holding on to her ghost with all his strength, unable to face life without her. It felt like he was living with a shell of his wife. She still looked the same on the outside, but everything on the inside, where it mattered the most, was completely different. He had no idea what to do. As he stared straight up, counting the little craters in the ceiling one by one, he let the "what ifs" run rampant in his mind.

10

Henry looked at his wife in the passenger seat, her face blank and distant. For a moment, he was reminded of how she used to be, so full of life and joy. But that seemed like a lifetime ago now. Since the Alzheimer's diagnosis, everything had changed. He knew it would- he wasn't naïve enough to think that things would stay the same forever- but he wasn't prepared for how quickly it felt like things were evaporating around him.

It had been almost a full year since their first appointment, and Henry was struggling to cope with all the extra responsibilities it brought about. He tried his best to maintain a sense of normalcy for Clara's sake, but he could feel himself slipping up more and more - neglecting basic tasks like cleaning or cooking dinner for them both. He became agitated and upset whenever he had to repeat things or move a little slower for her to catch up.

Taking care of Clara was draining him physically and emotionally, leaving him feeling exhausted all the time, no matter how much sleep he got each night. Most nights, he couldn't sleep. He would stare at the popcorned ceiling in their bedroom and count how many ways he pitied himself and their current situation. He would often have to sneak and catch a nap at work. Exhaustion settled into his bones and in the very framework of his body. It was a part of him now.

The one bright star in all of this was Anya. She had been becoming more than just an assistant and coworker. She was becoming his sounding board. Their conversations were his cathartic release. She seemed to know exactly what he was going through. She would often stop by his office in the mornings to chat and see how he was doing. At first, it felt intrusive and annoying. Didn't she have her own family to worry about? Wasn't her father struggling with the same diagnosis as Clara? Why wasn't she focused on him? But he grew to appreciate her friendship.

In some ways, she felt like his only friend. He spent his days working so much and neglecting everything other than his responsibilities that most of the friends he made disappeared over the years., slowly fading into the background as they settled into their own lives. Anya was a surprise. She was much younger than him, but from how she responded to him and listened without judgment, he could tell that life made her much wiser beyond her years. Whatever her struggle was, it was profound. He could almost see it in the way she held herself during their conversations.

Sometimes her face would crumple, and for a split second, she would look like she wanted to burst into tears. Henry never knew what to say in those moments. He was always terrible with emotions. He would just stare awkwardly and wait for it to pass. She noticed immediately whenever something wasn't right with Henry as soon as she saw him. Most days, he couldn't even keep eye contact while talking to her, terrified that she would see too deep into his soul. Instead of skirting around the problem, like everyone else in the office, she asked what was going on directly, waiting for him to find the words to explain.

As soon as Henry began to let the words out, it felt like a dam bursting inside him - suddenly, every emotion held back came pouring out until there was nothing left but exhaustion again. Tears streamed down his cheeks and soaked the collar of his shirt. He snuffled, embarrassed yet again for letting the emotional wall he struggled to build collapse around him. Anya took him into a hug without hesitation, knowing precisely what he needed at that moment, even if he could never bring himself to admit it out loud. Their morning talks were the only times he allowed himself a few minutes to let everything go and lay it all bare in front of him.

Afterward, when he was able to calm down long enough to stop the tears, Anya offered to give him the number to the therapist she used, but Henry politely declined. Even though she saw him crumble like a cookie in front of her, his pride wouldn't let him accept help. She remained patient, telling him about her support group meetings and how they were helping her. The thought of opening himself up to a room full of strangers and letting them witness his innermost thoughts felt gross. What could a meeting do to help him figure out how to handle losing his wife while she was still alive? She wasn't physically gone just yet, but it still hurt like she was. She didn't speak much anymore. He tried to engage her in conversation, but the Clara he had fallen so desperately in love with all those years ago was gone.

The person left was a husk - a shell. What he missed the most, and he never thought he'd say it, was her humming. The woman used to hum all the time. There was never a quiet moment in the house until recently. If she wasn't humming a tune, she was belting the lyrics at the top of her lungs. She was never scared to dance to the beat of her own drum. She always tried to get him to join in, begging him to relax and let his hair down. He would force a smile and shake his head, not wanting to make a fool of himself in front of anyone, even his wife.

She would attempt a few times, shrug, and return to making noise. At first, it used to irritate him, especially after an incredibly long day at work when he just wanted to come home to a quiet house and unwind. The sound would stomp on his last nerve. He would go into his office and close the door sometimes to block out the sound, just for a second of quiet. Now, she was always quiet. No matter what he tried, he couldn't get her to sing, dance, or hum. He would hum her favorite tune, and a flicker of recognition would spark in her eyes. He kept humming, desperately hoping that she would be able to finish the song or yell out the lyrics in her offkey singing like she used to, but then the flicker would fade. He mentally kicked himself for not being able to relax enough to enjoy the noise. He took it for granted while it was here, and now that it was gone, he would have given anything to get it back.

A big thing that Henry had been unprepared for when they were told that their lives would be different was the guilt that followed every single emotion he experienced. Whenever he snapped at his wife for not catching on as quickly as she used to, he would immediately be inundated with guilt so intense he could feel it in his chest. In the split second where Henry contemplated sending her off to a nursing home and letting someone else deal with her decreasing independence, the guilt would almost bring him to his knees. He felt guilty on days when he got angry at someone for something small. Henry began to feel like his personality was eroding and chipping away, only to leave a skeleton of who he used to be, especially when it felt like he was trapped in his own mind, just like Clara.

Now, out of desperation, he poured through Google hysterically, determined to find some information about The Memory Concierge other than what Sullivan had told him. So far, Henry had found nothing to support either side. The idea that Sullivan got one over on him made Henry want to wrap his fingers around Sullivan's neck and squeeze until his jowls popped.

Your search for The Memory Concierge- did not match any documents. Please make sure all words are spelled correctly or try different keywords to expand your search.

Henry stared at the Google page in frustration, trying to swallow back his anger. He felt like he was being taunted by the lack of information. Sighing, he closed the window and pushed back from his desk. Sullivan should be available in the next few minutes. Most of his meetings took place first thing in the morning. He'd planned it like that to have time to putz around for the rest of the day. Henry found him in his office, reading a book. He looked up in mild annoyance when Henry pushed his way in without knocking.

"Did you lie to me?" Henry demanded, fixing Sullivan with his best death glare. Sullivan glanced up at Henry, looking utterly unbothered by the outburst. Henry waited, saying nothing.

"Probably; be more specific," he said finally, placing his book down on his desk. Henry crossed the room to stand directly before him, annoyed that he even had to be in there in the first place. He'd much rather sit in his office and find the information he needed in his own time, but his patience was waning rapidly these days.

"This Memory Concierge bull! Did you lie to me?" The smug smile across Sullivan's face made Henry wish he could take back the question. The way his face lit up in satisfaction made Henry almost nauseous. He wouldn't have had to come here if he could have found something on Google to confirm or deny.

"Oh! That. No, I didn't lie." He spoke carefully as if he was sifting through responses in his head. "Do you really think there would be available information on the internet? The identity of the concierge is concealed for a reason." He smirked at Henry like he should have known this information already.

"How am I supposed to find him then?"

"I can tell you how, but it will cost you." Sullivan crossed his arms, willing Henry to keep pushing.

"I'll work overtime for the next month," Henry offered. Sullivan barked out a laugh and shook his head. "I couldn't care less about your work ethic, Tubeck." He flicked his hand, exasperated. "I'm talking about money. It's going to cost you money."

"How much?" Sullivan grinned and looked at the ceiling, pretending to consider his answer. Henry could tell that he was briefly calculating how much he could get away with asking for without getting in trouble for extortion and bribery. Embarrassment heated Henry's cheeks. He knew from the beginning not to trust this imbecile, but he allowed hope and desperation to convince him otherwise.

"A hundred will be fine," Sullivan said with a slight shrug. Henry stared at him for a moment, debating whether he should even bother. Henry could feel Sullivan's smug satisfaction in being able to hold information over his head. Henry knew he would never live this down, especially if it worked. Sullivan would try to take the credit for saving Clara. He would even expect a thank you of some sort in return. The idea made Henry's lip curl in disgust. Was it worth the risk? Sullivan stared at him, sensing the hesitation.

"Think it over. I've got nothing but time," he said with a disinterested shrug. Henry felt jealous of Sullivan's ability to be so carefree. He mentally added it to the growing list of reasons why he disliked the man, even though he hadn't done anything to Henry specifically. He carried an entitled air of ease that got under Henry's skin, like he knew everything would work out in his favor because he'd never experienced a situation where it had done anything else.

Meanwhile, Henry felt he had to scrape, claw, and fight his way forward on a good day. Henry wanted to say something else to explain his frustration, but the words wouldn't come. Instead, they swirled around in his head, jumbling and crashing together. He had trouble voicing his anger at that moment. Defeated, Henry turned on his heels and returned to the office. He'd find information on the memory man on his own. He didn't need anyone's help but…

"Hey! I was wondering where you'd gone." Anya's voice disrupted his thoughts. She sat perched on the edge of the chair in front of his desk. Since he had confided in her about his wife's health, she visited his office more frequently. She seemed genuinely interested in checking in and seeing how he was doing. He appreciated her thoughtfulness. Sometimes it was nice to have someone to talk to who understood what he was going through.

From what Anya told him, her father was deteriorating quickly. He was no longer able to remember her or her siblings. Henry was terrified of those days with Clara but he knew they were coming whether he wanted them to or not. She had moments where her memory slipped and she couldn't remember his name, but it never lasted longer than a few minutes. The thought of her looking at him and being unable to remember made him sick. He clutched his side gently, hoping Anya hadn't noticed him wince.

"Anya! Hello." He managed to smile, pushing away the reel of dark thoughts playing in his mind. He didn't want to think about Clara being unable to remember him. That was too much at the moment. It was too excruciating to think about or allow his mind to grasp. Anya smiled back at him and gestured toward his messy desk. "Are you working on a new project?" He crossed the room and scooped up the haphazard strips of paper that littered his desk. Days of angry scribbling filled the crumpled pages.

"Something like that. I was talking to Sullivan about something."

"Anything I can help with?" Her tone was innocent, but he couldn't help feeling embarrassed. He didn't know how to explain that he was searching for a mysterious, mystical man with a fancy drug that may or may not be able to restore his wife's memories. He wanted to - what if she knew something that could help? He stared at her for a moment, unsure of what to do. She held his gaze, waiting patiently for him to answer her. That was something he admired about Anya. She was always so patient. Whenever he was stressed and having a particularly snippy moment, she never held it against him.

"If I tell you, you can't tell anyone else." He started, closing the door. "This is top secret information." The smile on her face widened as she sat forward in her chair, looking like she couldn't wait to hear what he was about to say. "I'm serious, Anya; I need you to promise that you won't breathe a word." Henry stared at her, not wanting to utter another sound until she promised. With a quick wave of her hand and a nod, she urged him to continue.

"Yes, yes, okay. I promise. Now what is it?"

"There is a person- a doctor- that can restore memories." He held his breath as he waited for her response. She stared at him quietly, her head slightly tilted to one side. He could tell she was studying him, trying to gauge his seriousness. "How?"

"I don't know how just yet. Sullivan knows, but he won't tell me how I can find him. I was hoping you could help me look. Maybe he could even help your father too? Depending on what the price is?" The look she was giving him made him uncomfortable. He couldn't tell if she believed what he was saying or thought he was full of crap. His body was buzzing with excitement. He couldn't wait to start looking, especially with Anya's help. The two of them could work together and solve all of their problems.

"Are you sure Mr. Sullivan was being serious?" Anya asked carefully. He expected some pushback, but her question still got under his skin because he wasn't entirely sure. Sullivan was a douchebag; he'd always been but lying about something like this was next level. He lied about stupid things that didn't matter in the grand scheme, but Sullivan was mainly honest when it counted. In the years Henry had known him, he felt he could count on Zander Sullivan to tell the truth when it truly mattered. But could he really? Henry took a deep breath and glanced down at the scraps of paper that were scattered on his desk but now sat in a small heap. Different and mostly incorrect spellings of the concierge covered the pages. Henry hoped that he could find the information he needed independently if he changed some letters around. No such luck. "I'm sure." He answered after a moment.

Anya shrugged. "What's the catch?"

"I'm not sure. I will have to ask the memory man when I find him. So will you help me?"

"That's a beautiful picture of you, and... what did you say your wife's name was again?" She asked, ignoring his question. Henry stared at Anya, his annoyance bubbling under the surface. She wasn't usually this indirect with her conversation, but instead of answering him, she asked about the picture that had been on his desk since she started here. He swallowed back the urge to yell at her in frustration; maybe she needed more time to process. It was a lot to drop on someone without warning. He could understand that.

"It's Clara." "Right. You never told me how you guys met." She picked up the photograph and brought it closer to her face. Henry smiled at the memory her statement conjured up.

"I was at a Halloween party with another woman." Anya's head snapped up in surprise.

"Wait, really?" she asked; the corners of her mouth twitched as if she was trying not to laugh. Henry nodded and leaned against the corner of the desk. It was a ridiculous story that people would always shake their heads at whenever Clara told it. He used to be embarrassed about it; he wished they had met more conventionally, but over time he grew to love their awkward love story. It was special. It was them.

"I was dressed as Fred Flintstone."

"Let me guess, she was dressed as something sexy? Like a kitten or something?"

"No, actually... she was dressed as a dirty pad." Anya stared at Henry with her mouth open in shock. That was the usual reaction whenever someone heard what Clara's costume was. At the time, it seemed weird. It was still odd if he was honest with himself, but her refusal to do what was expected was one of the things he loved most about her. She was never afraid to be out of the box. As a result, there were a few questionable fashion and hair choices over the years.

"A dirty pad?" Anya placed the picture back on his desk. "That's disgusting, and now I must hear this story." Henry nodded and inwardly smiled at the pure interest on Anya's face. He never minded sharing this story. He would tell it every day if he could.

11

What makes you think you can save her?" Anya asked. The question caught Henry off guard. They were sitting in his office talking like they did most mornings, and she blurted the question during a stretch of silence. Henry stared at her, unsure of how to answer.

"I'm sorry?" he spluttered, drawing his brows together in confusion. Anya sighed heavily and glanced at the ceiling. Her eyes glistened wet with unshed tears.

"Alzheimer's is a disease with no cure. Instead of spending all your time obsessing-"

"I am not obsessing!" He snapped, interrupting her. She paused briefly. They stared at each other; a silent battle contained in their gazes. He watched her, unmoved by the tears slipping down her cheeks. Anya broke their look first and swiped at the tears in her eyes.

"There is no cure," she began, her voice softer, "why are you so determined to find this Memory Concierge?"

Henry looked down at the muffin Anya had brought him. Their talks and morning muffins were sometimes the only bright spot in his day, but there were moments when Anya would blurt out something that made him uncomfortable or make a comment that would cause him to regret opening up to her. Henry knew Anya was only trying to help, but he would much rather have her support instead of her criticism or judgment. Henry steepled his hands and placed them against his lips. He chose his words carefully, not wanting to be rude to her while she was crying in his office.

"If you had the chance to save your father, even if the chance was slim, wouldn't you take it?" he asked. Anya said nothing. "Wouldn't you?" He repeated more firmly than the first time. Anya flinched; it was quick, but Henry caught it.

"I would." Her voice came out in a hoarse whisper. Henry nodded and pinched off a bit of his muffin.

"So, then you can understand I would do whatever I can to save my wife," he replied, glancing up at her. The pain on her face made his heart clench. It was a pain that he understood.

"What if it's too late?" Anya asked; a single tear slipped down her cheek. He watched as she wiped it away and took another bite of her muffin.

"If it's too late, then at least I'll know I tried." Henry shrugged and leaned back in his chair. He knew that people thought he was crazy for believing The Memory Concierge was a legitimate thing that could help, but that didn't stop him from trying. He couldn't let it.

"Tell me about your father," Henry said, desperate to break the uncomfortable silence. Anya shifted in her seat and looked up at him, startled. He realized it was the first time he had bothered to ask about her father. Guilt washed over him. He had been so focused on his own struggles that he didn't bother to stop and take notice of Anya. She never blamed him for it, but he could tell she needed to talk. Henry folded his hands across his stomach and waited.

"He was always working when I was growing up," Anya began, a wistful smile brightening her delicate features. "He worked hard to make sure we had everything we needed. Even with mom's high-paying job, Dad always ensured my siblings and I had it all."

"Were you all close?" Henry asked.

"He tried, but he was always working so much that he missed out on a lot. I don't think he really knew how to relax."

"At least he provided, right?" Henry couldn't tell why he felt oddly defensive of a man he hadn't met.

"As an adult, I now understand that men, especially black men, were only taught to love by providing. Ensuring we had clothes on our backs and food on the table was how Dad showed love, but all we really wanted was to have him there." Anya looked at him, and the intensity of her gaze made him fidget in his chair. He suddenly felt uncomfortable meeting her eye, so he focused on picking the lint off his shirt.

"I probably should have been more available for my children, but it's hard," he said. Admitting it out loud made his chest tighten. Before Clara's diagnosis, one of his goals had been to spend more time with his children and get to know them.

"What's hard about it?" Anya asked.

"Emotional availability wasn't a thing when I was a child, especially not from my father. Being too emotional made you soft, which was the worst thing you could be as a man. Men are strong. Men provide. That's it. Nothing else. I'm sure your father can understand."

Anya nodded and grabbed the trash from their shared breakfast. Her expression was pained like she wanted to say something else but was holding back. Henry wished to press; he wanted to know what she was keeping from him if only it would make her stay and talk to him a few moments longer.

"I should go." She said with a stiff smile. Henry wasn't sure what he said that upset her, but he nodded without asking. As soon as the door clicked behind her, his mind drifted back to The Memory Concierge. He was unable to think about anything else for very long.

Henry was losing his grip on his health. He was so focused on finding The Memory Concierge and juggling things with Clara that everything else had become severely neglected. He forgot to shower; he could never remember whether he had eaten. Sleeping became incredibly difficult; whenever he closed his eyes, his brain jumped into overdrive.

Did he give Clara her medicine? Did he hide the keys so she couldn't take them? When was the next doctor's appointment? Did he schedule it, or did they move it to another day? He could feel his body screaming for attention. At work, there would be moments when it got too quiet, and he would accidentally drift off to sleep at his desk. He'd always pop awake a few minutes later, embarrassed that he allowed himself to get this bad off.

Clara was not getting better. Her personality collapsed in on itself. She was quiet and timid, unsure of herself and her movements. Gone was her vibrancy and everything that made her unique. Henry's heart broke every time he saw her on the couch, staring into the distance. He wanted to be able to reach into the murky waters in her mind and pull her out and save her from drowning.

He increased his efforts to find The Memory Concierge, but with the limited availability of information and Sullivan's sudden tight-lipped behavior, Henry felt stuck in the same spot. All his work conversations centered around Clara and Alzheimer's and The Memory Concierge. People were beginning to avoid him, but Henry no longer cared. If he had to pour his entire paycheck into Sullivan's pocket to convince him to talk, he would.

When he entered the office, clothes wrinkled and disheveled, Sullivan glanced up at him in surprise. Usually, Henry would never allow himself to leave the house looking like this, but his body and mind were exhausted, and he couldn't see an end in sight. Sullivan stared at him before sighing and folding the newspaper he was reading.

"Alright. You want information about the concierge?" He asked. Henry nodded, shifting in his seat to keep his anxiety at bay. Sullivan paused before shaking his head.

"Fine. but before I tell you anything, I need you to promise me one thing." Sullivan said, crossing his arms. Henry waited, hoping that Sullivan wouldn't ask for any more money. His account was looking slim until the next payday rolled around. "Whatever happens from here and whatever you end up finding is completely on you whether you like it or not, you hear me?" Henry nodded again.

"Rumors say he is working out of the abandoned Newk Hotel." Sullivan's eyes bore into Henry, a smile played at the edge of his chapped lips. "That's where you'll find him."

"What do I say when I find him?" Henry asked, suddenly feeling nervous. He hadn't thought he would get this close. Sullivan tilted his head to one side and rolled his eyes in exasperation.

"Do I need to tell you what to wear too? I don't know! Look, Tubeck, I've said all I'm going to say. Figure it out." With that, he leaned back in his chair and stared at Henry as if dismissing him.

Henry sat in stunned silence for a moment, unsure what to do next, before heading back to his office with a sigh. After a split second of hazy contemplating, Henry decided to go to the hotel that night once Clara was asleep.

He didn't want to worry or confuse her by trying to explain what he was doing. He would explain it when it was all over. Henry could not focus on anything else for the rest of the day. His steps felt lighter and full of energy, invigorated by a newfound sense of determination within himself. He was so close to the finish line.

That night, when everything was quiet, Henry slipped out of bed and headed for the front door. He hesitated for a moment, wondering whether he should take the car. Instead, he slipped out on foot. The building was about a thirty-minute walk heading out of town. He passed by the Newk Hotel many times over the years and never paid much attention. When passing, he could have sworn he saw light in one of the windows every now and then, but he never stopped to check. After the building began to crumple and age, Henry wondered why it was never removed.

The night air was crisp, and the sky was full of stars as he walked down the deserted streets alone. He smiled up at them, thinking of the times he and Clara had pulled out a blanket and watched the stars from their backyard. Those used to be his favorite nights. When the kids came along, they didn't get to do it as often but had picked up the habit once again when all three children were grown and out of the house. So many peaceful nights were spent under the stars talking about what they wanted to accomplish in the next year and what their goals and plans were for themselves and their marriage. It had been such a long time since they did that. It had been a long time since they did anything that didn't revolve around Alzheimer's.

That's something they don't really tell you. In all the pamphlets with the smiling faces and the inspirational quotes and the dos and don'ts of Alzheimer's, they always seem to forget to tell you that it will slowly eat away at everything you once enjoyed until there is nothing left but emptiness. It erodes the happy moments, the simple moments, and even the angry moments. Henry and Clara hadn't argued that often during their marriage, but now, he preferred arguing over silence. At least he would know she was still in there.

He propelled forward, powered by hope, determination, and slight desperation. He ignored the cars driving on the road as he walked. A few stopped to ask if he needed a ride, but he shook his head and kept going. He used the walk to clear his mind and think about the good things that had happened in his years on this earth. He had regrets. His most significant regret was not spending enough time with his family.

His kids were grown and starting families of their own. They barely checked in. He spent so much time working while they were growing up that he missed the critical moments. He knew how to provide, but Clara was the one to kiss the scraped knees and bake the birthday cupcakes. He always told himself that he would get to it next time, but the next time came and went, and he never quite learned how to be vulnerable with his children. That may be why conversations with Anya meant so much to him. He could pretend she was his child and make up for the lost time with his kids.

Henry always struggled with denial when facing situations, he couldn't fix. He would pretend they weren't there until they eventually sorted themselves out. That was his biggest struggle with this situation - knowing the problem but being unable to fix or ignore it. All he could do was sit back and watch his wife fade into the background, powerless to do anything about it.

Her outward beauty was still there, unaltered by the disease. Her skin was still velvety, and her hair was still an enviable length, but her eyes no longer held the same light. They were empty and lifeless. For the longest time, he thought there was nothing he could do. He believed that Clara would slip through his fingers, and he would be stuck living in the past, trying desperately to cling to the memories they made when everything was simple.

The air grew colder as he walked, his throat dry and painful with each swallow, but he kept pushing - one foot in front of the other - one breath at a time. He had almost given up by the time he had made it to the hotel building. His heart pounded with anticipation and nervousness. It was dark. It was cold. It was late. He wondered briefly if this was a suicide mission, and he was willingly offering up his life. He stared up at the building, intimidated by how tall and ugly it looked against the other buildings on the same street. He wasn't sure what to do next. Should he knock or just burst in like the police? Would it be unlocked? He stepped forward, and the automatic doors remained closed, which was no surprise. He didn't expect that there would be electricity.

Henry placed a palm against the dusty door of the building. It was cool to the touch. He pushed his shoulder gently into the door, unsure how much force to use. It caved inward under the weight of him, allowing just enough space for him to slip through. He was surprised at the state of the room in front of him. The lobby was luxurious and pristine with shiny marble floors and velvet curtains framing the windows looking out onto what Henry assumed would have been beautiful gardens at one point in time. Everything looked untouched – almost as if time had stood still since its last visitors left many years ago. But when Henry stepped entirely inside, he immediately noticed something off. Despite its beautiful architecture and lush decorations, an oppressive silence and an odd smell - like death and rot - hung heavily in the air.

He shivered as he walked further into the hotel's grand lobby; even though the moonlight streaming through the stained-glass windows above him allowed him to see where he was planting his feet, the room was still dark and ominous. Henry's teeth chattered loudly. He couldn't tell if it was from the frigid air in this abandoned lobby, nerves, or a combination of both.

He felt like someone, or something was watching him, but he couldn't see anyone. Anxiety and paranoia crept up his back. He whipped around to make sure nothing was sneaking up on him, but nothing was there. He mentally cursed himself for not bringing a weapon of some sort. He was so focused on getting here he didn't think about protecting himself. He never thought he would get this far. He hadn't planned what to do from here but was determined to keep going forward. He had to at least try. If it didn't work, he could rest knowing that he had done everything within his power. Not many others could say the same.

Henry began exploring each room until finally coming across what appeared to be some kind of reception area at the very back of one hallway. A large wooden desk sat atop richly patterned yet dusty carpeting, while two leather chairs faced away from him towards a wall adorned with old portraits. He wondered why no one bothered to remove them when the place was evacuated. They looked valuable.

This room was in a much poorer state compared to the lobby. Yellowed wallpaper peeled from every corner, revealing streaks of grey beneath it all that seemed almost alive and moving up towards the ceiling like tendrils desperately reaching towards the ligh or towards escape. The smell of death was more pungent here, like it was trapped. It was so strong that Henry felt he could taste the sickly sweetness of it with each sniff. He took short breaths, hoping to get less of the smell trapped in his lungs. It didn't help.

"You shouldn't be here." A voice suddenly echoed around him breaking his thoughts. Henry jumped and turned toward the sound; in his fascination with the room, its rancid smells, and the abandoned artwork, he didn't notice the dark figure huddled in the corner. He couldn't tell if it was a man or a woman - young or old. Henry cautioned a step closer. All lessons of self-preservation and safety evaporated from him like water.

"Are you...are you him?" He asked quietly, not wanting to believe what he was seeing - or not seeing. He couldn't really tell anymore. The figure remained in the corner, concealed by the shadows. The hair on Henry's arms prickled. The air grew thick with tension. His mind and body told him to run, to turn around and get out before something happened that he couldn't control, but he pushed forward anyway.

"Am I who?" the figure asked. The voice made Henry uncomfortable. It felt too loud - his eardrums wanted to block out the sound. He resisted the urge to place his hands over his ears.

"The Memory Concierge?" Henry said quietly. His confidence in the situation was draining quickly. Had Sullivan sent him on a wild goose chase? Who was this person? Would they hurt him? He tried to remember a few basic moves from when his brothers taught him how to fight. It was years since he'd been in a fight. He wasn't even sure he could appropriately defend himself anymore. He glanced around the room, trying to find something he could use as a weapon. The only thing in the room besides the two of them would be much too heavy to lift. The figure stretched to its full height, which made Henry freeze in shock. From the shadows, the figure stretched to be almost able to touch the ceiling. It looked too tall to be human.

"Why are you here?" It demanded, staying hidden.

"I- I came because I was told you could restore my wife's memories. She has Alzheimer's. She- She can't remember me anymore." Tears began to pool in his eyes, blurring his vision of the figure. "I just want my wife back." The figure remained quiet for a moment; it seemed to be considering Henry's words.

"Please," Henry whispered. His voice cracked with desperation. The figure stepped toward him, revealing only half of its face. It was wrinkled like it was old but somehow looked young at the same time. The skin was an ugly grayish-greenish shade that made Henry want to turn away in disgust. Blueish veins pulsed through the spindly arms. Panic coursed through Henry's veins. His feet felt frozen to the floor. The figure smiled, revealing rows of sharp and rotten teeth.

"Hello, Henry."

12

An overwhelming, angry buzzing in his ears made it difficult to hear what was happening around him. The smell of rotting flesh stung his nose hairs and stuck to his clothes and skin. He could feel it on him. He could taste it. It made his eyes water and his stomach flip with nausea; every muscle in his body screamed at him to turn and run. The Concierge regarded him with a curious expression. Its white, pupil-less eyes were fixed on Henry, studying him closely as if looking for the perfect moment to strike. The creature looked like a mixture of a human and a snake, like a horrible science experiment gone wrong. Henry gulped nervously, his throat dry and sandpapery.

"How did you know my name?" he asked, cursing himself for sounding as terrified as he felt. If he thought he was putting on a good front before, the tremor in his voice ruined it. His heart thumped in his chest. The Concierge tilted his head and sniffed.

"That's not really what you came to ask me, now is it?" Henry didn't respond. He felt childish in front of this monster; after spending so much time hunting it down, he was unsure what to do or say. Sullivan had warned him that he might not like what he found. He had let the warning slip in one ear and out the other.

Now, standing in front of this nightmare in physical form, Henry wished that he had taken some kind of precaution instead of running headfirst into an unfamiliar situation. He kept his eyes glued to his feet. "Please… my wife, she-"

"You need memories restored." It wasn't a question. Henry nodded quickly. The Concierge's face shifted upwards as if it were lifting an eyebrow that it didn't technically have. "That's going to cost you."

"I'll pay whatever you require. I have money." The Concierge leaned towards him.

"I have no use for your currency." It snapped. Henry flinched at the aggression in its tone. He had somehow angered it and wasn't sure what he had said wrong.

Henry kept his eyes on his shoes, terrified to meet the gaze of this creature. He vaguely thought about Medusa and how she would turn her victims to stone if they looked at her or that Bible story about Lot's wife who turned into a pillar of salt because she turned and looked back.

Henry felt like something would happen to him if he stared directly into the eyes of The Memory Concierge. Maybe he would melt into a puddle. Maybe his bones would crumble.

"Some memories are better left hidden," it said simply, bringing Henry back to the present moment. Henry's head snapped up; he met the eyes of the creature, completely forgetting his earlier concerns about eye contact.

"I need her back. I won't be able to let go until I get her back."

"Playing with fate is a dangerous game, Henry."

"I'll take the risk!" Henry almost stepped closer but then thought better of it. The Memory Concierge looked tall enough to close the distance between them with little effort, but Henry wanted to keep from giving it any ideas. He was having trouble reconciling his thoughts with what he was seeing in front of him. He expected a doctor or at least a human, not this...thing.

"You may not like what you get."

"You don't understand. I need her back! Please! I have come all this way. I can't live without Clara. I need my wife! She looks at me and doesn't even remember who I am. I can't keep living like this!" His own voice grew louder and more emotional with each word. Desperate tears slipped down his cheeks; snot bubbled in his nostrils, temporarily blocking the smell of decay.

The Concierge remained unmoved. Instead, it watched Henry curiously, like it was studying him for a test or to see if he would make a good meal. Henry couldn't be sure which was closer to the truth.

"Forgetfulness plagues your family, but not in the way you know to be true."

"What does that mean?" Henry's brow furrowed in confusion. Why was this creature speaking in riddles? Irritation bubbled in his throat, and he furiously wiped at the tears still slipping down his cheeks. He wasn't prepared to solve a puzzle. What was he supposed to do with that? The Concierge seemed to sense his annoyance and let out a chuckle. It was a deep and eerie sound, like bass rumbling and vibrating the windows.

"Things aren't what they seem, Henry. Are you sure you want to lift the veil? Once you do, you cannot come back." That didn't sound good. He knew there would be consequences, and until now, he thought he was prepared to deal with them, but standing here looking at this nightmare in physical form, he wasn't so sure anymore.

Part of him wanted to turn back, but he had come so far. Could the consequences really be that bad? Henry tried to imagine what life would look like if he had given up and decided not to come. Clara would continue to get worse until her body ultimately betrayed her. It would forget essential functions like breathing or swallowing, and then she would die.

He couldn't process what life would be like without her in it. Nothing would make sense. The sun would cease to shine. People would grieve with him for a while, but then they would slowly drift away. They would go back to their own lives and move on one by one leaving Henry stuck deep in grief and sadness. He would be expected to move on with his life as if his heart was not buried in the casket with his wife. He couldn't go through that. He refused to go through that. Not now. They were still young. They deserved more time. Whatever hardships came their way, they could deal with it together. If he had Clara and his children were okay, they could figure out the rest.

"I'll do it. I want to move forward. Tell me what I need to do."

"Each memory comes with a price, Henry. And it is nonnegotiable." The Concierge crossed its lanky arms and stared at Henry with empty eyes. As much as he wanted to turn his head, Henry stood firm and held the gaze, wondering if this creature just hung out in the corner of this room until someone ventured in, looking for its help. How many people sought out The Memory Concierge? This had to be a lonely existence. The creature's tongue flicked across its teeth, making Henry shiver with fear and disgust.

Henry was proud of himself for not wetting his pants. Fear settled deep into his bones and sweat pooled at the small of his back. No one would believe this story if he tried to tell it. He wasn't even sure if he trusted this story, even as he stood here in front of this grotesque humanoid, begging for it to change his life back to normal. He felt sick just looking at it, even more so when he thought about the possible scenarios this could turn into. Maybe his wife didn't love him, and this distant version of her was better than the real version. Maybe his kids secretly hated him, and if he went forward with this deal, he would know just how much. Perhaps his marriage hadn't been as happy as he had imagined.

She may leave him for the next-door neighbor. He had seen how the man would practically melt into a puddle whenever Clara was nearby. He may have to live out the rest of his days knowing he allowed his wife to leave him behind and move on. Could he live with that? Henry contemplated the possibilities, but even if, in another life, Clara never loved him, he would give anything to replace that fire in her eyes.

If it meant she was truly happy with someone else, at least she would be happy. She would be alive. And that's what counts at the end of the day, right? Henry took a deep breath, filled with new resolve. Come what may, he had to try. He tilted his head towards The Memory Concierge, who hovered over him and watched him with mild curiosity.

"Well?" The Concierge said after an uncomfortable stretch of silence. It stared at Henry expectantly, waiting for the answer. Henry was vaguely aware that he was standing there staring at The Concierge with his mouth slightly open while his brain lagged, struggling to understand what was happening.

"What's the catch?" he asked skeptically. He glanced up at the dusty windows covered in cobwebs and dirt. It was a wonder this building was still standing. The Concierge sighed and stared at him. Henry knew he was pushing his luck, but he had to at least ask. This was a big decision to make at this moment. One that apparently had the potential to end in a way he wasn't expecting.

"There are consequences, of course. Everything has consequences." The Concierge offered Henry a smile that was probably meant to be comforting but only increased Henry's unease. The overwhelming number of teeth were sharp and pointy like a piranha. It was a wonder that it could close its mouth without slicing through its lips. A sheet of paper resembling a scroll appeared between the boney fingers. It held it out for Henry to take, but he made no move to reach for it. From what he could see, the pages were blank except for the word **CONTRACT** in big black letters.

"I don't understand."

"It's not meant for you to understand right now, Henry, but you will soon." An eerie chill filled the air, and all sound felt muffled as if someone had reached in and turned down the knob on the volume in the room. Henry begged for months to be here. He pestered Sullivan at every turn for any information he had on The Concierge.

Still, now that he was looking at this beast, something niggled at the corners of his brain - something dangerous. It felt wrong. This entire ordeal felt off, but he couldn't quite put his finger on how or why. It was a gut feeling. The smell in the air began to overwhelm Henry, making it difficult to take deep breaths. He was so sure before. On the walk over here, he had no doubt in his mind that he would make a deal with The Memory Concierge and then go on about his day.

He couldn't bring himself to do it now that he was here. He wanted to, but something was holding him back. Something was screaming at him to go back home where it was safe. Henry could tell the Concierge's patience was growing thin with his waffling. He thought back to Clara and the empty way she stared at him when he was trying to tell her he loved her.

He thought about the way she had flinched when he touched her, no longer recognizing that he was her husband and meant no harm. Fear flashed in her eyes momentarily before the empty, soulless look she always wore returned. It was a similar look to the one that The Concierge wears now. He didn't think he could take much more of that look. It ate away at his heart, leaving it cracked and bleeding in his chest. It hurt. His desire for his wife began to overpower the rest of his senses. If he tried and it didn't work, he could say he did all he could. He just hoped that he wouldn't regret it.

"Okay. I'll do it. Where do I sign?" The Concierge considered him for a moment before nodding toward the contract. The creature held it out again, expecting Henry to know where to sign. Henry subconsciously patted his pockets in search of a pen. The Concierge watched him, mild annoyance dancing across its grotesque face.

"You won't need a pen. Fresh blood is all that is required." At its words, Henry froze. Blood? Was he signing his life away?

"Okay, wait, I have questions. What are the consequences? Will Clara die? Will I die? Will I wake up tomorrow morning with talons and a long tail?" The Concierge let out a booming laugh as if Henry's questions were absurd, but when Henry didn't join in, its eyes narrowed.

"Are these serious questions?" Henry waved a hand at the room they both stood in as if to say: *do you see where we are right now?* "Completely serious."

"For Christ's sake, Henry, you won't have a tail. This isn't a movie." It sighed. Henry snorted. If this was a movie, it would make more sense. He stood for a moment, contemplating. The Concierge made a sound similar to a grunt, grabbed Henry's hand, and brought it toward the contract. It was then Henry noticed that his hand was bleeding. He stared at his fingers, confused. When did that happen? The Concierge touched his finger to the paper; the blood soaked into the fibers and spread like ink. He watched with fascination and fear as the blood looped and swirled. Until his name was written in thick, bold letters.

Henry D. Tubeck

"There. It's now complete." The Concierge tucked the paper into a flap of fabric that hung loosely on its body like a cloak. It flashed another unsettling smile at Henry, the sharp teeth glittering like knives against the moonlight. The unease settled into the pit of Henry's stomach like a lead bomb. His throat became dry, and his vision tilted. He felt as if he would pass out if he didn't sit down soon.

A deafening grumble filled the air. The smell of death and rot, already potent, got worse. Henry felt the ground rushing towards him, ready to swallow him up. Was he falling? He flailed, frantically trying to reach for something to steady himself. "What's happening?" His voice was panicky and hoarse. The Concierge didn't respond; it just watched as Henry continued to fight for air. It felt as if the walls were getting closer. The room seemed to shrink around him. Henry turned, desperately searching for the exit. His feet wouldn't move. They felt glued where he stood. He looked down at his feet but couldn't make sense of what was happening. He couldn't see them.

"This is what you wanted, Henry." The Concierge's voice was softer and muffled, like it was traveling through a tunnel before it reached Henry's ears. He wanted something else, not this. Not at all. He thought about Anya, who had been concerned about him from the moment he started talking about The Memory Concierge. She encouraged him to find a different route, but he didn't listen. He couldn't imagine why it would be a bad idea to come. He wanted to look into Clara's eyes and know she remembered him. That desire fueled him and clouded over any sound judgment. He never considered that coming would be a bad idea. All he wanted was to have his wife back. He didn't want to die.

"No... please...do *something!*" He gasped. The corners of his vision began to blur. The Concierge grinned. The smile stretched unnaturally across its face sending a wave of terror through Henry. He wanted to scream for help, but the words wouldn't come. Who would hear him anyway? He was all alone in this abandoned hotel. Everyone else was sleeping. He sank to his knees; dirt from the un-swept floor coated his pants and the palms of his hands. His heart thumped wildly in his chest. Henry couldn't catch his breath. Is this what having a heart attack felt like? He was terrified and had no way to call for help. Henry couldn't even remember if he brought his phone with him.

"It's too late, Henry."

"I feel like I'm dying. I need help. Please help me; I don't want to die! I want to see my wife. Where is my wife? Clara! Oh God, Clara!" As he continued to scream, he felt oxygen leaving his body. Breathing was becoming more complex. He couldn't see. The smell of death and decay was overpowering. The Concierge remained still, watching Henry slowly lose consciousness. It gave no indication if it had the power to help; it just watched silently.

Henry's thoughts jumbled together in a clump of confusion and desperation. They say that your life flashes before your eyes right before you die. All Henry could see was Clara and all of the missed opportunities. And all of the moments he wished he could redo. Deep in his subconscious, he wondered who would take care of her if he didn't return home. Would their children step in to protect their mother? Would they tell her the lengths he traveled to save her? She'd never know what happened to him. She'd never know why he left the house in the middle of the night. He worried that she would think he had finally abandoned her, even though he promised to always be by her side, no matter what happened.

He wondered if his children would miss him. It had been so long since he'd had a moment to catch up with them. He wondered if they knew how much he loved them and how quickly he would do this all over again if it was one of them suffering from memory loss. Henry spent so much time working when they were children; he never considered it would damage the relationship with his three heartbeats. His family was always his world, but he never told them. Here in this dusty hotel, he could only hope they could see past his actions and hear his heart to know just how much he loved them.

13

Henry woke up with a start, sweat covering his back and shoulders and his heart pounding in his chest. The sheets under him were drenched. Sunlight shone through the window to his right leaving dots in his vision as his eyes tried to adjust. He squinted, trying to make sense of what was happening. He was disoriented and confused. It took him a few seconds to realize where he was - in the bed of his own home. How had he gotten here? The last thing he remembered was being on his hands and knees in front of that awful creature, accepting his death as it watched him fight to breathe. Is this what death is? Is this just a dream, and he's actually on the floor of that hotel covered in dust and bugs? Would any-one find his body?

He glanced to his left and saw Clara sleeping peacefully beside him. She looked beautiful. Her arm was casually thrown over her face to block out the sunlight. Did it work? She didn't look any different from what he could tell. She looked peaceful as she slept, her face relaxed, and her mouth slightly opened. Her chest rose and fell gently with each breath.

His heart thudded against his ribcage as he reached out a trembling hand to touch her, praying that this wasn't a dream. She felt real under his fingertips. Her skin felt normal. He quickly checked for a tail or another sign of being somehow different, and when he found none, he let out a sigh of relief. He rubbed her arm and let out a shaky breath, trying and failing to reel in his surging emotions. Clara stirred beside him, her eyes fluttering open as she looked at him in surprise.

"Henry? Are you okay? What time is it?" She sat up and rubbed her eyes. He glanced at the clock on the nightstand next to her side of the bed. A small yawn escaped her lips, and she stretched her arms toward the ceiling. He blinked, trying to understand what had happened since he left last night - was it last night? It all felt like a dream. One moment, he was walking through the Newk Hotel's dimly lit corridors, and then suddenly... he was here, back in his bed, like nothing had happened. The last thing he remembered was talking to an ugly creature called 'the Memory Clerk,' who claimed they could help restore Clara's lost memories.

He remembered being warned about the consequences and being terrified the creature had somehow killed him without touching him. He was lying on the floor in a crumpled heap when everything around him faded into black. He was confident that was the end, yet here he was.

As he struggled to find the words, Clara pulled the covers back from her side of the bed and came around to sit next to him. He watched as she moved just as gracefully as she used to before, each step full of confidence. She placed a warm hand on his cheek. He caught a glimpse of her yellow acrylic nails in the corner of his vision. Henry closed his eyes and leaned into her hand, savoring the touch. It had been a while since she had done something so simple yet so comforting. He didn't realize how many things he missed about her.

"Sweetheart, let's go ahead and get you ready for the day. As soon as we get you dressed, I'll get breakfast started. Does that sound good?" she said gently. She rubbed a hand on his back in gentle circles. The unease he felt seemed like a distant memory next to this moment. Henry was so happy to see Clara with that familiar spark in her eyes. He stared at her, unable to talk but wanting her to feel how much he loved her even though he was too choked up to find the words. Relief washed over him in waves. She was back. She was here. She recognized him again. He wanted to return to that hotel and hug the creepy snake creature around the waist to thank him for giving the Clara he fell in love with back to him.

Yet deep down inside himself, despite his happiness and the seemingly normal household, something didn't feel right--it felt almost like a puzzle piece that was in the wrong puzzle. The colors were similar, it looked okay from a distance, but up close, it didn't quite fit like it was supposed to. The edges were hazy and out of focus. Something was off. He just couldn't put his finger on what it was.

"Are you hungry? We have some extra time this morning. I can make your favorite." Clara stood up and gently pulled Henry up into the standing position. He didn't need the help, but he let her assist him anyway. Henry stood, feeling choked up and emotional. His muscles felt stiff with sleep, and his brain felt fuzzy, but he was happy… so happy. Tears slipped down his cheeks and soaked into the collar of the ratty pajamas he was wearing. It was his favorite pair. The seams had worn from overuse, there was a hole in the armpit, and the pants had a patch sewn into the knee, but they brought him comfort. Henry knew he needed a new pair, but he couldn't bring himself to try any out, and he wouldn't let Clara throw them away.

"Honey? Why are you crying? What is it?" She searched his eyes, her own full of concern, swiped at his tears, and planted a sweet kiss on his forehead. God, he loved this woman so much. She was the sun in his sky, the air in his lungs. The sunlight from the window bounced off her skin, making it glisten. Her purple bonnet, worn thin around the elastic edges, was pushed back a little, and her beautiful hair peeked out at the top. It was a little grayer than he remembered, but it was still gorgeous. Thick and full of healthy curls. He lifted a hand to touch a coil that was hanging out. She grabbed his wrist and kissed it; her eyes were full of love.

She was known for her fashion sense and ability to pull together an outfit for any occasion, but his favorite moments came before the glitz and the glamour. When her hair was disheveled, and her eyes still crusted with sleep. She was always beautiful, but in his eyes, she looked stunning in those moments. The vulnerable moments that belonged only to the two of them, together in their bedroom and away from the rest of the world.

The two of them headed into the kitchen. Clara chattered happily about their plans for the day and what their kids had been up to after their usual phone conversations. Clara demanded that their three children call at least once a week to keep her abreast of what was going on in their lives. No negotiations. Once a week. They would complain, but in the conversations that he listened to, he could tell their children appreciated it. He couldn't keep up with the weekly phone calls, and after a while, they stopped expecting him to participate. It had been a while since he heard from them.

The fact that they just assumed he wouldn't be able to join hurt his feelings - even if it was true. Even if he was busy or struggling to care for Clara, he still missed his children. He still loved them. Henry realized Clara had been talking to him, but he still hadn't opened his mouth to respond. He rolled his tongue around in his mouth, trying to come up with something to say, but he couldn't. As hard as he tried, the words just would not come. He moved his lips, but no sound came out. It must be the influx of emotions. His brain was tired and in shock. He was overwhelmed, that was all. The whole search for the memory collector was exhausting. The trip to the hotel took a lot out of him, and he just needed a little time to gather himself — only, that didn't seem right. Memory Collector? Henry shook his head slightly. No, that wasn't the right name for it. It was close, but not quite. Memory Cleaner? Henry shook his head again and squinted. No. That wasn't it either.

Clara led him to the chair at the dining room table. She placed a hand on his shoulder and kissed his cheek quickly. His entire body flinched away from her touch. The look on her face made him feel bad almost immediately. He hadn't withdrawn because of her. He was so wrapped up trying to figure out the name of that entity he had spoken with that he didn't realize what she was doing. Before he could turn to her and tell her, the look on her face vanished, replaced with a cheerful smile.

"Let me grab your meds." She turned and reached for the cabinet closest to the table. He watched, bewildered, as she took out bottle after bottle of medication. Each one was a different size and pill shape. She moved through each bottle, taking two out of one and three out of another. She placed them on a paper towel before him and turned towards the refrigerator to grab a water bottle. Clara opened the lid on the bottle and handed it to him, the smile never leaving her face. Henry paused before reaching for the bottle.

Right before his eyes, the smile twisted a bit. The corners of her mouth turned up in a way that almost seemed evil. The air around her head turned black and circled like a halo. He thought he caught a glimpse of a thin, snakelike tongue flicking behind her teeth, but the image was gone when he blinked and looked again. Replaced with Clara's usual expression. He hesitated, unsure of what to do. Henry had never taken medication before; when had he started? He blinked, confused. He could feel his head shaking back and forth in refusal. Panic coursed through his veins and turned his blood cold like ice.

Clara sighed quietly and urged him to take the water bottle. "I know you don't like taking your medicine. It's not fun, but the pills are meant to help you, honey. We've talked about this, remember?" He didn't. Not really. He stared up at her, the words still stuck in his throat. He wanted to say no, to shake his head... to tell her these weren't his pills and there had to have been some mistake. The doctors had gotten everything mixed up.

Instead, he nodded stiffly and brought the medications up to his lips one by one. Each pill was chased by a gulp of water, some dribbling down his chin. Before he could reach for it, Clara snatched a napkin and wiped at his mouth. She was so attentive. It made him feel loved and protected in a way he had recently missed. It had been a long time since Clara could care for him how she used to. He didn't mind stepping up and taking over the caregiving reins, but he had to admit that this felt nice. Not having to worry, being free to focus on the bigger picture rather than having to remember the small details. He had never been good at this part.

Once satisfied that he had taken all his medicine, Clara turned to the cabinets and pulled out different pots and pans. Henry watched, trying to work up the nerve to say something, but his mind fell blank. He felt he was missing key details like he entered a room in the middle of the conversation, and no one would help him catch up.

Nevertheless, Henry chose not to dwell too much on the things that didn't seem quite right and instead savored being back with the woman he loved most and would give anything to see smile. He was glad that she was back. Her voice took on the familiar lilt that he was used to. Her eyes had their usual sparkle. Her step had that same bounce he had grown to love over the years. Taking solace that everything seemed alright, Henry embraced the familiar warmth radiating throughout their home.

Pots clinked and clanked together as she prepared to make breakfast for them. Henry's stomach growled in response to her preparing the kitchen. He couldn't remember the last time he had eaten. It took only a short time until the smells wafted throughout the house.

"I'm making pancakes. Is that okay?" Clara called over her shoulder.

When Henry didn't respond, she turned to look at him. He smiled at her and nodded silently. This satisfied her enough to continue cooking. He tried to make sense of the last few days as he waited for his food. Was it real? Did he travel through town on foot in the middle of the night to an abandoned hotel covered in dirt and ruin from years of non-use? Did he make a deal with the devil in exchange for his wife's memories? Are there going to be consequences for the deal he made? He looked down at his hands, where he had been bleeding the night before. The blood had oozed from his fingers to sign the contract and seal his fate. There was nothing there now besides the same old scars he had carried with him into adulthood. He turned his hands over, searching for signs that he hadn't imagined the whole ordeal.

"The truth might be more than you can handle." A familiar gravelly voice filled his ears. Henry jumped at the sound, turning left and right to locate the source of the voice. He found nothing. He glanced over at his wife, wondering if she was the one who said it. Clara continued to cook as if she hadn't heard anything unusual. His heart raced, and his pulse thumped in his ears. He struggled to swallow; his throat felt dry and coated with grit.

He wanted to return to the hotel and demand answers, but he remembered that the creature had said that once you leave, you can't return. He didn't want to make that trip again anyway. The building was dark and ominous, covered in a thick layer of rot. Even if the interior was mostly preserved and untouched, an unease permeated the air. Being in that hotel had made the hairs on his entire body stand to attention. Henry was lucky that he made it out of there, even if he wasn't quite sure how he managed it. Clara set the plate in front of him and pulled out her chair.

"Rose called last night to check on us," she said, taking a bite of the pancakes on her plate. Henry waited for her to continue. "I told her we were doing fine as usual. She offered to sit with you for a bit so I could run some errands. I'm sure you don't want to come with me to the store." Clara chattered happily as the two of them ate. He briefly wondered why she thought someone needed to sit with him while she left the house as if he wasn't an adult, but he brushed it off. A few things didn't make sense, but he needed help figuring out where to start.

He had just taken a hefty gulp of orange juice when he heard it. He thought he had imagined it at first, but as Henry sat quietly, he heard it again. Clara had begun to hum. It was initially quiet, a sound low in her throat but unmistakable. The same sound that had irritated him so many times during the earlier parts of their marriage soothed a wounded spot deep in his soul. He missed that sound so much more than he could have expressed in words.

Clara absentmindedly hummed and ate as she scrolled through the messages on her cell phone. Henry stared at her, completely in awe, too scared to look away for fear it would vanish. He didn't want to believe it, in case it wasn't entirely true, but it was becoming harder to ignore. The eye contact, the affection, the caretaking, the humming… it worked. All of the months of research, the trip, the near-death experience… all of that brought Clara back to him. As her humming progressed into full-blown singing, he felt tears slip down his cheeks. She belted the words to a song he didn't recognize, but the sound of her voice, bright and full of life, brought joy to his heart.

He wanted to jump up and hug her around the waist, but he didn't want to scare her. He couldn't explain how he had traveled into town searching for a mythical creature to make a deal and return her memories. He wondered if he could ever tell her the lengths he had gone to. Would she believe him? He couldn't wait to return to work and tell Sullivan what happened.

Clara. His Clara. The love of his life was home, not just in body but in mind. He wished he could freeze time at this exact moment and live in it forever. Her hair was covered by the bonnet, the sleeve of her pajama top hanging slightly off her shoulder, the bit of toast crumbs by her mouth, and the bright sparkle in her eyes as she watched him eat… all of it seemed so beautiful and so normal. These moments had passed while he was too busy to realize and appreciate them for what they were. He had a second chance to do it right and would do everything in his power to avoid messing this one up.

14

The smell of death was back. Just when Henry had begun to let his guard down a little, it filled his nostrils and made him sick to his stomach. He lurched back from the table in surprise, recoiling as if he had been slapped. Clara flinched at his sudden movement, shocked that he reacted so violently. He was sitting at the kitchen table with Clara, listening to her hum as she ate when it assaulted his nose. He tried to ignore it, but it seemed to grow stronger with each passing moment until it overpowered his senses. He couldn't breathe without smelling it. It coated his tongue. He sniffed at his plate, wondering if the food was the cause, but the food smelled fine. Clara turned to him, concern and a hint of hurt on her face.

"Is something wrong with your breakfast?" She asked, looking at down at his plate in concern. She leaned toward it and sniffed as well then shrugged as if she couldn't smell anything. Henry sniffed again and then he shook his head slowly. He still couldn't seem to find the words to answer out loud. This was beginning to frustrate him. He was never one for idle chatter, but this was getting ridiculous. It was like his mouth forgot how to form words; instead, they stayed trapped in his thoughts in a garbled clump of confusion. She watched him for a moment and then finished her food.

When she leaned over to grab his plate and put it in the sink, the smell hit him even stronger. It was coming from Clara. It seeped from her pores like she had bathed in it. It was on her clothes, in her hair, on her skin, and on her breath. He jumped back, desperate to put distance between the two of them before he got sick all over the floor. A look of hurt contorted her features. "Oh, Henry," she whispered, her eyes glistening with unshed tears.

She didn't speak to him for the rest of the morning. He missed her voice already but didn't know what to say or how to apologize. He couldn't explain. As he sat in his favorite armchair in the living room, staring blankly at the television screen his mind struggled to sort through what was happening. He was having trouble grabbing onto the words and making sense of them. They floated in the corners of his subconscious, just out of reach. He grabbed for them, but they seemed to fade just as he got close. Like the words were on the tip of his tongue but he still couldn't place them.

Clara flitted around the house, cleaning and prepping for the rest of the week. She meal prepped, washed and folded laundry, and checked in with her coworkers at work. He silently admired how she tackled everything that needed doing and she didn't complain once. Since he recoiled from her touch earlier, she hadn't said much to him. He could tell that he hurt her feelings, even though she tried to hide it. Whenever he caught her eye, she offered a small smile and turned away. She would no longer hold his gaze. Knowing he hurt her made his heart clench in his chest. If he could just figure out what was going on, maybe he could fix it.

"He's not doing much better. I think he's getting worse. He hasn't talked in a few days." Henry snapped awake. He was still in the chair in the living room, but this time he had a thick blanket draped over him. He didn't realize he had fallen asleep. He looked around, searching for Clara. He felt a mild sense of panic when he couldn't locate her immediately. She was no longer in the room with him, but as he strained his ears to listen, he could hear her voice.

"He seems worse off today than he was even yesterday" She sounded tired, exhausted even. "I'm afraid I can't take care of him much longer." His heart sank as he inched closer in the direction of her voice - what did this mean? Was Clara getting ready to leave him? Is this what that thing was talking about when it said that the truth might not be what he really wanted? Was it trying to warn him that she would get tired of him and leave if she had her memories back?

The sound was coming from the office. The door wasn't completely closed; it was cracked open enough for Henry to be able to see Clara slumped behind the desk with her head in her hands. Her curls fell around her face in a tangled heap. The phone sat next to her. She hadn't noticed him in the doorway.

"What do you want to do?" the voice on the other end of the phone asked. It was a woman's voice. It was gentle and sweet, and made him smile slightly. It sounded familiar for some reason. He knew the person it belonged to, but he couldn't remember who it was.

"I'm not sure, honey. I can hold off a little longer maybe a few more months, but I am so tired. I need more help." When she reached up to wipe at her eyes, he realized that she was crying. She never would have let him see this. Whenever she was around him, she kept a smile on her face, determined not to let him see her upset. His heart broke at the pure exhaustion in her voice. He knew that feeling.

"You've been doing it all by yourself, Ma. Let us help you." said the voice. Ma? It must be one of their children. Henry shifted his weight and winced when the movement caused the floor to creak under him. Clara glanced up, a look of guilt flashed across her beautiful face. She wiped her eyes again and dried her hands on her pants leg.

"Oh! Hi honey, everything alright?" She asked in a fake cheerful voice. He wanted to tell her that she didn't have to pretend for him. He wanted to tell her that he understood her exhaustion and didn't need her to care for him like she had been doing. He wanted to tell her that she needed to take a moment for herself, otherwise she would run herself into the ground… all of the things people had been trying to drill into him when the roles were reversed. All the advice that he ignored or said he would listen to later came flooding back to him.

As she looked at him, he saw her in a clear light for the first time since he had woken up that morning. She was tired. No, she was completely burned out. Exhaustion settled under her eyes. Her skin, while still gorgeous, wasn't as vibrant as he remembered. Her curls were pulled up in a messy bun on the top of her head, gone were the perfectly hydrated tendrils that he was used to. Loose strands of it hung around her face and some littered the desk in front of her. Her hair was falling out, or she was getting so stressed out that she was pulling it out. She had lost weight. Her pajama top wasn't hanging off of her shoulders because she was too lazy to push it back. It was hanging off because it was too big. After everything he had done to save her, he still couldn't stop her from wasting away in front of him. She watched him intently, sniffling a little. They gazed at each other with so many things unsaid between them.

"Mom? What's going on?" the voice from the phone made him flinch a little. He forgot that Clara was talking to someone. The woman sounded concerned, a little frantic actually. Clara glanced down at the phone and then moved it to her ear to take it off of speakerphone.

"Everything is fine, baby. I have to go, okay? I'll see you when you get here. I love you." She hung up the phone and then turned back to Henry. Her expression was bright, despite the bags under her eyes and her crying just a few moments earlier. His heart twisted in his chest. What had he done? In his desperation to get rid of the burden for himself, had he given the burden to Clara instead? That's not what he wanted. He wanted to remove the burden from them both and give them some happy years back.

"Rose is on her way to sit with you while I get some errands done, okay? Won't that be fun?" She asked, getting up from the desk and coming towards him. He was craving her touch, but as she got closer, he froze. Her smell greeted his nose immediately. His stomach flipped. He took a big step back, bumping into the doorframe. Clara's face fell. "That's okay, honey. Everything is okay," she whispered, a small smile on her lips. Her voice was soothing, meant to comfort him, but her eyes were sad. He wanted to reach out and comfort her, but he had forgotten how.

He hated himself for making her look so sad. He opened his mouth, wanting desperately to tell her how sorry he was and how he made a mistake - a mistake that he now had no idea how to fix. He wanted to explain it all to her, but the words refused to leave his lips. He stood there struggling, trying to force his vocal cords to cooperate, but it was no use. Clara gave him a look of pity but took the hint. She didn't push for him to talk, and she didn't come any closer.

He had his wife back, but she couldn't get close to him because of the smell, and he couldn't seem to make his voice work to communicate with her. The distance between them seemed to have multiplied. He felt lonely and isolated, trapped in his own mind. He wanted nothing more than to have his wife hold him and stroke his hair, like she used to whenever he was feeling sick. He wanted to go back to normal, but what was normal? Things had changed so much so soon; he was no longer sure what normal meant for them. When a few moments passed without his response, she stepped around him and left the room. All hope of conversation gone.

"Hey, he's in the living room. Please watch him for a minute so I can go out and take care of some things. I won't be gone long."

"Sure. I'm off today, so take your time." The voice from the earlier phone conversation echoed through the kitchen about an hour later. Henry planted himself back in front of the television but had no idea what he was watching. He stared at it blankly, contemplating whether he should try to find his way back to the hotel. He was starting to feel sick as the day progressed.

He wondered if it was all the medicine Clara had him taking. So many pills at once couldn't be good for his system. Or maybe it was another consequence of the deal he made with the devil incarnate. His head was pounding so hard that it hurt to move his eyes and he felt an intense wave of nausea he couldn't shake. His body felt cold, but he was starting to sweat. If he had to guess, he would say he had a pretty high fever.

"Hi, Daddy." A soft voice said from behind him. He didn't move to look, his head hurt too much to turn. Instead, he leaned back in his chair and closed his eyes, hoping to stop the room from spinning. The owner of the voice didn't say anything else. Clara crossed the room and came to kneel in front of him. She placed a hand on his forehead and snatched it back with a gasp.

"Oh! Henry you are burning up. Let's get you to bed." Clara helped him stand up and led him back to their bedroom. He noticed a young woman standing near the doorway. She strongly resembled a younger version of Clara. They had the same texture of curly hair with similar noses and almond shaped eyes. Their skin was the same shade of mahogany. She smiled gently at him but said nothing. He gave her the best smile he could muster in that moment, which felt more like a grimace. She seemed vaguely familiar. He felt like he should know who she was, but he couldn't remember her name.

"He was fine this morning. I'll call his doctor in a bit, to see if we need to bring him in. I was just getting ready to run to the store, but maybe I shouldn't go out." Clara's brow furrowed as she tucked him into bed. She seemed to have aged a few years in that one day. Henry felt a small flush of guilt. He was the reason she was so stressed out. The young woman shook her head and came to stand next to Clara.

"No we will be fine, Ma. You need a moment to yourself. Go ahead. I'll call you if anything changes."

"Are you sure?" Clara asked skeptically. The young woman wrapped her arms around Clara and gave her a squeeze. He couldn't ignore the way Clara melted into the hug, almost as if she had been dying for physical contact from someone. He closed his eyes.

"He's my dad. Of course I'm sure." Her dad? He opened one eye to look at the young woman. She was watching him intently. The intensity of her gaze made him uneasy. He didn't like being watched so closely. He felt like he was a toddler and the young woman had been called in to babysit. The thought made him huff in disgust. He wanted to protest and beg Clara not to leave but he had no energy. The young woman had such a familiar face, but he couldn't place her. She smiled at him and reached for his hand. Henry combed through his mind, searching desperately for a clue as to who she was and what her name was.

She had called Clara mom, so this must be his daughter, but which one was it? Clara sighed and ran a hand through her hair. Between breakfast and now, she had taken a shower and changed her clothes. Patches of the day slipped away from Henry. So many hours he couldn't account for, while he sat staring into space. He felt trapped in the same spot, while the world moved on around him. Clara turned towards the young girl and shrugged. She still looked worried, but she leaned down to plant a kiss on his sweaty forehead.

"Henry, I'll be back okay sweetheart? Rose will be here if you need anything." He felt too weak to nod, but instead gave her hand a quick squeeze. The young woman watched the two of them interact, a small sad smile on her face.

When Clara left, the young woman came back into the bedroom and sat next to him on the bed. The bracelets on her wrist jingled with her movements. According to Clara, this was Rose and she was his daughter. Her face looked vaguely familiar, like he had passed by her during an event in the past, but he felt no connection to her. She seemed to sense that he didn't want to say much.

"Get some rest, Dad. I'm right here." Her words brought him comfort. He had exhausted himself trying to make sense of his world now. Little details escaped him and he had been chasing them all morning in a battle against himself. It felt like someone was dangling the information in front of him like a carrot on a stick, and then snatching it away as soon as he tried to reach for it.

Instead of continuing the fight, he decided to give his mind a chance to rest. He had no other choice than to relax. His mind had been overworked in the past few days. He felt confident that he would feel better soon, he just needed to give his body and his mind a chance to catch up. He felt a wave of sympathy for people who struggled with memory loss. He briefly wondered how Sullivan's ex-wife had dealt with it in her own family.

Did they struggle as hard as he and Clara seemed to? He thought about the support group meetings his assistant told him about and briefly wondered how she was doing. He never really took the time to be there for her or ask her how she was coping. He had been so wrapped up in trying to help Clara, he had little brain space for anything else. The articles he obsessed over when he was trying to prepare for Clara said that those who suffered with it likened it to feeling as if they were stuck in a foggy version of their own brain. It made sense. After just a day of being disoriented and slightly confused, he was ready to pull his own brain out of his skull and give it a quick shake or press the reset button somehow.

Henry tried to focus on the current moment if for no other reason than to calm his anxious nerves. He was sweaty and cold, and it felt like the blood was rushing in his ears, but the room was calm. The television hummed softly in the background. Whatever show Rose was watching made her chuckle quietly every few minutes. The sound calmed his nerves even more. He allowed the television and her soft laughter to lull him to sleep, hoping that tomorrow would be an easier day for everyone.

15

Henry was feeling worse and worse with each passing day. He hadn't been able to speak since he woke up that morning after his throat became too swollen to allow the words out. As Henry lay in bed, he felt a deep dread; something inside him seemed off and it scared him. He was losing control of his body. His limbs twitched back and forth periodically. He hadn't been able to eat in a while. Every time he tried to get some food in his system, he would choke on it since he could not swallow.

While he was getting sicker, Clara seemed to be aging by the minute. It took her longer to get from one room to the other. She was unable to carry heavy objects on her own. He saw her dragging the laundry basket behind her, unable to lift it with both arms. He could have sworn she had more wrinkles today than a few days ago. Her skin had lost some of its shine. Her eyes were constantly bloodshot. And the smell… the smell was horrible. He saw her step into the shower a few times over the last few days, but it seemed like no matter how much she bathed, her skin smelled like acetone and the unmistakable stench of the rotting flesh of a corpse.

It felt more challenging and more demanding for him to breathe. He could barely keep his eyes open. At first, he thought he was having trouble sustaining deep breaths because his wife smelled like roadkill, and it was taking the wind out of him, but even when she was no longer in the room, he struggled to take in the air. Each breath was more jagged than the last. It terrified him. He wanted to cry out for help but no longer felt he could control his body. He was trapped in a prison.

The only parts of him that moved without difficulty were his eyes, and they were rapidly losing focus as the days passed. He felt he needed to go to the hospital but had no idea how to alert Clara. She continued to move around the house, taking care of the endless tasks. Her body seemed to hunch lower and lower each time she passed in his line of vision. Rose promised to return with reinforcements, but nothing happened over the past few days. He was beginning to panic. Something was wrong. His throat burned like fire, and every breath felt like an eternity; he wondered idly if this was how dying felt.

The people who tried to assure others that dying felt peaceful had to be lying. This was not peaceful. This was miserable. If he was dying, he wanted to speed the process up and get it over with. It couldn't be worse than what he was feeling right now. Maybe this was a consequence of trying to manipulate how his life ended up. Perhaps he should have just left well enough alone. The Concierge said that the truth might not be what he wanted; at the time, he shrugged it off, but now he was beginning to wonder. Things weren't happening as he expected them to.

Time seemed to tick by slowly as if mocking Henry's weakened state. He hadn't seen anyone come back to help Clara, and sometimes, while he was drifting in and out of consciousness, he thought he could hear faint sobs coming from another room.

Clara always tried to look cheerful whenever she thought he was looking, but he saw how her shoulders drooped, and her body seemed to fold inward. He saw how she looked like she could collapse at any moment.

Henry couldn't remember the last time he saw her eat a full meal besides the breakfast they shared when he returned from the hotel. He hoped he would feel better after a few days and the two could return to normal, but he seemed to get worse by the minute. So did she.

A sudden wave of fear hit him as he lay in the bed, dragging his breath through his body. His anxiety skyrocketed in a matter of seconds. He suddenly felt like he was in danger. He forced his eyes open to look around the room. Clara stood in the far corner by the closet, folding clothes like nothing was happening. She struggled to put one of her dresses on the correct hanger and juggle a pair of his jeans in the other. A black sock was draped over her shoulder. It looked completely innocent, yet something felt amiss. Like it was the calm moment right before disaster struck - the eye of an incredible storm.

As if on cue, he saw a flash of movement out of the corner of his eye. A familiar dark figure loomed in the corner on the other side of the room. He didn't realize that The Concierge had the power to leave the hotel, but if it could mess with memories, being able to teleport or materialize wherever it wanted to be seemed trivial. Henry momentarily held eye contact with the creature, praying that it wouldn't get any closer.

"Hello, Henry," it whispered. Its voice sent chills down Henry's spine. He looked over at Clara frantically, but she continued to fold clothes, having no idea that anything was happening near her. Henry opened his mouth to warn her, but the words lodged in his swollen throat. The creature tilted its ugly head and followed Henry's gaze. Through his murky vision, he could see its cracked lips spread back to reveal its sharp teeth in a terrifying smirk.

"She knows nothing." It stepped towards Henry. "Do you want to see the truth now?" Henry stared at it but said nothing. It grinned and nodded back in Clara's direction. He glanced over just in time to see her clutch her chest in pain and fall forward. Her head knocked against the dresser's drawer, sending clothes flying everywhere and hangers clattering in different directions.

"NO!" A hoarse and broken voice cried, followed by strangled sobs. It took Henry a second to realize that it was his voice, finally, after days of being unable to talk. He pulled himself to a sitting position. Clara remained in a heap on the floor, covered in a pile of clothes and hangers. He watched in horror as her body began to age before his eyes. It began to bloat, and the blood began to pool in her body parts pressed against the floor. It looked like rigor mortis had set in. How long had she been lying there? To Henry, only a few minutes had passed, but he couldn't be sure of anything - not anymore.

"What's happening?! Help her! Clara! Oh my God, Clara, please!" Henry yelled. He willed his body to move, but it felt stuck to the bed. His heart pounded against his ribcage; his breath caught in his throat. "Wake up, baby! Please wake up! You can't leave me like this!" Tears poured down his cheeks and into his mouth, spittle flying from him whenever he spoke. The Concierge seemed to chuckle at his panic. Amusement contorted its hideous face.

"Don't you remember, Henry?" the creature taunted, leaning forward. It had to hunch over; its figure was too much for the small bedroom. Henry shook his head; his vision darkened and closed in around him. Spots dotted his vision.

"Remember...what?" He managed to choke out. The Concierge said nothing; It stared at him with that ugly, twisted grin.

"You haven't figured it out by now, Henry? Are you this far into denial that you can't see what's in front of you?" it shook its head in mock disappointment.

"I came to you so you could restore my wife's memories."

"There was nothing wrong with your wife's memories." The creature glared at him, its white eyes unblinking. Henry's breath quickened in his throat. It was coming out in short bursts, making him dizzy and unfocused.

"My wife...has-" He started but was unable to finish the sentence. His vision blurred completely. His heart felt like it was exploding in his chest. Faintly, he could hear a frantic and persistent beeping in the distance. He could hear footsteps in the background rushing toward him, but Henry couldn't figure out where they were coming from. He reached out for Clara, demanding his body get up and get to his wife. The sight of her crumpled body made his heart cleft into a thousand tiny pieces. A blinding pain overtook him as he struggled to fight through the muck and find the truth. Had Clara needed him, and he wasn't there for her? His thoughts swam around in his skull, but nothing took root. He couldn't focus on anything other than Clara.

Clara.

Clara.

Clara. His lungs burned as he gasped and gulped for air. He struggled even more to breathe. The creature stood unbothered and rooted in the corner, watching him with a smile on its ugly lips. It was enjoying watching Henry struggle to hang on to consciousness. It crossed the room in a flash and was right next to Henry, leaning down toward him. Its rancid breath tickled his ear with each word.

"You're too late, Henry. Clara is dead."

16

Clara (3 Years Before)

Clara glanced at Henry, who sat hunched over with his arms crossed, trying to make himself smaller than his five-foot-eleven frame would allow. The house was eerily quiet aside from the faint ticking of the clock on the wall. Tension settled in the back of Clara's neck, making her muscles stiff and uncooperative. Her heart fluttered in her chest, a new addition to everything else her and Henry had going on, the stress of the situation making her heart thump wildly against her ribcage. She had been trying to practice yoga and breathing techniques to calm her palpitating heart, but it wasn't successful. Clara made a mental note to visit her primary care physician in a few days.

A sharp sigh brought her back to the current moment. The three of them sat in the living room, saying nothing. Henry and Clara sat together on one couch, and their eldest child, Rose, sat before them; confusion and concern clouded her face. When Clara called and asked her to come by for a meaningful conversation, Rose wasted no time. That was the one thing Clara loved most about her oldest child; she was the type to drop everything and come running at the first sign of distress. Whenever someone needed her, Rose would always be there.

If you were someone this young woman loved, you had an army of support behind you whenever needed. Clara absentmindedly wondered if Rose knew how valuable she was. She wondered what their kids would look like when Rose and her husband were ready to conceive. Clara always wanted grandkids, but she didn't want to pressure any of her children to start a family before they were prepared. But as soon as Rose got married, Clara was counting down the moments until she told her they were expecting. She wondered if she or Henry would be around to meet them. They were still relatively young, but after the countless doctor visits over the past few weeks, mortality was heavy on her mind. Clara glanced up at Rose, noting how she looked like the mirrored image of her face at that age.

Clara swallowed, unsure what to say or how to begin the conversation. As strong as she had been pretending to be for her husband, she felt broken and afraid. Clara felt like she was on an island by herself that was slowly sinking into the ocean surrounding it. Henry had faded into himself as soon as they got the results. He'd chosen to slip into his thoughts while Clara busied herself with scheduling appointments, learning about medications, and preparing herself as best as she could for the days ahead.

"Mom?" Rose leaned forward and touched Clara's knee. The slight contact snatched Clara out of her thoughts. She met her daughter's gaze, trying hard to swallow back the tears threatening to flood her eyes. "You're scaring me. What's wrong?"

"I know you've expressed concerns lately after noticing some odd behaviors." Clara began. "We wanted to wait until we got a second opinion before we dragged you and your siblings into this."

"Mom, just tell me what's going on."

Clara shot another glance at Henry and sighed. "It's Alzheimer's." She said quietly. Clara took a deep breath and looked up at Rose, refusing to let herself break. Her children and her husband needed her to be strong. And she would be for them.

"Alzheimer's? Are you sure?" Rose asked. Clara nodded. "Mommy! What are we going to do?!" Rose wailed. She clamped a hand over her mouth to stifle a sob. The sound of her daughter's pain made Clara want to sink into the chair and disappear, but she remained where she was. Clara leaned forward and wrapped her arms around Rose, rocking her back and forth gently while she sobbed. Henry sat stiffly beside her on the couch, unable to participate in the conversation.

Clara couldn't bring herself to be frustrated with him. He had been in denial that there was even a problem, and now that they knew just how big of an issue it was, he was having trouble reconciling things. Clara patted Rose on the back and pulled away to look into her daughter's tear-soaked eyes.

"We will get through this as a family. It will be tough, and we will need a lot of support, but we can get through this." She smoothed Rose's curls and gave her a tight squeeze. Rose nodded and swiped a hand under her nose.

"Because family shows up," she whispered. Clara smiled, listening to her daughter parrot the phrase she had tried to instill in her children from their early days. 'Family shows up.' Clara's parents taught it to her when she was small.

"Exactly, baby. Family shows up."

"I'm sorry." Clara and Rose turned to look at Henry, who had been silent until now. He was still staring down at his lap, but they both heard the unmistakable rumble of his voice.

"Sorry for what, Daddy?' Rose asked. "None of this is your fault."

"It's my job to protect this family, and now-" Henry's voice broke. He cleared his throat and shook his head. Clara's heart fractured in her chest. She thought Henry was stewing in denial, but maybe he had other reasons for being quiet. She reached forward and grabbed his hand. A deep pain in his eyes made her breath catch when he looked up at her.

"You can't protect us from this. It's out of your control. The only course of action now is to try and make the best of things." Rose wiped her eyes and pulled away from Clara's embrace. Her sadness dissolved and morphed into a stubborn determination. Clara smiled gently at her oldest child, admiring her strength in this moment of vulnerability. She allowed herself to break for a few moments and then pushed forward. Her level-headedness and caring spirit would be something Henry would need to lean on, on the days when things became tough.

"Junior, your father and I need to talk to you. Do you have a moment to stop by the house?" Clara adjusted the phone between her ear and her shoulder while she cooked. Rose had left about an hour ago, and Clara wanted to ensure they had some food in their stomachs before the following conversation.

With her children's wildly different schedules, getting them all in the same room outside of holidays and special occasions was almost impossible. So, Clara was forced to go through this challenging conversation three times. She silently hoped that Henry would be more vocal during this one. He and his son had a special relationship that only existed between a man and his father. Clara could only pray that it would come in handy for this conversation. She heard Junior sigh quietly.

"Can you just tell me whatever it is now? I have a swamped day ahead of me," Junior said. Clara could hear the slight exasperation in his voice. Her son was always on the move. She admired his work ethic, something he inherited from his father, but she worried that sometimes he was working too much - something else he inherited from Henry.

"Absolutely not. I know you're busy, but this cannot wait. I expect to see you here in the next two hours." Clara didn't always take on such a demanding tone with her children, but when she did, they knew that she was not to be questioned. Junior was quiet for a moment; if she knew her son, she could bet money that he was rolling his eyes.

"Give me twenty minutes." The line went dead before Clara could respond. She wanted to call him back and fuss him out for hanging up on her; it didn't matter how old he got, he was not too old to get smacked, but she let it go. Clara was asking him to disrupt his plans to come over. She would allow him a little anger.

Junior arrived at the house twenty minutes later, as promised, and let himself in the front door. Clara got up to greet him, his bulky arms encircling her in one of his famous bear hugs.

"Hey, mama." He murmured into her hair. Clara gave him and squeeze and smiled up at him.

"Thank you for coming on such short notice."

"You didn't give me much choice," he snorted. "Hey, pops!" Clara turned to see that Henry had entered the room. He had a faraway look in his eyes. When Henry didn't respond, Junior's brows furrowed.

"What's wrong with dad?" He asked, glancing back down at Clara. Henry shuffled into the living room and sat down on the couch. His movements were stiff and choppy like he had been sitting still for too long and cramped up. Clara's shoulders sagged as she watched him.

"Let's talk for a second." Clara pulled Junior by the hand and led him to the living room, where Henry sat, picking at his fingers.

"We went to the doctor," she started. Her voice was wobbly. Junior nodded, urging her to continue, and shot another confused glance at his father. He glanced down at his phone, looking like he was trying hard to pay attention, but his focus was split between what he had going on and what was being said to him.

"It's Alzheimer's plus something called Anosognosia," Clara whispered. Junior's head shot up. His face crumpled for a split second before he shook his head in refusal. She could see him struggle to place his emotions behind a wall.

"What does that mean?" he demanded.

"It means that there is Alzheimer's but there is also the added neurological condition where the person doesn't always realize that they are sick. It can make things a bit more difficult."

"This is ridiculous," Henry grumbled, irritated. Clara sighed and opened her mouth to respond, but Junior interrupted, his voice flat and emotionless.

"Alzheimer's? No. No, I won't accept that. We'll get a second opinion and-"

"We've done that already." The sound of Henry's voice made Junior fall silent. Just like it had with Rose. His voice was still gruff with emotion but less broken than it had been with Rose. Junior looked back and forth between them, his expression growing stricken. Clara wanted to shield him from the hurt she knew he was feeling, but she didn't know how. All she could do was watch as his handsome face contorted into different expressions. Confusion. Hurt. Anger. Pain.

"What? When? Why is this the first I'm hearing about this?" he demanded. Clara tried to reach for him, but he shrugged away angrily. "Dad?" Junior asked, planting himself in front of Henry and folding his arms. Henry stared blankly at the television.

"We didn't want to bother you until we knew for sure," Clara said; the silence in the room was thick and uncomfortable. She fidgeted in her chair, longing for this to be all over so she could withdraw and think. She didn't get the luxury of being able to collapse in on herself like Henry was doing. Someone needed to be strong for their children. Junior glanced over at her, his face still twisted in anger.

"What doctors did you see? Maybe we can find someone else. A specialist or something. We can keep trying!" The desperation in Junior's voice made Clara's heart clench. She stood up and wrapped her arms around him. She half expected him to pull away, but she felt his arms slide up and wrap around her.

"I'm sorry, baby. I know it's hard to hear, but we wouldn't have concerned you with this had we not already been certain," she whispered. They stood like that for a long moment. It felt like everything was moving in slow motion around them. Henry sat frozen in his seat; a pained expression replaced the blank look he had been sporting recently. Clara knew these conversations were difficult for Henry to cope with. Still, she wished he would participate more instead of leaving her to carry the emotional burden for the entire family.

"I really can't deal with this right now," said Junior, stepping out of Clara's embrace. "I have to go." She wanted to protest and demand that he stay longer to talk it out, but she knew he needed time, just like his father. They just needed more time.

"What time is Rue coming?" Henry asked. The two of them had just finished dinner. Clara knew their youngest would probably come over much later due to her fluctuating schedule. Clara was emotionally and mentally exhausted. As she cleaned up the plates and dishes from dinner, she prayed this conversation would go better than the first two. Maybe one of them had already given Rue the heads up on what to expect.

"She should be here in another hour or so," said Clara. She had just leaned over to begin wiping the counter when Henry approached her. An involuntary sigh escaped her lips as his strong arms encircled her waist.

"I'm sorry," Henry whispered, resting his head against her back.

"For what?"

"I wasn't there for you during either of those conversations. I should have been more vocal; I just-" Henry gulped. "It's so much to take in."

Clara turned around so they were face to face. She could see in his eyes that he was lost. The past few months, their entire lives felt like they had been turned inside out. Nothing looked the same anymore. Doctor's appointments, new medications, new routines, and so many cognitive tests had given Clara something to focus on. Still, during the downtime, in moments when everything went quiet, her worries would take over.

What would their relationship look like a year from now? Two years? Three? She had seen countless articles about how the once loving relationship would transition into a patient-caretaker relationship as the disease progressed. She didn't want that for them.

"What are you thinking about?" Henry asked, studying her. Clara smiled at him and rested her head against his chest.

"Nothing important." She lied. Henry tilted her chin so he could see her eyes. He scanned her expression. He was always able to read her in ways she didn't think possible. Small inflection changes, silence that was a beat longer than usual… he always picked up on it. Clara loved that even after decades of life together, Henry could still tell when something was amiss.

"Tell me anyway," he said, tracing her jaw with his thumb.

"I'm scared," Clara whispered. Henry's brow furrowed for a moment.

"Scared? Of what?"

"Us. Life. What things will look like years or even months from now." A tear slipped down Clara's cheek. She wiped it away quickly, not wanting to break just yet. There was still one last conversation to get through. Henry wrapped his arms around her waist and pulled her close. She breathed in his scent, allowing it to calm her nerves.

"Do you love me?" Henry asked after a moment of silence. She lifted her head to look at him.

"Of course, Hen. With everything in me. You know this."

He nodded. "And I love you. So come what may, we will figure it out. We always do." Henry leaned in and gently pressed his lips against hers. Clara melted into the kiss. He still had the power to make her weak in the knees.

"Gross! Get a room!"

Henry and Clara snatched apart to see their youngest daughter grinning at them. They had been so engrossed in their conversation that neither had seen or heard Rue come in. She stood in the doorway with wild hair draping her shoulders and tattoos circling her arms. The tattoos had been a sore spot for them initially, but Clara began to enjoy the artwork that covered her daughter's arms although she would never admit that out loud. Clara smiled at her and held out her arms for a hug. Rue stepped into them and gave her a squeeze. She smelled like a mixture of vanilla and lavender. It was a calming smell. Clara used their embrace as a moment to steady herself, in preparation for the difficult conversation ahead.

"Hi baby, we didn't hear you come in."

"Clearly, you two were busy sucking each other's faces," Rue smirked; she reached up and wrapped her arms around Henry's neck. He squeezed her back.

"Lucky you came in when you did; otherwise, something else would have been getting sucked," said Henry, wriggling his eyebrows and laughing at his own crass joke. Rue gaped at him, shock and disgust evident on her face.

"Disgusting! Ya'll are way too old for that!" She shrieked, laughing. Henry grinned at her and shrugged. Clara watched the two of them as they all headed into the living room. Henry always struggled with connecting with Rue. Her eclectic and ever-changing tastes made it challenging to find common ground. It took a while for them to find their rhythm, and now that they had, Clara felt a sense of devastation that it would no longer be possible.

"What did you guys need to talk to me about?" Rue asked, looking back and forth between them. A lump lodged in Clara's throat, making it hard for her to speak. She opened her mouth, but no words came out. Rue tilted her head. "It must be serious," she said gently.

"We went to the doctor." Henry's voice surprised Clara. She expected him to be quiet like he had been with their other two children. She glanced up at him, grateful that he was navigating this conversation. Rue nodded slowly, processing the information.

"Okay. You went to the doctor. What did they say?" Henry and Clara both felt silent. They looked at each other in a quiet battle, trying to decide which would break the news. Clara pleaded at Henry with her eyes, silently begging him to step forward. He swallowed uneasily and nodded.

"Guys! Enough with the telepathy. Talk to me! What's going on?" Rue demanded. She placed her elbows on her knees and leaned forward, staring at the both of them. Clara smiled inwardly. Rue had her father's impatience.

"We've gotten second opinions and have taken a bunch of tests, but unfortunately, it's not looking too promising, sweetheart." Henry began.

"What is it? Cancer? Some rare disease that gives you five legs and a tail? What!?"

"It's Alzheimer's," said Henry; Rue's mouth fell open in surprise. "I have been diagnosed with Alzheimer's disease."

PART THREE

17

Anya

Good afternoon, everyone; thank you for coming. Let's get started."
At the sound of Aaron, the group leader's voice, Anya settled in her
seat with her purse against her chest. This was her fifteenth support group
meeting. She decided to come when caring for her father was too much
to handle alone. When her mother, who had been his caretaker, passed
suddenly, Anya felt it was her responsibility to step up. On the days when
the overwhelm threatened to swallow her completely, these meetings were
a godsend. It allowed her to express her frustrations healthily without
getting upset with her father because of a disease he couldn't control. She
had been trying to get her brother Deven and her little sister Drusilla to
come to a meeting, but neither were receptive. After a bunch of unanswered text messages about meeting information, Anya stopped trying.

"Who wants to start us off today?" Aaron asked. He was a middle-aged
man with a kind face and an unnaturally large bird shirt collection. During
her first meeting, he launched into a long-winded tale about how many
shirts he had covered top to bottom in birds. For some reason, it made
Anya feel a little more comfortable. Aaron crossed his legs and looked

at the group expectantly. His long brown and honey-tipped locs hung loosely over his shoulders. Anya looked around, hoping that someone would speak up. This part of the meeting always activated her anxiety about public speaking, but hearing everyone else's stories made her feel like she wasn't crazy for struggling like she had been.

"My wife was just diagnosed about six months ago. I've been trying to handle everything independently, but it's getting harder as the days and months pass." Anya glanced to her left at the man that had just spoken. His face was partially covered by his hat, but something felt familiar about him. She squinted at the nametag where he had written his name in a shaky scrawl.

Hen.

A few others in the group nodded in agreement. Everyone here had similar stories. A loved one was diagnosed, and they willingly took on the burden of caring for that person, not knowing just how much work it would take. As the oldest child, Anya felt responsible for her father. She tried to help out as much as possible when her father was first diagnosed, but her mother had taken on the lion's share of the responsibility. She would tell Anya to go live and enjoy her life and her new marriage. Luckily, she married a man who understood her devotion to her family. Her husband, Luca, was more than accommodating, especially after her mother's unexpected death.

They had just moved to the next town over and settled into their new home when she got a phone call from her hysterical baby sister saying she had gone to check on their parents to find their mother dead in her closet. She died of a sudden heart attack while folding laundry. Anya tried to hold on as long as she could, commuting back and forth almost daily, but Luca noticed the strain all of the extra driving was putting on her and offered for them to move back home. The following week, they searched for apartments that would put her within twenty minutes of the nursing home they placed her father in.

Anya remembered his conversation with her shortly after their mother passed. He'd sat her down and told her to find a nursing home to put him in because he refused to be the reason someone else he loved wasted away. Anya protested at first, determined to handle his care on her own, but her father was adamant.

"Alzheimer's is not a diagnosis that you can take lightly," Aaron began, breaking Anya out of her daydream. "It can transform your loved one into someone else entirely." The group murmured in agreement. Anya watched as Hen sniffled and wiped his nose on his sleeve. She wanted to get up and hug him, but she remained seated. She could tell he was the type that didn't take too kindly to affection from strangers.

"I thought I could handle this, but I don't think I can." His voice was thick with emotion. The woman beside him reached out and placed a hand on his knee. He shifted in his seat away from her touch but didn't look up.

"Have you thought about hiring someone to help? We have an excellent home health care team that takes referrals from us-"

"I should be able to care for my wife on my own. What kind of man would that make me? To tell her that she's become too much for me to deal with?" Hen looked up from the floor and stared at Aaron. Even from across the room and with his face partially covered, Anya could feel the pain emanating from him in waves. Aaron smiled and leaned forward in his chair, pulling his hands together in a steeple in front of his face.

"I want to say this lightly because I can tell you feel a great sense of responsibility for your wife, but...this is not what you signed up for." Aaron took his silence as a cue to continue.

"Like I said, Alzheimer's is a great deal trickier than people initially realize. Your loved one doesn't look sick, so you try to operate as if everything were normal, but it's not. You are tasked with remaining devoted to them as their personalities shift by the day and their memories fade. It is normal to feel overwhelmed and need help. It doesn't make you any less of a devoted husband. It doesn't make you any less of a man."

Hen held Aaron's gaze for a moment, with a look that started off as stubborn indignation but quickly crumpled into brokenhearted sobs. The groups sat quietly as Hen folded into himself, letting out gut-wrenching cries from deep in his belly. This wasn't the first time someone had broken down in the middle of a meeting.

After the meeting ended, Anya headed out to her car feeling a little lighter than when she first arrived. Alzheimer's Support Group was always heavy, but it made her feel good to know that a community of people understood. Her biggest struggle in the beginning, when she took on caring for her father completely, was feeling like she was going through it alone.

Her brother and sister were determined to do as little as possible but depended on Anya for updates and to take the lead in their father's care. She had no idea how to do any of this. Most days, it felt like she was making it up as she went along. Like clockwork, her phone buzzed in her pocket. It was her younger brother, Deven, calling. He always wanted to know how meetings went and what they discussed.

"How did it go?" he demanded as soon as she clicked the button to answer. She chuckled and pulled out of the parking lot. She spotted Hen looking forlorn in the driver's seat of his car as she pulled off. Part of her wanted to stop and talk to him, but she could sense that he wasn't ready for that just yet. People who let such intense emotion out for the first time usually need time to process it afterward. She would check in with him at the next meeting.

"It went fine. You should come instead of demanding a play-by-play from me every week."

"Mhm. Any changes?"

Anya could hear commotion on the other end of the phone. Most likely, he was standing in the middle of the kitchen at his restaurant, fluctuating between telling his staff what to do and trying to do the job himself. He sounded distracted.

"No changes. Dad is settling well into the nursing home. Especially now that he has the desk and computer in his room. Makes him feel like he's back in the office."

"Great. Okay, I'll talk to you later, sis. Love you." The soft click of the call's end responded before she could. She sighed and tossed the phone on the passenger seat next to her. She couldn't blame him for being distracted. He had spread himself thin by opening a second restaurant and refusing to take on extra help. He was determined to hang on to his success in his first year, even if that meant working himself to death. That workaholic habit is something he picked up from their father, who refused to slow down until life forced his hand. Sometimes Anya worried her brother would suffer that same fate instead of learning to relax.

By the time she made it home, darkness had fallen. From the driveway, she could see her husband standing in the window over the kitchen sink. He was most likely washing the dishes after cooking dinner. He would always pitch in and help when Anya had a meeting or would be at the nursing home late with her father. She was so grateful for him. There was no way she'd be able to juggle any of this without his help.

He looked up from the dishes when she entered their home. He offered her a small smile and nodded at the microwave to his left. "Your plate is in the microwave; just press the button." Anya pressed the start button and plopped in the chair at the kitchen island with a sigh. "Long day?" Luca asked, planting a kiss on her forehead.

"Yeah. There was a new member at the meeting today. He spoke for a bit before completely breaking down. It was heavy."

"I bet. Have you heard from either of your siblings?"

"Yes. Deven called after the meeting as usual, but we didn't talk long." Anya shrugged. The microwave pinged behind her, signaling that her food was ready. She grabbed the plate out of the microwave and sat down to eat. Luca sat beside her as she ate, his brows furrowed in concentration. Something was bothering him, but he struggled to say what it was. Anya stopped eating and looked at him.

"What is it?" she asked gently.

Luca sighed and ran a hand over his face. "It just bugs me that neither one will step in to help. It's not fair to you."

Anya said nothing. She wasn't in the mood to have this same argument again. There was nothing to say that she hadn't already said. They had this conversation multiple times, but it did nothing to alleviate the stress of the situation. His fussing about the lack of assistance from her siblings only made it worse. It wasn't like she didn't know what was happening.

She hated that she was the only one concerned with their father's progress and made sure to go to each doctor's appointment. She pushed forward by herself even when it bled into her work schedule and personal life.. As grateful as she was for his help, Luca pointing out the absence of her brother and sister every chance he got did not help the situation. He turned to her and stared expectantly, waiting for a response.

With a sigh, Anya rubbed her temples and stared down at her plate. Her appetite suddenly disappeared. "Luca, honey, what do you want me to say? They have their own lives. I am the oldest, so-"

"That doesn't mean you must take this on yourself!"

"I know that!" She hissed, standing up from the table. Luca stared back at her, surprised by her outburst. She didn't mean to snap at him, but he kept poking and prodding at her soft spot. It was impossible not to get annoyed. He said nothing as she wrapped up her plate once more and stuck it in the refrigerator. Maybe she would be hungry later, but her appetite was gone right now.

"Anya, babe, I'm sorry. I don't mean to push, but I hate that you are shouldering this burden alone. I get they have their own relationship with your father, but they could still help! If not for him, then for you, at least."

Luca gently grabbed her wrist and pulled her towards him to keep her from leaving. She allowed her body to melt into his; his hugs always made everything better. Plus, deep down, Anya knew he had a point. She tried to be understanding. Things could have been better in their house growing up. Dad was always working, so it was mostly just the three of them and their mom. Their dad tried his best, but he was raised believing that the man had to take care of the house. There was little room for anything else. Her grandfather was the same way.

When her dad was diagnosed, her siblings didn't seem that bent up about it. Anya tried her best to tag along to doctor's appointments and to be there for her mom whenever she had extra time, but she would always shoo Anya away and tell her not to worry. Anya was the one that noticed their mother's health declining. She let herself burn out taking care of their father, and in the end, when her mother was found in their bedroom, dead of a heart attack, Anya chose to step up.

Later that night, Anya sat in front of her computer, willing the words to come. She promised herself that she wouldn't sleep until she had written two thousand words of her debut novel. So far, Anya had two hundred words, but nothing else worked. She turned on the sound machine in her office to block out the sounds of the heavy bass in the music her husband was listening to; she had lit her favorite calming candle and dimmed the lights just enough to give the room a nice vibe but not too much that she made herself sleepy.

None of that was working.

Since she was a little girl, it was her goal to become a writer. She put off the dream for something more practical when she went to college, settling for an unfulfilling career in accounting and bookkeeping, but recently she decided to pick it back up. She started with a blog about her personal life and struggles with her father's diagnosis. The blog gained some traction, a few loyal subscribers commented on every post she made, and the uptick in popularity with the comments on how beautifully written her work was fooled her into thinking she could write a novel. Anya snorted to herself as she thought about how she claimed she would write the ninety thousand words in two weeks and get it published by her next birthday.

How ridiculously naive she had been. That declaration was months ago, and now she fully understood why it took some people years to write an entire book. You had to account for the time when the words wouldn't come. Lately, more often than not, the words evaded her completely. She would write a few hundred and then eventually delete it because she disliked how it sounded.

Luca asked why she didn't just publish the blog posts about Alzheimer's that she had written and turn them into a book of short stories, but Anya wasn't ready for that. Putting her heart on the pages for the few readers she had was one thing but publishing it as a book and allowing strangers from all over the world to read her deepest, most personal thoughts and judging them based on whether or not they were interested, seemed like cruel and unusual punishment.

Sometimes she envied her siblings. Deven had gone to culinary school and opened a restaurant that had just added a second location after only two years. He fell in love with cooking when he was younger. He would be in the kitchen with their mother, being her little helper. Eventually, he learned enough from her to take over dinner on some nights when their mom needed a break.

Drusilla, lovingly called Dru by close friends and family, was the baby and was making a name for herself in the interior design industry even though she was only in her late twenties. Anya watched her morph into the daring and beautiful young woman she was turning out to be. It was no surprise. When Dru was younger, she wasn't afraid to take risks with her clothing in ways that Anya wouldn't have imagined. Dru was always the oddball of the three of them, choosing to march to her own beat.

Her passion for colors and patterns turned into an interior design career. Barely scraping twenty-six years old, Dru had already participated in designing and creating some well-known locations in the city - even a few in neighboring locations. Her success was impressive for someone her age, but to be this successful as a young black woman was completely unheard of. During their brief weekly conversations, Anya could barely contain her pride in her little sister. Even if most of the time, it felt like Dru was embarrassed to be seen associating with her, let alone related.

Anya's brother and sister made their own names in their industries. And then there was her, wandering around, trying to decide her place in the world while it moved on around her. She was only good at taking care of the people who needed her. When Deven needed somewhere to crash when he could not make rent after pouring his life savings into his restaurant, she was more than willing to let him stay with her until he could get back on his feet. When Dru's engagement fell through just weeks before the wedding, Anya wiped her sister's tears and promised to flatten Eric's tires the next time she saw him.

When her dad needed her, she dropped everything, ready to be there for him in whatever capacity. As soon as she became overwhelmed with the burden of looking after her father as his condition worsened, she reached out to her siblings for help; no doubt in her mind that they would drop everything and come running just as she had done for them so many times in their lives.

But they didn't.

Suddenly, things were too hectic for them to be able to come to the house. Suddenly, they were too busy to pick up the phone. They missed appointments. They didn't return her calls. They rarely checked in to see how everything was going. When she had no choice but to admit their father into a nursing home for around-the-clock care, neither bothered to reach out to see what was needed. They never worried about anything because they knew their big sister Anya would take care of it.

She put her dreams on hold without a second thought because someone needed to ensure everything worked out now that their mother was gone. Their father couldn't take care of himself. It made sense that it fell on Anya's shoulders. She happily grabbed the burden and carried it on her back. She was the dependable one - the eldest. The one who would happily sacrifice herself to be the caretaker for the people she loved.

As she sat in front of her computer, staring at the blinking cursor on the half-empty Word document, Anya wondered if that was all she was destined to be.

18

Deven

Dee, we need to talk." Deven froze at the sound of his girlfriend Camila's voice. This couldn't be good. That phrase always preceded a breakup, and he wasn't ready for that. He might have laughed at how cliche that simple phrase sounded if he wasn't so nervous about what she wanted to talk about. It has been used to death in romantic comedies since the beginning of time. That's not to say he was watching romantic comedies. Still, he did grow up with two sisters who loved to sit in front of the television and squeal over their corny love interests. So, he had learned a thing or two about romantic movies against his will.

He stood in the middle of the restaurant with the phone pressed to his ear, trying not to freak out. The restaurant's noise faded into the background as soon as the words left Camila's lips. He was only absentmindedly paying attention at first, but he was now zeroed in on the conversation. His mind raced, trying to figure out if he had done or said something wrong. They hadn't been together long enough for an anniversary. Did he miss her birthday? Did he forget a date they had set up? Why was she breaking up with him already?

"Dee! You still there?" He had been running through so many possibilities that he forgot to respond.

"Sorry, sorry. Yes, I'm here. What's up?" he asked. He slipped past the guests and the waitstaff in the main dining area. He kept going until he stood in the little manager's office in the back of his restaurant, Le Fugue. He wasn't scheduled to come in today since he had been at his other location, but the manager here called him in a panic. The dinner rush was about to start, and Deven couldn't make any sense of the schedule.

The manager had redone this thing at least four times, but they still ended up being three servers short for the night, and no one was willing to come in on their day off. So here he was, the restaurant owner, preparing to cover a shift. If he didn't love this restaurant like it was his child, he would probably have been annoyed about spending another day pulling a double shift.

A good leader will get in the trenches with his team when needed. That's what his mother and his father had always taught him. His father led by example, showing Deven what a hardworking man was supposed to look like. When Deven opened this place, he was determined to show his parents, especially his father, just how hard of a worker he could be. He had desperately wanted to make them proud. This was the only way he really knew how to do it - food and business.

"I can tell you're distracted. Call me when you get home; I'll come over."

"We can't just talk now?" he asked, running a hand through his thick beard. He didn't want to cook tonight because that meant he'd need to wear a hairnet on his head and face; they made his face break out. He had been meaning to find a different brand, but he was so busy lately opening the new location that he didn't have time to eat a decent meal, let alone search for a new hairnet vendor. Camila sighed in his ear, bringing him back to the conversation.

"No. We need to do this in person." His palms felt sweaty. She was definitely breaking up with him. He was willing to bet on it. In the back of his mind, he worried that he was spending too much time working and not enough time with her. He meant to cut back on the hours some, but he hadn't yet.

"I'll call you when I get done," he replied, trying not to let on how nervous he was. When they hung up, he slipped his phone back into his pocket and sighed deeply. He would be anxious about this conversation for the rest of the night. These were the moments he wished he could pick up his phone and call his father. His dad always had sound advice when it came to women. The man was a hopeless romantic underneath the endless hours spent working.

He worshiped the ground Deven's mother walked on for as long as Deven could remember. He'd lost count of the times he saw his dad, an intimidating man in his own right, staring at his mom with a dopey-eyed grin. Deven wanted a love like that. He almost craved it. He and Camila had only been together for a few months, but something about her differed from the other women he dated. It made him wonder for a moment if this was it. Although, there was no reason to consider that now since she was breaking up with him.

He glanced at the clock and then grabbed his phone from his pocket. The phone rang twice before the line clicked, indicating that his sister had answered.

"How'd it go?" He knew she would be leaving the Alzheimer's Support Group meeting now. The idea of sitting around with a group of strangers and divulging his personal feelings made him want to throw up, but Anya claimed they helped her out.

"It went fine. You should just come instead of demanding a play-by-play from me every week." He rolled his eyes just as the office door opened, and his head chef stuck his head in. Deven held up a finger to signal that he would be there in a minute. Noise from the excitement in the kitchen filled the room.

"Mhm. Any changes?" He sat on the corner of the desk. Should he just go home early and get the conversation with Camila over with? He could return to the restaurant and use the last part of the dinner rush as a distraction. Or, if it was a particularly humiliating conversation, he might be able to sweet talk one of his older servers into covering the shift so he could stay home and sulk. It was tempting, but he vowed to never let his personal life bleed over into his business. They needed him, so he would be here.

"No changes. Dad is settling well into the nursing home. Especially now that he has the desk and computer in his room. Makes him feel like he's back in the office." Deven smiled at that. He knew how much pride his father took in his work. It was one of the lessons he drilled into Deven's head as a kid. *No matter what you decide to do, you must work hard. You have to work twice as hard to be twice as good. Don't let them catch you slipping.* Deven allowed that phrase to fuel him. He wished his dad could see how well he was doing now. Granted, he could always visit and tell his father how everything was going, but he couldn't bring himself to enter that nursing home again, not after that first time. Deven kept telling himself he would return one day, but he didn't see the point.

Henry had stopped recognizing Deven. Now, he would stare right through him as if he were invisible. It didn't feel good. It had been almost a year since their mother passed, and their father declined rapidly since the day they told him she died. It was like he stopped fighting and let the disease take over. He kept forgetting that she was gone, and each time they reminded him, it was like watching his heart shatter into a million pieces all over again.

She was still alive in his mind, and he clung to it, refusing to accept that she was no longer here. The last time Deven went to see him, he was obsessed with talking about saving his wife. Deven couldn't ignore the pang of jealousy he'd felt each time. He remembers their mom. Why couldn't he remember Deven? His son? His flesh and blood. Wasn't he important?

"Great. Okay, I'll talk to you later, sis. Love you." He hung up before she could respond. This entire thing was a lot to process, and Deven hated dealing with it. He kept putting it to the back of his mind and focusing on other things. It was a problem for another day, but it was getting more difficult to ignore. His dad used to be his hero. The man could walk into the room, and all heads would turn. When he spoke, people would get quiet and listen; they'd hang on to his every word as if it were law. He was full of knowledge and wisdom about life. He was the one that gave him the courage to pursue the restaurant when the funding had fallen through on the first project. He listened intently whenever Deven wanted to talk business, only offering his input when asked.

Deven used to love whenever they talked. His father always offered something new that Deven could try, or a different perspective on a situation. Now, every time Deven looked at him, all he could see was weakness and emptiness. There was nothing behind his eyes anymore. He no longer stood as tall. He was unsure of himself. He didn't look like the same man, and that broke Deven's heart more than anything else. He couldn't look at his father and into his vacant stare without wanting to collapse on the ground and sob. He already felt as if he had lost both parents.

Alzheimer's meant having to say goodbye and grieve the father he once had while his body was still alive. That's a different kind of pain that

Deven wasn't sure how to navigate yet. Anya believed that he had never been to visit, but that wasn't true. He had gone. After Anya told Deven their father was doing well, Deven rushed to the nursing home, hoping for that spark of recognition. But when he got there, all their father talked about how to save his wife. He didn't even remember Deven. He didn't stay long. He tried, but it was hard to pretend what he was rambling about made sense. Too hard. Deven put his phone on the desk and tried to put it out of his mind. He had a restaurant to run.

He was exhausted when he made it home that night. Every muscle in his body ached. He wanted nothing more than to lay in bed and sleep for the next day and a half, but he knew he needed to call Camila back. He was tempted to go to sleep and call her in the morning. He could claim that he had gotten in super late and had forgotten. She'd never know the difference.

Instead, he dialed her number and flopped backward on his bed. He wanted to see her, even if she was about to break up with him. Maybe, if he tried hard enough, he could convince her not to leave him. If he promised to spend more time with her and made more of an effort to be present when they were in the room together, she would see that he wasn't a bad guy and would not give up on him. If he said this and made the conscious effort to try, she might give him another chance.

He had fallen asleep by the time she made it to the house. He didn't mean to, but the chaos from the dinner shift had taken a toll on him. It had been a while since he worked as a server. It was exhausting work, especially when stuck with a table that could never be satisfied. It seemed like for every table he had that was dope, two more sucked the energy out of him.

Luckily, Camila had a key to his place and could let herself in. His friends admonished him for giving her a key to his home so early, but he assured them it was just convenient. She worked nights and could come and go as she pleased without waking him up. In reality, it was both. He was moving too fast, but it was too convenient not to.

He popped awake at the sound of her footsteps on the stairs. His anxiety had already started to creep up his neck. He still couldn't figure out what he had done wrong. She entered the bedroom with a surprisingly pleasant smile on her face. Her black hair flowed down her back in one long braid, which accentuated her cheekbones. He sat up, taking in her simple pink tank top and jeans that seemed almost tailor-made to fit her body. The jeans hugged her curves in a way that distracted him immediately. He reached for her, and she happily stepped into his arms.

"How was work today?" she asked, nuzzling his chest. She rubbed her hands up and down his back and smiled as he shuddered under her touch. Goosebumps popped up all over his arms.

"It was hectic." He sat down on the bed and pulled her with him. "So, what do you want to talk to me about?"

"Dang. You can't ask me how my day went first?" She laughed. "I had a good day, too, in case you were wondering." Deven rolled his eyes and tried to hide his smile, but he couldn't resist. His phone vibrated, and he instinctively reached for it.

Scale of one to ten, how much do you love me? It was his younger sister Dru.

Zero. What do you want? He replied. Camila let out a sigh beside him. Her irritation was palpable.

I need more cash until payday. Deven was getting ready to reply when Camila touched his arm. He stopped and looked up at her, feeling guilty. How quickly he had just pushed her to the side to focus on something else had to be the main reason why she was dumping him.

"Just make it quick and painless," he said, closing his eyes and bracing himself. When she said nothing, he opened them again and looked at her. "You're breaking up with me, right? That's why you insisted we talk in person?"

"What?" She laughed. "Why would you think I was breaking up with you?"

He shrugged, trying to hide the smile of relief that was pushing at the corners of his mouth. "That's what 'we need to talk' means, Camila!"

Her expression grew serious as she looked at him, studying his face. He held her gaze, unsure of what to do next. She said she needed to talk, but how she looked at him made him want to do other things instead. He leaned forward and planted a soft kiss on her lips. He could taste the lipstick she was wearing, fully aware that it was probably smearing all over his lips. It tasted terrible, but he didn't care.

"Dev..." she whispered against his mouth. He groaned and deepened the kiss, wanting to feel her hands on his body. She shifted so she could throw a leg over him and opened her mouth wider against his to invite his tongue. She always knew exactly what to do to drive him wild. After his day, he could use a little special attention. Whatever she wanted to talk about could wait until later.

An hour later, he tumbled off her, panting and deliciously spent. His chest rose and fell rapidly with each breath he took. He only felt mildly guilty about distracting her from why she had come over in the first place, but he was happy to know that it wasn't to dump him. Whatever she wanted to talk about had to be serious. She didn't usually hesitate to say what was on her mind.

It was one of the things he liked most about her. It didn't matter how you felt afterward; she spoke her mind. It was up to the other person to decide how to deal with it. Her habit of being blunt made it so he never had to guess with her. He never had to try and read between the lines to figure out what she wanted. When she had a need, she expressed it.

He glanced over at her, smiling from ear to ear. Her hair was tousled, and a light sheen of sweat coated her arms. He gave himself a mental pat on the back for being able to tire her out the way he had, even though she had sufficiently exhausted him. He would have tried to push for another round if he hadn't already been beat from working at the restaurant. She smiled back at him and wrapped the blanket around her naked body. Purplish hickies dotted her neck and chest, evidence of how good she tasted to him. He reached down, grabbed his boxers from where he had tossed them earlier, and put them back on.

"What did you want to talk to me about again?" He asked, turning to look at her. She sat up, keeping the middle of the blanket over the front of her body.

"Come." She said quietly, patting the bed next to her.

He raised an eyebrow. "It must be serious."

"Deven...you know how much I care about you, right?"

He narrowed his eyes. "Yes."

"And... I know we haven't been together very long. but I feel like what we have is special." She took a deep breath, "and I hope you know this wasn't on purpose. It was a complete accident."

"Camila! Out with it!" He prodded, frustrated. He was growing tired of her dancing around what she wanted to say. She sighed and closed her eyes. He watched as a single tear slipped down her cheek, followed by the one phrase that made his heart stop beating in his chest.

"Deven...I'm pregnant."

19

Drusilla

Don't look now, Dru, but that guy over there is staring pretty hard." The bartender nodded over Dru's shoulder in the crowded club. She glanced up from her Kindle in surprise. She had been so engrossed in what she was reading that she had completely forgotten where she was. The noises and sounds of the crowded public space had blurred into the background. That snap back to reality made her a little disoriented.

She blinked, letting her eyes adjust to the dark bar. Spots dotted her vision. Her hair: black, shoulder-length, and reminiscent of a lion's mane, was pulled into a ponytail at the nape of her neck to expose her angular face. She wore a knee-length, sleeveless black dress that showed off the multiple tattoos creeping up her arms. She was a thicker woman. By society's standards, she was considered plus-sized, maybe even obese, but she had never felt insecure about her size. Any chance she could get to flaunt her curves, she would take it. Anyone who had an issue with it was someone she didn't feel like she needed to associate herself with in the first place.

She had come out, only as a favor to the owner, Bryce, for the club's grand opening. Bryce was a friend she made while briefly studying business before switching majors. Everyone in their circle knew he always had the biggest crush on her, but to Dru, he was just a good friend, nothing more than someone to get a drink with after a long day, or someone to laugh with when she needed to take her mind off the stress of life for a night. They had never gone further than being just friends, but that wasn't for lack of trying on his part. He graduated two years before her and took over the club that had been in the family for years.

Under his ownership, the club had undergone an entire, and frankly much-needed, rebranding. Everything from top to bottom was remodeled or wholly done away with. He trashed the outdated furniture and decorations and donated some to charity. He brought Dru in for the interior designing, an opportunity she got only because of how infatuated he was with her. She knew this but still accepted the job, not really caring about the true motive behind the offer. She put her heart and soul into redoing the place. By the time she was done, it was a completely different atmosphere - a better one. Something more modern that could be viewed as a hangout spot for people in town. The outdated look of the building had been completely restored to something straight out of a movie.

After everything was finalized and ready to go, Bryce begged her for weeks to ensure she came by for at least a little while on opening night. So far, she was there for an hour and a half, hoping to at least see him so she could fulfill her promise and go home. He was so wrapped up in the behind-the-scenes hustle and bustle of the grand opening that he had yet to come out and see her. Usually, she would be irritated, but she enjoyed seeing how everything came together. All her hard work created a beautiful, finished product.

She smiled as she stood there, taking in the minimalist yet unique decor she had chosen. She was proud that she finally found something that sparked her passion and creativity. It had been a long journey, full of half-started degrees and projects that she had no intention of returning to, but once she found design, everything felt like it clicked into place. The club was crowded; Dru heard more than a few whispers about how much the guests loved the blacks and whites of the interior with the subtle pops of color.

"Oh, he's coming over. Be nice! He's actually pretty cute," the bartender hissed at her before busying himself with wiping the counters. She was so content while taking in the vibes and the atmosphere that she forgot why her attention was taken from her book. A man was approaching her. Dru rolled her eyes at the bartender and focused on her drink, not even bothering to turn around and see who he was. She wasn't interested.

A moment later, the intense scent of a spicy, woodsy cologne filled her nose. A thick, muscular arm came into her peripheral vision. She was tempted to stare straight ahead, but curiosity got the better of her. She turned to see who the arm belonged to.

A man who looked to be in his late twenties or early thirties sat down next to her. He had dark brown locs with dyed blonde tips cascading down his back and a sharp jawline with almond-shaped eyes that were currently fixed on her. The bartender had undersold how attractive he was. She bit her bottom lip, hoping her sudden snap to attention wasn't noticeable and didn't seem weird. She briefly glanced down at her outfit to make sure nothing was out of place. So far, so good. She hadn't eaten anything, so there was no risk of having food stuck in her teeth, but just in case, she ran her tongue over her teeth to wipe off any lipstick that could have gotten smudged there.

"Hello," she said, smiling politely. He smiled back, showing rows of perfectly whitened teeth. It was unsettling how attractive and put-together he was. He could have easily been some type of male model. He couldn't have been from around here; men this pretty didn't live locally. He reached out his hand for her to shake.

"Hello. I'm Kenan. I hope I'm not bothering you, but I just had to speak to the woman reading in the middle of the club." He nodded at the Kindle on the bar counter with a bemused smile. Dru felt herself blush. She knew she probably looked weird to other people, but she wasn't here for fun. She was here out of obligation, but that didn't mean she had to sit and twiddle her thumbs until it was time to leave.

"I bet you think that's weird, huh?"

"Not really. What are you reading?" he asked. Dru picked up her Kindle and flipped to the cover page to show him. He leaned forward; his interest seemed genuine. She caught another whiff of his cologne from the movement.

"It's called *Beneath the Burrow* by Lauren W. Roach," she said, closing the Kindle. "She's new, but I appreciate her writing. I didn't think I would enjoy the story, but so far, I can't seem to put it down and-" Dru looked up to see that his smile had grown wider. She clamped her mouth shut. He had to be laughing at the nerdy girl in the middle of a social event reading. After a moment of silence, he tilted his head, confused.

"Why'd you stop?" He asked.

"You don't want to hear it; it's unimportant," she replied, shaking her head. She didn't usually struggle this badly talking to members of the opposite sex, but there was something about this man that made her melt into a puddle of word vomit. He placed a hand on her arm; his skin was softer than she expected.

"If it brings you joy, then it is vitally important." He signaled for the bartender and ordered a drink. "Tell me, what's your name?" Dru wanted to kick herself for not telling him her name. Here she was, rambling on about a book she had been reading, but didn't even bother to tell this man what to call her. Embarrassment made her skin flush.

"My name is Drusilla, but you can call me Dru," she replied. He flashed that smile again, and her breath caught in her throat. It had been a while since a man could make her feel anything.

Not since...him.

She blinked, trying to force away thoughts of her ex-fiancé. The wound was still fresh from the end of their relationship, and allowing herself to think about it would bring her to tears. If reading on her Kindle in the middle of a busy club didn't make her seem odd enough, crying her eyes out in front of a stranger would do the trick. She didn't want to scare him off. Not yet.

"It's nice to officially meet you, Dru." Hearing him say her name made her stomach tighten in the best way possible. The way he looked at her made her want to divulge her deepest and darkest secrets, even the things she was sure he wouldn't want to hear. "What brings you to the club if you are more intent on reading?" A question like that would typically irritate her, but he seemed genuinely interested so she didn't mind.

"I came as a favor to Bryce. He's-"

"My brother." Kenan interrupted with a smile. Dru paused, surprised. As long as she had known Bryce, he had never mentioned having a brother. Especially not one that was this easy on the eyes.

"He's younger than me by a few years." Kenan continued, sipping the drink the bartender had just placed before him. Dru watched, noting how his muscles flexed through his simple, solid-colored T-shirt. He caught her staring, and his smile widened knowingly, but he said nothing.

"I designed the place," she admitted waving a hand around the room. For some reason, she was shy to share that with him. She wanted to seem nonchalant about it, but inside, she was still excited at the fact that she had designed an entire business by herself. It was his turn to look surprised. His eyes grew wide for a second before he let out a low whistle, impressed. Dru felt her insides grow warm.

"Wow. Beautiful and incredibly talented. They don't make them like you anymore, do they?" His eyes traveled down her body, taking in each inch of her hungrily. The heat behind his gaze made her feel weak. She was happy she had been sitting down; otherwise, she would have fallen over in a swoon worthy of a cheesy romance novel. The intensity of her attraction to this man, this complete stranger, confused her and excited her simultaneously.

"Do you want to get out of here?" she asked, surprising both of them. She didn't mean to say that, but it came out of her mouth when she opened it. Now that it was out there, she did not intend to take it back. Her brother always picked on her about being too forward with people. He would tell her that some people don't know how to handle a woman who is as matter of fact as she is when she wants something. She stared at Kenan, holding her breath and waiting for his answer. He held her gaze briefly, then a broad smile cracked his thoughtful expression. She breathed a sigh of relief as he signaled to the bartender for the tab and grabbed his keys.

"Absolutely."

She slept with him.

The plan had been to find a quieter place where they could talk. They found a more peaceful spot, but talking was not at all what they ended up doing. One thing led to another, and they ended up back at her apartment, tangled in a heap of body parts and bedsheets. Dru didn't expect to go that far with him so quickly, but being able to turn her mind off for a little while felt incredible. As she ran her fingertips gently up and down his chocolate-colored chest, she had no regrets. She tilted her head back to look up at him, and he met her gaze with a lopsided grin on his gorgeous face.

"I'm not usually like this," she said with a sheepish grin. She sounded like the worst rom-com type, but she didn't care. He let out a hearty laugh that made her smile. The sound of it made her heart thump a little harder. She wanted him to laugh like that more often, especially if she could be the one to make him do it. She blinked, surprised at herself for thinking about future interactions with a man she had just met and had already slept with. One-night stands don't usually turn into reoccurring dates. That gets too close to a relationship, which she didn't want to deal with any time soon.

"I was about to say the same thing. You are something different, Drusilla. Something special." He played with one of her curls that had come loose during their night. His hand gently brushed against her bare shoulder and made the rest of her tingle with excitement. Dru couldn't ignore how comfortable she felt lying there in his arms. She felt like she could stay there forever. She shook her head slightly, pushing the thought out of her mind. If she focused too hard on it, she would start to panic, ruining the moment. She could obsess over what happened between them later when she was alone. She could call her therapist or maybe even her friends, someone who would tell her she was being crazy and she needed to get a grip.

"I'm sure you say that to all the girls who throw themselves at you." Dru smiled.

"Nah." He planted a kiss on her temple and let out a contented sigh.

Dru fought back a smile. She knew that sigh. It meant Dru had done her job well. She wanted to fist bump the air, but instead, she let her head settle onto his chest and listened to the steady sound of his heartbeat until sleep took over.

Dru popped awake, covered in an icy sweat. She'd had a nightmare. The same nightmare had been playing on a loop in her head for the past few months. It randomly started one night and refused to let up. She glanced to her right and almost jumped out of her skin. Kenan was still lying next to her, fast asleep.

His chest rose and fell with each breath. His mouth was slightly open in a light snore, and his locs were spread out on the pillow behind his head -a perfect picture. Dru gazed at him for a moment, letting her rapid breathing calm down before she disturbed him. She didn't expect him to still be there. She expected him to slip out in the middle of the night like the other guys she hooked up with in the past. They never spent the night. They never made themselves comfortable in her bed like they had some right to be there. She reached over and shook him awake.

"Is everything okay?" he asked, rubbing his eyes. She ignored how adorable he looked while half asleep and threw his shirt at him.

"You need to leave." Her voice was cold and stiff, even though she wanted nothing more than to crawl back into his arms and shut her brain off for a little longer. She felt safe in his arms during the brief moment she allowed herself that comfort.

"What? Why?" He was fully awake now, looking at her with a confused expression mixed with something else she couldn't quite place. Was that... hurt? He seemed genuinely upset at her reaction. It confused her. Why hadn't he left? Why did she want him to stay? She turned away from him, feeling guilty for telling him to get out but inwardly pleading with him to understand that she needed him to go.

He couldn't be here when the nightmares came back. He was lucky she didn't wake him up screaming like she did most nights. That's too much to show someone so soon. She liked him, but she knew that he would run if he got a glimpse at the real her with all of her bruises and brokenness. They always run. Panic began to swell in the pit of her stomach. She clamped down on her tongue to give herself a pain she could pinpoint and focus on.

"Please. I just need you to go." Her voice was soft, broken.

He reached for her but then changed his mind and nodded. "I understand. Will I be able to see you again?"

The hopefulness in his voice made her want to shrink away and hide. It wasn't supposed to be like this. Dru mentally kicked herself for allowing things to get this far. She should have just gotten his number and then not called him. The same way she had with every other guy that hit on her since she and her fiancé split. There was safety in being alone. She didn't have to worry about letting someone else get close enough to shatter what was left of her mangled heart.

She pulled the covers up around her body and stared at the wall over his shoulder, unable to answer his question or meet his gaze. Dru knew she would crack into a million pieces if she looked into his eyes, and it was taking all of her strength to hold herself together. After a moment, he sighed and slid off the bed. She couldn't look at him as he put on his clothes and headed towards the front door. Instead, she lay with her back facing him, staring out the singular window in the bedroom. She heard him pause by the bedroom door.

"If you change your mind, I'll be at the club again tonight. I'll wait for you." She didn't move or respond, just held her breath until she heard the soft click of the front door closing behind him.

As soon as she knew she was alone, she let the tears come.

20

Good morning, Mrs. James! You here to see your father?" The woman at the front desk, a skinny blonde with blinding white teeth and wide blue eyes, greeted Anya as she stepped through the front door of Wimbledon Farms Nursing Home. Anya smiled at her and nodded. Although pleasantly decorated, the building smelled faintly of pee and heavy antiseptic. No matter how often she came, it was a smell that Anya could never get used to.

Still groggy after a long night of forcing herself to write, she blinked back the sleep from her eyes and tried not to take too deep a breath. Anya always felt like she could taste the horrid combination of smells that lingered in the air if she opened her mouth for too long. She signed her name on the guest sheet and headed down the familiar hallway to her father's room.

"You wearing them pants, miss lady." A gruff voice spoke up from behind her as she walked. Anya turned to find Zander Sullivan leering at her from his wheelchair. He made a show of letting his eyes travel down the length of her body and back up to her breasts. She instinctively folded her arms across her chest and rolled her eyes. His teeth had yellowed after years of coffee drinking and chain-smoking, and his skin sagged around his face and neck, but his eyes were as bright as ever. Anya shook her head and smiled politely.

"Good morning Mr. Sullivan. Have you seen my dad?"

"Maybe, but I'm more concerned with seeing what you got under that blouse. Make an old man's day and shake those titties for me." Sullivan flashed his teeth in what was supposed to be a grin but looked more like a sneer and licked his chapped lips. Anya resisted the urge to push his wheelchair in the opposite direction and watch him spill out of it. If he was this disrespectful and gross as an old man, she could only imagine how insufferable he was in his younger days. She turned and walked away from him, ignoring the grumbling she heard from him in response.

She found her father sitting behind the desk in his room, clicking away on the laptop she had brought him. The walls remained undecorated, and the television played quietly in the background. There was a bookshelf full of random books to the right of him and a small room to the left opened to reveal his bedroom with the bathroom in the corner by the door.

The staff at this facility told her that when she moved her father in, they did whatever they could to make sure the residents felt like they had a space of their own that was bigger than just a bed and four walls. They would spend the rest of their lives there; giving them some semblance of home-made sense. She lightly rapped her knuckles against the open door to announce her entrance. He stared blankly at her momentarily when she came in before smiling politely and motioning to the chair near his desk.

"Mrs. James, good to see you. How was your weekend?" He asked, tilting his glasses up on his face. Anya swallowed, debating whether to go along with the conversation as it was or to just remind him who she was. His doctor had mentioned that sometimes, trying to correct someone with Alzheimer's can confuse them even more. This confusion can cause outbursts.

According to the nurses, whenever she tried to convince him she was his daughter, he would be violent and belligerent toward the staff for the rest of the day. He had been doing so well lately. She didn't want to risk causing an outburst if she upset him. He stared at her expectantly, waiting for her answer. After a moment of debate, she smiled and settled into the chair.

"Good morning, Mr. Tubeck. My weekend went well. How was yours?" He shrugged and looked down at his hands, clasped tightly in front of him.

"It went alright. Clara and I revisited the place where we got married. She- She couldn't remember the date." Anya watched, unsure what to do, as tears spilled down his cheeks. Alzheimer's had completely morphed her father's personality into someone she could no longer recognize. He used to be so strong, so stoic. She could count on one hand how many times she saw her father cry growing up. Watching him now, in front of her, blubbering so freely, made her uncomfortable. She shifted in her seat.

"I'm so sorry to hear that, Da- Mr. Tubeck." If he heard her slip-up, he gave no indication of it. This dynamic that started between them, pretending to be coworkers, had its upsides and downsides. On the upside, she could share things with her "coworker" that she wasn't able to communicate with her father, but in those moments when Anya wanted to reach out and hug him or tell him she loved him, she had to remind herself of the situation. It was tricky to navigate; sometimes, it took so much out of her that all she could do was sit in her car and weep afterward.

Obligation wouldn't let her stop coming, but she wasn't sure how much more of it she could take. She handed her father a tissue from the box on his desk, which he took gratefully and dabbed at his eyes. After a moment, he seemed to snap out of his sadness and straighten.

"How's your father doing? Has his condition progressed?" She had shared with him before that her father had Alzheimer's. He listened intently, utterly oblivious that he was the father she was referring to. Even in moments of clarity, glimpses of reality, he didn't seem to remember who she was.

"Not...Not so great. He no longer remembers me," she whispered, looking down at her hands. He let out a low whistle and leaned back in his chair. "That must be tough," he said after a beat of silence. Anya said nothing. What could she have said at this moment? Yes, Dad, it is 'tough' that you don't remember me. Or how long are we going to play this charade, Dad? It's me! I'm your daughter! Look at me! So many times, she wanted to scream at him. One time, she actually did. After a particularly stressful day at work, she'd come in and snapped at him, frustrated that he couldn't remember who she was.

"Dad! Let this go! I'm your daughter. It's me. I'm Rose! Anya Rose!" She yelled with tears streaming down her face.

He shook his head and replied, "I'm sorry honey, you must have me mistaken. I don't know who you're talking about."

The blank look he gave haunted her for weeks afterward. That night, she went home and cried in Luca's arms. He held her, rubbing her back and kissing her hair while she sobbed until her eyes were almost swollen shut.

They tell you about these moments during group. They try to prepare you for what it will be like, but nothing can prepare you for that feeling. Nothing can steel you for that moment when your loved one looks you in the eye without recognition or familiarity in them. After that visit, she started going to the support group because she felt like she was drowning in a diagnosis that wasn't hers. She sobbed, wailed, and screamed about how unfair it was while other group members listened silently. When she finally let it all out, throat sore from screaming and crying, Aaron patted her knee. He assured her that she wasn't alone in what she was feeling.

Even knowing that it would happen never fully prepares you for it. Each time you realize that the person who's supposed to love and protect you from the world doesn't even remember your name, it is like another punch to the gut. Even here, at this moment, listening to her father speak to her as if she were a coworker and acquaintance instead of his first-born child, hurt more than she could articulate. Instead of yelling at him as before, she smiled at him, the man who looked like her father but was no longer him, and nodded.

"It is tough."

They sat together for a while, talking and catching up; her father continued to refer to her family and his family as if they were two different things. He referred to his wife as if it wasn't her mother. She kept up the charade because it was the only thing that seemed to keep him in a good mood. When he was confused, he got mean. And that was the last thing she wanted. None of this was what she wanted.

How's Dad doing? The text message pinged on her Apple watch on the way to work. Anya had texted her brother and sister in the group chat to tell them she was stopping at the nursing home before work to check in on their dad. She didn't text them every day, but she would let them know when she was visiting every now and then in hopes that one of them would offer to tag along.

They never did.

Most of the messages in the chat consisted of her giving them the updates they asked for and them turning down her offers when she wanted to get together or wanted them to come up and see their father for a little while.

Of course, neither wanted to visit, but they would always check in when it was time for new information. They wanted to know what was happening at all times but wanted to be as far away from it as possible. Dru was the only one to respond to the group chat this time. It was still early; Deven was most likely still asleep, while Dru probably hadn't been to sleep yet. She usually spent her nights at flashy industry events or working on projects that took her time and energy. Anya drove into the parking lot at the firm and pulled her phone out of her purse. She contemplated not answering, but she knew that would be mean.

He's the same. Still thinks I'm his assistant, not his daughter. She responded. The bubbles immediately popped up in the chat, letting Anya know that someone was typing back. She gathered her belongings and exited the car while she waited for one of them to send the following message. The subsequent response came from Deven. She was surprised he was even awake.

That's tough. His response sounded similar to what their father said when she spoke to him. Anya snorted and then tossed her phone back in her purse. Part of her wanted to stop responding to their requests for updates, especially when they suddenly stopped responding when she needed them, but she couldn't bring herself to be that cruel. Even if they were taking advantage of her caring nature, the family was the most important thing to her.

"Anya! Hey! How is Pops doing?" Her coworker and best friend, Daphne, stepped beside her as she headed to her office. Her blond box braids were tied up in a neat bun on the top of her head, and her makeup was perfectly done, accentuating her flawless beauty. Her light pink eye shadow matched the pink flowers in her blazer. Daphne was one of the few people she confided in other than her husband. They had been friends for most of their lives. When Anya's mother passed, Daphne showed up at the house with an overnight bag and a pint of ice cream for each of them. Whenever Anya felt overwhelmed and undervalued by her family, Daphne let her vent and helped her cook and clean.

When they graduated high school and moved on to college, they applied and got accepted at the same school. They even finagled their way into being roommates. Daphne was Anya's right hand. Since the beginning of time, it was the two of them against the world. She was the maid of honor at Daphne's wedding and vice versa. You couldn't have one without the other. When Daphne got the job here at the firm, she immediately brought Anya on board when the company was hiring. She was one of the only bright spots about this job. Anya sighed and shook her head.

"This whole thing is a mess. He still thinks I'm his coworker or his assistant. I'm not clear on which."

"You can't tell him?"

"He gets so irritable and angry whenever you try and tell him what's actually going on. The nurses have practically begged me not to ruin his mood. He becomes insufferable."

"What about Deven and Dru?"

"Girl, what about them? They don't help. All they do is harass me for updates. They can't bother stepping away from their lives for a second just to sit with him." Tears pushed at the back of her eyes, but she blinked to keep them from spilling over. She had already cried enough over the last few months to last a lifetime. The last thing she needed was to start blubbering at work. Daphne leaned over to give her a hug and rubbed her back.

"I'm sorry all of this is on your shoulders. What have you been doing for yourself? Have you been making your self-care a point?"

"Self-care? What is that?" Anya laughed bitterly. Daphne said nothing, just waited for Anya to respond. After a second of silence, Anya took a deep breath and shrugged quickly.

"I have been trying to get some writing done."

"That's great!" Daphne clapped her hands excitedly. She had always been one of Anya's biggest supporters. Every blog post she submitted was met with so much positive feedback and love from her readers, but also from Daphne. Days when she was convinced that she was taking on too much and should just drop the idea of writing, Daphne was always ready to build her back up and convince her to keep pushing. If she ever finished this book, whatever it was, she would mention Daphne and Luca in the acknowledgments.

After eight hours of mind-numbing calculations and spreadsheets, Anya shut down her computer and grabbed her stuff. She had promised Luca that after she left the nursing home, she would grab some Chinese food since it was her turn to figure out dinner. She hadn't been cooking as much lately because she spent most mornings and evenings at the nursing home with her dad. Luca made no complaints other than wondering why her brother and sister were not helping.

The blond woman from earlier was replaced by a chubbier woman with a less pleasant face. Anya smiled at her, but she only nodded and looked back at her computer screen. As Anya made her way down the hall to her father's room, she spotted a familiar face standing outside one of the rooms further down the hallway.

"Mr. Hen?" she asked quietly. He flinched, seeming startled, and turned to face her. His eyes were puffy and tired looking. His skin had a grayish tint. He was obviously not taking care of himself and seemed to be struggling with his wife's condition. He looked more downtrodden now than he did at the last meeting.

"Oh. Hi. You're from the meeting, right?" He looked around nervously. "What are you doing here?" He rubbed a hand over the back of his neck.

Anya tried to give him a reassuring smile. "My father is a resident here. Henry Tubeck?"

"The guy that thinks everyone is an employee in his office?"

His comment stung. "Yes. That's him."

Mr. Hen studied her for a moment. He looked to be deciding whether he could trust her. Anya briefly wondered what had happened in his life to make him so untrusting. "My name is Anya, by the way." She reached out to shake his hand. He stared at it for a moment and then grabbed her hand.

"You can call me by my full name now. It's Hendrickson - Hendrickson Andrews." After moments of awkward silence, she turned to find her father. She was halfway down the hall when she heard his voice again.

"Does it...does it get any easier?" There was a sense of desperation in his tone that made her stop in her tracks. Did it get easier? It hadn't for her yet. It felt the exact opposite. It felt like it was becoming harder and harder to stay afloat. She turned back to face Hendrickson, taking a moment to choose her words carefully.

"No. It doesn't."

"What's the point in continuing to show up then? She doesn't even know who I am anymore," he asked. His voice cracked towards the end of the sentence. Anya closed the distance between them and placed a hand on his shoulder.

"You know who she is, though. She's your family. And family shows up." Hendrickson took a deep breath and nodded. Anya stood and watched as he steadied himself and headed back into what she assumed was his wife's room. Anya stayed put for a moment, trying and failing to encourage herself.

Family shows up. That's something her mother used to tell her when she was a young girl, mad that they had to go to Dru's fashion shows and Deven's cooking competitions. Her mother would always place her hands on her shoulders, look her in the eye and tell her they would be there. They would show up because family shows up. Anya lived by that simple phrase ever since.

Even now, after her mother died and left them struggling to figure out which way was up. Anya was always there, willing to step in when her family needed her. She was ready to show up, even though she knew that if situations were reversed and it was her in this nursing home with her memories fading by the minute, none of them would do the same.

21

Pregnant? How far along are you?" His voice came out in a breathy whisper. His stomach dropped to his knees. Of all the possibilities running through his mind, pregnancy hadn't even crossed the list. He stared at Camila. His brain ran a mile a minute, trying to form coherent thoughts. They twisted and jumbled together in a big clump, trying and failing to make sense of the situation.

"About ten weeks. I missed some of my birth control pills. My cycle has always been out of the ordinary; I figured I was just stressed out with the job," she shrugged. "I took the test after my friend told me that she sensed a difference in my moods and eating habits."

"How long have you known?" He was almost afraid to hear the answer. He knew he had been too preoccupied with Le Fugue, but how could he have missed this? Panic set in, stiffening his muscles. He ran a hand over his face. Deven didn't know the first thing about raising a child. He didn't particularly care for them if he was being candid. They were needy and tended to get in the way a lot. Plus, children were expensive. He'd seen the prices for daycare and formula. Camila placed a hand on his leg.

"Not long but talk to me. What are you thinking?" she asked quietly. He dragged in a deep breath and released it slowly. Anxiety flipped his stomach as he tried to quickly calculate what it would cost to have a child in this economy. A business was bad enough; now he had to factor in a baby? He was thinking about how he didn't want kids but didn't know how to tell Camila this without making it seem like he was abandoning her to figure it out herself.

Deven wanted to be with Camila and travel the world. There was so much wrong with this situation. His mother was no longer here; his father was no longer coherent. Neither one of them had met his girlfriend, and neither one of them would meet their grandchild. Camila didn't have an easy childhood. Her parents weren't in the picture. Her father was never around, and her mother was in and out of rehab for drug addiction. Camila spent most of the time at her grandmother's house. Her grandmother passed a few years before Camila even met Deven. Who were they supposed to lean on for guidance?

"We... I'm not ready to be a father."

"I will take care of everything myself. I'm not expecting anything from you."

Deven shot her a crazy look. She didn't honestly expect him to sit by and not participate in his child's life, did she? He cupped her face in his hands and kissed her lips.

"Camila, please shut up. You're out of your mind if you think I will let you do this yourself." The smile that spread across her lips made his heart warm.

"I just wanted to make sure. I know you have a lot going on right now with the restaurant. And with-" she widened her eyes and stopped, but he knew what she meant. She meant to say: with your father. She was the only one he talked to about his father's poor health. Deven had lost count of the times he cried in her lap over the last few months. He gave her a sad smile and nodded.

" I get it, but we're here. We're doing this." He sounded more confident than he felt at the moment. His heart was racing, trying to decide what to do next. He had so many plans for his life and a baby was not part of it.

"Thank you," she whispered. He glanced at her, unsure of what she meant. "Thank you for not being angry." His head still felt cloudy as he tried to imagine either of them holding a small child or hearing a child cry at night instead of being able to sleep. Life as he knew it was about to flip on its head -- again. After everything that happened recently with his parents, he wondered if he pissed someone off in a past life. Deven wrapped his arms around Camila and pulled her into his chest. Her body felt warm and comforting against his. He closed his eyes and focused on his breathing. He tried to imagine them as parents. The idea was almost laughable. He could barely remember to care for himself some days, and now he would be expected to care for two people: Camila and their new baby. He didn't have the slightest idea where to start.

"Henry Deven Tubeck, you got a girl pregnant?" Dru hissed into the phone. Deven winced at the tone of her voice and her use of his entire government name. It wasn't often that anyone called him that, so he knew he had messed up big time. He planned to sit on the information for a few days before telling either one of his sisters, but he caved and called her immediately after Camila left.

Deven needed someone to talk to about it, and he knew that Anya would be too busy trying to lecture him instead of listening to what he had to say. His friends would be trying to give him hell for getting a girl he just started dating pregnant. Dru was the least judgmental, so she was the next best bet.

Even though she was still in her twenties, she was surprisingly wise for her age. Some days Deven had to remind himself that she wasn't the older one of the two of them. Deven sighed and stared at the ceiling; the small white lumps in the paint seemed to dance around each other in a blur the longer he looked.

"Yes, but she's not just any girl, Rue!"

"Are you going to marry her?"

The question caught him off guard. He let out a startled cough and then laughed. He shook his head but then remembered she couldn't see him.

"No! I mean- I don't know. It's still so early."

"You skipped a few steps, Dee," she said, "Major steps, actually. None of us have met her. You haven't introduced her to Dad-"

"What would the point of that be? He won't remember." Deven snapped, interrupting her. Deven had considered taking Camila to meet his father, but he was embarrassed. He didn't want to have to remind his father of who he was. It bothered Deven more than he was willing to admit out loud. In some ways, he felt angry with his father and guilty for being angry.

"That's not fair. You know that's not Dad's fault."

"I know that, but it doesn't change the fact that I have to introduce myself to the man who raised me! How are you so cavalier about this? It doesn't bother you?" Deven rolled over on his side and grabbed his phone from where it had been perched on the bedside table while he talked on speaker. He scrolled through his Facebook timeline while he and Dru talked. He wasn't really absorbing any of the posts he was looking at. His mind was racing too much to focus on anything, but it gave his hands something to do. He heard Dru shuffle around on her end of the phone before she responded.

"Yes, it does bother me. Dad and I could never really connect when I was growing up, and now we'll never get the chance. It angers me when I think about it for too long, but he's still our dad. We know who he is, even if he doesn't remember us anymore."

"When was the last time you went to see him?" Deven knew from the way Anya complained that neither had been going often enough. Dru didn't respond right away. He heard her hesitate and then let out a quiet sigh. It was heavy, full of words she hadn't been able to say out loud just yet.

"Things have been hectic lately with work and life in general. I'm trying," she said softly. He knew what that really meant. Their father deteriorated much faster than any of them anticipated. When their mother died, the last bit of him holding on to the real world had broken off and sent him floating into his warped reality. No matter how self-evolved and self-aware Deven and Dru pretended to be, it was hard to accept that their father was gone.

Dru was the one to find their mother. She went to the house intending to give their mom a break to get her hair done - a treat from the three of them- when she saw her. She was lying on the floor in the closet in a crumpled heap. It looked like she had fallen forward while folding clothes. The autopsy told them that she suffered a massive heart attack. There wasn't anything anyone could have done to save her.

To make it worse, their father had been sleeping not even ten feet away. The medication the doctors put him on made him sleep more often than usual. He didn't hear a thing. When they woke him up and told him, he was distraught. The anguish on his father's face kept running through Deven's mind when things got too quiet and he got a chance to think. He had never seen his Dad look so broken. It was painful.

Dru faded into herself for a while after that. Deven couldn't blame her. He probably would have been messed up, too, if he had been the one to find their mother dead in the middle of doing something as ordinary as folding clothes. Anya told them that she noticed their mom had fallen out of the habit of caring for herself. She was so wrapped up in caring for their father that she'd forget to eat, go days without showering, and neglect her hair and doctor's appointments because she couldn't leave him alone for more than a few minutes without Dad panicking when he couldn't find her. Hearing about how far his mother, who never had a hair out of place, had fallen made no sense to Deven. Their mother prided herself in her appearance for as long as he could remember.

Deven thought that Anya was exaggerating when she called him in a panic; he felt he had more time. He planned to make it a point to help out a little more once things at the restaurant calmed down, but he never made it there. She was dead two weeks after Anya notified them about their mom's declining health.

"How are you dealing?" Deven asked when he realized neither had said anything in a few minutes.

"I'm fine. Hashing it all out in therapy," Dru replied. He didn't push; when she was ready, she would talk.

In the meantime, he had more than enough on his own plate to try and sort through. Camila gave him the dates for her next few doctor's appointments. She said it was still early, and they didn't have to figure out the living arrangements, but he had been looking at some of the listings on Facebook since she left. Deven wanted to be sure they had enough space and were comfortable before the baby arrived.

Once Deven hung up the phone with his sister, he lay back on the bed and stared up at the ceiling. On the outside, he seemed like he was handling things well, but his emotions were an ugly storm cloud on the inside. He had no idea how he was supposed to do any of this. His first instinct was telling him to run far and fast, but he fought against the urge. They had both gotten themselves into this situation. It was up to both of them to figure it out.

At this moment, he craved a conversation with his mother. She would have smacked him in the head for getting a girl pregnant early into the relationship. Still, she would have given him some priceless advice. The two of them most likely would have baked cookies or made a cake. She would decorate it while he watched her skilled hands move around the dessert like she was performing surgery. While she worked, she would listen to him vent, and then they would laugh about how mad his father would be when he heard the news.

It was small moments like those that Deven had taken for granted; he would give anything to have them back. Simple conversations where he could pick his mom's brain about life or discuss music with her… moments when his Dad was playing around with the latest technology and showing Deven things he didn't even know his iPhone could do. He should have spent more time with his parents while he could when they were both still alive and doing well. He had wasted so much time ignoring their calls and missing family dinners to hang with his friends or be with whoever he was dating at the time. His heart ached, wishing he could get that time back.

"I'm sorry," he whispered into the air. The regret is what had been eating him up the most, but instead of facing it and learning how to deal with it, he pushed it to the back of the closet in his heart and pretended like he couldn't see it or feel it. If he didn't acknowledge the guilt, then it wouldn't be there. It wouldn't make his heart throb in pain whenever he thought about his family.

The following day, Deven's phone pinged loudly next to his head. He didn't remember falling asleep. The last thing he had been doing was looking at parenting websites and reading stuff like **Tips for First-Time Dads** and **Things No One Told Me When I Had My First Kid.** After a while, all the articles started to bleed into each other.

Deven glanced down at his phone with one eye open. Dru had texted the group chat he and his sisters had about their Dad. He waited for a moment to see if Anya would respond. She mentioned that she would stop by and see him before she went to work that morning.

He's the same. Still thinks I'm his assistant, not his daughter. His heart sank reading Anya's response. He was hoping he could sneak over and bring Camila to tell his father he would be a grandpa, but it didn't seem like a good idea if he couldn't even recognize Anya. She saw him every day. What would his father do if Deven showed up bringing in a woman he had never met?

He quickly typed his reply while pulling himself out of the bed. He wasn't sure what else to say that hadn't already been said at some point during their many conversations. Anya would complain about how Dru and Deven needed to be more involved. He would agree because he knew he needed to, and then feel guilty when he could not get away from work. It was the same old song and dance. He couldn't figure out how to stop it.

He wondered why Anya wouldn't just tell him who she was. When he was googling what to do when a loved one had Alzheimer's or some other form of dementia, he saw a lot of conflicting information. Some said that you were supposed to tell them what was happening while others said it was best to just let them be. But she claimed the nurses in the facility said he became too angry and belligerent when they told him the truth. So, they just played along to keep him calm. That seemed cruel.

They were placating him just to talk about him behind his back later. It felt like they humiliated him, even if he didn't know what was happening. The idea that people were pitying him and just going along with what he said, even though they knew it was wrong, would have pissed their father off back in the day. It would make him furious to see that they were making him out to be a spectacle or treating him like he needed to be coddled and handled with kid gloves. He had always hated to be pitied.

Deven sighed as he rubbed the sleep out of his eyes to get ready to go into the restaurant. He had inventory to review and schedules to fix, but all he wanted to do was crawl back in bed and close his eyes. So much was happening around him, and he had no idea how to control any of it. There was a nagging feeling in the base of his brain that he couldn't seem to shake, no matter how hard he tried to distract himself.

Alzheimer's can be genetic. So, what happens if he becomes a father and ends up in the same boat as his own dad? What if he starts to forget everyone and everything he ever loved? What happens, then?

22

Drusilla (1 Year Earlier)

When Dru stepped into her parent's house, she immediately knew something was wrong. A pot of something on the stove had begun to burn and boil over, spilling onto the stovetop. The charred smell hit her when she opened the door and entered the kitchen.

"Mom? Dad?" She called out. No answer. She could hear the television playing from the bedroom. The hair on the back of her neck rose as she took the steps up to the second floor of her childhood home. When she reached their bedroom, she knocked on the closed door, still waiting for an answer. They couldn't still be sleeping. Her mother had asked her to come over to sit with her dad so she could get her hair done. She pushed open the door; her father was still asleep in bed. She could see his foot peeking out from under the blanket.

She slowly walked over to him and knelt down beside the bed. He didn't stir or acknowledge her presence; her mom had mentioned that the new combinations of medications made him a lot sleepier than before. She took a moment to watch him, her heart squeezed at how normal and unaffected by disease he looked while he slept.

Alzheimer's can sometimes be difficult to spot from the outside. Earlier in his diagnosis, her dad would try to go out in public and function as usual. He denied being sick and needed assistance until he was struggling in the middle of the grocery store, trying to remember the name of an item. People would become frustrated with him because they couldn't tell he needed help just by looking at him. He didn't look sick. So, therefore, he must be okay.

Dru sighed to herself while she watched him for a few minutes. He seemed smaller and more fragile than she remembered. Her father had always physically been a large man with a booming voice to match, but Alzheimer's chipped away at the parts of his personality that Dru loved until all that was left was a shell of the man she remembered. She reached out, getting ready to wake him up, when her gaze shifted to the closet.

That's when a strangled scream left her throat.

Her mother lay in a crumpled heap, half in and half out of the closet. Dru rushed over, yelling for her mother to wake up, but she didn't budge. Her body was cold and stiff. She must have been here for hours.

"Oh, Mommy! Mommy, please wake up! You can't leave us like this! Mommy please!" Dru sobbed, reaching down to pull her limp body closer. The seat of her pants was dark from where her muscles had loosened in death. Anya mentioned that their mom hadn't looked good the last time she visited. This is why they convinced her to just go out for a day and take care of herself, to pamper herself and enjoy the things she used to. None of them knew just how serious it was until then, when it was too late.

Her screaming woke her father, who sat staring, trying to process what was happening. Dru grabbed her phone and dialed 911, not letting go of her mother's body. She knew this was the last time she would be able to hold her. Dru remained there, cradling her mother while her father began to wail in agony. He finally realized what happened. The heartbreak in his sobs made her own eyes well up once again.

By the time the paramedics arrived, the swell of emotions between them calmed down. A dull acceptance fell over the room. Dru stared at her father, who sat quietly in the corner of the bedroom. He stopped wailing, but now he seemed empty and far away.

His eyes were vacant, and his skin was pale. He hadn't spoken since Dru woke him up with her panicked screams. Paramedics rushed around him as if he wasn't sitting there; their main focus was her mother. Dru called her brother and sister to let them know what happened. Anya rushed over immediately, and Deven said he was on his way.

Dru felt numb, but just under the numbness was an anger that surprised her. It bubbled up underneath the surface, dangerously close to spilling onto everyone else in the room - people who didn't deserve any of it. She couldn't pinpoint her anger. She was angry at herself for not noticing her mother's suffering. She was angry at Deven for being so absorbed in his restaurant that he left his family to deal with the stress of everything else. She was angry at Anya for not telling her just how much their mother had been suffering, but most of all, she was angry at her father.

In a way, it felt like he had abandoned them. She knew it wasn't his fault, but it did nothing but feed the anger. His disease demanded so much of everyone around him. It required everything her mother had until nothing was left but a shell of bones and flesh. And what made it worse was he wouldn't even remember doing it.

It was almost a year since that day, and the memory of her mother on the floor haunted her dreams more often than Dru really cared to admit. Being unable to see or talk to someone who has died is the worst thing about death, but regret is the next worst thing. It sneaks up at the most inconvenient times possible. Conversations you knew you should have had but never got around to and stuff you knew you should have done but pushed off until later because you believed you had all the time in the world, those moments came in and took over. They seep into happy moments and ruin them like that one rotten fruit in the bowl. Eventually, it turns the rest of the fruit rotten too.

Dru was struggling not to let her mother's death turn her cold, but it was hard. It seemed to influence everything she did lately. It inspired her to seek out therapy, something that her brother and sister should be doing as well, even though they refused to. Anya claimed that the support group was enough for her. At the same time, their brother drowned his sorrows in work. He avoided talking about anything that dealt with emotions because he was a carbon copy of their father. They even had the same thick build and hickory-colored skin.

"So, how have you been feeling since we last talked?" Dru's therapist, Dr. Hatcher, crossed one knee over the other and looked at Dru, waiting for her to respond. Truthfully, she had no idea how she felt. So much happened since her last session. She was still reeling from her brother telling him he had gotten his new girlfriend pregnant. She didn't even known he was seeing anyone or that it was that serious.

"I'm... confused, I guess," she replied, looking down at her arms. Original artwork from Roya, one of her favorite tattoo artists, and her best friend, covered them. The vibrancy of the purples and blues of the flowers against her skin always made her smile whenever she looked at them. It was important to her to find an artist who specialized in black skin. When she found Roya Jude, a Persian and black tattoo artist, she didn't expect they would bond over the many tattoo sessions. Dru confided in her as if she were a childhood best friend. Something about discussing the things that hurt while the needles penetrated the layers of her skin was therapeutic. It was a form of release.

Dr. Hatcher studied her for a moment before writing in the notebook in front of him. The pen made a slight scratching sound against the paper as he scribbled. Dru watched him write, noting how his muscle flexed under the pen's grip. If she was honest with herself, he was attractive, but having a crush on the therapist was painfully cliché. Her rational side knew that being vulnerable with him gave her a false sense of closeness. It was one of the lessons she retained when she briefly considered becoming a therapist. But it didn't change the fact that this man was gorgeous. He was tall, broad-shouldered, and his skin was a rich shade of brown that seemed to almost sparkle under the light. Black male therapists weren't as common as they should be. Dru was excited to find him.

"What are you confused about?" he asked after the silence stretched out. She leaned forward, making sure her cleavage was visible. She licked her lips and put on her sexiest smile. If he was tempted to look, he gave no indication. Instead, he kept his eyes trained on her face, a look of amusement on his own.

"Do you think I'm attractive, Dr. Hatcher?" She used the most seductive voice she could muster. His expression twisted, and he paused momentarily as if running through his list of appropriate responses. She smiled, confident that she could hook him if she wanted to. She didn't, but she enjoyed having the advantage.

"Ms. Tubeck, you're deflecting." His response caught her off guard and hacked at her self-esteem. Maybe she didn't have the advantage. She felt uncomfortable with being so easily dissected. Dru sat back in her chair, immediately embarrassed. "Have you noticed that you default to sexual intimacy in order to keep from having to be emotionally intimate or vulnerable?" Dru felt her cheeks grow hot. Had she really become that much of a mess?

"My brother is having a baby."

"And that confuses you?"

Dru chewed her bottom lip. She was irritated that her brother and sister seemed to be moving forward in their lives while she was still stuck here, reliving the same painful moment repeatedly. She glanced at the mahogany brown desk Dr. Hatcher usually sat behind and shrugged.

"It's so easy for them," she whispered, her voice thick with sudden emotion. He remained silent, allowing her to continue. "Anya started a blog and is actually focusing on her writing career, Deven has a new girlfriend, and his restaurant is thriving so much so that he was able to open a second location. And I'm...I'm here." She waved a hand at the office.

"What's wrong with being here?" Dr. Hatcher asked, feigning offense. Dru glanced up at him, alarmed, but then saw the smile on his face. She grinned back and shook her head.

"Nothing is wrong with your office; I'm just...I don't know...I guess-" She hesitated, unable to finish the thought.

"Do you feel like they're moving on and leaving you behind?" he offered. She nodded; hot tears slipped down her cheeks and dripped on her lap. Dr. Hatcher grabbed the box of tissues from the corner of his desk and offered them to her. She took a few, keeping her head down in embarrassment. What kind of person gets jealous of their own family? She felt guilty for even thinking it and even worse for admitting it out loud.

"You suffered a significant trauma, Dru," he said, "Trauma has the habit of freezing us to that one spot until we take the steps to heal, which you are doing."

"We all lost her."

"Yes, that's true, but you were the one to find her. That couldn't have been easy to see." Dr. Hatcher studied Dru as he spoke; she stared straight ahead, letting his words sink in and swirl around in her mind. He had a point. Dru was the one that found their mother, which added an extra layer of hurt and pain to what was already there. At first, she tried to push it down and keep moving like nothing was wrong. She made it for about a month before she had a complete breakdown in the middle of the store when she wanted to bake the strawberry cake her mother would make whenever Dru was sad and realized that the store was completely out of the cake mix. People swerved around her and refused to make eye contact. Later on, after calming down, she realized that the alcohol and extra naps she had been using to cope weren't enough anymore, so she reluctantly started therapy.

Therapy had been the one thing to keep her from completely losing her mind. Between the nightmares and the intimacy issues she couldn't pinpoint, Dru felt like she was a walking ball of trauma and emotions. She wore her pain like a wall of protection, allowing it to speak for her in relationships or in situations where she felt herself becoming too attached. If she could chase away those who wanted to get close by allowing them to see the aching, bleeding parts of her soul, then she didn't have to worry about anyone else having the power to hurt her like her parents... or Tarik.

Tarik was her fiancé before he decided that she wasn't what he wanted and left her a few weeks before they were going to elope. He decided, more specifically, that she wasn't what he wanted because he wanted her best friend instead. Well, her ex-best friend now.

Dru came home one night early from work and found her fiancé and best friend sleeping naked together in her bed. The room reeked of sex and sweat. When Tarik realized he had been caught, he showed no remorse. He actually acted relieved. As if he had only been tolerating her up until that point, and now he could finally tell her the truth. This happened a month and a half before she went to her parent's home and found her mother sprawled on the floor in a pile of laundry.

She lost everyone she would have confided in, in one fell swoop. Her fiancé, her best friend, and her mother. And now her father was trapped in the closets of his own mind, existing in a reality where her mother had not died a tragic death. Part of Dru wished she could live in that reality, too. She wanted to get lost in a place where none of this had happened and no one had abandoned her.

Both Anya and Deven seemed to have a firmer grip on their lives, or at least, they were better at faking it. Sometimes she wanted to confide in Anya, her only big sister, but Anya had never been good at not judging. When Dru ended up on her doorstep, broken into a million pieces, Anya took that opportunity to remind her that she was too young to be married anyway. She stayed on her couch for a few days until she could no longer stomach the lectures.

She never told either of her siblings why the engagement ended. She wanted to talk to her mom first, who always knew exactly what to say to make everything seem like it would work out. Dru kept it to herself at first, preferring to lick her own wounds rather than worry her family, but she finally cracked and was planning to talk to her mom that day after her mother returned from her much-needed hair appointment.

Life clearly had other plans.

Maybe that was why she was confused and a bit jealous of her siblings. It seemed like they were handling their mother's death much more gracefully than she was. Like Dr. Hatcher reminded her, they weren't the ones to find her the way Dru did but even still. It felt like life kept knocking her down. Growing up, her mother constantly repeated that cliche when things got tough: God gives the largest battles to His toughest soldiers.

But when did she sign up for this war?

After sufficiently embarrassing herself in her therapy session, Dru picked up a call from Roya on her way home. Dru heard the familiar buzzing of the tattoo gun in the background. Roya was probably still in the shop.

"Can we talk about how I threw myself at my therapist like a trashy hoe from a bad BET movie?" Dru groaned into the phone. She pulled her car out of the parking lot and headed toward her apartment.

"You did what?" Roya laughed, disbelief coating her voice.

"Please don't laugh. I'm already mortified."

"Sorry, okay, tell me what happened. Spare no details." Roya replied. The buzzing grew louder. Dru sighed, hoping that whatever client Roya was working on couldn't hear her.

"Things have been spiraling out of control lately. Dad isn't doing well. Anya is still nagging us about pitching in, and Deven got some random girl he's been with pregnant."

"And you met a gorgeous man that laid down the pipe, and you let him slip away. Right?" Roya added. She pushed when Dru didn't respond. "Right?"

Dru sighed loudly, regretting that she had told Roya about Kenan in the first place. She had hoped to put him out of her mind with everything else she had going on, but Dru couldn't help wondering if he had actually shown up to the club that night like he said he would.

"Fine. And I met a gorgeous man that I let slip away," Dru conceded, "But anyway, I was in my session with Dr. Thatcher, and I threw myself at him."

"Physically or sexually?"

"Roya!" Dru laughed, rolling her eyes.

Roya chuckled. "Sorry, sorry. I'll be serious. Did he take the bait?"

"No, but that's not even the point. I didn't even want him to take the bait. He's attractive, sure. But I don't actually have feelings for him."

Silence passed between the two of them as the tattoo gun buzzed quietly. Dru waited, hoping her best friend would say something that made her feel better.

"It sounds to me," she began, "that you felt out of control and were looking for a situation that you could control."

Dru sighed. That was precisely what Dr. Thatcher had hinted at during the session. She was embarrassed at herself for being so reckless but thankful that Dr. Thatcher diddn't hold it against her. She was making too much progress to start over with a new therapist.

"I'm a mess."

"You're not a mess, best friend. You're just hurting. You lost a lot of people at one time."

Tears pricked at Dru's eyes at her best friend's words. She wiped at them frustratedly, not wanting to cry again after spending her session blubbering like a baby. She pulled into the parking lot and cut the engine. Instead of going home, she sat in the parking lot of Wimbledon Farms Nursing Facility.

"I should see my dad," she said quietly.

"You should." Roya agreed.

Dru glanced around, looking for her sister's car. It was still early. She probably still needed to make it here from work. Dru slipped out of the car and headed towards the door. It would be a quick visit and then she would go home.

"Here he is." the kind nurse said as she pointed in her father's room. Dru peered in to see him sitting at his desk, furiously typing on his computer. He glanced up when she walked in, his face blank.

"Hello."

"Hi. What are you working on?" Dru tentatively stepped into the room.

"I'm working on something to help my wife. She has Alzheimer's." He mumbled, turning his attention back to the computer screen. Dru froze. Anya had mentioned that he was still thinking that their mom was alive and that she was the one sick.

Earlier on, when their dad kept denying that he was ill and projecting it onto their mother instead, they consulted the doctor with their concerns. It turns out that he had something called anosognosia. Not only did he have Alzheimer's, but her father also didn't realize he was the one sick. According to the doctor, he has no knowledge of being diagnosed with the disease.

"I'm sorry, who are you again? Are you a new employee?" her father asked, his face twisted in agitation as he stared at her. Dru swallowed, utterly unsure of what to do.

"No, I don't work here. I'm...I'm me. I'm Drusilla." She said in a shaky voice.

"Who?" He asked.

"I'm your daughter. Your youngest. I'm Rue," she replied, blinking away the tears that threatened to fall from her eyes. He paused, watching her. Dru held her breath, praying for a spark of recognition, even if it was small. Just something that would let her know that her father was still in there and still loved her. Time seemed to freeze around the two of them as she waited, with bated breath, for his answer. Finally, after what felt like an eternity, her father shrugged.

"Sorry, I don't know anyone by that name."

23

Anya

It was the first time their family had been together since their mother's funeral. Anya begged her younger brother and sister to come to dinner with her. They both reluctantly agreed to meet at Deven's restaurant after it closed for the night. He would make them something quick from what was available in the kitchen. Initially, Anya was excited to finally see Dru and Deven, but chronic exhaustion had become an old friend. It settled into her bones like it was coming home after a long trip. She wanted nothing more than to crawl into her bed and sink into a deep, dreamless sleep.

She had just come from visiting their father; as usual, it had gone the same. He still thought she was his assistant, but now he was talking about something called The Memory Concierge. She had no idea what it was, but it seemed to take over their father's every thought. She googled it sneakily, and something about a medical trial popped up. But it was nothing substantial - nothing that warranted her father's all-consuming obsession with it.

The three of them sat at a table, waiting for the food. Anya's stomach let out a loud growl, reminding her that it had been a while since she'd eaten anything. She smiled at her little sister, wanting to say something but unsure what. Deven's head cook exited the kitchen carrying three plates of jumbo lump crab cakes. It was their father's favorite dish here at Le Fugue. He claimed that Deven's restaurant was the only one that used real crab instead of imitation. Anya didn't think this was true, but she wasn't one to burst anyone else's bubble.

She glanced at the two of them. Deven kept pulling out his phone to answer text messages. Dru was chewing on her bottom lip, wholly preoccupied with whatever she was thinking about. At this moment, Anya realized she had no idea what her brother and sister had going on in their lives as of late. She had been so absorbed in their father's care that she didn't have time for anything else.

"I'm sure you two are wondering why I've gathered you here today," she started. Both of them shot her a weird look. "I feel like we have drifted apart since Mom passed, and Dad is-"

"Lost in his own version of reality?" Deven offered. Anya and Dru both glared at him; he shrugged.

"We haven't spent much time together recently. I feel like I don't know anything about you two anymore." Anya took a bite of her crab cake and resisted the urge to let her eyes cross in delight. It was delicious. She had to admit that sometimes she was jealous of how well her little brother could cook. Their mother taught them a few things, but Deven had really taken to it. When he told the family he was going to culinary school, Anya thought there wasn't much of anything he could learn that he didn't already know. His current knowledge of culinary arts proved her wrong.

"Have you told her yet?" Dru asked, looking pointedly at Deven. Anya glanced between them, suddenly hurt that they had things they talked to each other about and not her. Deven shot Dru a look and shrugged again.

"It's not a big deal," he said, staring at his plate.

"Not a big...?" Dru started. She rolled her eyes and turned to look at Anya. "He got his girlfriend pregnant." Anya almost choked on her food. Pregnant? Girlfriend? Since when was he even dating anyone?

"I didn't realize you were seeing anyone," she said, trying to recover from the shock. He wouldn't meet her gaze. Instead, he kept it fixed on his plate. Anya remained silent, waiting for him to respond. The silence was uncomfortable.

"It's still new," he mumbled, still not looking up. "I was going to tell you; I just needed some time to process." Anya watched him for a moment. He was the spitting image of their father, especially from the photos she had seen when their parents were younger. Part of her ached for her mother's advice. What should she tell her brother? As the oldest, shouldn't she be the one with the sage advice? The one her younger siblings would turn to when they needed a wise opinion? She didn't know the first thing about raising children or being a parent.

"Why didn't you say anything?" she asked. Dru knew before she did; if she was honest with herself, that hurt. She always prided herself in being someone her family could count on. Deven glanced up at her with an expression on his face that resembled a smirk.

"You're kind of judgmental, sis. Let's be honest," he replied. Dru snorted.

"No, I'm not!"

They stared at her for a moment and then burst into laughter. She felt hurt, but she let it slide. Anya was opinionated, but that was only because she wanted the best for her baby brother and baby sister.

When Dru noticed that Anya wasn't laughing along with them, she placed a hand on her arm. "Don't be upset. The oldest always thinks they're the third parent." Anya glanced over at her but didn't respond. Dru cleared her throat to break the awkward silence that had fallen over them.

"I met a guy the other day," she started. "He is my friend Bryce's older brother."

"Dang. Bryce has been pining after you for years, and you haven't given him the time of day. But you entertain his brother? Ruthless." Deven laughed. He sat back in his chair and pushed his now empty plate away. Dru stuck her tongue out at him and rolled her eyes. It was true. The few times Anya has seen Bryce and Dru in action, the poor guy swooned the entire time. She was surprised when Dru chose Tarik over him instead. Bryce turned into a heart-eyed emoji around her. Most men did.

"I'm glad you're getting back out there after-"

"I kicked him out after we had sex." Dru blurted and then turned red. Anya and Deven both stared at her with their mouths slightly open. Neither one had expected her to say that - not if she was comfortable mentioning him. Dru never brought up a guy unless it was serious. Deven glanced at Anya and widened his eyes slightly.

"Why?" Deven asked. Dru shrugged and ran a hand over her face.

"I was having nightmares," she whispered, "and I panicked. I feel terrible." Dru had mentioned having nightmares about the day their mother died before, but Anya didn't realize how serious they were. It had been almost a year since she died. Anya naively thought she would have been over them by now.

"I'm working it out in therapy, but still, he was...he was special. I probably ruined it." She let her head drop in her hands. Her wild curls draped over her face and arms like a curtain. Anya felt so out of touch with them both. She wanted to be the sister with all the helpful advice, but as hard as she wracked her brain, nothing came out. Her thoughts were blank - wiped clean like a dry-erase board. She opened her mouth, desperately scanning her mind for something to say, but the words wouldn't come.

"Maybe you should just talk to him?" she said after a while. Dru groaned from under her hair. "I can't be that vulnerable with him. We just met!" she wailed. Deven tilted his head at his sister, even though she couldn't see him.

"He's already seen you naked, sis. I don't think you can get much more vulnerable than that."

"Emotional vulnerability and physical vulnerability are two different things." She waved a hand down her body. "I have no problem being naked in front of anyone. I mean, look at me." A look of disgust crossed Deven's face, but he said nothing. Anya admired her sister's confidence.

"Well, if you like him enough to tell us about him, then obviously, it's worth taking the risk," Anya said gently. Dru sighed loudly and lifted her face from under the thick curtain of hair. A warm feeling washed over Anya as she sat here catching up with her brother and sister about their lives. She had missed them more than she realized. She wished she could freeze time just to bask in the conversation that didn't somehow involve Alzheimer's. She knew it wouldn't last long, but it was just what her bleeding heart needed for now.

"How's dad?" Dru asked. The three of them had talked through all of the recent events in their personal lives. Dinner was finished, and now they were working on coffee and dessert. Anya sighed. She knew the conversation would end up here eventually. The exhaustion creeped out and planted on Anya's shoulders like a coat. Deven was looking down at his phone, furiously texting someone.

"He is obsessed with something called The Memory Concierge," she said quietly. Deven's head snapped up, and Dru raised an eyebrow.

"What?" they both said in unison.

"The Memory Concierge. It's supposedly some mythical creature that can restore Mom's memories," Anya explained with a shake of her head. Deven barked out a laugh and put his phone face down on the table in front of him.

"There was nothing wrong with *Mom's* memories," he said bitterly. "And besides, she's *dead!*"

"I know that!" Anya snapped, frustrated.

"Why are you entertaining this, Anya? Tell him the truth!" Deven's voice rose. Anya flinched and blinked away the tears that suddenly threatened to spill. She wanted to tell him the truth.

"The nurses-"

"They're not his family. You are! We are! You know that Dad hated to be coddled and talked down to when we were growing up. Letting him live in this fantasy world is cruel." Deven pushed back from his chair; Anya was surprised at how angry he seemed about it. Dru sat quietly, letting her two older siblings argue. Anya wanted to disappear. She wanted to be able to snap her fingers and be back in her own home in comfortable pajamas instead of dealing with this. Her anger bubbled up under the initial shock of Deven's outburst. She stood, ignoring the loud scrape of her chair against the floor.

"How dare you!" she exclaimed, "When was the last time you went to see him? Or even called him on the phone? I am there every day with him. Every day! And where are you?!"

Deven blinked, stunned. He didn't expect Anya to respond that way. She spent their lives being the one that took the bull and shouldered the burden with a quiet smile on her face. Anya was always the one that stayed calm no matter what was happening. But now, she was tired of being calm. She was tired of shouldering the entire burden and being the punching bag when they disagreed with her choices. She was tired.

"Maybe I'm not as strong as you." His voice fell. "I tried. When he first went to the nursing home, I tried. He looked right through me. I couldn't take it."

"His eyes were so empty the day Mom died," Dru whispered from her seat. Anya and Deven turned to face her; they had forgotten she was there. She'd let the two of them argue without saying a word. Anya's heart squeezed. She had been so wrapped up in everything else she never stopped to consider that maybe her brother and sister were hurting in their own way. She reached over and put an arm around Dru. Tears slipped down her baby sister's cheeks.

"That look has haunted me since that day. I went to see him in the nursing home a few days ago after my last therapy session," she said, wiping her eyes with the heel of her palm. "He told me that he didn't know me."

"I didn't realize you two had even been to see him." Anya was crying now too. She was feeling raw and overwhelmed with emotion. Dru rested her head on Anya's shoulder. Deven crossed his arms and leaned against the bar behind him. He looked like he was barely holding it together himself; his eyes glistened with unshed tears.

"I'm not as strong as you, Anya. Dad was my hero. To see him waste away into...into" tears slipped down his cheeks. He swiped angrily at his face and sniffled. "It's too much."

Anya looked at him, seeing the little brother she had grown up with -

the sensitive, big-hearted boy that craved approval from his father. The little boy that hung on his dad's every word. The teenager and the young adult had gone to their dad for advice before all the big moments. Her heart broke for him.

"You don't think it's hard for me? Having to pretend that he's not my father? Listening to him talk about mom as if she isn't already dead?! It's hard! Unbelievably hard!"

"You don't have to! You can tell him the truth, but you won't do it. You keep him in the dark. How is that fair to anyone?" Deven demanded.

"I'm protecting him!" she yelled. Her voice cracked from the volume change. If their father knew the truth, he might give up. She couldn't stomach the idea of losing both of her parents. Deven scoffed and shook his head.

"No! You're protecting *yourself!*" He spat the last word out with so much venom Anya took a step back as if she had been smacked. She turned to Dru, who cowered in her seat like a small child.

"Is this how you feel too?" she asked her sister. Dru cried harder and reached for her, but Anya stepped out of her reach, emotions making the air in the room thick. Anya had come here, hoping to reconnect with them, but instead, she felt as if she were being ganged up on.

She had done what she thought was best in the situation, and maybe it wasn't the right decision; perhaps she should have made a different choice, but she made a choice! Anya wasn't the one to stick her head in the sand and block it out because it was too hard to deal with. Their father needed someone to be there for him, whether he remembered them or not. She was the only one who had been there for her father while the two of them were busy making a mess of their personal lives. Angry tears blurred her vision.

"I am not perfect, but at least I'm there! He needed us, and neither of you could get past your feelings to be there for the man who raised you!"

"Anya..." Dru whispered. Anya held up a hand to cut her off. The two of them watched as she angrily snatched up her purse and phone. She stomped towards the restaurant's front door but then turned on her heel to face them again.

"Until you two show up, instead of using your fear as an excuse, you have no right to tell me how to care for our father." Her voice was quiet and firm. She swallowed, so they couldn't hear the pain she was feeling. Neither one of them responded. For a moment, it was a standoff. Deven stood with his arms folded, looking like a much younger but equally as stubborn version of their father, and Dru sat planted in her seat, her face contorted with conflicting emotions and pain. Anya looked at them both for a moment, her heart cracking and splitting open in her chest, and then shook her head in disgust.

The sound of the bell chiming over the front door as she left was the only noise in the room.

24

Deven

She stormed out and left you guys there?" Camila asked, her voice was stunned. Deven had just finished filling her in on that disastrous dinner he had with his sisters a few nights ago. They were currently on the way to Camila's ultrasound appointment. He couldn't sleep at all the night before. The conversation at dinner, plus the excitement for the appointment, kept him wide awake and staring at the ceiling all night.

Deven was nervous, his hands trembling slightly as he gripped the steering wheel. He used the drama from his family to distract him, recounting the events, hoping that his girlfriend could shed some light on what his sister could have been thinking. Even though he had been outnumbered by women in his home growing up, he still felt he did not understand how their minds worked. Anya said that he and Dru had no right to speak on her decisions for their father as if she was the only one who cared about his well-being. That comment stung. Even though the dinner was a few nights ago, he couldn't get it off his mind.

"Yeah. It was awful. She's being selfish. She won't listen to anyone else when it comes to Dad." He shook his head. When Camila didn't respond, he looked over at her, confused. "What?"

"She has a point," Camila shrugged. He glanced in her direction to see her staring straight ahead. His first instinct was to protest, but he remained quiet, letting her continue. "You and Dru don't contribute anything to his care. You don't really have the right to get upset about it if you're going to sit back and let her do all the work." Her words stung. Deven knew she had a point, but it still hurt to hear her say it. He focused on the road, preferring not to continue the conversation.

When they arrived at the doctor's office, his hurt was replaced with nervousness. He had no idea what to expect. As Camila checked in and offered the front desk clerk her insurance information, Deven glanced around at the other couples in the waiting room. Some were clad in sweatpants and hoodies, looking more like they had just rolled out of bed than purposely dressing for the occasion. He looked down at his outfit, dark blue jeans with a buttoned-down shirt, suddenly feeling overdressed and overwhelmed.

"Are you okay? You look pale," Camila whispered, sitting down next to him. No, he wasn't okay. He was beyond terrified. Deven had no idea what to do with a kid. He had never even babysat before. At most, his interactions with children began and ended with kids that came into the restaurant. He would smile at them and bend down to their level before speaking, but that was always under the watchful eye of their parents. If they cried, someone else was there to handle it while he awkwardly backed away out of view. Now, people would expect him to handle it. How do you tell the difference between a food cry and a wet diaper cry? Instead of divulging any of this in the middle of the crowded waiting room, he turned to his girlfriend and forced a smile.

"I'm fine." He avoided her concerned gaze and busied himself with checking in on the restaurant. He recently hired a new manager to help him run both locations. He was a man close to Deven's age with a passion for management. Deven interviewed him a few months ago and was impressed with his resume. Plus, he was a black man, and Deven always looked for opportunities to put his people on however he could. It was a sense of community that his mother and father had drilled into his and his sisters' heads since they were little. You have to look out for your own. His mind drifted to when he was younger, talking to his dad about his dreams of opening a restaurant one day.

"You've got to stay focused. You can't take your eyes off the end goal for a second. The minute you do, you get distracted. You can't do big things if you're distracted by small things." He had said. At that moment, Deven had nodded, not really taking any of what his father said to heart. He was young and was only concerned about making the drawings of his dream place look as cool as possible. But now, the words pinged around in his brain. Did this count as a distraction? Would his father have been proud or disappointed? His parents were traditional when they were both alive and in their right minds. They likely would have expected him to marry Camila, just like Dru asked. He loved her; he knew that much, but marriage? That was a big step, no matter how much Deven cared about her and loved being in this relationship. When he thought she was breaking up with him, he was devastated. But did that mean marriage?

He turned to look at Camila, taking in the stretch of her nose and the smoothness in her skin, the loose curl pattern of her hair that hung well past her shoulders. She always smelled like a combination of vanilla and roses, something that he never thought would work together, but it somehow did on her skin.

"Where is your head at, babe?" she asked. He blinked, realizing she was looking at him while he stared at her and daydreamed. He nodded, reaching for her hand. He brought it up to his lips for a soft kiss.

"Let's get married," he whispered gently. He was only half joking. Her eyes widened. The couple sitting within earshot glanced at each other, a knowing expression on their faces.

"Married? What? Deven, you can't possibly be serious!" she hissed, casting an embarrassed look at the couple. They said nothing, but out of the corner of his eye, Deven saw them scoot a little further down on the bench like they were trying to increase their distance and give them privacy, or maybe they wanted to get away from the argument.

He gave Camila a sheepish grin. "I know it's a lot, but why not? We're already having a baby together."

"This isn't the fifties, Deven," she scoffed. "We'll talk about this later when we're not in the middle of a waiting room." He had imagined a different reaction, one with more excitement. He pulled out his phone and sent a quick text to his best friend.

I asked Camila to marry me. He typed. It took a few seconds for the text bubbles to appear under his message.

You proposed in the doctor's office?

Yes. I asked in the waiting room. The bubbles popped up and disappeared. In the distance, Deven heard Camila's name being called and felt her shift beside him. They both stood and followed the nurse back for the appointment. As they settled into their room to wait for the OBGYN to come in and start the visit, his phone vibrated in his pocket. His buddy had texted back. He pulled it out to look at it, hoping his friend had something to say to calm his nerves about the situation.

You are an idiot.

The appointment went well, and the baby was developing as it should. Still, Camila's face was pinched and uncomfortable throughout the entirety of the doctor's visit. Deven stayed quiet as they drove back to his apartment. He had time to think since he blurted out his marriage proposal, and now, he felt embarrassed, but that didn't mean he wanted to take it back.

"Explain yourself," Camila said, her voice tight.

Deven hesitated. "Well, we love each other, and now we have created life to bring into this world. Why not bring that child into a stable home?"

"Marriage doesn't guarantee a stable home, Deven."

"That's true, but still… we could be...a family." His voice cracked on the end of the sentence. Camila paused and he could feel her gaze burning a hole in the side of his face. Minutes passed without her saying a word. She stayed quiet so long he thought the conversation had ended. His mind drifted to a mixture of baby names and ideas for the restaurant.

"This baby and I can't be a replacement for your family." Her voice was quiet and matter of fact. Her words surprised him. He gazed at her face, narrowing his eyes slightly as he picked through the first batch of responses to find the appropriate one.

"What is that supposed to mean?"

"Your family is going through it right now. You lost your mother last year; your father is struggling with Alzheimer's, and you don't see eye to eye with your sisters. You don't think that has something to do with why you suddenly want to get married?" She folded her arms across her chest. "You're trying to replace them with me and the baby so you feel less guilty about not stepping up like you were supposed to."

His first reaction was to deny it. Deny, deny, deny. He opened his mouth to protest, but the words seeped into him and settled in his heart.

He had been feeling guilty, although he hadn't voiced it to anyone. Was he trying to replace his family? At first glance, it seemed absurd. He wanted to marry Camila because he loved her and she was currently carrying his child, but the closer he looked at the situation, maybe she had a point.

"Is that so bad?" He asked.

"Getting married can be something we revisit in the future, but I don't want to be used as an excuse to not fix things with your family. Just sort it out because if you don't, that regret will eat at you for the rest of your life."

He pulled into the parking lot of his apartment complex and turned off the engine. He had no idea what to say. In his mind, he knew he needed to see his father. It was an uncomfortable situation, but the guilt that was building up from avoiding him for so long had gotten heavy. It settled on his shoulders and walked with him through every day. While he was at the restaurant or lying in bed with Camila, a little voice in the back of his head would scream at him to see his father, or yell at him to try to help Anya with the responsibility. He may have disagreed with how she'd chosen to handle things but, it wasn't fair to her to try and control the narrative without putting in any effort.

Camila reached up and cupped his face with her hand. He gazed into her eyes, feeling his heart swell with affection for the mother of his unborn child. "I do want to marry you," she whispered. "Just sort your family drama out first."

Together, they headed into his apartment to relax for the night. Camila brought an overnight bag so she could sleep over. He wanted to start looking at bigger places; his one-bedroom apartment wouldn't be enough for the three of them. While Deven cooked dinner, he thought about his older sister and how tired she looked the last time he saw her. His mother looked exhausted in the same way, and he was so fixated on his own thing that he didn't stop to ensure she was okay. When Dru called him hysterical and crying to tell him that their mom was gone, a wave of remorse washed over him. It felt like his entire world tilted on its axis.

He stuck himself headfirst into his businesses, using the restaurant to cope with the loss, and tried to stomp the pain down and out of sight. He figured if he stayed busy and worked himself until he was too tired to function, he wouldn't have to think about how his heart ached for his mother. He wouldn't have to acknowledge the grief and regret that took him over whenever he thought about her last days with them. Hindsight is 20/20, and if he had known what was getting ready to happen, he would have dropped what he was doing to see her. He'd give anything to be able to hug her one last time; to smell her honey and ginger-scented soap that she would get from her favorite little shop a few blocks from the house. Even today, the scent of honey and ginger makes him want to curl into a ball and sob.

What he didn't tell his sisters because he was too ashamed to admit it was that she had left him a voicemail two days before, begging him to come home and see them. He was so preoccupied with the restaurant that he sent the call directly to voicemail, telling himself he would call her back as soon as he got a moment. He listened to the voicemail in the middle of the crowded restaurant, with the noise of the place muffling the sound of her voice in his ears.

He'd forgotten about it after that, until days later when Dru called to tell him what had happened. He turned on his heels and walked out of the building without bothering to tell anyone where he was going and when he would return. Deven would only let himself react once he was home alone. That's when he pulled out his phone and listened to her voicemail again. There was a hint of desperation in her voice that he missed the first time. When he heard it again after her death, the exhaustion in her voice knocked him to his knees.

"Hi, Dee. It's mom," she had started, *"Look, I know you're busy, but I... I really could use some help with your father. He's starting to forget who I am and... I don't..."* there was a muffled sob, and then she blew out a breath. *"Come by as soon as you can. Come say hi to your mama. I miss you."* Two days later, she was dead. Sometimes, that voicemail played in his head at night when he was trying to sleep. He would kick himself for not dropping everything and running to be by her when she needed help. Now here he was, doing the same thing to his sister.

"Where's your head?" He had been so absorbed in his thoughts, using muscle memory to cook dinner, that he didn't notice that Camila entered the kitchen. He flinched in surprise, sending a droplet of the sauce onto the counter. He grabbed a towel and wiped it up before it could leave a stain.

"I think…" he said, stirring the sauce, "…that it's time I see my dad."

25

Drusilla

So, are you going to avoid my brother forever?" Bryce demanded. Dru groaned and rolled over in her bed. She had picked up the phone without looking to see who was calling. Big mistake. She assumed it would be Roya, who usually called on her way to work to vent about the other artists in her shop. Instead, it was Bryce, and he sounded annoyed.

"You're calling me," she pulled her phone back and squinted at the time on the clock, "at seven-thirty in the morning to talk about your brother?"

Bryce hmphed on his end of the line. She heard shuffling in the background as if he was moving the phone from one ear to another. "He's been here every night since you met, looking like someone kicked his puppy."

Dru sat up in the bed, shocked. She and Kenan had hooked up almost three weeks ago. She had gone on with her life, assuming she ruined her chance.

"What?"

"You heard what I said. My brother has been in here looking for you every night for almost a month. I wasn't going to say anything because I am still pissed that he got farther with you in one night than I have in the past five years, but I can't take it anymore. Come get him out of my club."

Dru smiled at the irritation in his voice. Even though Bryce had a crush on her, she had made it clear that she was only interested in friendship with him. He was okay with it, but that didn't mean he wouldn't bring it up every chance he could.

"Come to the club tonight and put him out of his misery. Please. He is bringing the mood of the entire building down."

"I made such a fool of myself that night," Dru said softly, embarrassed. She stared up at the ceiling.

"Well, whatever you did, it didn't stick. I'll see you tonight." Bryce hung up before she could respond. Dru thought about Kenan while dragging herself out of bed to prepare for class and then work. She had a new project for a selfie studio that was opening soon, an opportunity that only came around because of the work Bryce had let her do on his club.

Dru expected Kenan to return to the club the following night since he said he would, but she figured he would drop it when she had yet to show. It had taken all of her willpower that night not to just race down to the club at the last minute. Instead, she sat on her couch and absentmindedly flipped through Netflix, searching for something to watch.

There was too much going on in her life to entertain a relationship or even a situation-ship as much as he intrigued her. Her heart was still too broken and too fragile to let him in. She had thrown herself at her therapist to try and avoid being vulnerable. If that didn't scream, 'this girl has issues,' then she had no idea what did.

Her thoughts drifted to her father. On her 18th birthday, Dru brought a boy home to meet her parents. He was a boy in her senior class named Darien. She barely remembered what he looked like now, but she was head over heels for him then. Dru's world revolved around his every move, and she hung on his every word like most teenage girls around that age. In her eyes, her world began and ended with Darien.

He was her midnight moon and her morning sun. Deven and Anya ignored him for the most part, but her parents zeroed in on him, analyzing everything about him. Dru's father interrogated him like a detective most of the night. Darien squirmed around in his seat, obviously uncomfortable, but that only made her dad question him harder. Her mother was silent most of the meal, observing him quietly rather than participating in the questioning.

Later that night, after he had left, she pulled Dru aside and whispered: "I know you like him, baby, but that isn't the boy for you." She was so hurt then and was determined to prove her wrong.

Only about a month later, Dru discovered that he had been cheating on her the entire time they dated. She found out on Valentine's Day when they were supposed to go out together. He forgot to cancel and left her sitting outside on the porch, waiting for him to pick her up. When she called him, terrified that something terrible had happened to him, a giggly girl with a high-pitched voice answered instead. The girl told Dru he was with someone who made him happier and to let go of the idea that Dru and Darien would ever be together. He never even bothered to speak to her.

Devastated, she tried to hide in her room and cry it out, but both of her parents had noticed her sullen mood change. That night, her mother slipped into the room and crawled into bed beside her. She said nothing. She just laid next to Dru, allowing her presence to comfort her youngest daughter. While they lay there, saying nothing, her father knocked on the door holding a giant teddy bear and a balloon.

"What's this for?" Dru asked, wiping the tears from her cheeks. Her father shrugged and offered a sheepish smile.

"It's still Valentine's Day, and ending it on a sad note didn't seem right." He offered her the teddy bear and tied the balloon to her desk chair in the corner of the room. When her father turned back to face them, Dru caught a glimpse of the look he gave her mother. There was so much love and devotion in that glance that new tears began slipping down Dru's cheeks. She desperately wanted love like her parents. She wanted a man to look at her the way her parents looked at each other.

"Wait for the man who makes even the simple moments seem magical, Rue," Henry said. That moment, in her room, sandwiched between her parents, Dru felt more support and love than she had in the years leading up to it. There was barely enough room on her queen-sized mattress for the three of them. She snuggled up to her father and allowed him to swallow her in his arms like a forcefield, shielding her from the rest of the world. He didn't say much else. He never had much to say during the emotional moments. He just held her and let her cry for as long as she needed.

Dru always remembered that day. It was one of the few times she and her parents seemed to be on the same page. In the years before and following that moment, it felt like there was a crack in the earth around them, and each of them stood on the opposite side, reaching for each other but never quite able to touch. Dru loved her parents, and she knew in theory that they loved her too, but there was always so much distance between them.

Dru craved more of those moments with them but never knew how to say it – she never knew how to ask for it without feeling selfish or needy. Instead, she chose to suffer silently and sort through her demons alone.

Dru and her mother had grown closer as Dru aged, like most mothers and daughters do, but there was still so much left that she had wanted to tell her and so much she still had left to learn.

Dru felt robbed of special moments with her parents, deprived of the chance to make them proud. She was still trying to sort things out when her mother died, and now, her father was even farther away. He was in a place almost impossible to reach, which made her angry. It was irrational and unfair; she knew this already, but it didn't squelch her anger.

Deven and Anya had a different relationship with each of their parents, but Dru always felt like a castaway.and a misfit. She knew it was hard for her parents to relate to her growing up. She definitely hadn't made it easy on them; she just wished they hadn't given up so soon. Maybe Dru wouldn't have felt so much regret and anger towards them long before either had fallen ill. Deven would talk about how hard it was to look at their father and know he didn't recognize them, but that part hadn't bothered her so much. Her father never truly recognized her to begin with.

"You know, this entire thing screams Hallmark movie." Dru slid into the seat next to Kenan with a smile. She ignored the whoosh of giddiness she felt at the look of pure relief on his face when he recognized her. They had hooked up once… just once. There wasn't even much of a conversation that night, so there was no need for Dru's body to respond this way. It made no sense.

Kenan gave her a once over, taking in her outfit and letting his eyes linger on each part of her body. Her neck, arms, breasts, waist, and legs all sizzled under the heat of his gaze.

"You look beautiful," he replied, completely ignoring her joke. Dru blushed. She had almost chickened out again like she did the first night, but something in her pushed her forward. Maybe it was curiosity? According to Bryce, he had come to the club almost every night in search of her. In any case, her nerves were excited about seeing him again. So here she was. Dru leaned forward to give him a hug, taking in his scent. It was a spicy scent this time, with hints of amber. She briefly wondered what his cologne collection looked like.

"Thank you." She smiled, her voice breathy and flustered. "You look nice too." She gestured towards his outfit, a simple black sweater with dark jeans. "Is this cashmere?" She reached out and ran her hands along the fabric of his sleeve, feeling the quality of the material. The look on his face made her freeze and pull her hand away in embarrassment. "Sorry."

"No need to apologize. It's good to see you." Looking at him, Dru felt the room around them fade away. All she could focus on was how he looked at her like every word out of her mouth was a treasure. She had never been looked at like this before, not even by her ex-fiancé. It reminded her briefly of how her father looked at her mother. Dru pushed the thought away before it could take root. It was way too early to be comparing right now. She knew nothing about Kenan. The jury was still out on him.

Pace yourself, Dru chided inwardly. Nothing chased off a man faster than being desperate. Even if her heart yearned and ached for love and acceptance, she couldn't project her neediness onto Kenan. Not in the first real conversation, at least. Dru was so entranced in her thoughts that she barely registered her phone vibrating in her back pocket. She ignored it, choosing to focus on Kenan instead.

"I'm surprised you kept coming back," she said. "I figured you would be pretty much done after how I acted that night."

Kenan shrugged; his eyes never left her face. "I knew that whatever that was had nothing to do with me."

"How could you possibly know that?"

"I can see the way you look at me." He grabbed her hand and brought it up to his lips. She resisted the urge to close her eyes at the soft touch of his lips against her skin. "Like that." He grinned at her triumphantly.

Embarrassed, Dru snatched her hand away and turned her head. She tried to reel in her emotions, but this man spun her insides to jelly. Her phone vibrated in her pocket again, but she narrowed her eyes at Kenan instead.

"I don't know what you mean."

"I think you do, but that's fine. If you want to feign ignorance, that is up to you. Just know that I can wait."

"For how long?" she countered, looking away again. He paused, reached forward to place a gentle hand under her chin, and turned her face back towards his. She reluctantly met his gaze, willing herself not to cry.

"I've been in this club every night since we met, hoping to run into you. I'll wait for however long it takes." He patiently held her gaze. His words made Dru emotional in a way she couldn't quite understand. She somehow felt a connection to him, like he understood her before she explained herself. He knew the song of her heart before she even sang it to him.

She wanted to hug Kenan and thank him for not giving up on her, but she also wanted to turn and run. Instead, she sat where she was, too scared to breathe in fear that she would find out that she had been sleeping and this was just a dream. She wanted it to be real. She needed it to be real.

"I came to tell you that I am damaged. You're better off with someone else, and you should stop wasting your time on me." Even as she halfheartedly said the words, Dru prayed that he would see past them. He made a face and leaned forward on his barstool.

"Everyone in here has been damaged by life in some way. Does that mean that they are somehow less worthy of love?" He waved a hand. "Perfection doesn't exist. A life without scars and bruises is not a life actually lived." She stared at him, unsure of what to say. There were enough bruises on her heart to last a lifetime, maybe two. "Why me?" She asked.

"Why not you?" Kenan leaned forward, closing the distance between them, and softly kissed her lips. His kiss made her entire body grow weaker yet stronger simultaneously.

Wait for the man who makes the small moments seem magical. Her father's words rang in her head. At the time, she didn't know what he meant. It seemed like something that belonged in a movie or a book… something make-believe like a fairytale. Something that couldn't possibly be real. But as Dru sat in the club, kissing this man she had barely been on one date with, the floor felt like it was opening to swallow her whole. But before she could sink, Kenan wrapped his arms around her waist and pulled her closer. Dru felt like she was finally beginning to understand what her dad meant.

"I'm sorry," she said breathlessly, breaking away from his intoxicating kiss. Her phone had been vibrating consistently in her pocket, distracting her from thoroughly enjoying the moment. She reached for it while Kenan signaled to the bartender to refill his drink.

Her lock screen was filled with texts, missed calls, and voicemails from her sister. Dru's stomach sank as she unlocked her phone and pulled up the voicemail option. Her sister's voice was increasingly frantic with each missed call.

Dru, it's Anya. Call me back. This is an emergency! Call me!

Drusilla Tubeck! For God's sake, where are you? I need you to call me immediately. Please!

Please! Call me. It's about Dad.

Dru's stomach dropped to her knees. Was he dead? It was too soon for that, right? Anya said he was doing well. Dru held up a hand to Kenan, signaling that she would be back in a minute. He nodded, his eyes filled with concern. Dru didn't have time to explain; she knew something wasn't right. She ran to the bathroom and checked to see if any stalls were occupied before calling her sister back. Satisfied that the bathroom was completely empty, she dialed Anya's number, praying that whatever was happening could be fixed. Maybe Anya was just being dramatic, and nothing was actually wrong. Dru's hands trembled as she dialed her sister's number. She quickly prayed, begging God to please make everything okay.

Her sister picked up on the second ring. Before she could speak, sobs echoed in Dru's ear. Her heart sank.

"Dru! Oh my God!" Anya sobbed. "I can't believe this is even happening!" There was a commotion in the background, something that sounded like a siren. Either the police or an ambulance. She couldn't be sure which.

"Breathe, sis. Tell me what's wrong," Dru replied, her voice belied a calm that she did not feel. Anya took in a few air gulps but couldn't control her crying. The sound of her sobs brought tears to Dru's eyes, even though she had no idea what was happening.

"It's Dad. He's... He slipped out of his room sometime last night when they were short-staffed, and none of the nurses could locate him. They have no idea where he went. He's gone!"

26

Anya

Mrs. James?" The nurse's voice sounded nervous. Anya had stopped by to see her father on her way home from work as usual. She hadn't been able to stop by that morning because she woke up late and needed to head straight to work, but she made plans to stick around for a little longer that night. As soon as she stepped inside the building, she felt something was off. A police officer was milling about in the hallway, and the residents she could see in the front lobby seemed tense, worried. She headed to the front desk to sign in and smiled at the lady behind the counter. Instead of returning the smile, the lady glanced down at the name Anya had written and then turned pale.

"Yes?" Anya replied, her own nerves making her heart thump against her ribcage. The lady swallowed and looked down the hall, almost as if searching for backup. The Director of Nursing for the facility, Eleanor came out of another patient's room, spotted the two of them at the counter, and rushed over. Anya's anxiety soared even higher. The D.O.N was usually absent during the later hours.

"Mrs. James, oh! Hello! Can you come with me for a moment?" She ushered Anya into her office, where the police officer she had spotted earlier sat waiting. The walls were painted a rich emerald green with a woodsy brown trim. Family pictures dotted the walls and the space in front of her desk. Gap-toothed children in various stages of growth grinned back at Anya.

"I'm sorry that we are chatting under these circumstances," she began, "I can assure you that we are doing whatever we can to rectify the situation." Eleanor paused; her lips pursed as if she wasn't sure how to phrase what she needed to say. Anya's heart was in her throat. Was something wrong with her father?

"I'm afraid... your father slipped out of the facility early last night. We haven't been able to locate him. He's had a decent head start, but I can assure you he hasn't gotten far." Anya stared at Eleanor wordlessly; her brain felt like it was overheating.

Eleanor continued to talk, but her words sounded like they were being warped and distorted; Anya felt like she had been submerged underwater. The ground had opened up and swallowed her whole. Her mind was reeling; her dad didn't seem all that lucid lately. Every time they spoke, his conversation drifted to that Memory Concierge thing - whatever that meant. He told Anya that he was going to find it. At the time, Anya had just shrugged it off, thinking that he would be safe behind the walls of the nursing home. Plenty of nurses and staff were here to keep an eye on him and determine his safety. Now, it looks like he wasn't safe here after all.

"My father is...missing?" Anya narrowed her eyes. "How does that even happen? Was no one watching him?" Eleanor blushed; the skin under the collar of her shirt flushed a bright pink.

"We are short-staffed. Yesterday, we had a lot of callouts, and we weren't able to make sure that-"

"So, my father just got up and walked out, and no one saw anything?"

"I know this is upsetting, and I completely understand if you want to take legal action. My biggest concern is making sure we find your father before...um- before he-" Eleanor blushed even brighter and swallowed nervously. Anya sat staring at Eleanor as she struggled to find the words. Tears pushed at the back of Anya's eyes and spilled down her cheeks. She could only imagine what Deven and Dru would say about her caregiving skills now. It had been a few days since that dinner. A few times, she wanted to be the bigger person and apologize, but her pride kept her from making the first move. She grabbed her phone in her back pocket.

"Do you have any idea where he could be? Where he could have gone? Has he mentioned anything recently?" The officer remained quiet at first but spoke up when Eleanor's voice faltered. His pen was poised above the small notepad he was holding. Anya blinked up at him, her vision blurry and unfocused. She needed to call her family. She needed to find her father. She needed to talk to Sullivan.

"Excuse me, I need a minute." Anya pushed herself up from her seat and left the room before either could respond. Henry mentioned Sullivan in passing, saying that he was the one that had told him about the whole Memory Concierge idea. Sullivan was a jerk and a creep. Sullivan often messed with other residents and gave the nurses a hard time, especially the younger ones.

Anya could see right through his prickly exterior. He was a lonely old man with no friends or family to visit him. When he wasn't tormenting others, Sullivan spent most of his days in his room watching old movies by himself which is exactly where she found him now. He looked up when she burst in, and the look of guilt on his face told her everything she needed to know.

"Sullivan, what have you done?" she hissed, glowering at him.

He cowered under her glare. "Look, before you get crazy, I can explain."

She wanted to throttle him, but instead, she calmly closed the door behind her and sat on the chair near his bed.

"Tell me everything. Start from the beginning."

Anya typed a frantic text to her siblings while Sullivan talked. She called them before he started his story, but they didn't answer. Typical. She left voicemails. She sent texts but got no response. She was going to have to do this alone.

"Henry is confused. You know that. All the nurses beg us to play along with his foolishness like they do with most of the crazy patients. I don't know why they get the special treatment when the rest of us don't get to live in our fantasies," he scoffed. Anya narrowed her eyes at him, and he cleared his throat awkwardly.

"Sorry, um...there's a new drug out for what he's got. I told him about it and that he needed to get on the list for the trial. He kept rambling about his wife and how he wouldn't give her any experimental drugs - ain't she dead anyway?" He looked at Anya with his head tilted, asking the question. She confirmed with a curt nod.

"Anyway, I told him about the guy that administers the medication during the trial. Some doctor does the work under the table because they can't get approval from the FDA. Something like that. They were calling him a memory assistant or a memory collector. I can't remember the word. "

"Concierge?" Anya offered, annoyed. Sullivan clapped and pointed at her. "Yes! Concierge. Exactly! I figured that would be the end of it, but he kept pushing me for details. He offered to pay me."

"You were taking money from my father?" Anya demanded.

Sullivan's eyes widened, and he threw his hands up, trying and failing to feign innocence. "He kept offering! What was I supposed to do?"

"Say no! You knew he was confused!" She yelled, her entire body shook with rage.

"Look, I ain't perfect, alright? I ain't proud of it, but I did it!" Anya took a deep breath and sent another text. Someone needed to answer soon. She didn't have the strength to handle this all on her own.

"He kept asking me where to find the concierge."

"And what did you tell him?"

"I told him he could find it in the abandoned hotel building in town. I didn't think he would actually go!" Anya balked at him; her mouth open in shock. Sullivan dropped his head in shame. Her phone vibrated in her pocket just as she stood to exit the room. It was Deven.

"Sis? You okay? Your voicemails sounded upset. Is Dad okay?" He asked hurriedly. Anya explained the situation to him in one breath. He was quiet, taking in every word as she talked. With everything he had going on, this was the longest she had held his attention in a while.

"I need your help, Dee. I can't deal with this alone. Luca is stuck at work still and-"

"I'm on my way." He hung up before she had a chance to respond. Dru called not even a minute later. Anya was so overwhelmed with everything that was happening that she could barely get the words out without crying.

"He slipped out of his room sometime last night when they were short-staffed, and none of the nurses could locate him. They have no idea where he went. He's gone!" She sobbed into the phone; she pressed her body into the wall and slid down, letting her legs give out from under her. A young couple heading to one of the resident's rooms sidestepped her, murmuring to themselves as they walked. She was sure that her family was the talk of the nursing home now.

Anya placed her head in her hands and continued to cry. She had vaguely registered that Dru said she would be on her way too. So many emotions bounced around inside her, and she couldn't seem to grasp any of them. She was worried about her father and she was chronically exhausted but under all of that, Anya felt relieved that her siblings were finally coming to help.

"Mrs. James?" a gentle voice asked. She glanced up at the sound, feeling slightly embarrassed for bawling on the floor in front of everyone. Eleanor crouched down beside her and rubbed a hand on her back, trying to be soothing. In any other circumstance, Anya would have appreciated the gesture, but she was so furious with everyone in the facility she wanted to shrink away and scream.

"Check the abandoned Newk Hotel," she whispered. "He could be in there." She placed her head back in her hands and let the exhaustion take over. There was a shift in movement beside her, and the officer that had been in Eleanor's office with them rushed out, speaking into the device on his shoulder.

All she could do was pray that her father was safe.

"Anya? Anya!" She heard a familiar deep voice. "Move, man! That's my sister." Anya didn't bother to lift her head. She had been curled into this position on the floor for what felt like hours, her body finally succumbing to exhaustion.

"Anya, hey. We're here. What's happening? Any word?" She slowly dragged her head up to see Deven, Dru, and some guy she had never seen before. He was attractive and standing unusually close to her little sister.

"Who is he?" she asked, ignoring the questions. She knew she was being rude, but she didn't have the strength to care at that moment. Dru glanced nervously at the man and offered an awkward smile.

"Kenan. I'll explain later. Have they found Dad?" Anya shook her head, tears welling up in her eyes again. Dru sat down next to her and wrapped her arms around her. Deven stood, looking around the room with an expression bursting with rage. He looked so much like their father in that moment that Anya wanted to reach up and hug him. It had been so long since she'd felt the support of her siblings. She was grateful to have them with her, even under these circumstances.

"I know you mentioned Dad being fixated on something called The Memory Concierge, but to this extent? To leave the nursing home?" Dru asked, shaking her head.

"Some medicines prescribed for Alzheimer's can cause intense hallucinations and visions," Kenan spoke up from where he stood leaning against the doorframe. All three of them turned to him. He shrugged sheepishly and smiled. "I'm a doctor," he admitted.

"You are?" Dru's mouth gaped open in surprise. Anya gave her a confused look. Wasn't he with her? How did she not know what he did for a living? The group gathered in their father's room, waiting for news from the officers that went to check out the hotel. Anya prayed as hard as she could that they would find him, and he would still be alive. She wasn't ready to lose him. Not yet.

They had been there for hours, waiting, hoping, and praying for good news. By now, Luca had gotten off work and rushed over. He scooped Anya up in his arms and held her as tight as he could as soon as he saw her. Deven sat on their father's bed, furiously texting on his phone while Dru and Kenan sat at his desk and looked through his search history.

"He's been on Google search engines typing in some variation of The Memory Concierge. Or the 'creature that can restore memories,' pretty much every day for the past few months." Dru said. "No one thought to check on this?"

"I didn't think he was serious. He hadn't mentioned it in a while. I didn't know." Anya shook her head, her voice breaking towards the end of the sentence. "I didn't know." Luca hugged her tighter and stroked her hair.

"She shouldn't have had to deal with this by herself. Both of y'all dropped the ball here." Luca said, looking pointedly at each of them. The anger in his quiet tone made Dru look up from the computer, and Deven put down his phone mid-text. Deven sighed heavily, shaking his head.

"You know what, man?" he started as Luca braced himself, seemingly ready for a fight.

"You're right." Deven waved a hand at Dru and then looked at Anya. His expression was remorseful. "Dad has always been my hero. Seeing him deteriorate like this has been harder on me than I realized, but that's no excuse. I'm so sorry."

"I was angry at him," Dru admitted, "we never really connected while I was growing up, and now...it feels like we won't get that chance." Kenan looped a large arm around her shoulders. Anya stared at her siblings, shocked that they were apologizing. Anya felt terrible for assuming they weren't coming around because they didn't care. The three of them may not always see eye to eye, but Anya knew better than to think they were being heartless.

"I'm sorry too. I know I haven't made things easy for you guys to come to talk to me." She unfolded herself from Luca's embrace and reached for her brother and sister. Dru grabbed one hand, and Deven held the other. Anya's heart swelled, even amid the tragedy; finally, feeling like they were all on the same page for the first time in a long time was beautiful. She missed them.

A sharp knock on the door interrupted their bonding moment. All of them turned towards the noise. A police officer, different than the one that had been there earlier, stood at the door. Anya's heart dropped to her knees.

"Are you all the family of Henry Tubeck?" He asked. Anya nodded and stepped closer, daring herself to hope.

"We dispatched a few squad cars to the area you suggested." The officer smiled gently; his eyes tired. "He's at the hospital being treated, but we found him. Your father is alive."

27

Deven

The officer's words made Deven's knees give out. He sank to the chair nearest him and blinked at the ceiling, trying to keep his tears at bay. His father was alive. He was safe. Anya let out a choked sob and collapsed into her husband's arms. Dru quietly put her head in her hands; her shoulders shook imperceptibly, letting Deven know she was crying. The man she had called Kenan wrapped an arm around her shoulders, trying to comfort her. Deven observed the two of them, mentally noting the questions he was going to grill her with later.

She had invited this strange man into their family business, giving him full access to their most vulnerable moments. It felt like an invasion of privacy, but it wasn't his place to demand that the strange man leave. Dru seemed to want him here, and Anya hadn't mentioned anything even though Deven had caught her staring at him curiously more than once.

Deven briefly wished he had asked Camila to come, he had been texting her with updates, but she didn't been feeling well that day, and he didn't want her to risk her or their baby's health. But Deven could really use a hug from her right now. He crossed his arms to wrap himself in an attempt to self-soothe and steady his shaking.

"Was he hurt?" Anya asked after a moment. The officer cleared his throat and looked around the room at everyone gathered. Deven briefly felt terrible for some of the other residents in this facility who didn't have the same amount of people that would pull up ready to burn the building down on their behalf. Living in a nursing home had to be lonely, even though it was full of people constantly. Anya filled him in on the man, Sullivan, partially responsible for this mess. She told them all that he had no family to visit him. At first, Deven didn't care and wanted him to suffer for what he had put their father through, but the more he thought about it, the sorrier he felt. Deven would hate to live in a place like this.

"When we found him, he was unconscious and bleeding heavily from the abdomen. It looks like he fell and cut himself open on a jagged piece of wood. The building we found him in is in dire shape. It's a wonder he didn't injure himself much worse. They took him to the hospital to assess his injuries and provide care." He looked around the room once again. "May I offer some advice?" They all stared at him expectantly.

"Sue this place. Sue them for everything they are worth and then some." He didn't wait for anyone to respond before turning on his heels and walking out. Deven looked over at his sisters, trying to gauge their reactions. Dru looked relieved, and Anya just looked tired. This was the first time he had looked at his oldest sister in a long time.

Deven recognized the same fatigue and exhaustion in his sister that he had seen in his mother. As they all gathered their stuff to head to the hospital, he vowed to do what he needed to protect his sister. Anya had shouldered the burden on her own for too long, and they all saw what happens when someone becomes so consumed in the care of others that they forget about themselves.

"We can all ride together," Anya offered quietly. Deven pulled out his phone to text Camila quickly to let her know what was happening. He smiled faintly at the picture of Camila smiling up at him from his lock screen.

They found him. On the way to the hospital now. May not be home until later. She had been staying with him recently, and even though they didn't technically live together, he loved coming home and seeing her there. He had been searching for somewhere they could move that had more space for their growing family. The text bubbles popped up almost instantly.

Thank God! Do you need me to be there? He hesitated. He wanted her there so badly but felt like it would be selfish to ask that of her when she wasn't feeling well. He glanced up at his sisters. Luca held Anya's hand and whispered to her as they walked out to the parking lot. Dru and Kenan followed behind. He had an arm protectively around her waist, and she leaned into him.

No. I'll be fine.

The hospital was crowded but quiet, filled with sadness and anxiety. Families huddled together in sections of the waiting room, hoping for the best and expecting the worst. Deven swallowed the lump in his throat, suddenly overcome with emotion he wasn't ready for. Anya headed to the front desk to find out the information for their father's room while the rest sat in the lobby looking forlorn and out of place.

"Hey Dee," someone softly whispered behind him. Deven turned to see Camila's face smiling down at him. He stood and wrapped his arms around her, bringing her as close to his body as possible. He took a deep breath, inhaling her familiar scent of vanilla soap.

"What are you doing here?" He murmured against her shoulder. Camila pulled back and looked at him.

"I could tell you needed me." She said it as if it was common sense. He hugged her again, resisting the urge to weep in the middle of this dreary hospital lobby. A soft wail grabbed his attention. The couple sitting in the corner nearest the window held each other for dear life. A young doctor stood over them, whispering something Deven couldn't hear. His heart broke for the couple; whatever news they received couldn't have been good. He and Camila sat, clasping each other's hands. He noticed Dru and Anya looking at him curiously, probably wondering if this was the girl he had been telling them about. He ignored them; introductions would come later.

"Are you the Tubeck family?" A young doctor in a blindingly white lab coat approached them. Deven took a deep breath, bracing himself for the worst. Anya stood and shook his hand.

"Yes, we are. How is he doing?"

"We are out of danger right now, but he has a long road to recovery. When he was brought in, he was bleeding profusely from the abdomen. We stopped the bleeding, but we had to sedate him. He was disoriented and confused." Camila squeezed Deven's hand. He was incredibly grateful that she decided to come; Deven felt like the longer he was here, the weaker he became.

He felt a new respect for his sister, seeing her absorbing the information from the doctor. His brain felt like mush, but Anya stood tall and confident like she had been in this situation before. No wonder she always looked like she had been awake for nights at a time. He felt horrible for leaving her to deal with their father on her own. As the doctor filled them in, explaining their father's situation and what he would need, Deven reached out and grabbed his sister's free hand. She glanced at him, surprised, but then her gaze softened.

"Can we see him?" Dru piped up from where she sat. Her voice was shaky and broken. She sounded like a little girl. The doctor nodded and offered a sympathetic smile.

"Yes. He's still sedated, but you can go in and see him. Just make sure it's only two of you at a time." Anya nodded toward Deven and Camila.

"You two can go first if you'd like."

"Are you sure?" Camila asked, looking unsure. Deven could tell that she felt like she was overstepping on a family moment. Camila's family had only consisted of her grandma until she passed away, so she wasn't used to this. Anya reached for Camila with one arm and reached for her brother with her free arm. Deven stepped into her embrace almost immediately. All of their tension and anger towards each other before this moment melted away in that embrace. He knew that was wishful thinking, and they still had work to do, but he was glad they found a way to reconnect.

"Yes, I'm sure. I'll probably be here for a while," Anya replied with a gentle nudge. Luca yawned beside her but nodded. Deven smiled, thinking about how Luca snapped at him and Dru earlier at the nursing home. He couldn't blame Luca for being pissed at them. Had situations been reversed and Camila needed help from her family, he probably would have done the same, if not worse.

He guided Camila into the hospital room where his father lay. Nerves twisted his stomach into knots. It had been a while since he and his father were in the same room. Deven used the distance he created between them to ignore the situation's seriousness. Out of sight, out of mind. If he never looked at or spoke to him, then Deven could forget how much his father had changed. He could pretend that none of it existed. He had become comfortable in his denial, and now that he was being forced to step out of it, his first instinct was to protest, to fight against the change.

When Deven stepped into the room, he froze. The small, frail body in the bed looked nothing like the father he remembered. He glanced at the name on the whiteboard to make sure he was in the correct room. His father's name was scrawled across the top in choppy handwriting confirmed that he was in the right place. Camila studied him as he stood, frozen in one spot.

"Go say hi," she whispered as encouragement when she noticed that he still hadn't moved. Deven took a shaky step forward, blinking away the tears that threatened to slip down his cheeks. He missed out on so much time with his father, time he would never get back.

Deven took another step. His father's dark, tightly curled hair was speckled with gray - even more gray than the last time he had seen him. His skin had a dull cloudy tint, and the muscles on his arms and legs looked emaciated and thin. His father was disappearing before his eyes, and he had been too busy trying to avoid him to notice.

"He's so thin," Deven whispered to no one in particular. Camila kept her distance, allowing him to have this moment with the man he had spent his childhood and teenage years looking up to and desperately trying to emulate. After looking up to him for so long, he was scared to face him in his vulnerability; Deven was terrified he would view his father as less than or smaller than he was. Standing there in the hospital room, listening to the machines beeping and the background noises from the nurses bustling around in the hallway, he only wanted to grab his father in his arms and apologize.

"Can he hear me?" Deven asked, turning to look at Camila. She shrugged and smiled at him sadly.

"Maybe. Maybe not, but there's no harm in trying just in case." Deven nodded; she had a point. He reached for his father's hand. It was clammy and cold, but he held onto it, praying that wherever he was, he could hear what Deven wanted to say for so long. Deven gave his hand a slight squeeze.

"Hey, Dad...it's me." He paused, hoping for a response, but when none came, he kept going. "I haven't been fair to you lately. I think...I think I've been punishing you for being sick." Deven swallowed the lump that formed in his throat, threatening to snuff out what he wanted to say.

"I don't know if you can hear me, but if you can, I just want you to know I love you." He glanced up at Camila, who smiled gently at him in return. Her curly hair was backlit by the light from the hallway. "And I'm sorry."

Deven thought about when their parents first sat him down to tell him about his father's diagnosis. He only half listened at first, more interested in scrolling through his DMs on Facebook than really hearing what was being said to him.

"Dee, your father has been diagnosed with Alzheimer's and Anosognosia," his mother had said. The sadness in her voice is what caught his attention. He looked up from his phone and gaped at his parents.

"What does that mean?" he'd asked, looking back and forth between his parents. His father had been sitting quietly, with his hands clasped tightly together as if he were praying. Deven looked at him, hoping to meet his eye, hoping he would explain that it wasn't as serious as it sounded and that everything would be okay in the end but he wouldn't look up.

"It means that your father is having trouble with his memory, and trouble understanding that he is sick. We're going to have to help him, understood? I know this is hard to hear, but we can get through it." His mother said, reaching for him. Deven skirted her grasp and shook his head angrily, not wanting to accept what was happening before him.

"I don't have time for this right now," he'd said.

The tears that had pushed at Deven's eyes since he first arrived at the nursing home finally slipped down his cheeks. Camila came to stand next to him, resting her head on his shoulder.

Deven stood over his father and wept. His entire body shook with each sob. He had been selfish. He understood that now. All the doctor's appointments he missed, and all of the phone calls he ignored; the text messages that he didn't answer were proof that he had put the people who raised him, the best way they knew how, last on the list of priorities.

He understood now why Anya had been so angry. That day, he promised his parents that he would be with them every step of the way. Deven didn't live up to that promise. At the time, he meant it wholeheartedly. Still, as time passed, the restaurant and his personal life took over the spot in his mind where his family should have been.

He had no idea when things switched, and he started putting *Le Fugue* before his family, but one day he looked up and realized he had no idea what was happening with his parents. When his mother passed, he promised himself that he would step up and do what needed to be done, but as soon as he took one look at his father in that nursing home, his heart couldn't take it.

As he stood there and watched his father, hooked up to all of the machines in a bed that almost completely swallowed his frail body, he realized that he had failed them. He failed Anya and Dru, he failed his father, and he failed his mother.

"I've been selfish lately," he began, his voice quivering as he spoke, "but I'm here now. I showed up. That's what family does."

28

Drusilla

Is he awake?" Dru jumped up as soon as she saw Deven and his girlfriend come out of their father's room. She could feel the heat from Kenan's stare. It was weird that he was here; she knew it, but deep down, she was glad he was willing to come. His presence was keeping her grounded, even if it was odd that he didn't have anything else to do.

Dru's heart sank when her brother shook his head. When she heard Anya's panicked voice earlier on the phone, her heart started thumping wildly in her chest. It hadn't stopped since. She knew that her father was at least safe now that he was at the hospital, but Dru wouldn't truly be able to relax until he opened his eyes. Even if he didn't remember any of them, she would find a way to figure the rest out as long as he was alive. She shot a quick glance in Kenan's direction. He was watching her; no, he was studying her closely. She felt almost as if she were under a microscope with the intensity of his gaze. He clocked her movements with a look that seemed ready to pounce at the slightest chance he could assist.

"I appreciate you being here," she whispered to him, patting his knee.

He placed his warm hand over hers and gave it a light squeeze.

"Of course," he whispered back with a smile. Even amid this upsetting moment, the sight of his smile made her knees buckle. She tried to keep her mind focused on what was happening around her, but whenever she looked at him, her mind drifted into distraction. Dru blinked and looked away. It was ridiculous to focus on anything other than her father right now. She felt embarrassed that her mind was elsewhere.

"Dru?"

She had been so caught up in her mind that she missed Anya asking her a question. When she brought her attention back to the room, everyone was staring at her expectantly.

"Hmm?" she asked, trying not to look like she was daydreaming in the middle of the hospital. Anya raised an eyebrow but didn't press.

"I said, do you want to go next?" she repeated with a bemused smile. Dru nodded and stood, swiping her sweaty hands on the front of her outfit. Kenan moved to stand, but she placed a hand on his shoulder.

"I'd rather do this alone. Will you wait for me?" He looked deflated, but he nodded immediately. Unlike Deven, Dru couldn't imagine bringing her -whatever he was- in to see her sick father. It felt like an invasion of the family's privacy. She knew that just having him here was pushing it a bit.

Dru took a deep breath and headed down the hallway to her father's room. The sight of him pale and small made her want to curl into a ball and sob. He had been larger than life for as long as she could remember. Now, he looked like he was being swallowed by the hospital bed, the blinding white sheets engulfing his thin frame.

She hadn't really seen him up close in a while. The last time she visited him in the nursing home, she was barely able to step entirely into the room. After that, she couldn't work up the courage to go back. All of that felt silly now. She gave so many excuses to keep the distance between her and the man who raised her while he wasted away in a nursing home. She felt ashamed of herself.

When her mother first told her about his diagnosis, she was supportive. She would research holistic medicines and foods to try. She would come over to help him exercise and ensure they were caring for themselves. As time passed and his mental capacity decreased, she started easing out the door, frantically searching for something else to do instead of witnessing his decline. She would have done more if she could go back and relive that moment. She couldn't help but wonder if she could have extended her mother's life by helping out more often.

Dru silently blamed her father for taking her mother away when in reality, her mother was so burnt out from taking care of everything herself without help from her children. Her cries for help were ignored or brushed aside until it was too late. Dru shook her head and pulled the one chair in the room up to the side of her father's bed.

"Hey, Dad. I've been a terrible daughter lately. I'm sorry." His hand twitched, but he made no other moves to acknowledge her presence. Dru let the tears flow freely; the emotions from the day were overwhelming.

"I was angry with you. It felt like you took my mom away from me. Your disease is so selfish. It takes everything from everyone it encounters. It siphons the air and the energy out of the room." She reached out and touched his arm, surprised at how cold his skin felt. "It's not your fault, and it was selfish of me to blame you for something you couldn't help. I shouldn't have been so mad at you for being unable to remember."

"Anya told me that you thought mom had Alzheimer's, and you were so hellbent on finding a cure for her that you snuck out of the nursing home." Even though she was crying, Dru smiled at the thought of her father being stubborn enough to chase after something like that. He was always ready to burn the world down for her mom without hesitation. Dru always admired that and wanted it for herself. Her thoughts drifted to Kenan. A man who she hadn't even gone out with yet but couldn't seem to shake out of her mind. The same man who grabbed his keys and was ready to run out the door with her when she said her father was in trouble. He hadn't even questioned whether she needed him.

"Wait, what are you doing?" she asked Kenan, watching him grab his things and pay the tab. She had come rushing back to where he sat after her conversation with Anya. She'd had every intention of rescheduling and heading out on her own but he nodded once and grabbed his things. At her question, he turned to her and gave her a funny look.

"Didn't you just say your family was in trouble?"

"Yes, but that doesn't mean-"

"Look, I can already tell that asking for help is something that you struggle with, so I don't plan on giving you a chance to ask. I'm just going to help." He jingled his keys. "I can drive so you can call your family and figure out what's going on without having to focus on the road." She stared at him in shock with her mouth open. She wanted to trust that he was just a good person, and it was finally her turn to experience real love, but part of her had trouble accepting it. It made Dru feel vulnerable and seen in a way she hadn't experienced before.

She stayed quiet the entire ride to the nursing home. Her brain was an indistinguishable bundle of emotions and thoughts. Was Kenan just genuinely this nice of a person, or was all of this just a big red flag? Was her father going to be okay? So many different questions bumped into each other, making the two sides of her world that she managed to keep separate for so long collide in a big bang inside her head.

The ease with which he slipped right into the family dynamic increased the questions' speed and intensity. When he admitted he was a doctor, it reminded her that she didn't know anything about him other than that he was Bryce's brother and unbelievably talented in the bedroom.

Now, she was vaguely aware that he was sitting in the lobby with her family at the hospital when they hadn't even gone out together. Had this been her friend, she would have asked: 'Girl, what are you doing? This is too much too fast!' But there was just something about him and the way he seemed to be able to sense what she needed that made her want more. A little sparkle of hope settled in her heart. She hoped this was long-term and not just a passing relationship. It was still too early to tell, but as she sat in this hospital room looking at her father's sickly body, she couldn't help but hope that Kenan would be her Henry and she could be his Clara. Her parents were madly in love from the moment they laid eyes on each other.

Growing up, she and her siblings used to shriek in disgust at any display of affection between the two of them, but Dru secretly loved it. She often caught her father staring at her mother in lovestruck fascination as she completed menial tasks around the house or told him about the surgeries she had assisted with during her days at the hospital. Dru used to watch the two, utterly content in each other's company. She modeled all her relationships after it, telling herself that if they didn't treat her like her daddy treated her mom, it wasn't worth it.

When her mother died, something inside her father snapped and broke off. Even with Alzheimer's clouding his reality of what was happening around him, it was like his body and heart knew that his person was no longer alive. His last grip on reality disappeared, and he was stuck in the loop of thinking her mother was the one with Alzheimer's. He was stuck thinking that she was alive and that he could help save her. Dru always wondered if this was regret manifesting itself as something else. She had been so angry at her father for not knowing what his diagnosis did to her mother, but maybe, deep in his subconscious, he did. Perhaps this was his way of trying to fix the situation, even though it was muddled and misguided.

During the funeral, he was in such a heavy fog that Dru was almost sure he had no recollection of it. At first, she wondered if his medications made everything hurt worse, but she realized now, sitting next to him in this room full of machines and wires, that it was love.

As cliche as it sounded, love was what severed his last grip on reality because that reality meant that he was genuinely alone- no more Clara- and his heart couldn't take it. In the little bit of research Dru had done on Alzheimer's, she read that sometimes, those who have it latch on to one person. That person becomes their everything. They sometimes become clingy and stick to their person like a shadow. Their mother was his person. Dru watched helplessly as his disease progressed. He went from being a man closed off in his affection to becoming needy, almost like a child. He went from being a physically intimidating man to a fragile one that would wet himself without realizing it.

The stress of the changes in her parents and their dynamic contributed to her backing out of helping with the care. It had become too much to see him following their mother around the house, unable to be without her for more than a few seconds.

It became too much watching him soil himself or struggle to remember to get dressed and be unable to recall simple information. Dru could tell it started to stress her mother out, but instead of voicing her feelings, she swallowed it and smiled through it, making it easier for everyone else to pretend it didn't exist.

The machines hooked up to her father, keeping him alive, beeped loudly. It was the only noise in the room other than Dru. She watched as his chest rose and fell.

"Dad?" Dru called gently. When he didn't respond, she nodded and leaned forward, hoping that maybe somewhere in there, her words could reach him. "Guess what?" She allowed herself to smile. "I met someone… someone great. He reminds me a lot of you."

When Dru was finally done visiting with her father, she returned to the lobby. She felt strangely lighter like she had purged herself of the guilt she was carrying for months. When she spotted the familiar faces of her family in the lobby, she stopped short. Kenan sat next to Anya and Luca. Deven and his girlfriend stood nearby, and Kenan seemed to be in the middle of a profound explanation about something. His hands moved animatedly, punctuating the words as he spoke.

"In my experience with a disease like this, sometimes the specific cocktail of medications can be revisited. Especially if the person is experiencing vivid hallucinations or delusions." Anya seemed to cling to every word he said. Dru raised an eyebrow, suddenly embarrassed.

"What did I miss?" she asked, looking at each one of them. Anya clapped her hands and smiled at her little sister while Kenan gave her a look that made her insides sizzle. She avoided eye contact with him and focused her attention on everyone else.

"Your boyfriend was giving us some amazing medical advice. Did he tell you that he works in this hospital as a neurosurgeon?" Anya's smile was mischievous. She already knew the answer to the question.

Dru had no idea that Kenan was a neurosurgeon. She wracked her brain, trying to remember if Bryce had ever mentioned it. Dru couldn't remember, but that didn't mean he hadn't. She had the tendency to zone out of conversations with him. The man could talk for hours without stopping to take a breath.

"No, I don't think we've had the chance to discuss it," Dru replied, risking a glance in his direction. As she feared, he watched her, studying her face with unsettling intensity. A smile tugged at the corners of his mouth. She wondered, if he was truly a neurosurgeon, how did he have time to wait for her at the bar for so long? Weren't those types of doctors notorious for working incredibly long hours? How old was he? She felt locked in his gaze; they didn't break eye contact until Deven awkwardly cleared his throat.

"I'm going to get Camila home," he said. Dru's gaze slid to Deven's girlfriend. They had yet to officially meet with everything that was going on. Camila gave her a small smile, and Dru returned it hesitantly. They would get a chance to meet later. "Make sure you call me if he wakes up. I don't care what time it is," Deven continued. A look of relief flickered in Anya's eyes.

"I will! Drive safely, you two." She gave Deven a hug and squeezed Camila's hand. When they left, whispering quietly to each other as they walked, Anya focused her attention on Dru. "I'm going to go visit with Dad." She shot a pointed look in Kenan's direction. "Clearly, you guys need to catch up," she chuckled. Dru smiled sheepishly.

Over Anya's shoulder, Dru spotted Luca and Kenan huddled over Luca's phone. If Dru knew her brother-in-law as well as she thought she did, Luca was most likely showing Kenan some of the latest photos he had taken. With a small wave, Anya turned, grabbed her husband, and headed toward their father's room. Leaving no one else there to use as a buffer between Dru and Kenan. He put his hands in his pockets and grinned at her. She folded her arms and narrowed her eyes at him.

"So, when were you going to tell me you are a neurosurgeon?"

Anya

Sue this place." The officer's words had been echoing in her mind since he said them. She felt conflicted about what she wanted to do. The nursing home had absolutely dropped the ball with her father. Anya was still having trouble wrapping her mind around him just getting up and walking out of the nursing home without anyone seeing him. He stayed gone for hours without detection until the next day. Even then, when they discovered their mistake, they failed to immediately notify her, hoping they could rectify the error before anyone noticed. The thought of her father wandering alone, confused and determined to find something that didn't exist, made her angry.

She wanted to see to it that Wimbledon Farms burned to the ground, but her empathetic side saw how stressed out the nurses were. They were short-staffed and struggling to keep up. Numerous times, Anya had come in looking to visit her father, and she spotted a nurse quietly crying in one of the empty rooms. It was a lot of work with not enough people there to help.

She understood how overwhelmed some of those nurses felt. She had been feeling it herself with the care of her father. It felt like she woke up one day, suddenly responsible for so many things that she had no idea how to do. Dru and Deven had gotten upset with her for not making decisions they would have made, and her husband fussed about allowing them to shirk their responsibilities by not stepping in.

Anya allowed too many people to dictate from the sidelines for too long. It's easy to point fingers without realizing how overworked and undervalued someone can feel. Luckily, Sullivan was willing to tell her where he had told her father to look for this Memory Concierge. Otherwise, who knows how long it would have taken to locate him?

Anya shook her head as she surveyed the hospital room. Her father in the bed looking limp and lifeless. The beeping of the heart monitors and the steady *pfft* of the ventilator were the only indicators that he was still alive. She wanted to be angry at him for putting himself in so much danger, but she couldn't bring herself to feel anything but relief and maybe some admiration. Her parent's relationship had always been full of intense support and love. She tried to model her marriage after the one true example of love she saw growing up. Luca was a fantastic man, but he couldn't hold a candle to Henry Tubeck's devotion to Clara Tubeck.

Even in his confused haze, she was his main focus. Part of Anya didn't want to correct him whenever he talked to her like a coworker because she would only see him come alive during conversations about his wife - her mother. He seemed so far away and out of reach every other time. Even though it made her heart ache for him to look at her with the reserved politeness that one would look at someone they weren't familiar with, she went through with it. Trying to explain that to Deven and Dru had been difficult.

At the time of their conversation, she didn't even have a good reason for not telling him the truth. She blamed the nurses, saying they begged her not to, but in reality, it was clouded by her selfish reasons. Anya could pretend that things were normal. She didn't have to face the heartbreak and devastation that crossed his face whenever she told him his reason for pushing forward was no more. She didn't want to tell him his sun and moon were gone.

The idea of there being a creature that could restore memories gave him something to focus on daily. He was so convinced of the existence of a Memory Concierge that she, for a moment, almost believed it herself. She would never admit it if someone were to ask her, but after his continual insistence that it was real, she had gone home and googled it herself. For weeks straight, she tried every word combination she could think of and came up with nothing other than the brief mentions of a medical trial that had no success.

She didn't have the heart to tell him it didn't exist, so instead, she would try to steer him in a different direction. She thought it was working, but clearly, it wasn't. Her father caught on to her diversion attempts and just stopped bringing it up entirely. Anya placed a hand on her father's arm and sighed. Luca hovered by the door, giving her the personal space she needed but would never have the courage to ask for.

"Daddy, why did you do this to yourself?" she whispered, even though she knew exactly why he had done it. A love that stretched beyond the boundaries and limitations of memory loss had guided him to the hotel that night. The guilt of knowing that caring for him sucked away the life their mother was supposed to live.

Even if he had been confused about the small details, one thing remained constant: no matter how far away he had gotten. Clara, their mother, was the love of his life, and he wasn't ready to let go. One thing that Anya never shared with her brother or sister was that brief clarity their father had right before he was put in the nursing home and chose to stop fighting to remember.

"I don't think I can do this," he whispered to no one in particular. It had been a gross day outside, constantly raining, while Anya bustled around trying to get everything ready for the realtor to come to look at the house. It was such a quiet declaration that she wouldn't have heard it had she not been walking directly behind him at that exact second.

"Can't do what, Daddy?" Anya asked, pausing in her mad dash around the house. He turned to look at her, and the crushing devastation she saw in his eyes made her chest squeeze. He swallowed, the muscles in his throat flexing.

"I miss her." He turned fully to show that he was holding the bonnet their mother used to wear around the house. His hands trembled as he gripped it so tightly that the elastic band was stretched to its limit. Anya watched as he lifted it to his nose.

"I miss her too," Anya replied, her voice crackling with pain. He didn't seem to hear her. He turned back to the window and stared out at the rain. The entire earth seemed to weep for their family. It had rained for the entire week, even through the funeral, like the world itself mourned the loss of Clara Tubeck.

"I won't live in a world where she doesn't exist," he said. Anya tilted her head at him, unsure what he meant by that. When she didn't respond, he turned back to look at her once more. "I won't." The determination in his eyes scared her.

Sometimes, it felt like he chose not to remember because it hurt too much. Instead, he held on to his idea that she was still alive, and it had been her all along that needed The Memory Concierge. He convinced himself she was forgetting him because he couldn't fathom a world where she would no longer exist in his reality or mind.

It made no sense how he could just cherry-pick specific memories and discard the others, but according to the numerous specialists she had spoken to, while she was desperately searching for answers, there was still so much that science needed to learn about Alzheimer's. Even with the disease clouding each moment, it was becoming more challenging to figure out which moments were due to actual memory loss and which were due to pure soul-crushing grief.

During her support group visits, the members would sit and listen to her vent but had nothing to offer when she asked for advice. They knew about the intimacy issues, the anger, and the struggles with dependency, but as soon as she begged for advice about what to do when he conjured up a creature in his head that could magically erase all of his problems, they would shrug helplessly.

She felt like she could no longer relate to the stories from the people in the group. They were either in the beginning stages of the diagnosis and grappling with the idea of their loved one changing, or they were at the very end stages when their loved one forgot how to breathe or feed themselves. Her father was in a league of his own, stuck between remembering some things and omitting others. It didn't make sense. She didn't know how to help. She had no idea what to do.

"Sweetheart, he's awake."

Anya had been so stuck in her thoughts that she had forgotten where she was until Luca's soft voice cut through. She blinked at him, and he nodded toward her father. The squeeze of his hand made her almost jump out of her skin.

"Dad?" She was almost scared to ask. After everything that happened recently, she didn't think she had the strength to call him Henry anymore. Pretending he wasn't the man who had given her life and raised her was becoming too much. He blinked a few times and then turned his head in her direction slowly, painfully.

"Dad? Can you hear me? It's me. It's Anya." She leaned forward, bringing her face closer to his, hoping that spark of recognition would flicker in his unfocused eyes. He squeezed her hand hard. Luca left the room to try and flag down a doctor. Tears slipped down Anya's cheeks and fell on the thin sheet of the hospital blanket. Her father was gazing at her now, fully aware of her. His cracked lips curled into a smile around the tubes protruding from his mouth. The tears fell harder, a mixture of relief, sadness, and joy.

"Hi, Daddy."

"How long have I been out?" Her father's voice was scratchy and hoarse when they removed the tubes that were helping him breathe. Anya frantically texted Dru and Deven to return to the hospital now that he was awake. It had been a few minutes, and neither of them answered. They were probably sleeping by now. It had been an extremely long night.

"They brought you here about five hours ago," Anya replied. She resisted the urge to curl up in the hospital bed beside him. It had been so long since her father looked at her and truly saw her. She wanted to be selfish with his time and keep it all to herself, but she knew her brother and sister deserved to see him like this. It wouldn't be fair to keep it all hidden.

"Brought me here?" he asked. "Brought me here from where?" Anya paused for a moment. She had no idea how much to tell him.

"You were looking for something called The Memory Concierge." She saw his eyes flicker at the name. "They found you in an abandoned hotel."

"Did I find it?" he whispered. Anya held his gaze, unsure what to say or how to respond.

"You tell me." They stared at each other for a moment, their silence thick and full of emotion. Skepticism lay heavy in the air around them. Anya wanted to question; she was dying to know what happened when he left the facility. Henry gazed at her, his expression clearly overwhelmed and confused. She worried, for a brief moment, that she had lost him again, but before she could ask, a voice in the doorway made them both turn. It was Deven.

"Dad?" His voice was quiet, void of the confidence that usually colored his tone. He stepped awkwardly into the room, nodded at Luca, who sat reading a book in the corner and smiled quickly at Anya. She watched as their father turned in Deven's direction and studied him momentarily. Everyone in the room froze; even Luca put down his book to see what would happen.

A slow smile spread across their father's face.

"Hello, son." He held out his arms weakly, and Deven rushed to them, body shaking with sobs. Gone was the thick-shouldered, imposing man that Deven had grown to be. Anya watched as he melted into a little boy again, hugging his dad as tightly as he could without hurting him. Silent tears slipped down Deven's cheeks. Anya felt her own cheeks wet with tears that dripped down her face and onto her neck. She had hoped against everything for this moment.

"How?" When Deven lifted his head, his face was still wet. His eyes were hopeful yet skeptical, the same way Anya had been feeling since she first heard their father acknowledge her as his daughter. He swiped at his nose and looked at Anya, who shrugged and shook her head.

"I...I'm not sure. The doctor said we should monitor and see how things go." She smiled at her father. "I have been enjoying having him back too much to really try and explain it all away."

A small part of her wondered if they should be concerned, but she ignored the thought, choosing to enjoy the moment. After so long, it felt like a weight had been lifted from her shoulders. For however long it lasted, their father was back.

"Where's Rue?" Anya's heart warmed at the pet name for the youngest Tubeck child. It was a name that their father had come up with that just seemed to stick. "Is she coming?"

"Yes, I am sure she's on the way." Anya hadn't heard from her, but if she was anything like the sister she knew, she would burst through the room in a flurry of perfume and curly hair at some point. Her father nodded, seeming to accept that answer, but still looked unsure. Anya touched his arm and smiled reassuringly when his gaze flickered toward her. "She'll be here."

"Clara," he whispered with a wistful smile. She wasn't sure what to say in response. Deven looked at her, panic contorting his expression. Had he forgotten already? "You remind me so much of your mother. Taking care of everyone; at the expense of yourself." A lump formed in her throat, painful and hard to swallow. She glanced around the room, trying to focus on the beeping machines and the IV drips instead of letting the words sink in. They hurt too much to hear.

"I no longer want you putting your life on hold for me."

"Dad, I-"

"No, listen to me." Even though he was much weaker than the version of her father that had raised her, he still knew how to command her attention. Her mouth clamped closed out of habit. "You have done enough."

"But family shows up," she squeaked helplessly.

"You need to show up for yourself." His words cut through the emotional wall she had been struggling to hold up and settled into her most vulnerable parts. Anya nodded, in a mess of emotional turmoil that she couldn't verbalize. Deep down, she knew she needed to stop letting herself put her desires and dreams at the bottom of the list. She wasn't sure when she had convinced herself that she was not good enough to chase happiness, but she knew her father was right.

It was time to choose differently.

30

Deven stared at the scene in front of him, playing out like some type of lifetime movie. He felt slightly embarrassed for becoming so emotional at the sight of his father recognizing him, but as soon as it happened, he felt his insides break into a million little pieces – a grown man reduced to feeling like a little boy again. The rational part of him knew this wouldn't last long, but he still held on desperately to the hope that maybe everything was alright. As soon as he heard his father's voice, his resolve crumpled, and every emotion he had been fighting to stave away these last few months came tumbling out front and center. Before he could reel it in, he was a blubbering mess of snot and tears.

He wanted to say so many things, but he couldn't figure out where to start. Instead, he just said nothing, too afraid to trust the moment. Anya was handling it better than he was. He admired the strength she exuded that seemed to elude him completely. She moved through the room and spoke with the doctors with ease, handling all the information thrown at them as if it were a regular conversation while Deven struggled to keep up. He felt like this was the final exam, and he had skipped all the classes leading up to it. He wanted to puff his chest out and be stoic. He tried to push down this overpowering sense of dread and anxiety and be calm. He wanted to impress his father with his strength and ability to deal with everything, just like his big sister, but all he could do was cry.

"I'm sorry," he said, sheepishly wiping at his eyes. "I'm crying like a little kid." Each tear he wiped was replaced by a new one until he felt he was chasing his own tears.

"Nothing to be ashamed about." His father offered a sad smile. Deven stared, unable to form a response. There was a stark difference between the father he had been raised by and the father currently in front of him. Deven had read that the condition could sometimes alter the person's personality, and intellectually, he knew his father was different now. His sharp edges were molded down by grief, loss, and pain, but knowing his father was different and seeing it unfold in front of him were two very different things. Deven shot a confused glance at Anya.

"Are you hungry?" she asked, focusing her attention on their father. Deven knew that was something they should be concerned about. His father had been refusing to eat and wasn't interested in it. He was already rail thin, and this couldn't be helping. The machines he was hooked up to pumped him full of nutrients, so he wasn't starving his body, but still. Deven turned to his father, opening his mouth to try and convince him to at least try a little bit of something, but before he could, his father shook his head, staring at something over their shoulders. His eyes widened in fear.

"It's here." His whisper was tense and urgent. Deven and Anya turned to see what he was staring at, but the corner of the room was empty. The intensity of his fear made Deven nervous, even though he couldn't see anything wrong.

"What do you see?" Deven asked, narrowing his eyes. Had something flown past the window? Had he misunderstood?

"Memory Concierge. It's right there. Don't you see it?" He pointed a shaky finger at the empty corner. Deven swallowed nervously, unsure of what to say.

"Dad? You're in the hospital with me and Anya. Remember?" Deven placed a hand on his father's arm and gave it a gentle squeeze. His entire body tensed under Deven's touch, but after a moment, his gaze refocused. He gave the two of them a shaky smile and shrugged.

"It must have been my imagination."

"Why don't you rest for a little bit? We'll wake you up when Dru gets here."

"Who?" His brow furrowed in confusion.

"Rue," Anya replied, ignoring the panicked look Deven shot her. The familiar nickname connected the dots for him. He nodded and laid back against the stiff-looking hospital pillows. As he made himself comfortable, Anya motioned for Deven to follow her into the hall. As soon as they were alone, she gave him a hug.

"Thank you for coming." She murmured into his shoulder. He hugged her back and shrugged.

"Of course, I came. Why wouldn't I?" Anya narrowed her eyes at him; embarrassment made him feel flushed. He had wasted so much time avoiding this inevitable situation and even though he was here now, it felt like there was almost too much to learn in a short period of time.

No wonder Anya looked like a pro when she spoke with their father, gently guiding him in the right direction, while Deven felt clumsy and unsure of what to do or say. She had been here from the beginning while he cowered in the background, too scared to face the reality of the situation.

There was a bit of pressure behind his puffy, swollen eyes - evidence of so much crying after spending so long without allowing himself to feel his grief. His entire body felt spent like he had just finished running a marathon or lifting heavy weights at the gym.

"You can't let him see you panic."

"I'm sorry, he just started talking about a Memory Concierge, and I didn't know what to do. Was I supposed to pretend I could see it even though I couldn't?" His question had more bite than he meant, but Anya continued as if she hadn't noticed. Her long braids swung as she moved her arms while she talked.

"No. You were right about that; I should have been more honest with Dad from the start," she sighed, "but he just looked so at peace talking about Mom. Even if it was hard to hear, I-"

He put a hand on her shoulder. "You don't have to explain it to me. I get it. I had no right to speak on it since I was absent for pretty much everything. I let you take the reigns but still kept trying to drive from the backseat. That wasn't fair to you." He was embarrassed about how he acted during that dinner. Seeing Anya now, unshaken and completely confident, he understood exactly how much she had to power through on her own.

"How do you...how do you handle this?" he asked quietly. Anya turned to him, her eyebrows raised in question. He sighed and ran a hand over his face. "You're handling all of this so well. Dad talked about a creature in the room with us, and you didn't flinch."

Anya smiled wistfully at him. "I've had a lot of practice."

Things fell silent between the two of them; he stood with his back against the wall, watching the nurses bustle up and down the hallways tending to other patients that could possibly be in similar situations. A sick loved one with a family was trying to mend fences and come together before it was too late. His phone buzzed in his pocket, and he grabbed it, ensuring it wasn't Camila.

His manager at the newest restaurant location asked if he would be in that day at some point. His first instinct was to say yes and head over there now, but he had already missed so much by letting the restaurant be his number one priority. He quickly typed out a response, telling the manager to handle as much as he could, and they could figure out the rest later, and then slid the phone back into his pocket. When he looked up, Anya stared at him, clocking his movements with the phone.

"Do you need to leave?" she asked. There was an edge to her voice. He shook his head and gave her as much of a reassuring smile as he could muster.

"No. I'm here. Nothing I can't handle later on." The relief that flashed in her eyes made him feel guilty. He had lost count of the many times he disappeared in the middle or didn't show up at all when she called. If he could go back in time and kick his former self for being so selfish and self-centered, he would.

His only hope would be that he had enough time to make it up to the people he loved.

Dru showed up later in a flurry of wild hair and flailing limbs. Deven and Anya had just made themselves comfortable in their father's room with the takeout that Luca had stepped out to grab for them. Their father slept peacefully in his bed while Deven and his sister used this time to catch up, just the two of them.

"I came as soon as I got the message!" Dru exclaimed breathlessly, bursting her way into the room. Anya flinched, caught off guard by the sudden noise. Deven glanced at their father to see if he had been disturbed by Dru's yelling. He hadn't. Deven smiled; that man has always been able to sleep through even the loudest noises. "Is he...?" She hurried over to his bedside.

"He's just sleeping," Deven clarified, gesturing towards the takeout containers on the small table in front of them. "Are you hungry? We have plenty." She nodded. She snatched the fork from his hand and stuck it into the side of the lasagna he was eating.

"Gross. Get your own; I don't know where your mouth has been recently!" He grumbled, reaching for the fork. She held it above her head and laughed, mouth full of lasagna. He rolled his eyes, trying to suppress the smile tugging at the corner of his lips.

"Where's Kenan?" Anya asked, making a point to look around the room. Dru narrowed her eyes at her sister and pulled up the only other empty chair in the room.

"This is a family affair," she replied with a shrug. Anya glanced at Deven, clearly wanting to laugh. Dru gave them both a pointed look, her expression laced with irritation. Deven placed a hand on his belly, full of lasagna, and laughed so hard he couldn't catch his breath.

"What?" she snapped. Anya was able to compose herself quicker than Deven, who was still snorting in amusement.

"He sat with us the night they found him. He was here offering advice on Dad's medications like he had been in the family for years, and *now* you want to establish boundaries? It's a bit late for that, isn't it?" Anya pointed her fork at Dru as she spoke, accentuating words with a quick jab at the air.

"Things are moving so quickly." She looked down at the takeout plate she was eating; Deven had officially given up on getting his lasagna back. He reached for the container of breadsticks and took a bite out of the largest one. The buttery, garlicky taste was comforting; it reminded him of spaghetti nights at the house growing up - the three siblings fighting over who got the last breadstick while their parents watched in amusement.

"Do you want them to slow down?" he asked.

"No, but they should, though, right?" Dru glanced between them, the confusion and uncertainty clear on her face. "I mean, this isn't a movie or some fairytale. Shouldn't I be concerned that I feel so strongly so soon?"

"Not necessarily. I'm not saying marry the man, but you don't have to figure everything out right now." He snuck another bite of lasagna when she was distracted.

"You've had a rough go at love, so nervousness is expected, but just enjoy it. See where it goes."

"He is obviously just as crazy about you," Anya chimed in, closing her takeout container and sliding it toward Deven. He accepted it greedily, finishing off the last of her food.

"It's the crazy part I'm worried about," Dru grumbled. "Did I tell you that Kenan sat at the club every night for three weeks straight, waiting for me?" Her voice feigned disgust, but the way her eyes sparkled gave her away.

"Weird. What did you do to him to get him that sprung?" Deven asked, then shook his head. "Wait, never mind. Don't tell me; I really don't want to know." Dru threw her head back and laughed.

"I love seeing my three together." Henry's voice was still hoarse, b ut it caught their attention. They had been so enthralled in their conversation that none of them noticed their father awake and quietly observing them. His voice was gravelly and weak but unmistakable. An air of seriousness fell over the room. For a moment, they had forgotten where they were.

"Hi, Daddy," Dru said quietly, getting up from her chair to stand beside him. He smiled up at her, tired but alert. Deven breathed a quick sigh of relief. He wanted his little sister to get her moment with their father while he was lucid, however long that moment lasted.

"What's this I hear about a boyfriend?" he asked, raising an eyebrow. Dru blushed and widened her eyes in embarrassment.

"Um. We don't have to talk about that right now. Did Deven tell you he got a girl pregnant?" Dru shot an apologetic look in Deven's direction. He glared at his little sister, irritated that she blurted his business before he'd had a chance to say it himself. He felt his own wave of embarrassment when he caught sight of the stern look on his father's face. He felt like he was in trouble, even though he was a grown man. No matter how sick he became, his father could make his kids wither in shame with just a look. The same look he was giving Deven at that exact moment.

"No. He must have forgotten to tell me." Panic rose in the back of Deven's throat, making him want to run out of the room, but he stood his ground.

"I was going to," Deven waved a hand around the room, "but I felt like there were more pressing things to address first." He stared daggers into the side of Dru's face making a mental note to fuss her out later.

"I trust that you are going to step up and-"

"Dad, you don't have to worry about me taking care of my responsibilities. You raised me well."

"Girls, can you give me a moment to speak with Deven?" Dru and Anya got up without another word and left the room, leaving Deven almost too scared to look his father in the eye, he steeled his shoulders and met his gaze anyway.

"I won't be here much longer-" Deven opened his mouth to protest, but his father held up a hand to quiet him. "It's the truth, and there is something I need you to know. I spent your life telling you that as a man, you must always be strong. I kept telling you that you had to work hard to provide for your family - providing was all that mattered." A single tear slipped down his father's cheek. Deven tracked the tear, unsure of what to do.

"I was wrong. Providing is important, but it's more important to be present for your children. I missed out on so much with you guys when I didn't need to and now it's too late to get that time back. Don't be like me; don't let anyone tell you that you aren't allowed to feel because you're a man. Be with someone who you can feel with; someone who won't criticize you when you break every now and then." A silent tear slipped down Henry's face as he talked. Deven nodded, bewildered. "Your mother was that for me."

"I know," Deven whispered. He thought about the times he had broken in front of Camila and how she scooped him up in her arms and held him.

"As a father, you aren't going to know what to do all the time, but be present for your family. I let you three think that work was more important than you, and that has never been true." He waved a hand around the room. "When you're on your sick bed, your work won't be there to comfort you. Family will. Because-"

"Because family shows up." Deven finished for him. His father nodded and then fell silent. "We'll be okay, Dad." Deven wasn't even sure if that was true, but something told him that it at least needed to be said. His father let out a shaky breath and nodded, closing his eyes again.

"You'll be a wonderful father." His whisper was so soft that Deven almost didn't hear it. The words washed over him, cloaking him in a layer of comfort he didn't know he needed. Ever since he first found out

Camila was pregnant, he wondered if he could raise a kid. He had wanted to ask his sisters, but felt dumb for needing that type of reassurance. Deven had questions that he'd needed his father's wisdom on and without even having to ask, Henry had sensed his uncertainty and addressed it in a way that didn't make Deven feel incapable.

Deven felt ridiculous for thinking Henry had been weak for being vulnerable. In this hospital bed, covered by blankets and hooked up to multiple machines, his father still looked ten feet tall in Deven's eyes. Guilt and sadness flooded his body, making his knees feel wobbly and unsteady. It had been a while since he admired his dad; he had been too busy looking at the diagnosis instead of the man his father has always been.

"Thank you," he whispered back, just as softly. His father's face remained blank, giving no indication that he had heard him but the quick squeeze on Deven's arm told him he had.

He'd understood Deven's fear without him having to voice it. Standing there, watching his father rest, Deven promised himself he would do whatever he needed for his child, the same way his father had done whatever he needed to do for him and his sisters.

"I'll make you proud, Dad. I promise."

31

Dru hadn't been able to stop thinking about Kenan since their first encounter. And now, sitting next to him as he drove her home from the hospital, she felt even more confused and unsure than she had before. Instead of returning to the club to grab her car after leaving it there, Kenan offered to drive her home so she could rest. He promised that he and Bryce would drop her vehicle off later.

Exhausted, Dru immediately took him up on the offer. She had never been around anyone who was so in tune with her needs so quickly. It felt unreal, and her first instinct was to try and scare him off. If she convinced him they were a bad idea together, she could lick her wounds now but still come out of the situation virtually unscathed. She knew that the longer he stuck around, the harder it would be to swallow when it all fell apart. She could handle it now if they called it quits.

"I was engaged once," she blurted as Kenan drove. He momentarily took his eyes off the road to study her face. She stared straight ahead, refusing to meet his gaze and hoping he couldn't hear her heart thumping wildly in her chest.

"What happened between you two?" he asked. Dru hesitated, unsure of how much to share. It felt weird opening up to Kenan when she usually kept her feelings close to the vest. Normally, whenever someone tried to get too close, she would shoot them a stern look and tell them to mind their business. With Kenan, however, sharing felt completely natural. She felt like she could open up to him without fear of it being used against her later.

"He cheated on me with my former best friend," she said bluntly, surprised at herself for being able to say it without collapsing into a puddle of tears. She hadn't allowed herself to think about the situation for so long, and now she was watching it play in her head, almost as if it had happened to someone else. Kenan let out a low whistle, bringing her back to the moment.

"How long ago was this?" His hand rested on her knee, which sent a shockwave of electricity through her body.

"A year or so ago. About a month before I found my mother dead on the floor of her closet." She didn't mean to blurt out *that* much. Dru bit her lip, immediately feeling stupid for letting that slip out. Embarrassment heated her cheeks. She didn't dare chance a look in his direction, but she knew he was staring at her again. She could feel the heat from his gaze on her face.

"That's... wow, that's a lot to process at one time. How have you been dealing with it all?"

"I'm in therapy," she admitted. Out of the corner of her eye, she could see him nodding.

"Good. You should have an outlet to discuss your feelings." This time, her head whipped in his direction, and she narrowed her eyes suspiciously.

He glanced between her and the road, a blank expression on his perfectly sculpted face.

"An outlet to discuss my feelings? Okay, who *are* you, and what planet did you materialize from?" she demanded, folding her arms, and glaring at him. He laughed, the headlights from the passing cars illuminating his sharp cheekbones. A smile pushed at her own lips. The sound of his laughter warmed her. This was a beautiful man. Unnaturally beautiful, and now she was expected to believe he was also emotionally adjusted? Something had to be wrong.

"So, I'm from another planet now?" When he met her eyes, there was a twinkle in his. Dru resisted the urge to smile even wider. She hated and loved how he made her feel so carefree in his presence. It had been a long time since she could feel anything but sadness.

"You have to be. There's no way you're this attractive and this well-adjusted. Do you have kids and a secret wife somewhere? Bodies in the basement? Running from the law?"

"Hm? Sorry I didn't hear anything after you said I was attractive." His grin broadened. Dru shook her head and turned to face the window so he wouldn't see her smile. After a moment of silence, she glanced back at him.

"I have a lot of pain."

"You've told me."

"That doesn't freak you out?"

"Should it?" he asked. Dru didn't respond. She didn't know how to.

"I'm not naïve enough to believe that people don't come with some kind of hurt and baggage they are trying to sort through. Live long enough, and you will have trauma. How you deal with it is all I'm concerned about." Kenan said, offering her a gentle smile. He pulled his car into her driveway. She was so enthralled by his words that she hadn't noticed they arrived at her place. She hopped out of the car and rushed inside. She barely turned around to watch Kenan pull off. She would see him later when he came back with her car.

"Dr. Hatcher?" she huffed into the phone. "I'm so sorry to bother you at this hour. I know you said this number was only for emergencies, but I'm...I'm spiraling." She heard rustling in the background before Dr. Hatcher cleared his throat.

"I'm listening."

"I told you I met a guy, right?" She began. Dr. Hatcher grunted his acknowledgment. Dru paused for a split second; his gruff response made her self-conscious about calling. She knew it wasn't the best idea, but she had been freaking out since leaving the hospital with Kenan. "Well, he seems too good to be true. How do I know he's the right guy?"

"You won't."

"What?"

"Forgive me for being a bit forward, but considering what time it is, I will get straight to the point. What you're asking me is how to predict the future. You can't. All you can do is just living one day at a time."

"I could get hurt again."

"You could. Or you could establish a real connection with this person and find the relationship you have been trying and failing to convince yourself you don't actually want."

Dru scowled at his words and sank down on her couch. "You're not very friendly outside of office hours."

"I use all of my good manners for work," Dr. Hatcher chuckled. Dru couldn't help but smile as well. She was grateful he had even taken her call.

Dru's phone buzzed in her ear, letting her know she had a text message. She pulled her phone away from her ear to see a message from Anya at the top of her screen. Her stomach flipped, immediately worried that something was wrong with her father.

Dad is awake. Get back to the hospital as soon as you can.

"Hello? Dru? You still there?" She had been so stunned by the message that she had forgotten she was on the phone. She put it back to her ear and, after a promise to schedule her next session for some time that week, ended the call. Dru felt weird. Seeing her father unresponsive in the hospital bed was one thing, but being able to talk to him made her nervous. Would he remember her?

If he did remember her, would he be angry or upset that she hadn't come around as often as she had initially promised she would? Her mind was a flurry of different thoughts and emotions that all bounced against each other in a heap of nonsense. Instead of turning around and heading back to the hospital, she slid off the couch and wandered numbly into her bedroom. Everything was too much at the moment… too real… too raw… too vulnerable. She slipped under the cool sheets and tucked the blanket under her chin.

She would deal with everything when she woke up, but first, she needed a nap.

Dru popped awake, covered in sweat, with her hair stuck to her forehead. Her bonnet had fallen off in the middle of her fitful sleeping. The sun showing through her thin curtains let her know she had slept much longer than planned. She grabbed her phone to check the time.

2:00pm.

She scrambled out of bed and reached for the first clean outfit she could find, not caring if it matched, as long as it was clean. She slapped on some lotion and tied her hair up as well as she could into a messy pineapple on the top of her head. She was vaguely aware she was zooming through her apartment like a tornado, but she only meant to sleep for an hour - not almost ten. The entire next day was nearly gone already. Her brother and sister were most likely at the hospital with their dad, giggling about how she was always late to everything.

Even as a somewhat self-sufficient adult, Dru still struggled to make it places on time. Thankfully she had a job where the supervisor wasn't such a stickler for punctuality, as long as the work got done and turned in when she was supposed to and her professors rarely cared, as long as she came in and sat down without causing too much of a scene. That was the only thing that saved her from getting fired and failing some of her classes. She was talented, she was creative, but she was habitually late.

When Dru made it to the hospital, it was closer to the evening hours than she would have liked. She burst into the room, taking in the sight in front of her. Anya and Deven were sitting at a small table in the corner of the room, huddled over takeout boxes and laughing animatedly. Their father lay asleep in the hospital bed to their right. His skin had regained color and looked better, but he still seemed dangerously thin.

"I came as soon as I got the message!" she exclaimed. Her sister's raised eyebrow told her that she knew Dru was lying but wouldn't push. She was grateful for that. How do you explain that you didn't come because you decided to take a nap that lasted most of the day? She knew that deep down, they probably all thought she was irresponsible. She didn't want to give them any more evidence towards that point.

"Is he...?" she glanced at her father again, suddenly worried that maybe something was actually wrong. She stepped closer to his bed.

"He's just sleeping," Deven said, his reassurance sending a flood of relief through her body. She didn't realized how tense her muscles had become until she felt herself relax. Her stomach let out an aggressive growl, and Deven gestured toward the takeout containers they had stacked on the small table. She was already eyeing the food before either one of them offered.

"Are you hungry? We have plenty," he asked. Dru nodded, swiped his fork from his hand, and slid the lasagna toward her. The garlicky smell made her stomach rumble again. She hadn't eaten since the afternoon before. She had planned to order some food after she and Kenan left the club, but then they left in a whirlwind of emotion and frayed nerves when Dru got the call that something happened to her father. The stress made her appetite disappear entirely.

"Gross. Get your own; I don't know where your mouth has been recently!" Deven grumbled, trying to snatch his fork back. She leaned away so he couldn't reach it and shook her head; her mouth was full of lasagna as she giggled at him. She always loved to annoy her brother. It was one of her favorite things to do. Deven pretended to be annoyed, but she could see he was fighting a smile.

They had been so absorbed in their conversation that they almost didn't hear their father when his voice cut into it. Dru's heart lept in her chest. Wordlessly she rushed to his side of the bed, wanting to crawl into his arms and sob. Now that he was awake, she wanted to keep him all to herself. Anya and Deven had spent time with him all day. She felt selfish for even wanting to ask them to leave. Instead, she focused on her father, who was finally looking at her like he knew who she was for the first time in such a long time.

"Hey, Daddy." She smiled. He placed a shaky hand on her cheek and smiled gently when she leaned into his touch. He was rarely so tender with her. It made her chest squeeze uncomfortably.

"What's this I hear about a boyfriend?" he asked, raising an eyebrow. His tone was playful and light, but Dru could still feel herself blush. She wasn't ready to talk about Kenan. Not yet. Not here.

"Um..we don't have to talk about that just yet. Did Deven tell you he got his girlfriend pregnant?" In a flash of immature judgment, Dru blurted out the only thing she could think of to take the focus off her in that moment; just for a second so she could make some sense of her jumbled feelings. She could feel Deven glaring at her without even having to look. She would have to pay for that later.

Dru was irritated in a way that she knew was irrational but couldn't figure out how to stifle. After outing Deven's news, their father asked her and Anya to leave the room for a second. Jealousy crept around the edges of her mind, making her want to yell at the both of them. Deven and Anya already had their time. They'd been having their time since they were kids. Dru had always felt like the oddball that her parents sometimes avoided because it was just easier to pretend she wasn't there than to try and understand their quirky child.

Rationally, Dru knew that her father probably preferred dealing with Deven because they were both men. It was easier for him to talk to her brother and understand how to relate to him. Her father and Anya had their own relationship that had only grown stronger in a weird way after his diagnosis. He may not have remembered who she was, but he still confided in her.

It was Dru's fault for blaming him for her mother's death. The two of them had just reached a point in their relationship that made sense, a place she felt good about. She knew the tattoos and the wild hair had widened the gap in understanding between her and her traditional parents, but her mother had finally gotten to the point where she wasn't so bothered by it, and then she was gone. Dru didn't know where else to direct her anger, so she directed it at her father. She deprived herself of the chance to spend time with him while he was still somewhat aware of what was going on around him. Dru had no one to blame but herself.

After Deven and her dad finished talking, Anya and Dru returned to the room. They all crowded around the bed, chattering happily as a family. It was a moment that Dru had craved for so long; now that it was here, she didn't know what to do with it.

"Rue? Why are you looking at me like that?" her father asked. Dru blinked, completely thrown off. She had been so focused on stewing inwardly that she didn't realize she was staring at him. Dru could imagine how crazy her expression must have been. She shrugged and turned back to the small television on the wall in the corner.

Anya and Deven looked at each other and then back at Dru. She could feel her father's eyes on her, studying her silently. Tears pricked at the back of her eyes. She felt silly and childish but couldn't control it.

"Give us a minute," Henry said. She glanced up in surprise to see Anya and Deven getting up to leave. When the door closed behind them, he turned to look at her. As soon as their gaze met, the rest of her resolve cracked open, and the tears she tried to blink away dripped down her cheeks.

"Is this our goodbye scene?" she laughed drily, trying to force humor into the moment. He didn't smile or laugh at her attempt at a joke, and her stomach sank to her knees. She wasn't ready for this.

"It might be," his voice was solemn. Tears fell harder, blurring her vision. There was barely enough room for the two of them on the bed, but she curled against his side, the bones of his ribcage poking against her shoulder, bringing a fresh batch of tears into the mix.

"Daddy..." she sobbed. His arms tightened around her in a grip that was still surprisingly strong.

"Do you remember why I nicknamed you Rue?" he asked after a moment. Dru shook her head.

"When you were a little girl, you were always bouncing around from one thing to another like a little kangaroo." He chuckled. "Things were easier between us when you were younger. I didn't have to try as hard to bridge the gap between us. You were always so colorful, bursting full of life and creativity and I was just me. Dull and thriving on routine and structure." He stroked her hair as he talked, his voice hoarse but firm. "I always admired it but never knew how to relate to it so I stopped trying. That was wrong of me." Dru lifted her head to look at him, but his gaze was fixed on the window, staring out of it as he confessed.

"I thought you were embarrassed by me - the black sheep of the family," she whispered. His head whipped in her direction; his eyes flashed with an anger that surprised her.

"You are my child. I could never be embarrassed of you."

"I wish we could have been closer." Dru dropped her head, staring at the ugly white sheets that covered his waist and legs.

"Watch after your brother and sister, will you?" He asked.

"Me?" She squeaked.

"Yes. You've always been stronger. Anya is the caregiver, Deven is the hardworker and you, my little butterfly, were a leader." His words surprised her. She never felt all that strong, especially not these past few years. Dru felt the opposite of strong - weak and unable to function. "You doubt yourself, but you have a good head on your shoulders. You always wanted to do things your way. I never worried that you needed me."

"But I *did* need you, Dad!" Dru wailed, swiping at the tears on her cheeks. She scooted closer and placed her head on his shoulder. "I still do."

"I'm sorry I didn't recognize that then," he said quietly. The two of them sat together, letting the unspoken words remain where they were. Dru wanted to cry and yell that he was leaving her before she could show him what she could do with her career and life - before she got married... before she had children of her own. But instead, she chose to realize that her father was human, imperfect, clumsy, and full of flaws. He loved her in the best way he knew how and for that, even if it wasn't perfect, she would always be grateful.

Dru stepped out of the hospital room, wiping her eyes on the bottom of her shirt. So much crying left her feeling spent. She wanted nothing more than to sink into her bed and sleep away the rest of the day. Her father expected her to watch after her siblings. How? When she could barely get herself together?

"Hey."

Dru had been so enraptured in her thoughts that she didn't see Anya standing outside the hospital room. She swallowed, bracing herself for the criticism she was sure would soon come.

"How are you?" Anya asked with a sheepish smile. Dru's shoulders sagged. Fresh tears pricked at her eyes, even though her body felt spent from crying so much. She was surprised she had anymore tears left. Anya wordlessly wrapped her arms around Dru and pulled her in close. She smelled of vanilla, the same perfume their mom had worn.

"I'm sorry I haven't been here," Dru murmured into Anya's chest. "It's been so hard seeing him this way."

"I know," Anya replied. Dru pulled back and looked at her.

"I just couldn't do it. I'm not as strong as you." Dru whispered, letting her eyes fall. A soft chuckle made her look up in surprise. Anya smiled at her and shook her head.

"Sis, you're stronger than me and Deven combined, even after everything. After finding mom..." Anya's voice caught in her throat. "I should have checked on you more often. I was foolish to think that you and Deven weren't grieving and coping in your own ways."

"You kind of suck for that," Dru replied, then laughed at the look Anya gave her. "You've been handling it all by yourself lately. So, I get that you weren't necessarily in the headspace to process what we felt and everything else."

"You've got a good head on your shoulders, little sis." Anya wrapped her arms around Dru again and pulled her in for another hug.

"So, I've been told." Dru laughed sadly, thinking about what her father had just told her. She had no idea what he saw in her, but she was determined to prove him right, whatever it took.

32

Henry (35 Years Earlier)

Today was the day Henry would marry his bride. It had been six months since she said "yes" in the middle of his kitchen, covered in his ex-girlfriend's vomit. It wasn't the most romantic proposal, but Henry wouldn't have traded it for anything.

He glanced around the small conference room in the back of the church, his designated spot to get ready for the wedding, and smiled. This was the happiest day of his life. He felt like a kid in a candy store or someone who had just won the lottery.

Had someone told him just a year ago that he would be getting ready to walk down the aisle to marry someone who wasn't Lynette, he would have scoffed in disbelief. Henry was convinced that marriage wasn't in the cards for him back then, and he was satisfied with it. Henry was content knowing he was never supposed to be anyone's husband. His main concern was thriving, ensuring he could support himself wherever he ended up.

Especially after witnessing his brother Anthony's marriage crash and burn so quickly. Anthony had married someone he'd only known for a few weeks, and while Henry and Clara hadn't known each other that much longer, there was a glaring difference. Anthony was not in love with that woman. She convinced him that she was pregnant, and he had been trying to fulfill his duty as a man. Turns out, that was all a part of her ruse.

Henry glanced over at Anthony, surprised to find he was already watching him.

"What?" Henry asked.

Anthony narrowed his eyes, his mouth spread into a slow grin. "I've never seen you this happy before. It's good to see." He clapped a thick hand on Henry's shoulder.

"You won't lecture me about how she and I haven't known each other long? After everything that happened with you and-"

"There is no need to talk about her," Anthony interjected. "We're having a good day. This is a happy occasion."

"It's a good feeling being here." Henry grinned. His excitement reverberated through him and filled the room. The door opened behind him, and his mother stepped in wearing a calf-length blue skirt with a matching suit jacket. Silver buttons adorned the front of the coat jacket, and the sleeves puffed slightly, making her shoulders appear higher than they were. A string of pearls that Henry gave her for her birthday was around her neck. As soon as she laid eyes on Henry, she smiled.

"Henry, baby, give your mother a hug." She opened her arms, and Henry stepped into them and kissed her hair.

"Have you seen Clara?" he asked when she pulled back to look at him. His mother nodded as tears welled in her eyes.

"She's absolutely stunning." Her nose wrinkled. "I'm so glad you found her and got rid of that awful Lynette."

"Ma," Henry admonished, "be kind. Lynette's been through a lot." His ex-girlfriend getting involved with Eric had sent her down a destructive path. Henry hadn't realized it then, but Lynette admitted to using drugs with Eric longer than before the Halloween party. She'd started when things had gotten tough, and Henry busied himself so much at work that he hardly noticed the changes in her behavior. It wasn't

until he saw her standing by his car, looking haggard and rough, that he realized what was happening with Lynette. The night Clara helped her get situated, Lynette slipped out in the middle of the night in search of her next fix. To know that she was so far gone made Henry sad.

Drugs had very rapidly altered his neighborhood into something dangerous. Leaving the house at night meant risking being shot by dealers and rivaling gangs but leaving during the day meant witnessing his people wandering the streets like zombies searching for the next hit of the drug that had quickly ruined their lives.

Lynette was now one of the zombies. In less than a year, she had gone from a relatively decent girl with a good head on her shoulders to an addict willing to sell her body for a few dollars. Henry had run into her a few more times in the past months, and his heart broke at the state of her appearance.

The first thing he wanted to do after he and Clara got married was move her away from the crumbling ruins of this town. They had to escape before the plague that had already taken so many lives and ruined many others sunk its fangs into either of them.

Henry shook his head to clear any thoughts of his ex-girlfriend. As badly as he felt for her, today was not the day to focus on how her life turned out. Henry stood in front of the mirror and adjusted his bowtie. His skin glowed against the powder blue of his tuxedo. He hated the color, but Clara had begged him to wear it. He would have worn a banana suit and sunglasses had she asked.

"Come. It's time to take your position," Anthony said. Henry reached over and squeezed his mother before heading out into the church's sanctuary. His father stood at the podium, ready to officiate. His dark eyes gleamed when he spotted Henry approaching.

"You ready for this, son?" His father asked when Henry was within earshot. Nerves buzzed in Henry's belly. He managed a nervous smile in response to his father's question, but before he could respond, the music started signaling Clara's entrance. Henry turned, and his breath caught in his throat. There, in the doorway of the sanctuary, stood love personified. His heart soared as soon as their eyes met.

Everyone and everything else faded into the background. All he could see was Clara as she sauntered towards him, clutching her bouquet of flowers. Her silky white, off-shouldered gown flowed around her. Intricate lace covered the front bodice, the bottom hem of the skirt, and the long train that flowed behind her.

Henry vaguely remembered hearing her gush about it to her friends. He hadn't cared much at the time, his main concern making sure that everything ran smoothly, but now as he watched her glide towards him, he realized just how much effort she put into picking the right dress.

When she finally reached him, she held a white-gloved hand for Henry to grasp. He swallowed his nerves and clutched her hand, vowing to himself that he would never let go of her hand no matter what happened in their life.

"I will love you until my dying day," he whispered. And he meant every word.

Henry was tired. He had never felt this spent before in his life. No matter how much he slept, his energy was still depleted. Holding his eyes open felt like he was running a marathon. Conversations with his children had wiped him out. Being alive was wiping him out. Pretending that the odious creature wasn't there in the corner of the room, scrutinizing his every move tired him out. Henry wanted to turn his head and meet the gaze of that ugly brute and tell it just to go ahead and finish the job. He had almost spoken to it a few times when the kids were still here, but no one could see it when he tried to point it out.

Instead, they could give him worried looks thinly veiled by tight smiles and nervous laughter. It made him feel like a circus animal or a spectacle in a museum - something to point and marvel at and take pity on. So instead, he just ignored the creature and pretended as if he couldn't see it. He no longer felt scared of it anyway, and he learned to ignore its dead eyes staring at him. The longer it stood, hovering in the corner, the more he could pretend it was just an ugly light fixture or a decoration that no one actually wanted.

There was still so much happening around him that he couldn't understand. As hard as he tried to make sense of it, it felt like he was trapped behind a corpulent film, and he could only make out the vague shapes, but as soon as he got closer, it moved farther out of reach. According to his children, the doctors, and everyone else, Clara had been dead for the past year. He was the one that had been diagnosed with Alzheimer's and not her.

He was the one that struggled to remember, and as a result, his wife had worked herself to death trying to take care of him. None of it made sense; thinking about it made him even more tired. The idea that Clara's death was real and possibly his fault made him sick. He pushed the thought away, refusing to let it sink into his mind and make him begin to hate himself.

Henry already struggled with the idea that he had failed his children. Hearing them cry and hurt made his heart heavy. Leaving this world knowing he failed everyone was too much to hold on to. It was too big for him to grasp. Henry had trouble meeting everyone's gaze, feeling guilty and ashamed that they were taking time out of their day to sit with him after he had injured himself so severely.

He wanted to tell them to go home and let him die in his shame in peace, but he knew they needed to be here more for their own sakes than for his. So he plastered on a smile, and pretended there wasn't a pit of anxiety deep in his belly. The nagging feeling in the back of his mind settled in since the moment he stepped into that hotel. The uneasiness hadn't left him. Trying to wrap his mind around Clara being dead was too difficult. Every time the door opened, his heart would swell with hope that it would be his wife, but it never was. Each time his hope was crushed, the crack in his heart grew deeper.

"They keep telling me you're dead," he whispered into thin air. This was the first time he had been alone since he woke up hooked to every machine imaginable. He had been in the hospital for weeks. Someone had been on rotation at all hours of the day and night. When one kid had to leave, two stayed behind. When two had to fulfill their adult obligations, one was glued to his side. Henry was grateful that his children still cared enough to visit, but it was a lot to take in at one time. The finality of this moment was burdensome. Henry knew that he would never see the outside of this hospital room, and he could tell his kids knew it too, even when they peppered him with surface-level smiles and positivity.

He had met boyfriends and girlfriends, even though he couldn't remember who they were or their names. Henry smiled when appropriate, nodded, and tried his best to follow along with their conversations, but everything was too loud, and nothing added up. The Memory Concierge lurked in the background of the conversations, hovering over his children like a dangerous shadow. He wanted to tell them to watch out, but he had been told so many times that nothing he knew to be true was reality. He was no longer sure what he believed anymore.

"Henry." The voice was soft, but he heard it as clear as day. He opened his eyes and searched around the room; hope filled his chest.

"Clara? Baby? Are you here?" A shadow in the corner of his eye made him turn. His breath caught in his throat, and tears obscured his vision. There, in the corner of the room, sat Clara. She was younger than he remembered; she looked like she did the day they met. Her wild hair swirling around her shoulders as if she were standing in front of a fan.

"Hi, Hen." She smiled. Peace flooded through him, calming his nerves and relaxing his muscles. Clara always settled him when he was stressing out about something going on in their lives. It never took much from her, a touch, a smile, a look, but it always worked. He took a deep breath, trying to hide the shaking in his voice. She stepped forward, cupping his face and kissing him on the forehead.

"They keep telling me you're already dead. How can this be?" he asked.

"I am," she said calmly. He shook his head, grabbing her wrists and pulling her closer. She felt the same as he always remembered. Warm. Soft. He brought her wrists to his nose and inhaled her scent. Vanilla. Like always.

"How am I able to touch you?" he asked, bewildered. Clara didn't respond, just sat on the edge of the bed and held his gaze.

"I tried," Henry whispered after a moment passed between them. "I tried to save you. I tried to get your memories back. I tried to make everything right."

"You really hurt yourself in that old building, Hen." Her voice wasn't accusatory like he was worried it would be. He had been so scared to let her down, but she didn't sound disappointed. She sounded sad. Remorseful. She shook her head. "You shouldn't have gone in there."

Henry dropped his gaze. It was his fault that he was in here. Henry wanted to kick himself for doing something so dangerous, but at the time everything felt so real. It still felt real. He couldn't reconcile reality with what he knew in his head to be true. He had gone into the hotel in the hopes of saving his wife and restoring her memories.

"I thought I could save you," he whispered with a shrug. Clara looked up at him and narrowed her eyes.

"I didn't need to be saved." Her words hurt even though he knew now that she was right. The truth behind them stung. He couldn't save Clara; he couldn't save himself. He couldn't save anyone. Henry felt like he had been chasing his tail for the past few years, believing that one thing was happening while the entire world gingerly stepped around him, trying not to disturb his fantasy.

"Do you think they'll be okay?" he asked. "Do you think- do you think they know how much I love them?" He was worried about his children and how they were coping with everything. He knew they were hiding the uglier emotions from him, trying to spare him in his moments of illness. He had done his best and provided for them as he had been taught. But he knew now that kids genuinely care about their parents being there for them. All the money in the world can't make up for being present in their lives. They deserved more of him, but he could only hope they understood his heart. He hoped they knew that he had nothing but good intentions.

"They're going to be fine." Clara smiled; her eyes were glassy with unshed tears. She grabbed Henry's hand and gave it a reassuring squeeze. "You did your best; they know that," she whispered, her voice shaking slightly, heavy with emotion. He nodded; his heart ached, thinking about how sad they all seemed. Sure, they smiled and laughed together these last few weeks, but there was a heavy sadness in the air that he knew they felt too. He wanted to wrap his arms around the three of them and protect them from the pain that was due to come.

"I'm so tired, Clara." She nodded and pulled his blankets up under his chin. His body craved sleep; he felt cold. He wasn't sure what was happening, but he knew it couldn't have been good. When he first found The Memory Concierge, there was a moment when he felt like he was losing his grip on his own life. He had been lying in the bed while Clara folded clothes, and the creature was in the room with them, telling him to look. He saw her collapse; he saw the life leave her body and vaguely, in the back of his mind, a dot connected. It was distant and if he focused too hard it vanished, but he felt like he had seen that moment before. He lived it before.

The kids told him that this must have happened while he was bleeding from the wounds he sustained on the hotel floor. His brain had been replaying the moments he couldn't remember, struggling to make sense of what actually happened. His brain had been searching for something to hold on to, struggling to decipher what was real from what wasn't.

Henry had been trying to assemble the pieces, but nothing connected like he needed it to. Anya told him that Sullivan was not a coworker but a patient inside the nursing home where he had supposedly been living for the past year of his life. The office was actually his room. Anya had been coming to visit him daily, but he had been convinced that she was an assistant and not his oldest child. As she explained, he nodded, trying his best to follow along and connect the scenarios she had given him. It didn't feel right.

He felt like a prisoner trapped in his mind, running around in circles and tiring himself out for no reason. People were trying to convince him of things he knew couldn't be true. He was so sure of everything when he set out to find The Memory Concierge. He took his keys and left the house while Clara slept. Only, now he wasn't sure. Had he been at home? Had Clara been in the bed next to him? Had she even been alive? Did he do all of this for nothing?

"Rest," Clara whispered, her lips close to his ear. She turned to leave, but he grabbed her hand, suddenly terrified of being alone.

"Please- don't go. I'm- I'm scared of what comes next." Wordlessly, Clara slipped into the bed beside him and wrapped her arms around him. He could feel her tears against the side of his head, but he allowed himself to find comfort in her arms. He had so much left he wanted to say, so much left he wanted to tell his children.

He wanted to be here to witness Dru marry one day or meet his grandchildren. He wanted to be able to see each one of his heartbeats thrive and chase their dreams. Henry had high hopes for all of them. Knowing he wouldn't be here to see it broke his heart, but as he lay there, comforted in his wife's arms, he knew he had done all he could. He just had to hope that it would be enough.

33

Anya

Anya took a deep breath, smoothed her skirt, and adjusted the microphone. The sanctuary was packed full of people in various stages of grief, but Anya felt an unusual wave of calm. Maybe she had cried all the tears she could cry, or perhaps it would all hit her later when she was in the comfort of her own home, but for now, Anya was doing okay. Her heart thumped at a steady rhythm in her chest as she looked out at the wet eyes of the congregation.

Sunlight peaked through the stained-glass windows, casting colorful shapes over the floors and faces of the attendees. The church smelled faintly of mildew from a leak after the torrential rains they had just experienced. The earth had wept for her mother's and now her father's loss. Anya caught Luca's eye from where he sat; his soft smile and a slight nod urged her to start. She sucked in another deep breath and closed her eyes before she began.

"My parents had a bond of love stronger than anything I had ever seen," Anya smiled down from the pulpit at the people gathered in the church. The shiny black casket sat between them, covered in gorgeous flowers. "It surpassed all forms of reality. It bulldozed through stumbling blocks that would have torn others apart."

Anya glanced at the casket in front of her. "A few years ago, my father was diagnosed with Rapid Early-Onset Alzheimer's with Anosognosia. When they first told us, we had no idea what that meant. We had no idea what to expect. Would it take months? Years? Days? Our mother devoted what was left of her life to making sure that her husband- our father- had everything he needed. Until her last breath, she remained a devoted wife to the man of her dreams. None of us were prepared to lose her so soon and so unexpectedly. Least of all, our father. I believe his soul died the day that she left us and he trapped himself in a world where she was still alive."

A lone sniffle momentarily distracted her from what she was saying. Dru sat in the front row, her head full of puffy curls, resting on Deven's shoulder, crying softly. Deven looked on, his face stoic and blank; the only indication he was listening was the glassy sheen of unshed tears in his eyes.

Their father's last few weeks had taken an emotional toll on all of them. He remained somewhat lucid until the end, in what the doctor called "Terminal Lucidity." It occurs when a person is in the process of dying and experiences moments of mental clarity. It can last somewhere between minutes, days, and in rarer cases: weeks before they die. They had mistaken it for a sign that he would be getting better, naively planning the following few holidays and making commitments in the future that they were confident that he would see. His death had come as a surprise to Deven and Dru, but Anya saw it coming. She knew that their father sensed it too. She saw it in his eyes and in the hunch of his shoulders.

In a way, his last few weeks felt like his way of telling his three children goodbye and assuring them they would do fine without him or their mother. His final moments were spent with Clara. At least, that's what his muddled mind had led him to think. Anya had forgotten her phone charger in the hospital room. She thought her father was asleep and planned to just slip in and back out, but when she turned to leave, he noticed her. He had called her Clara, his voice desperate and broken, his arms reaching for her. Anya didn't have the heart to correct him, sensing that he needed to have that conversation. Ultimately, he died peacefully while she held him, promising him that she and her siblings would be fine.

It was a moment she hadn't shared with Deven or Dru because she had been unable to find the words to explain what happened. After he died, Anya sat with his body for a moment, letting the situation's finality settle inside her. Her life had been solely devoted to his care for so long that she wasn't exactly sure what to do now.

She wasn't sure what it meant to be free. A piece of her felt guilty for feeling a quick rush of freedom when he took his last ragged breath. Maybe she would tell her brother and sister about his final moments one day, but right now, that was a special moment between them. She sobbed when she felt him finally let go, thankful he was finally at rest but heartbroken that both of her parents were no longer alive. She wasn't sure she could face what the world looked like without them.

Her father had made her promise that she would stop living life for others and finally take a chance on herself, but Anya had no idea what that looked like. She had no idea what it meant. Her days had started and ended with her father's care for so long that she hadn't stopped to prepare herself for what was supposed to come next.

It wasn't until he died that an idea for her first novel began to take shape in her mind. After weeks of wracking her brain, desperate for a good idea, it all flooded her thoughts. She started to draft ideas and toy around with plot points during her nights after work and mornings before work now that she was free.

Aaron had stepped away from the Alzheimer's Support Group because his wife was offered a job in another state. Anya stepped up to lead the group, choosing to be a sounding board for those still struggling to cope with their loved one's health conditions. Her blog, as well as her meetings, added a sense of purpose to her struggle. Anya, Dru, and Deven had all gone through what they went through to help others and give back to a community that was hurting so deeply. It made Anya feel good to know she could still assist, even after her father passed.

Anya's gaze rested on Kenan, Dru's new boyfriend, sitting a few rows back. He offered her an encouraging smile and nod when their eyes connected. He was a surprise to everyone, not just Dru. He slipped into the family dynamic almost like he had always been there. The ease with which he cared for her little sister filled Anya's heart with joy. She wished their mother had been able to meet him. Anya had no doubt that she would have loved him.

A flash of orange-red hair caught Anya's eye as she glanced up from the notecards on which she had carefully printed her words, and she paused. Sullivan sat in his wheelchair at the back of the church, hunched over and trying desperately to blend into the background. As hard as he tried to become invisible, his pale skin and reddish hair stuck out like a sore thumb in a church full of various shades of brown skin.

Sullivan felt so guilty about his part in it that he had donated a good chunk of his savings to pay for the service. He had been a greedy, wealthy man with no children and a gaggle of bitter and estranged ex-wives. As hateful as Sullivan had been to her father, he begrudgingly admitted that her father was his only friend. In Sullivan's eyes, everyone else had written him off a long time ago, but her father was the only one that mildly tolerated him.

Anya locked eyes with him for a moment. He held her gaze, his expression flickering between guilt and defiance. Sullivan raised his chin for a moment, feigning a level of confidence she knew he didn't have. His jowls moved as he swallowed; guilt colored his expression. He broke their stare first, glaring down at his hands instead. Anya's gaze settled on Deven; Camila, whose pregnancy was really beginning to show, sat on the other side of him. She rested a comforting hand on his knee. Anya smiled to herself.

In a roundabout way, The Memory Concierge had done its job. Their father wanted to find it to restore memories and give him his wife back. It did that. Henry and Clara were together again. It also gave them their father back just long enough to say goodbye. It had started mending the relationships between Anya, Deven, and Dru.

The three of them still had so much work to do, but for the first time, that didn't fill Anya with a sense of dread. She was excited to see what the future held for her and her siblings. All three of them had so much life left to live. Anya looked around at the people again before tapping her index cards on the podium.

"Our father wasn't perfect. He struggled with many things, but he loved us the best way we knew how. And when he could no longer remember that love, we remembered it for him. We showed up for him when he could no longer show up for us. Even if some of us showed up a little later than others." Anya grinned at her brother and sister.

"Because that's what family does. They show up."

Later that day, when everything had all been said and done, Anya stood in front of the abandoned hotel where her father was found unconscious. No matter how she tried to shake it, something constantly pulled her to this building. The air was thick and sickly sweet, with an intensity that made Anya's stomach turn with every step toward the building. She looked at it, examining its details, trying hard to see what her father had seen. Trying, without success, to make sense of it all.

As the night air swirled around her, gently ruffling her hair, she stared up at the building's empty bones, trying to imagine how scared her father must have been, walking into a situation he couldn't possibly have prepared for. Briefly, she'd had allowed herself to hope that there was a creature or a person in this building that could tamper with memories. It felt almost silly now, but she had been sad when she confirmed that The Memory Concierge wasn't real. The small seed of hope that had taken root in her heart finally dried out.

"Come, Chauncy," Anya whispered to the old dog, "it's way past your bedtime." As if understanding what she was saying, the elderly dog let out a yawn and wagged his tail. He sniffed the air one last time and then trudged beside her on the short walk back to her car.

Acknowledgments

First and foremost, I'd like to thank my extraordinarily talented husband and graphic designer, Jared Roach, for the fantastic book cover (of course) but primarily for your countless pep talks and encouragement on the days when I wasn't so sure I could tell this story. You let me bounce ideas off of you and talked me through many different versions of this plot before I finally found one that stuck.

When I got in my own head, you pulled me out and pushed me forward. Your unwavering support, love, and encouragement have kept me going more times than I can count. I definitely wouldn't be here without you. I've spent my life playing it safe until you came in and showed me there was more. Thank you for reminding me that flying is possible. I love you more than words can express.

Second, I'd like to thank my mom for instilling the love of reading into the fibers of my soul from very early on. The nights you would read chapters of *Little House on the Prairie* and *Tawny Scrawny Lion* before I went to sleep will always be some of my favorite childhood memories. You have constantly pushed me towards greatness and never doubted that I would accomplish whatever I had set out to do, even if you didn't always understand my choices. You are the physical representation of God's divine love and care for me. He handpicked you specially for me, and I wouldn't have it any other way. I love you so much!

Third, I would like to thank my Auntie, aka my second mom, for dropping me off at Barnes & Noble during our summer sleepovers in my teen years and being so supportive whenever I popped up with a new idea or something I wanted to try. You nurtured my creative side in a way that showed me it was okay to be a little different as long as I was still me. Thank you for all of the paint nights, the pizza, and for just being you. Everyone needs an "Auntie" in their corner.

To my friends turned family (but specifically my girls) Tiffany, Tamara, Emily, Qiana, Tonisha, and Shassha: Thank you for reading all of my short stories, consistently souping my head up to think that I could actually sit down and write a book, and lovingly telling me to shut up whenever I got in my head about this whole process. Good friends are hard to come by, and I am thankful you ladies are here for the ride.

There are so many people I want to thank specifically for helping me get this done, but for the sake of page space, I have to narrow it down to a select few. Otherwise, the acknowledgments would be longer than the book. That doesn't mean I don't love and appreciate you all the same! Charge it to my printing costs, not my heart! To everyone who took a chance on me and decided to read this book, you are all considered a part of my extended family for the foreseeable future. It's too late to run. You're stuck with me now, and there is no escape. Go ahead and get comfortable.

About The Author

Lauren Roach is a dog obsessed, true-crime loving, self-proclaimed book nerd that has always dreamed of becoming a published author. While most kids were frolicking in the sun, Lauren chose the path less sweaty and opted for the cool embrace of air conditioning while immersed in a book or busily penning fan fictions about whatever heartthrob boy band was on her radar.

Lauren's literary ambitions took a brief hiatus when she decided to venture into the world of criminal justice, earning both a bachelor's and a master's degree in the field. Even though she has yet to use either one of her degrees for anything career-related, she hopes to maybe use her criminal justice knowledge to one day write a really good mystery plot.

Fast forward to today, Lauren is happily residing in North Carolina with her lovely husband where she records episodes for her book centered podcast Lauren's Library and isn't afraid to break out a book in the middle of a social gathering. You can follow her work at

Instagram: @thebookybabe_
Tik Tok: @thebookybabe
Podcast: Lauren's Library Podcast
Website: www.thebookybabe.com